MONITORS
—OF—
DESTRUCTION

MONITORS
—OF—
DESTRUCTION

Book 4 of the Monitors Series

DARLEEN HAYBALL JOHNSON

Monitors of Destruction

Copyright © 2019 by Darleen Hayball Johnson. All rights reserved.

No part of this publication may be reproduced, stored in a retrieval system or transmitted in any way by any means, electronic, mechanical, photocopy, recording or otherwise without the prior permission of the author except as provided by USA copyright law.

This novel is a work of fiction. Names, descriptions, entities, and incidents included in the story are products of the author's imagination. Any resemblance to actual persons, events, and entities is entirely coincidental.

The opinions expressed by the author are not necessarily those of URLink Print and Media.

1603 Capitol Ave., Suite 310 Cheyenne, Wyoming USA 82001
1-888-980-6523 | admin@urlinkpublishing.com

URLink Print and Media is committed to excellence in the publishing industry.

Book design copyright © 2018 by URLink Print and Media. All rights reserved.

Published in the United States of America

ISBN 978-1-64367-654-8 (Paperback)
ISBN 978-1-64367-655-5 (Digital)

Fiction
08.03.19

PREFACE

The Monitors had come to Earth to observe the fall of what they called the "American Hegemony." They wanted to see what would be the direct result of the Great Yellowstone Eruption. They knew that life would become more difficult for everyone once the middle third of the American continent was buried in almost three meters of ash and dirt and the sky was blanketed with grey clouds of sulfuric acid-bearing ejecta blocking the sun.

In the five years since the eruption, over two billion people had died of starvation and the wars fought by displaced people, but not in America. The country was effectively cut in half and millions had died covered in ash, but after the horrendous eruption, each coast had managed to feed itself, the government had remained stable, and life had gone on, albeit without jet airplanes, which cannot fly through ash.

The Monitors were quick learners, whose natural bodies were aquatic, much like an octopus. Their minds had been transferred into ailing human bodies afflicted with some terminal disease. With more sophisticated biological knowledge, they were able to cure the ailment and take over the brain of the dying human. The personality, knowledge, and memories of the human died, and the body's new tenant took over. They were completely new personalities, unaware of their former family members, language, or culture. Thus, it was best if the deceased "disappeared:" lost at sea, burned beyond recognition, or sold into slavery. In the twenty-first century, it had become difficult to make a person disappear. "Lost at sea" had become the best method before Yellowstone buried millions. Now, many had no birth certificates, marriage licenses, or other proof of their identity.

Monitors' brains grew throughout their lives, so only the young could restrict their knowledge into a three pound organ constricted by bone. Few Monitors wanted to stay for longer than a human lifetime. Each human they inhabited had to disappear and reappear in a new and different location as a complete stranger. They needed to be integrated into a community, learn human language and skills and interact with the people they encountered. To spend two lifetimes required disappearing, allowing their bodies time to repair themselves into their youthful state, and re-establish themselves into a completely different community. By that time, being cramped within the human cranium was far too restricting.

They went to great lengths not to influence the cultures they were studying nor to kill or damage any life forms except the dying person whose body they needed to inhabit.

For centuries, Earth had been studied by these xenophiles who were willing to exist in human form and be limited by the constraints of the three-pound brains. Many had come and gone, yet they had no desire to take over the planet. One long human lifetime was usually all they could stand to be squeezed into that tiny cranium. They yearned to return to their own bodies so that their brains could expand and their knowledge and skills could continue to improve.

Marco Antonio was by far the resident expert at everything, having arrived during the period known now as the Middle Ages. He had solved the problem posed by a small skull and a short lifespan by replacing most of his abdominal organs with neurons of the cerebral cortex, so his brain had quadrupled in size. Unfortunately, he had become dependent on drinking blood and taking a few important oils and minerals required for his body to function. Although technically a vampire, he preferred the term, "sanguinary eater."

Over the years, he had helped thousands of Monitors take up temporary residency on Earth so they could complete a study rotation in human cultures. They were here now to watch how the American culture would adapt to the Yellowstone eruption, which they had known would be a mega-volcano. On a planet with seven billion inhabitants, any change in the world's dominant culture and primary food producer would affect the entire planet. In an effort to be in positions to observe the disruption and adjustments, both social and political, they had sent many extra observers to outposts all over the planet.

Gabriel and Ruth Smith were two of the Monitors sent to Earth to establish a base. They had moved into the house next to Tim and Ann Jacob, two retired school teachers who lived in Hanford, California. The location was chosen because it was far enough away from the initial eruption to be relatively undamaged. Plus, it was located in a farming community in the San Joaquin Valley, the area deemed most likely to be able to adjust rapidly to the weather changes resulting from the lengthy winter-like conditions caused by suspended ash. The Smiths quickly realized that they had overestimated their ability to refinish the Victorian home they had purchased. In order to establish a communications center near the West Coast, they needed help, and the Jacobs had stepped up and willingly given them advice and support.

Confident that neither of the Jacobs would over-react, Gabriel had decided to "come out" to Ann and Tim Jacob, who were neither shocked nor frightened once they realized that the Smiths were there to observe what Gabriel referred to as "the fall of the American hegemony." In exchange for the Jacobs' aid, Ruth reset their biological aging, and helped them prepare for the coming disaster.

It had been a wise choice. The Jacobs had dubbed them "Monitors" and had taught them social skills, food preparation, building and decorating and had established the Smiths' place as the Monitors' central headquarters. Ann and her son Ian had helped floundering Monitors in Pennsylvania and they had all worked to maintain peace in California.

Having learned from history, few had disclosed their real identities to any humans. In the past, many Monitors had been burned at the stake, attacked by angry mobs, or been tortured as spawns of the devil once their abilities had been detected. Hence, they kept a very low profile as they observed their neighbors or attended classes or religious services; their job was to watch and report human interaction, not to interact with them. Scientists should not have any effect on the creatures they are studying.

Barring accidents, Monitors could maintain their bodies indefinitely at any age they chose. Most "hosts" were older people who rejuvenated and retrogressed back to a younger age, as Ann and Tim had been allowed to do. Monitors only rarely got together to visit except at their main outpost at the Mariana trench, a site they had chosen to avoid nosy human explorers.

Since human bodies could not exist at that depth, their consciousness was transferred into a vial, their human bodies were put into stasis on the surface, and then they would be reunited with their actual bodies far away, in the deep water where those bodies were in stasis. Once returned to their eight-legged bodies, they would unite and share what they had learned with others. Their own body's nine separate brains communicated in color, lights, sounds, and smells, as well as telepathically. To be limited to a single three-pound brain inside a cranium which limited further growth was stultifying, to say the least. Nevertheless, in order to grow and understand other cultures and other species, Monitor youth subjected themselves to the onerous process of infusing themselves down to their basics and existing for a while in someone else's mind and body.

Most were eager to return to the Mariana Outpost as often as possible for visits with others of their species. For a while, those stopovers had been impossible, since a mudslide had covered their stasis chambers. When that happened, they realized that being stranded on a planet covered in volcanic ash meant that they, too, would inevitably suffer from the diseases brought on by constant ash and obsidian inhalation. They could battle pneumonia and other bacterial and viral infections, but most Earth creatures developed a bizarre arthritic condition called hypertrophic pulmonary osteoarthropathy, sometimes known as Marie's Disease. Extremely painful, all humans, including Monitors as well as other mammals, birds, and reptiles were subject to this condition.

CHAPTER 1

The party lasted well into the night, but at last everybody had found a bed somewhere. Towards the end of the evening, everyone was either drunk or their brains were so low on neurotransmitters that they were rummy.

Ann was tired, but very happy. The whole evening had been a success for everyone. For the first time, she had heard the Monitors laugh out loud. They had tried to dance and sing. Sometimes it was difficult to remember that they were youngsters, especially since most were in the bodies of middle-aged people. Granted, they had observed the demeanor of people in that age-group, and had adjusted their behavior accordingly. Inside, however, they were young enough to fit into a human cranium. Having been a high school teacher for 37 years, Ann thought they were far too young to be so serious.

When everyone was tucked in, Ann and Marco Antonio headed for their bedroom.

Thank you for tonight, Ann. You were right; they did need a chance to learn to celebrate like other people. It is part of the human experience that I have never taught them, and it was a grave oversight. For centuries, I have cheated others of the joy you taught this group to experience in one evening.

There is more to life than work, lover. Everyone needs some fun and a few giggles.

In the morning, Ann was up early. She knew better than to expect her Monitor guests to want to eat breakfast together. She cooked plenty of food and provided dishes and bowls for them to take back to their bedrooms.

This was one of the times she missed Tim; he would have had the coffee on and have the bacon sizzling by the time she had rolled out of bed. Marco Antonio had usually had a cook and/or a maid who invisibly made sure his coffee was ready, and Ann had *ipso facto* stepped into that role. In all fairness, she couldn't expect him to worry about cooking breakfast since, as a "sanguinary eater," he hadn't eaten anything but blood in over seven centuries.

Marco Antonio would have helped her more had she asked, but she decided she would rather listen to him practice the piano while she put the coffee on. She decided to make a pot of oatmeal, and she had plenty of bread, butter, and jam. Peanut butter had become hard to find, so she didn't put that out, but she was ready to make fried eggs, bacon, or sausage on demand.

As a sanguinary eater, Marco Antonio had to search for fresh blood every day, preferably twice each day, since he refused to completely drain the lifeblood from anyone. Ann could not help him because he wouldn't let her, but he did allow Miguel, his fellow vampire, to bring him blood in a plastic bag. They had hunted together for years, and Miguel was always able to procure enough for them both.

She could hear Beethoven's *Moonlight Sonata*. Unfortunately, Marco Antonio wouldn't have much time to practice the piano, his newest passion. She knew he had a big meeting planned with everybody to discuss the production and delivery methods they would be using to breed the tiny little worms and the slime-secreting bacteria which they had bred to ingest the solids that had invaded practically all the lungs in the world. The same tiny creatures would successfully clear the lungs of people and wild animals like deer and squirrels. Without these species working symbiotically, lungs would remain irritated and bleeding.

The world had changed, and the Yellowstone mega-eruption had up-ended more than dirt. Everyone's lives had changed, and she intended to adapt to whatever the situation demanded. Being Marco Antonio's woman made that adjustment even more imperative. These Monitors needed a human woman they could really count on, and she didn't intend to disappoint anyone, especially Marco Antonio.

MONITORS OF DESTRUCTION

As she cooked, she placed the food on the dining room table, and everyone took what they wanted and disappeared. The ones who had slept downstairs in the laboratory came up, took their food, and returned to eat their breakfast in the tiny bedrooms she had built when she and Miguel had completed the basement. The others came in the front door, put their food on plates, and tried to find a quiet corner where they would not be observed eating. They would rather eat outside in the cold fog than sit at the table and watch the others bite, chew, and swallow.

Gradually, the dishes seemed to reappear magically in the kitchen sink, where each Monitor thoughtfully placed them when they were empty. Ann quietly carried them around to the other sink near the dishwasher, rinsed them, and filled the dishwasher. Those who observed her helped by carrying the dishes for her to the other sink. Ann knew she would not have to mention which sink to place the dirty dishes into; they would tell each other, and lunch clean-up would be much easier. Several actually thanked her for providing the meal. Their social skills were improving.

Since Ann's living room was the largest open space, they started setting up folding chairs there. Apparently, they had already conversed about how they would handle everything, and this was just the assignment-dispensing stage. Quietly, Ann took a seat near the back and halfway into the dining room. She didn't want to be noticed, but she wanted to hear what was going on.

Marco Antonio was standing up in front of the north window near the entryway. He had everyone's undivided attention when Ann quietly stood at the opposite wall to listen. "Because this treatment is not a medical one, we are not going through the United States' F.D.A. To do so would add years to the production of these creatures. Instead, we are going to address the farmers and meat processors, and we're going to market this as a food supplement."

As she watched and listened, she once again marveled at the fact that these remarkable beings had settled in Hanford. Even more astonishing was that Marco Antonio, the leader of all these creatures, had fallen in love with her, among all the women in the world. She was under no illusion that she was his equal in any way; the entire relationship was, in her words, "one horse, one rabbit." She firmly believed that he loved her as she would have loved a favorite pet, but she'd take it. She felt honored to her toenails that he had even noticed her and was truly surprised that he had.

As he talked, her mind wandered back to when they had first met. She had been a 62-year-old, plump, married lady. She had invited him to stay with her and her husband Tim because the Smiths' house was undergoing messy reconstruction. Although she knew that he was a Monitor, like Ruth and Gabriel Smith, she had not known that he was a "sanguinary eater." When Tim had excused himself and gone to bed, Marco Antonio had approached her and had smothered her in pheromones which made her feel like a 16-year-old cheerleader in the backseat of her boyfriend's car.

She didn't know that he had caused this sexual response, nor did she know that she was completely incapable of resisting it. She only knew that they had had the hottest sex she'd ever had while he fed off her, and that she had been willing. Before he removed the memory, she had asked him not to; she wanted to remember, not as a treasured memory of a romantic moment, but as a guilty reminder of her own weakness, which had totally appalled her.

When Ruth had informed her that she had never had a moment of choice, never had any free will, nor could she have stopped him even if she had wanted to, Ann had felt assaulted. Ruth had been shocked that Ann had been as upset as she was, and urged her to have the memory erased. Ann was adamant, however. She wanted to remember, so as to maintain vigilance when the vampire Monitors were present.

That had been so long ago. Now, Ann loved him with a passion bordering on a compulsive adoration. She knew she was more beautiful than she had ever been in her youth, yet her belief in their inequality was only reinforced with the memory. Just as she would love a favorite pet whether it was young or old, her physical attractiveness was not relevant to his emotional attachment. She thought she was his favorite pet, but his pet nonetheless. Clever, cute, adorable—she was all those things to him, and she was sure that he loved her.

He loves his horse, too.

She realized she would have to stop musing about the nature of their emotional attachment when he suddenly looked right at her and thought, "*It's not the same!*"

"*Sorry!*" she thought back. Quietly, she got up and went into the kitchen, so she would be less of a distraction to him. He had a huge job to do, many people to organize, factories to build on every continent, and he didn't need to deal with a whiney bitch at the same time. If the pet comparison held true at all, that's what she was being right now, a whiney bitch.

"*You are in no way my pet. You are the woman I love. The only woman I love! Will you ever forgive me for having accosted you without your permission? I'm so sorry, Ann. Please forgive me!*"

He sent these thoughts to her in words, but the message came through so much stronger than any words could convey. Nonetheless, he continued to run his meeting with the other Monitors without so much as a pause. He didn't need to concentrate on any one thing; he was the master of multi-tasking. In his natural form, he had nine separate brains, all of which could function independently of the others.

"*This is not the time for this conversation. I'm sorry, Marco Antonio. Try to stay out of my head, and you won't be bothered by my silly thoughts!*"

Normally, Monitors had to be in physical contact with a human being in order to converse with them. Marco Antonio had become so attuned to her that he was nearly always aware of everything she was thinking. She, too, was able to receive a message he sent her; as far as she knew, she was the only human who could do that.

As quietly as possible, she wondered if, when, and how he had changed her so that she could receive his mental messages. It was becoming easier and easier to feel his presence, be aware of his moods, and receive his thoughts.

Ann started mixing some pumpkin bread. Pumpkin was something they had plenty of because it was one of the few crops which grew well under the overcast sky, and she liked to come up with things her guests could not get elsewhere. Besides, it was relatively easy, and it would focus her attention long enough to divert Marco Antonio's. She was learning that he was always aware of her thoughts, but most of the time, he ignored them. They were just more background noise that his brain filtered, unless she was upset, in need, or really focused on a certain subject. Like her own brain, mundane tasks like cooking diverted her attention so that her musings did not turn into messages or worry. She didn't want him to know how much time she spent thinking about him; he was vain enough as it was. She was vain enough herself to object to the lack of privacy; her thoughts were her own. So she dumped the eggs, flour, sugar, and pumpkin mash into the mixer bowl and tried to think quiet thoughts about the spices she would need.

Somewhat irked that she had to go to such lengths to keep him from nosing through her thoughts, she listened to his voice as he made the assignments. Like a general preparing for a battle, he gave each person their specific task. Those who had achieved the best social skills were appointed to deal with certain people to arrange the production of the organisms; others had to obtain the necessary buildings and equipment. Miguel would start breeding enough organisms so that they could provide many sites with an adequate supply of genetically viable creatures to serve as Adam and Eve at their site.

Ann drained the beans she had put on to soak the night before and put the beans, clean water, and salt into her biggest pot. She started chopping an onion, but it was a huge pot, so she decided that two onions would be in order, and then she would have to go pick up the ham she would serve for dinner. She had had the butcher order a pre-sliced, honey-baked ham, so she would not have to cook it. Instead, she planned on fixing a really big pan of scalloped potatoes, which would take up most of the oven for most of the afternoon. Tomorrow there would be beans left over, and probably some ham, so hopefully that would provide lunch for any who didn't take off early in the morning.

As she worked, she watched groups find their way downstairs to the labs. After receiving their assignments from Marco Antonio, each Monitor had to quickly get checked out on the requirements of growing huge colonies of the little critters which would save the lungs of her planet. Almost every Monitor base had been doing some research with them recently, but now that production was about to begin, they wanted advice and recommendations from Miguel, who was downstairs demonstrating some lab techniques. This was sort of an in-service day, where everyone could get together, talk to one another, and catch up on their projects.

Ann had been shocked to learn that they had never had a planet-wide get-together. In fact, they had remained isolated while Marco Antonio had been the only uniting force. He would drop in on them all from time to time, or come if there was some emergency. They conversed with one another only at the Mariana Outpost, deep beneath the Pacific Ocean.

"Without you, it would be impossible and far too risky to have so many Monitors in one place," suddenly popped into Ann's mind. Marco Antonio came into the kitchen and said, "Could I help you make a pot of coffee?"

"Good idea! I could use another cup myself. I'm beginning to feel very under-caffeinated, and I smell like an onion," Ann said. "I'll make some more lemonade, in case someone would like that," she said as she scraped the last of her chopped onion pieces onto the lid of the pot and then into the pot on the stove. In response to the sudden question that popped into her head, *"What else needs to be done?"* she responded, "Someone could empty the dishwasher," as she reached for the blue glass pitcher. Without a word, Gabriel came into the kitchen and walked into the breakfast room directly to the dishwasher and started emptying it. "Use the tea towel on the back of the chair to dry the cup bottoms, Gabe."

"Sure thing, Ann," he said cheerfully.

Ruth came in from the utility room with the broom and started sweeping up a few onion pieces Ann had dropped.

Ann turned from the stove to thank Ruth. Suddenly, Ann was reminded of the kitchen scene in <u>Snow White</u>, which they had seen recently with her grandchildren. In that scene, all the animals were helping Snow White clean the kitchen. Ann started whistling, and Marco Antonio joined her instantly, both doing "Whistle While You Work," while the others stopped and stared at them. After about ten seconds, Ann began to giggle, as Marco Antonio did a little hop from the coffee pot to the sink as he whistled.

The others didn't get it, which was probably a good thing. As it was, they thought it was something Ann and Marco Antonio did when they worked together in the kitchen. They certainly had never seen them play.

The smile never left Ann's face as she opened the lemonade powder mix and waited for Marco Antonio, who was still whistling, to fill the coffee pot so she could fill the lemonade pitcher. She started humming the words, but she had to give it up when the tune went well above her singing range.

"You two sound happy!" Gabe said, his hands full of coffee mugs he was putting onto the shelf next to the sink. "Happiness on this scale makes my stomach hurl!" Gabe said, rolling his eyes.

There was a sudden intake of breath at the doorway as Raul wondered what Marco Antonio would say to Gabriel for making such a reference to vomiting. That was a Monitor no-no of the grossest kind. Ann and Marco Antonio grinned widely, and promised to tone it down a few notches for him. Raul smiled, too, mostly from relief that it was apparently an "inside joke" as Ann had described them.

The play stopped when the house rattled. Almost immediately after, there was a huge explosion, and the glass in the kitchen windows threatened to shatter, as did their eardrums. Marco Antonio grabbed Ann and held her tightly as he stepped away from the window and towards the center of the house. The fan started to circulate, and the air compression nearly knocked them over. The living room window imploded in a shatter of glass, most of which was caught by the heavy drapes which were nearly closed, yet billowing. In front of the big, wide door, the other living room window facing Douty Street to the west shattered inwards as well, knocking over the plant stand as the bulging drape threw it aside.

"Everyone into the basement!" yelled Marco Antonio, pushing Ann in that direction. "Get away from the windows! Cover your head!" He pushed her to the stairs and tried to get everyone down the steps as quickly as possible.

MONITORS OF DESTRUCTION

Right after the shock came the heat, burning everything in front of it. Anyone outside got singed in seconds, some with their clothes smoking, or by inhaling flames. Those who had been eating their breakfast or drinking their coffee outside rushed indoors, looking like they were sun burnt.

When Ann felt the heat whoosh down the open door to the stairs, she immediately thought of Questor. She looked up the steps at Marco Antonio, who was still near the basement door, descending behind her and directed that one thought towards him.

Marco Antonio gave a slight nod, and his eyebrows shot up immediately. She knew that he had gotten a telepathic message from Questor, which she immediately assumed was a cry of pain.

Lemoore has been attacked with a huge bomb, possibly a nuclear device. So have several of the Western American cities!

Marco Antonio forwarded that thought, clarifying and amplifying it. All the Monitors froze in place, staring at Marco Antonio. They had received the same news from him that she had, and they were dumbfounded, as she was.

"Turn on the television!" Ann said. "Perhaps they'll tell us what has happened!" She looked back towards the stairs as Marco Antonio came down into the basement and thought, *"Is he OK?"*

"Yes. He's fine, but a little scorched. He's the one who told me Lemoore has been bombed," Marco Antonio told her. He stayed on the stairs, looking ready to move either up or down. He quieted a moment, then aloud, he said, "Everybody listen up! The Rovers have survived, but all have been burned externally to some degree. My rover, Questor, has informed me that Lemoore Naval Air Station has been the target of a large bomb, at least as large as a nuclear attack, as were several other military outposts in this state. These attacks appeared to be simultaneous, but more might follow. I do not know who attacked America, or where, so turning on the TV is a good idea. There might be more news available. Try CNN. See what you can get on your cell phones, too," he said, pulling out his own cell. Everyone's head bent over their telephones immediately. Ann didn't have her cell phone on her, so she went to the television on the workbench and took over the remote controls.

She was relieved to hear that Questor and the other rovers though singed, were relatively unharmed, since these "flying saucers" were every Monitor's main means of transportation. They were more than mere transports; they were friends, very much alive and sentient. They used the sun or hot volcanic underwater vents to extract energy, and they could fly across the continent in a few hours, much faster than a jet. Without a definite shape of their own, they could mold themselves into whatever form was needed, including seats, beds, or stasis tubes for their passengers' comfort. The Monitors had bred them eons ago for both underwater and aerial flight, and nearly all of them were cloaked, circling above Ann's house at the moment.

"Is there anything I can do for Questor or any of the others right now, Marco? If they have been injured, I will certainly put some balm on their burns or something. They might just need some lubbies. Should someone go out and comfort them?" Ann asked.

"Yes. Someone, but not you. I want you to stay here in the basement until we at least know what's going on," Marco Antonio said.

"Perhaps I could just go hose them down. If they've been singed, some water might be soothing. Unless you think it's radioactive out there, in which case, they should run for their lives!" Ann replied, ignoring his protectiveness.

"Good thinking, Ann. I'm sending them out of harm's way, out over the ocean."

"Excuse me, Marco Antonio. The MSM news service is saying that Los Angeles, San Francisco, San Diego—they've all been hit! Several major cities in this state have been hit with relatively small nuclear-sized bombs simultaneously. There was apparently a war, and we have apparently lost, since we don't know who to fight. So far, no one has taken responsibility for the attack, so there has been no retaliatory strike. It might even be the East Coast!"

"Seriously?" Ann asked Raul, who had made the announcement. "Civil war? I don't think so," Ann said. She doubted that she was so politically out of the loop that she was unaware of any separatist movements. People would have talked about it long before it escalated to war.

MONITORS OF DESTRUCTION

"Questor will tell us," said Marco Antonio, rushing to the Monitor's communications equipment. As he touched it, he started getting and sending messages to the two stations where there were Monitors who were not already in Hanford. One Monitor had remained at home in India, missing the party because of an injured foot, and the others were at the main station at the Mariana Trench, where the stasis chambers and main underwater laboratory were. They were still replacing much of the equipment that had been buried under the mudslide which had very nearly killed them all.

Monitors communicated with each other through very long, slow radio waves. Each radio wave carried other messages, entwined within the wavelength. The receivers and transmitters managed to transmit colors, odors, pictures, and sounds to anyone in physical contact with them. Once again, the Monitors had bred a series of creatures who worked in conjunction with one another to achieve this process. Ann had used the call system many times, but she was still uncertain of the physics behind it. Every rover on the planet was connected in some way to this system, which worked either above or below the water or air. All the Jacobs could use it, but if a stranger came in and put their hands on the receiver within the black box, nothing would happen until Marco Antonio or another Monitor connected them to the system. So far, only the members of Ann's family had been connected.

The entire communication system was part of the Monitors' technology, which was very different and far more advanced than anything the Humans had on Earth. Marco Antonio had explained to Ann that the Monitors had been an advanced species for over a million years, while humans had not even had domesticated cereals until about ten thousand years ago.

Actually, he had understated the age of his species by a great deal. His was an ancient race which measured time in entirely different units which were difficult to explain to humans, whose brains barely grasped anything greater than a few thousand years, anyway. He had not explained any of their technology to anyone in great detail; in fact, he had purposefully dulled Ann's curiosity about technological things.

As he tuned into Questor, Marco Antonio saw, heard, and felt what Questor did. Mentally joining the rover as it flew well into the troposphere, he could see the classic mushroom clouds above several cities along the coast of California, and he could tell that the entire state had been attacked. These were not nuclear bombs, as they had originally thought. There was no radiation, but the explosions were as big as those that had wiped out Nagasaki and Hiroshima.

That was both good and bad news. It meant that the planet would recuperate faster, and it meant that this was not a human war. This was an attack by a different species, and it was probably planet-wide.

Questor turned outward, away from the surface and towards the edge of the planet, looking for a spaceship. There must be one or more there, since these attacks did not come from this planet. Who were they? Where did they come from? What did they want? Marco Antonio really wanted those questions answered before he took any action.

Questor could perceive no extraterrestrial ships in the air above earth. That didn't mean there weren't any. It meant that they were probably on the other side of the planet, had ducked behind the moon, or they had fled immediately out of light-space.

Monitors had not waged war for hundreds of thousands of years. There was nothing to fight wars over, as far as the Monitor culture was concerned. They didn't collect wealth or material objects, they didn't need more territory, they had no religious beliefs that required defense, and they were not by nature pugnacious. Their major goal and greatest value was the accumulation of knowledge, not objects. With the ability to travel quickly from one star system or one galaxy to the next, conquest became unnecessary and juvenile. There were plenty of planets providing anything the Monitors might need.

Any culture which was still waging war or seeking conquests was clearly new to interstellar travel. They had not learned that war was wholly unnecessary; in the vastness of the universe, there was plenty of everything for everyone. Many planets had life, but relatively few had what humans would call sentient organisms. As the Monitors had discovered, intelligence was not a prerequisite to survival or longevity. In fact, the species that survived unchanged for billions of years were usually tiny, with no brains at all. Most intelligent, sentient species destroyed each other rather quickly. Humans had come very close, and Marco Antonio was among the few Monitors who believed that Earth's most intelligent species would survive. Most felt they would either destructively overpopulate their world or depopulate their planet in a sudden holocaust.

"Clearly, these attackers want to eliminate human beings, probably to take over occupation of the planet. They have bombed four major population centers in California that Questor can see. I have sent him to the east to ascertain if the East Coast is also under attack," Marco Antonio told everyone who had huddled in the basement, still anxiously studying the news services on their phones. Many were calling people they knew, with varying degrees of success.

"Should we send out other rovers in other directions?" Ann suggested. "Are they going out alone?" Knowing that they were living, sentient beings made Ann very concerned about their safety. Nonetheless, quickly ascertaining who and what was attacking the planet was of primary importance, she felt.

"Until we ascertain who the enemy is, I hesitate to risk the rovers' lives. It is possible that they will shoot down planes or other flying reconnaissance vehicles, assuming the planes will attack them in defense. Let's get some more information, putting the fewest possible number of creatures in danger. Until we ascertain the effectiveness of Questor's shielding capabilities, I don't want to risk more." Having come down the steps, he approached and put his arm around her waist protectively.

"You're right, of course. Let's see if there have been any demands made," Ann said, changing the channel on the basement TV. Everyone craned their necks to see the screen, which wasn't possible. Ann turned up the sound and tried several channels, while the others kept checking out their phones on their own, personally favorite news sources.

Marco Antonio turned and climbed the stairs. There had been no more explosions after the initial attack, and he doubted that the area rated more bombs, depending on the damage done by the first strike. He wanted to make sure everyone upstairs was safe. Ann turned to follow him, handing the remote control to the person standing next to her.

"Stay here, Ann. It's safer in the basement," Marco Antonio said.

"No one really needs me in the basement, but there might be someone in need of first aid outside or in the neighborhood," Ann said, ignoring his command.

His anger flared for a moment; he was not used to being disobeyed. The desire to have her with him so that he could protect her soon calmed him, and he nodded. Still, his eyebrows were furrowed, an expression Ann recognized but chose to ignore.

"Hanford Glass is going to have lots of business this week," Ann said as she entered the living room. The temperature had dropped, but the heater was trying valiantly to warm up the room. Since the two main "picture" windows were shattered, that was an impossible job, so she walked over to the thermostat above the piano and turned off the heat.

She started to pick up the larger pieces of glass, but Marco Antonio said, "Let the others do that. We need to find something to board up the holes. Is there any plywood in the garage?"

"Maybe there's a piece big enough for one, but not both. We can put a tarp over it, I suppose. Let's go next door and check on the Smiths' windows, too," Ann said, grateful for something to do. She was fighting panic, and thrashing around in the garage and workroom wouldn't help. She was much more interested in checking on her neighbors, but she knew her guests couldn't sit around without any glass in the windows. They'd freeze.

"I'll go check on them while you find the tarp. Take someone with you to carry it into the house. Tarps are heavy and usually dirty, querida."

Without further comment, Ann returned to the stairway in the hall and asked Mike to come help her. When Ramon came up the stairs with Mike, Ann asked him to start the glass clean-up while she and Mike went to find the tarp.

There were neighboring people outside, milling around, checking on each other and trying to see if anyone knew what had happened. No one knew anything, of course, and Marco Antonio was not going to tell them that Lemoore Naval Air Station had been bombed, since he would have no explanation for where he'd gotten the information. Under "normal" conditions, he would have access to information from every one of the Monitors' stations, but almost everyone had come to Hanford for the party. The neighbors were concerned, and some were afraid, but no one was injured or panicked. They speculated about gas explosions and plane crashes, but so far, no one had any inkling that it was far more serious than they knew.

Marco Antonio had encouraged the gas explosion hypothesis with the neighbors, but within moments that changed. "Los Angeles and San Francisco have been bombed!" shouted Bob Silva, the neighbor. He was looking at his phone, and apparently the news had been posted on the internet somewhere. "We're under attack!" he said, yelling to Mr. Stevens across the street.

"Who's attacking us?" Mr. Stevens roared back.

"Nobody knows yet!" replied Silva, still staring intently at his phone.

"Look at that!" yelled Mr. Stevens, pointing to the west, where a huge mushroom-shaped cloud could be seen rising into the sky. People had to walk up or down the street to see around the tall, thick trees on Douty Street, but eventually everyone got to a position where they could see the signature cloud of a huge explosion.

Marco Antonio left the small group and sprinted directly to the Smiths' house, noticing that the front windows were undamaged. The smaller panes had absorbed the blast better than the Jacobs' larger expanses of glass. He walked right into the house and bellowed, "Is everyone all right here?"

Ruth had been in the kitchen, and she walked through the dining room, a tea towel in her hands. "We're all fine. How are you all? What was that explosion?"

Walking right past Ruth, Marco Antonio headed for the door to the basement. "Nobody's hurt, but Ann lost her two front windows. She's looking for tarps and plywood so she can put the heat on again. Lemoore Naval Air Station was bombed, as was Los Angeles and San

Francisco. I've sent Questor east, and I sent the other rovers west so they can cloak over the Pacific until they're needed. No point in drawing attention to this location."

"Are their cloaks down? Were they damaged?" Gabriel asked, joining them in the kitchen near the basement door. Marco Antonio stood there, his hand on the doorknob.

"Questor was a little singed, but that's all. They're all able to cloak, at least against humans, but we have no idea how sophisticated the enemies' sensing equipment is. That's why I wanted them dispersed. Whoever bombed Lemoore, L.A., and San Francisco appears to possess some advanced, high-tech weapons capable of destroying a whole city or naval air base with a single blast. Questor says the bomb was not nuclear, so getting that much power in a single projectile or shell is impressive. They probably have advanced sensing equipment, too."

"So you think the planet is under attack? It's not the Russians, Chinese, or Pakistani assault? Maybe a coordinated terrorist blitz, like 9/11?" Gabriel shifted his weight from one foot to the other, his body displaying the excitement he was trying hard to keep from his voice. "Do you think it's extraterrestrial? Seriously?"

Marco Antonio noted the uncharacteristic tone and phrases Gabriel was using. His English had changed, as he had adapted his behavior to be appropriate for a younger man. When he had been put into a twenty-year-old's body and returned to Hanford as Ruth's son rather than her husband, Gabriel had adjusted admirably. Marco reached out his hand and touched Gabriel's shoulder, expressing his compliments for the adjustment. Aloud, he said "That was Questor's opinion. I'm heading downstairs to see what he's found out. He's looking for a mother ship, drones, or some evidence that will tell us who or what did this. Everyone is monitoring the human news services on their phones and iPads. Keep me informed if you learn anything." Without another word, he descended the steep stairs to the basement.

As he'd feared, there was no news on the Monitors' communications device. He sent what information he had to the Mariana outpost, took out his own iPhone, and started searching the internet for news. San Diego, Vandenberg Air Force Base, Long Beach, and San Jose exploded next, although there was still no word as to who was attacking California. The news from the east coast had not arrived; perhaps this was just a west coast invasion?

As soon as he had formulated that thought, the cities on the east coast started reporting that they, too, were under attack. Washington, Boston, New York—all the expected population and government centers were blown up, as well as Norfolk and other military bases. Clearly, the entire country was under attack.

Marco Antonio felt crippled by the lack of information. Why had he allowed all the Monitors to convene in one place at the same time? He had become inured to danger, and he'd been caught unprepared. The passing of decades since Earth's only atomic conflagration had lulled him into thinking that no massive attack, nuclear or otherwise, would occur. 9/11 should have made him more watchful, yet the cautious, mature response by the American government had in fact reassured him that they could handle it. The fact that they had not immediately started bombing other countries trying to find a scapegoat for their anger encouraged him. They had not overreacted; they had pursued every lead, followed every trail, until they had narrowed down the guilty party. Granted, they had taken the opportunity to find and kill Saddam Hussein, and many innocent people had died in that fruitless bit of retaliation for previous wrongs, but for the most part, the retribution had been measured and acceptable. In the U.S., there had been no holy wars or righteous saber rattling, and revenge had remained relatively focused.

Ann came down the steps at the Smith's house a few minutes later, saying "Getting anything?"

"The whole country is under attack. No news yet from Questor, and the other rovers are safely cloaked over the Pacific."

"I'm sure every missile silo is open and ready to go, but do we know yet whom to fire upon?" Ann asked. "If more California cities have been bombed, it would explain the sudden blackout on most TV channels. Most of the internet is still getting through on the phones, at least so far."

"Good! Apparently most TV stations are from cities which have been destroyed. There are no demands for surrender, either. We don't know if any other countries have been attacked, nor who is behind this. I can tell you one thing: these are new weapons. They're not nuclear, yet they seem just as powerful," Marco Antonio said, not looking up from his phone.

"So all the time we were worried about Pakistan and Iran getting hold of nuclear materials, they were researching some other kind of explosive?" Ann asked. Her tone of voice showed her incredulity.

"Perhaps, but I don't think so. This is far too well organized, too large and far too strong to be either of them. One or two cities, maybe. Dozens of cities across America? I doubt it," he said, his eyes never leaving his telephone.

"I agree. Do you think we've been invaded from outer space?" she asked, knowing that she sounded like someone from a B movie. "Have you heard of other cultures who want our planet?" *There, that sounded better.*

He could have shown her his thoughts with a mere touch, but he didn't want to frighten her. She needed to conceptualize the situation in her own terms, so he kept both hands on his phone while he guarded his thoughts. "No, I've heard nothing of another species wanting to take over Earth. Remember, I've been pretty isolated here for quite a while, so I really don't know, Ann. I do know that it's not us, my love. We do not seek an empire," he said, looking up at her at last. He observed her reaction to that statement and felt relief. She was not accusing the Monitors, even with vague suspicions.

"I know that, Marco. If you'd wanted this planet, you would have taken it centuries ago," she said as she walked over to one of the computers and sat down. She tried to look for news, but they kept reporting the same things over and over.

At last, one of the talking heads said, "This just in—London and twelve other European cities have been bombed. There is still no declaration of war. No nation has come forth to take responsibility for this horrendous loss of life."

Ann sat there staring at the screen. It didn't feel real to her. Who was doing this, and why? She hoped it was some nutty faction with a new toy. Crazy people with massive weapons could be dealt with eventually. Goodness always wins out, always. But if they were being attacked and systematically killed by another species, all bets would be off.

Are we being annihilated?

His slight shrug said, *I don't know.*

Ann waited, but he did not elaborate. She squelched a sudden pang of terror and maintained a composed look. She did not want him to lie to her just to comfort her fears. That would be unworthy of her. She would show him that she could face whatever came along without screaming like a girl. *Never mind if I am a girl, and I would like to scream.* Calmly, she resumed looking at the screen in front of her.

"I think I should get Questor back here so I can go see for myself what is happening," Marco Antonio said, rising from his chair. "He is not reporting in with enough information to answer my questions."

"Please let me go with you," Ann said in her most serene voice.

"Of course," he replied.

That surprised her. She had expected him to respond with over-protective excuses about danger. She had been preparing pre-emptive arguments in response.

You've just averted World War III, my love. Well, maybe World War IV.

I know.

Smart man.

He glanced up at her and gave her that half-smile he wore when he knew they shared a secret no one else was privy to. Ann's cheeks also dimpled, unconsciously mimicking him. She said nothing more, but headed right for the stairs. Marco Antonio put his hand onto the communication device and sent for Questor, his favorite rover.

CHAPTER 2

Questor was well to the east of the Rocky Mountains, but he had seen no evidence of any flying objects, human or otherwise. He had been flying at his top speed, not worrying about sonic booms because he was flying almost directly over the Yellowstone desert. Jets and commercial airlines had been grounded since the Yellowstone explosion five years previously; jet engines and heavy aerial dust and dirt make a bad combination. A few propeller-driven airplanes had ventured into the skies above Texas, Arizona, and the southern states, but they stayed low and made only short hops.

Every road across the central section of the northern Midwest was buried under at least three feet of ash, dirt, and lava, so the only routes across the United States were the most southern routes. Being subject to severe windstorms and "black blizzards" made travel even more hazardous, although many stalwart truckers had begun to make the attempt.

The major trucking routes along the I-10 were studded with dust-shelters, where travelers could park their vehicles and find protection. Unlike the coffee shops and gas stations which previously had clustered around freeway off ramps, these places were designed to provide a haven from the deluge of dust thrown across the countryside, travelling at speeds much faster than the vehicles upon the roads. When the black blizzards blew, everything sought shelter and huddled until the winds died down. To do anything else was suicide.

Kept busy, road clearing equipment much like snow plows fought an unending battle to keep the highways viable. Dirt was piled up on both sides of the highways, frequently blocking the view of the sage and tumbleweeds of the deserts through which they passed. The hills of dust surrounding the Interstate were dark grey, while much of the countryside through which they passed was several shades lighter. Where the roads were asphalt, it looked as if there were black waves curling up either side of furrows plowed by a giant. The huge eighteen wheelers waddled through these channels, while speedier little cars flitted around them to avoid the dust in their wake.

Gradually, the country was becoming reunited. However, most of the central section would never be uncovered except to reach the most important treasures buried by the Yellowstone cataclysm. Frozen in time, many small towns, farm houses, cars, and people had been buried where they were when the mega-volcano dropped the 100 square kilometers of dirt, ash, and ejecta upon them. Like Pompeii before them, they would remain hidden treasures to be discovered by later explorers.

The main effort for the last five years had been to reseed the hundreds of square miles covered in easily-pulverized dirt. Some success had been seen from the grass seeds dropped by airplanes, but in many places, a cement-hard crust had formed when the rain had dried and the snow had melted. Legumes like clover and alfalfa had been encouraged to trap nitrogen into the barren rock. Native seed repositories were essential, but reseeding was complicated by the fact that the environment had changed enormously.

No bombs had been dropped over the center section of the continent. Clearly, this enemy was only interested in bombing cities.

For Questor to return to Hanford would take at least an hour, because Marco Antonio had asked Questor to return via a more southern route to check on the status of the major interstate highway. He had to give the Monitors new instructions, so he could utilize the time. Gone were the plans to begin cultivation of bacteria and worms; first, they had to ascertain the status of their laboratories. He feared that most had no homes to return to. They had to call someone in their vicinity to check the status of their nearest city.

Without large pieces of wood, they settled for several boards and heavy cardboard to cover the main window. Using a staple gun, they were attaching flattened cardboard boxes to the boards, darkening the room but at least providing some protection against the cold.

Once again, everyone was gathered together in Ann's living room. They had to be careful of broken glass which kept appearing in the most unlikely places, despite their efforts to clean it out of the thick, dark brown carpet. Many were sitting on the floor, seemingly intent on picking out the tiny shards by hand. Ann suspected that they were actually in shock, and the carpet-grooming activity was simply soothing to them.

"At first, I was sorry that you were all centralized in Hanford when the first attacks started. I am accustomed to you being my eyes and ears all over this world. Now, I realize how lucky we were to all be together and safe, at least so far," Marco Antonio said.

He perched on the end of the piano bench very casually. "I have sent your rovers to safety. They have cloaked themselves and are hovering at least one hundred kilometers apart, above the Pacific Ocean." He spoke quietly, in a tone that sounded conversational, not like a lecture. "The abilities of the observational sensors of the enemy are unknown, so I thought it best to separate them and station them away from any city that might be attacked. We were lucky that the invaders did not spot them suspended above Hanford; they would have provided a big target bull's eye above this town, flashing 'Monitors Here!' Either they were not spotted, they were not recognized as being extraterrestrial in origin, or the invaders did not care."

Marco Antonio continued talking in his conversational tone, uninterrupted by the Monitors, many of whom were still studying the carpet. "Until we know what is destroying the cities of this world, we cannot organize a defense. The first order of business is to access information. We must know what we are up against. There may be no defense, in which case you will be sent home directly."

Several of the Monitors looked up at him, surprise on their faces. Others looked relieved, carefully checking the others, assessing their responses. To Ann, these looked the most afraid.

"The problems of this planet remain unchanged for the survivors who were not vaporized. In fact, pulverized buildings will only add to the dust suspended above the stratosphere. After you place your calls, I suggest that you go down to the labs beneath either of these houses and begin making bacterial and worm colonies so that those who do not have labs set up can begin immediately. Also, many of the labs you did have will have been destroyed in this attack, so you will have to establish new facilities. Prepare as if you do, but we will reassess the situation after we discover the extent of this holocaust." Several nodded in agreement.

Ann watched in silence, carefully watching the responses of the group. Clearly, this was not a conversation. This was a coach talking to his team, or an officer talking to his men. Marco Antonio was explaining the mission ahead of them, and she was honored to be included in the briefing. She just wondered what her position would be. Was she on the team or merely the aide-de-camp? Maybe she was only a camp follower, the general's whore.

Whatever. This was a war, and she'd do whatever she was asked to do to win it. She stood up and walked towards Marco Antonio. He stood and put his arm around her waist. She had decided to take a more active command position, at least in her own home.

"I think you will be safe here for the time being," he continued. "So far, no city smaller than four million has been bombed, so Hanford will probably not be attacked. We can hope so, at least. The city of Lemoore, of course, was not bombed, but the Naval Air Station near there was. That was the blast we felt."

He gave her a tiny hug, and looked down at her briefly. "Ann and I are going towards the east coast and then onward towards Europe if necessary. I will report in regularly to keep you informed. There is food and good water here, and you can stay wherever you were last night. Our bed will be vacant tonight, so you may use it, too, if necessary, but please don't use Ann's personal items. This is her home, and I hope you respect that," he said, turning towards Ann and smiling.

Unexpectedly, she stepped forward. "Many of you have lost your homes, your laboratories, and your human friends. I extend my sincere condolences. You may stay here as long as it suits your plans to do so. I have called my friend, Carmen, who is my housekeeper.

She is also a wonderful cook, and I have asked her to prepare at least one meal a day for you all. Remember that she does not know that you are Monitors, so she will not understand your hesitation to eat in public. You may have to sit down to a meal together in order to maintain your cover as she serves you." Ann paused and looked around. "Carmen speaks Spanish, but very little English, but be careful. I don't know how much English she really understands because I have used my conversations with her as a means for me to practice my poor attempts at Spanish."

She decided to give them some human advice. They needed to be warned about the human response to grief. "Be kind to one another. This is a difficult time for everyone, and you will be surprised at how powerful grief can be to humans. Of course, you may certainly count on my daughter, Samantha, or my sons, Alex, Paul, or Ian. My grandchildren, however, do not know anything about Monitors, so please do not enlighten them. Children cannot be trusted to keep a secret of that magnitude. Your emotional responses may be stronger than you are used to, and you may feel overwhelmed at times. If you do, please talk to the Smiths or to Miguel. They have helped my family cope with crushing grief, and they can help you, too. They are wonderful friends, and we are blessed to have them. "

Ann took a small step back, indicating that she was through. She could feel Marco Antonio's pride in her as his whole body seemed to beam like a father at his child's first ballet recital.

Relieved, she smiled at him, and he continued. "We will be back as soon as possible, but we may be gone several days. Miguel is in charge, and both of the Smiths can advise you as well. Do not stop working, and be sure to help with the domestic chores. This will give you a chance to experience being in a family. Make the best of it." He paused.

Anything else, querida?

No. I'll think of a hundred things after we're gone.

"Excuse us while we pack a few personal things while we await Questor's return," he said, and he pressed her waist, indicating that she was to lead the way between the people sitting on the floor. Her way was blocked by someone who had shifted his position, so she hesitated. Marco Antonio held out his hand to Ann, and she took it, feeling like Marie Antoinette being escorted in to dinner.

"How very formal!" Ann said quietly to him.

"You make Marie Antoinette look like a kitchen troll," Marco Antonio said out loud. Anne smiled, because she had not sent him a thought about Marie Antoinette, yet he had picked it up from her anyway, and they had not been touching.

Oh, dear. You can hear my thoughts even when we're not touching! More every day.

They both walked into the big bedroom they shared. Wordlessly, Ann headed for the bathroom to get the grooming products they would need, and Marco Antonio went into the closet to retrieve their overnight bags. Questor would be able to store their things in vacuoles, but sometimes a suitcase still made moving things into the rover easier.

"Thank you for letting me come with you. I want to be near you because frankly, I'm scared," Ann said, her hands full of plastic bags filled with toothpaste, toothbrushes and deodorants.

"Ditto. This is something no one has ever experienced before. This is not war; it is invasion, possibly annihilation. I don't want you out of my sight. If anything ever happened to you while I was out on some recon mission, I would never be the same. I think I would rather be dead than to be without you," he said, taking underwear and socks out of his drawers and placing them into a suitcase. His tone remained conversational, as if what he was saying was as unimportant as deciding which shirt to wear.

"Oh, nonsense! You got along fine without me for over 700 years, and you could do so again. Let's just hope neither of us has to find out how we would fare without the other," Ann said, going through her underwear drawer, looking for her best panties. She could be casual, too.

"That was before I had met you. I had no idea what I was missing. I didn't really understand that 'we' means more than me and some other person. It is so much more than that. When I am thinking of you and me, 'we' is a sum much greater than its parts. I would be far less than half of 'us' without you. I would be less than myself. I would be nothing." At last, he glanced up from the suitcase and looked at her.

"Wow! You're a fun man to pack with!" she said, tossing the bag of teeth cleaning accoutrement into the bag. "You really know how to take a girl's mind off invading aliens!" Ann knew that her banter would not hide the depth of her feelings for him, so she just gave up and stepped into his arms. Sometimes, nothing said it better than a hug.

She had caught him unaware, and when she held his body next to hers, she got a blast of emotion bigger than the four-hanky scenes of *Old Yeller, On the Beach, Steel Magnolias, Last of the Mohicans, Gladiator*—all of them rolled into one. He was afraid, sad, sorry—all of it. She nearly collapsed, but she clung to him and scrunched her eyes closed against the emotional onslaught.

Whoa!

Instantly, he backed off, at least emotionally, letting only the love through. "I'm sorry. I did not mean to project so many feelings. We shall get through this together, and in your wisdom, you have reminded me to remember the memories we have made together when I feel overwhelmed."

"Oh, there are other ways I have to take your mind off your troubles. When we get into Questor, I'll show you. There are a lot more memories we can make while Questor whizzes us across the continent. We must live in the moment and not dwell on our fears."

"If I think about what you are suggesting, and hold you like this, I will want to kiss you, and then throw you on the bed and ravage you quickly, and then slowly. Hmm," he said, his chin next to her ear.

"I think you could start with the kiss now," she whispered. "The quick and slow ravaging part can come later. It will give us things to think about while we pack."

His arm slid up her back and into her hair. He fisted her hair and pulled her face back so he could look into her eyes, and then he slowly placed his mouth on hers. The kiss deepened as he let her hair go and brought his other hand up to her jaw. He cradled her face in his hands and let the kiss grow deeper, his tongue invading her mouth. Her hands slid down his back to his butt, which she pressed into her abdomen. She could feel her breasts harden and become firm as she compressed her body into his, and she felt lust growing by the second.

"I love you, querida, and if you keep your hands on my butt, the only thing I'll get accomplished is locking the door. You weaken my every restraint," he said, pulling her face back and looking at her again. "What do you want me to do?"

"What I want you to do, and what I need you to do are two different things. I must call my children and make sure they're all right, and that would be easier if I were not making passionate love with you," she said, letting go of his butt.

"Alas, I suspected as much. But I will take that rain check," he said, letting her go. "I love it when you want to make memories in Questor. Or anywhere else."

She grabbed his phone and started to dial Samantha's cell phone. Because it was a school day, she knew she wouldn't get through, so she sent a text. The message was "I'm going with Marco Antonio in Questor to check out who's bombing us. He doesn't think it's another country. We'll be gone a couple days, but I'll be in touch." She sent the same message to Alex and Paul and to Ian, who was out at Pilgrim's Camp, teaching the migrant children there.

She knew the phone lines would be clogged, so she stuck to text messages, which could be sent much faster, freeing up the lines. What she hadn't counted on were the blackouts caused by the bombed-out cities. Local connections were fine, but any that went through San Francisco, L.A. or any of the other cities got messages saying that those lines were not in service. Both Alex and Paul still had Kansas City area codes, and they didn't go through.

The first response was from Ian. "What bombs?"

Ann texted back, "LNAS had been bombed. San Jose, Vandenberg AFB, San Diego, L.A., S.F. and ?? Questor is taking us East and up to see who's doing it. I'm going 2. Front windows blown out, need fixin. Check ur house, then come 2 mine & help. Mom."

Before she could put Marco Antonio's phone down, her cell rang. She could hear it in her purse, so she retrieved it. Samantha was on the line. "Oh my God, Mom! Who's bombing us? Do you know how many people in my class have fathers and mothers at the base?! Was the town of Lemoore hit, or just LNAS?"

"Whoa, girl! Let me answer one question at a time. Mostly, I have non-answers and a lot more questions. It was Lemoore Naval Air Station. They're not atomic bombs, which is good and bad. They don't appear to be from any of our former enemies. Marco Antonio and I are going to take Questor out and find whoever is killing our cities. Then we'll see what the Monitors can do."

"Jake's best friend's dad is in the Navy, the people across the street are Navy, the ones with the noisy pool parties behind us are Navy. Who the hell is bombing us, and why don't we bomb them back?" Samantha said.

"That's what we're going to find out. Please keep an eye out for the Monitors. I still have a house full, and some have no home to return to. My front windows were blasted in, and I asked Ian to take care of that for me, but give him a hand if he needs it. Miguel will be in charge, but I know that he'll help you before anyone else, so you can count on him."

"Tell Marco Antonio to kick them in the ass for us! The whole school is on lockdown until we find out what's going on. I'm letting everyone call or text home, so I did, too. We're going to turn on the TV's so we can keep up on what's happening. You take care, Mom."

"I will. I know you'll help when and where you can. Let me know if you hear from Da Boys, too. I haven't reached them yet."

"Where did they go? Oh, my God, Mom. They were going to San Francisco last week-end, weren't they?"

"They should just about be home now. They were driving, not in a rover, but in a car. They were going to come back this morning, so they could go out with a couple of the Monitors and help locate a good site for another lung cleaner production company. Please keep trying to reach them after I go." Ann suddenly feared that they might have been near LNAS or still in San Francisco. She could only hope that they were somewhere in between when the bombs started dropping.

MONITORS OF DESTRUCTION

Alex, her middle son, and his partner Paul had become very good at orchestrating projects for the Monitors. With Paul's expertise on writing medical studies programs, his input on the lung cleaner program had been invaluable. Alex made things happen. He put together the people or experts with the supplies they needed. Their efforts had freed up a great deal of Marco Antonio's time, enabling him to work in the laboratory sixteen hours a day.

They'll be all right. They're on the road, coming home. They're OK.

Ann kept reassuring herself that her son and his partner were between bomb destinations. She had so many people to worry about, as did everyone. No one could reassure anyone because no one knew what was going on. They only knew that entire cities had been blasted out of existence by someone, somewhere, for some reason.

It had happened today. Not in months, weeks, or days. Today. *Oh, my God!*

CHAPTER 3

Entering the rover, they settled into their seats, which automatically molded around their bodies. Ann placed her hand on the console, and Marco Antonio did the same. Questor answered Marco Antonio's questions in pictures, not words, and he went faster than Ann's brain could follow. She didn't want to ask questions and interrupt the flow of information, so she just hung on and tried to catch what she could.

She gathered that the destruction had started at the West Coast, with bombs, ICBMs, nukes—whatever they were—coming from both the west, over the Pacific, and from the north, over the Arctic. As if sweeping the northern hemisphere, the missiles delivering the bombs had come from the west to the east and north, gradually ceasing to come from the west. Marco Antonio headed Questor north.

"We're going to peek over the North Pole to see what's there, querida. I strongly doubt that we will be able to see anything with the naked eye, but perhaps Questor will be able to pick up a frequency that they cannot hide," Marco Antonio said aloud.

"I'm surprised that NATO, NORAD, SETI, NASA, or *SOMEBODY* couldn't see them coming towards us by now. They can't be tiny and still carry that much ordinance," Ann wondered.

"I agree. I should think it would be impossible to shield that much mass. They were bombs, not energy bursts. They came from a big ship. We'll find it, and then we'll see what's going on," Marco Antonio said. *Good observation, querida.*

"There's either mass or energy somewhere, of course. Basic physics, not worth mentioning. If it's not nuclear, it must be chemical, like dynamite. Electromagnetic fields or laser beams don't explode like that, do they?"

"No, but not one in a hundred would think of it," he mentioned abstractly. She knew his mind was actually on other things, not on her brilliance. He was just trying to reassure her, and she knew it.

"So all my hours of watching *NOVA* are paying off. I'm sure our military generals and admirals watched the same shows," she said dryly.

"The skies are filled with satellites peering around the planet, looking for a mother ship. Clearly, it has some type of cloaking device which is keeping it invisible," he paused, and reached out and took her hand. Once again, he was trying to comfort her, and this time, she appreciated the effort. "As soon as they find one, there will be jets flying through the dust clouds, looking for something to aim at before their engines flame out. There will be a bunch of ICBM's emerging from their underground silos like cicadas from the ground. All they need are a few coordinates. We may be able to help there," he said quietly.

Ann was not going to remind him of the Prime Directive at this point. Earth was under attack, and Marco Antonio could surely help in its defense. There was much they needed to discuss. Normally, the Monitors would not even consider helping any side during a war, even with coordinates. "You'll help us stop them, won't you Marco?" she said plaintively, trying hard not to whine.

"The only problem is that we don't have any bombs, my love. We don't fight battles or wars; we just get out of their way."

He got up to check on their stores. Normally, Miguel or Marco Antonio restocked Questor with water and blood as soon as they disembarked, so he would be ready at all times. Ann had packed her own food before they took off.

"What if their bombs are superior to ours? We might be only poking with a stick, since our jets are grounded and our nukes are sixty or seventy years old. Surely, you have some defensive weapons to use when bad guys get out of line?" Ann asked, trying to keep the terror out of her voice. She stood up and walked over to him.

"Oh, we have a few tricks up our sleeves," he said, eyeing the dried fruit roll-ups she had brought along with her sandwich.

"Anyone with eight arms should have enough sleeves to carry a lot of secret weapons. Now is the time to use them, my love." Ann felt herself getting angry, so she paused, calming herself, and became thoughtful. "They've killed millions, and they have yet to introduce themselves, or tell us what they want or why they're here." Turning to look at him, she almost begged, "They must be stopped, Marco Antonio!" Ann said, stifling a sob. *Stop it! He doesn't need an hysterical woman coming unhinged in front of him. Get a grip, girl.*

"You are entitled to be a little upset. I would worry if you were NOT upset when your entire planet is under attack. What kind of sociopath would I have on my rover?" He put his arm around her and whispered into her hair. "Try not to think of the people; just focus on the bombs, not the casualties," he said, giving her a hug.

"Good advice, my love. Thank you." Ann put her arms around him and took a deep breath. He smelled of Marco Antonio, the most reassuring smell in the world. "Will you do whatever you can to kill them? At least scare them away. Maybe you could negotiate with them on our behalf?" *Anything! Just help us!*

"Of course, querida. Let's see what we have to face before we start making strategies."

"Well, we won't just wish them away. We have to have a plan. Hope is not a strategy, you know." Ann said, trying hard not to cry or to squeeze him too hard. She could feel the tears coming down her cheeks.

I'm sorry, Marco Antonio! I'm sorry I'm such a sponge! I can't help but grieve for the millions of people who have died in the last few years! First Yellowstone, and now city-killers from god-knows-where. Not millions—BILLIONS!

Ann became incoherent at that point. The stress, the grief, the fear—it all became too much for her, and she just cried. Marco Antonio could have soothed her, but he knew that her brain needed to relieve itself of some of the neurotoxins that had swamped it for hours, if not days. She needed to cry, so he let her.

Before she was really through crying, she lifted her head from his damp chest and looked up at him. The tissue she had brought in her pocket had been totally used up and was now a sodden mass in her hand. He reached into his back pocket and took out his handkerchief and handed it to her. Wordlessly, he pointed to an open vacuole where she could throw her trash. She did so, and Questor closed the vacuole and assimilated the tissue. The activity seemed to calm her, and she said: "Better now. I was gone, but I'm back. I'll cry more later, when I have time." She tried hard to get a grip, remembering the old Scarlett O'Hara trick from *Gone With the Wind*. "Later" is always the best time to cry.

"That's my girl! Let's see what our city-killers are doing while Questor flies us over the pole," he said, taking out his I-phone and flipping through it, looking for updates. Sure enough, the cities east of Europe were being bombed, too. Poland, Latvia, Russia, Ukraine—a steady eastward sweep was progressively eliminating most cities over a few million.

While Ann watched the map on the I-phone, she thought it looked like a child was blotting out each city with his thumb, carefully wiping out each one. City by city disappeared in an inexorable march to the east. She tried to shut down the thoughts about how many people were dying. She focused on the cities and countries which were being hit. Even more important, perhaps, were the cities which were being ignored. How did they choose?

While they stood transfixed, watching the tiny map, Questor crossed the North Pole. Immediately, he sent out an alert to Marco Antonio, who asked him to please create a window so that he and Ann might get a visual on the city-killers' ship. Questor immediately complied, making the hull next to them as clear as glass.

The ship was huge, but dark. There were no lights shining, nothing that looked like a bridge or control center, nor were there windows, portholes, or blinking warnings signs. Without decoration or printing of any kind, it had no particular shape, either. It had bulges and indentations apparently placed according to function, not form. There had been no effort to make it sleek or beautiful; this was a utilitarian vehicle about as sexy as a Jeep on steroids, but without any degree of "cuteness" that all Jeeps share.

"Hail it," Marco Antonio said aloud to Questor.

Instantly, Questor heeled to starboard at an astounding rate. Ann had never felt him move so fast, and both she and Marco Antonio were knocked off their feet. Marco Antonio fell on top of her, so Ann was blasted with "Sorry! Are you all right?" from both Marco Antonio and Questor. From Questor, she got the message that the city-killer had tried to shoot them. It was a good thing that Questor had been trained to veer to another position as soon as he sent a message to an unknown vessel. Thus, if the stranger wished to shoot in their direction, Questor would not still be there to receive their retaliatory strike. Ann got this explanation in a mental blast as she started to formulate the question.

"I'm sorry, Ann! We should have been sitting down and strapped in before I asked Questor to send out a message. That was sloppy of me," Marco Antonio said as he disentangled himself from her and helped her to her feet.

"No problem. You've swept me off my feet before," she said, pulling herself up with Marco Antonio's help. "Did it shoot at our position?"

"Yes," he said, straightening her shirt in back. "They used some kind of force beam, rather than a projectile. Interesting," he mused, looking once again out the window at the huge black hulk.

With the controlled fury of a school teacher who's just been knocked on her butt, she said, "Then it doesn't want to talk. Sounds like it doesn't mean to play nice, either." She stared angrily at the black behemoth, leaning towards the window so she could see more of it.

"No, it doesn't," he noted drily.

"In fact, I get the impression that it doesn't care about making friends at all. It only wants us dead," Ann said, her anger making her words clipped.

"Apparently so," Marco Antonio answered thoughtfully.

She looked out the window at the ugly black hunk of metal and spoke directly to it. "Well, that's just rude," Ann said, putting her hands on her hips. She hated everything that hideous black metallic carcass stood for. Catching her own assumption despite her fury, she added, "Is that thing metal? Plastic? Or just solidified slime carrying evil and hatred?"

"Mostly metal, I think. I'm wondering if there's anyone at home at all? I get no feeling of life from that ship, nor does Questor." Marco Antonio leaned down and peered through the window thoughtfully. "I think it's a robot, not a ship. They've sent out a drone."

"Well, good then! I won't have to worry about inviting them to tea before we blast them out into space. We can send the Welcome Wagon home and just bring in the marines." Ann's chin moved sideways like a cocky gangbanger. She looked ready to take them on all by herself.

"Maybe not, querida. Just because it's not alive doesn't mean that it is not attached to another living set of entities." He turned and looked at her. "Before Yellowstone blew, your government sent out drones to locate and eliminate enemies, and they knew exactly where each one was, who it was attacking, and whether or not it succeeded. If we knock this one out of the air, more might come in its place. I think we should tread lightly here, my love." Marco Antonio remained very calm and thoughtful as he turned his attention back out the window.

Glancing in his direction, she said, "You sound like you have a plan. What are your thoughts? Mine are all violent," Ann still sounded angry. "Can we just gently blow it out of the sky and then say 'Oops?'" She put her hand to her mouth, mimicking someone who had just spilled some coffee on an enemy's report paper. "It isn't like they don't deserve it," she added.

"Let's get closer. It hasn't fired on us again; perhaps it's not designed to attack moving objects unless they attack it or try to get in touch with it. Let's see," Marco Antonio said. Questor resumed its slow approach towards the huge space ship as soon as Marco Antonio put his hand on the armrest of the chair.

Nothing happened.

"I think we should take a closer look," Marco Antonio mused.

Ann turned from the window and looked at Marco Antonio. "Well, I don't want you poking in or around that thing! Please don't get too close to it. I can't believe it wouldn't be tamper-proof. I think if we touch it, it'll make us go 'poof!' and disappear in a cloud of damp powder." She raised her hands, mimicking a blast. Putting her hands back on her hips, she said, "I don't want us falling to earth in a cloud of ash! I'm asking you not to do this, please!" Had there been room, she would have been pacing.

Marco Antonio could feel her tension. He didn't return her gaze, but kept watching the ship outside. "I don't think it will react to living tissue. I think it will vaporize metals or rocks, but not living tissue."

"Good! Then let's throw a chicken at it!" Ann said, looking at him.

"Don't have one," Marco Antonio said, still gazing at the ship.

"I'll go then. If one of us is going to die, it should definitely be me. Not you or Questor. I'm replaceable, and both of you are not," she said resolutely. "Just throw me out of the ship. 'Annie, the Human Projectile!'"

"Don't be silly. I would never put you in such danger. You know that, Ann." He had turned to look at her directly, his eyebrows furrowed. Her humor had not amused him.

"Ditto. It's my job to protect you, too. Let's think of another way," she concluded, much more seriously.

Marco Antonio grew quiet for a moment, a long moment. Ann wondered if he was planning a way to enter the ship, or thinking up a new plan. While they watched and thought, two more missiles took off from the mother-ship and flew towards their right.

"Oh, dear god! There goes another eight million more people who are about to be vaporized. That's two more cities pulverized, Marco!" Ann was beginning to feel frantic. She knew they had to do *something* immediately, and Marco Antonio's controlled silence was beginning to really bug her. She knew it wasn't fair to blame Marco Antonio because there was nothing he could do about it immediately. Questor had no guns or lasers; he couldn't even defend himself except by dodging. The fact that they kept approaching the black, silent pile of metal which was lobbing death towards Earth was making her extremely nervous. In fact, she was terrified, furious and sad.

Let's get out of here!

In a minute, querida. I want to try something first.

Questor accelerated until he was directly in front of the launching tube from which the latest missile had emerged. Gently, it sent out a tentacle which reached into the silo. The end of the tentacle broke off, leaving a piece of itself in the missile tube, and the rest retracted.

With big eyes, Ann looked at Marco Antonio, gasped and said, "Did that hurt him? Can Questor break off pieces of himself at will? Can he grow back pieces of himself, or is that loss permanent? Is it sentient, like he is? Is it his baby?" Ann's mind had more questions than she could list, and Marco Antonio answered them as they came in. The problem was, she could not process the answers fast enough, and she confused the answer to one question with the answer to another.

Turning to her, he took her hand and said, "I am confusing you, querida. Let me answer one question at a time. He can break off and replace small parts of his body, which he does frequently to repair damage. It will grow back. Yes, it hurt him, but not as much as losing a hand, say, would hurt you or me. It is vaguely sentient to Questor because it is part of himself, but it doesn't think as you or I or even Questor does. No, it is not strictly speaking his baby, since it will neither grow nor reproduce. It will weaken and die, especially under these conditions. Be comforted in the knowledge that it is in no pain, neither physical nor emotional. Neither Questor nor the piece of him are suffering." Marco Antonio said, squeezing her hand. "Questor just threw it a chicken to see how it would react."

Calmed by Marco Antonio's touch, Ann answered more thoughtfully as she watched the total lack of response of the big ship. "It seems to like chicken, at least Questor-chicken."

"I think I'm going to try to board her, if we can find an opening. Even if it is a drone, surely there is a maintenance hatch," Marco Antonio said, speaking to both Ann and Questor.

"Brought your space suit, eh? Mine's still at the cleaners," Ann quipped. "If the lack of air doesn't get us, the lack of pressure and the cold temperature surely will," Ann pointed out, dismissing the thought as impossible.

"That's one of the things I have up my eight sleeves. Questor has an EV suit which will give me about a half hour if I'm in a human body and twice that in my Monitor body."

She felt she had better back off. Marco Antonio didn't need schooling in science. "We'll bring that next time," Ann said, half joking. "I'd kinda like to meet you in your native state, with your eight arms and big old googly- eyes." It felt good to change the subject.

"Are you tired of this body already?" he said, looking at her out of the corner of his eye.

"Never!" she said, and she could feel his whole body relax. "I love you—all of you. In every flavor, color, or shape." Just to change the subject and to evade his insecurity, she said, "Is your Monitor body tougher than your human body?"

"Much tougher. It's not as subject to pressure and temperature variances, and it can go longer with no oxygen." Marco Antonio returned his gaze to the black hulk out the window, which had still not responded to the "Questor chicken" that was sitting in its bomb bay.

Looking out the window again, she said "Cool!"

"I'd probably scare you off, and you'd never speak to me again."

"Why do you think that?" she said, turning her whole head to look at him. He kept his eyes riveted on the ship outside. "Do you really think I love you just for your hot body? Think again, Romeo. It's your mind that really turns me on."

"That would be very nice. This body, hot or not, is not really mine. I just chose it, and then modified it to suit my needs." His tone was conversational, but she felt the insecurity in his body, especially since he refused to look at her.

"You were smart enough to 'choose' one of the most breath-taking men I've ever seen. You are absolutely gorgeous, so I compliment you on your choice. Besides, I'm sure he deserved to die, or you wouldn't have picked him, right?" she asked, knowing the answer. As casually as possible, she looked away from him and back out the window.

"Absolutely. He was a monster."

"He cleaned up pretty well, I think. Anyway—will this portable, instant EV suit have an oxygen tank? Or are you just supposed to hold your breath for half an hour?" The change of subject had calmed her, as he knew it would. Still, they had to get back to the monster that was killing their cities before it shot off any more deadly bombs.

"Questor will make me a tank from the same material the suit is made of. We'll all have to head directly home when I return, since he will milk some of the oxygen in this cabin, and some from his tissues." He stretched his back, and turned toward her. He put his arms on her waist and looked directly in her eyes.

"So this would not be a good time for me to do calisthenics?" Ann asked.

"This would be a good time for you to sleep. Otherwise, you might just end up in a coma after your calisthenics," he answered. "I am worried that we'll run short of oxygen. This is a terrible risk, querida, and I can do it later, on the next trip. No harm can come to you," he said quietly, "and I am not going to imperil your life in any way. Could you remain very still?"

"I was just kidding, Marco Antonio. I'll be just fine. I'll be very still, but there's no way I could just doze off while you're out climbing into a known killer. Besides, I forgot my jammies. Go get your suit on and I'll start puffing into your oxygen tank, if that would help." She felt much better. She tried to smile at him.

"No, you were right. I'll come back later."

"You'll do it *now*. While we've been here, this giant killing machine has murdered millions more of my people. There is no time to worry about one little old lady's breathing. I'll be fine if you put me to sleep. Let's go, Marco. We're burnin' daylight here!"

"Are you sure? If anything happened to you, I'd die."

"That's why I'm sure. Go!" she said in her best Mrs. Jacob tone. She had not forgotten the skills gained from being a teacher for 37 years.

Still, he hesitated. The look in his eyes was pitiful and full of fear. Ann had never seen him like this, and she swallowed. *It must be very dangerous indeed if it frightens Marco Antonio.* But in the next second she realized that he was not afraid for himself; he was afraid for her, and for the guilt he'd feel if she were harmed in any way.

She realized that she must take the responsibility for her own safety inasmuch as she could. She looked him right in the eye and said, "The longer we wait, the less oxygen there will be for either of us. I insist, Marco Antonio. We must find out as much as we can as quickly as we can. Besides, no human has access to non-metallic, non-electronic space gear. That's what you're counting on, isn't it? It will not be aware of you, since you'll give off so little electrical energy, and you're non-metallic. Right?"

A big grin flashed across his face. "Good for you! Yes, you figured it out. I think it will not be aware that I'm there. Its sensors are wired to defend against other mechanical weapons, not biological entities." He kissed the end of her nose. "You never cease to amaze me, Ann. I wouldn't want to have to lie to you; you'd figure out whatever I was hiding."

"This is not my first rodeo. Now, go, go, GO! Get out of here, so I can take a nap!" she said, nudging him gently with her hands.

"OK, I'll make it quick, if Questor can find an opening to this tin can," Marco Antonio said, putting his hand onto Questor. They both became still for no more than a few seconds, but Ann knew that they had had a long conversation during that time. Questor slowly began to move to the top of the huge metallic blob in front of them, and made his way to the space-facing side of the ship. Rather than reconfigure himself, he slowly rotated 180 degrees until they were also looking at the unconventionally shaped space ship with the sun at their back. Now, it floated between them and the Earth, which was completely blocked from their view. Gently, Questor floated "down," towards their feet.

With the sun shining behind them, the ship was brightly lit. Marco Antonio and Ann studied it carefully, looking for a port. Briefly, Ann wondered how Questor created the gravity she was feeling, but she decided not to bring it up.

She scrutinized the uneven surface in front of her, trying to decide where an entry might be found. Would it be just a crack? Would it have steps or a ledge? Would one of these boxy add-ons just swing outward (or inward), the hinges invisible? She had no idea what she was looking for, but eventually her roving eyes saw something she recognized. She studied it for a few seconds, and then she pointed and said, "There. What's that?"

A small ledge stuck out perpendicularly from the ship. She hadn't noticed it at first, because she was looking for a step or walkway, and this was oriented up-and-down. At the base of the step, there were two tiny lumps (hinges?) about a meter apart (although it was very difficult to imagine the scale of what she was looking at). On the other side, there was a slight line. It could be a door, turned sideways. Ann touched Marco Antonio as she turned her head to look at it sideways. Yes, it looked more like an entryway with an exterior step.

Marco Antonio thought it might also be something on which to attach a catwalk or rolling stairs. Since there was no reference to "up" or "down" in space, any doorway could be lined up with another object or ship at any angle. Of course, the door would be sealed or locked somehow, and they would have to open it using non-metallic instruments.

Perhaps there was a handle. Perhaps there was not. The only way to tell for sure was to get close enough to examine it carefully.

Marco Antonio got up and walked the few feet to the back of the transport. He reached into the wall and started pulling out a sheet of clear plastic, which he started wrapping around his body. He took another piece out of a smaller opening and ran his fingers down the side and bottom of the sheet. It stuck together as if it were taped.

Ann could see what was happening, so she said, "Let me help you with that. I have a pair of scissors, if that wouldn't be too plebian? I'll cut the pants legs and the arm holes if you'll model." She reached for her purse and took out a small pair of sharp scissors, after a few seconds of rummaging around.

"That would be great, Ann. I'll need to cover my feet and hands, which I could do if you cut some smaller squares or rectangles. The edges will stick together like tape, but then they'll bond in a few seconds and become impermeable. It will fit onto my body like a second skin with an air bubble attached to my chest and belly. My body temperature will remain constant, and the air should last about half an hour. Because it is under pressure, some will leak into by body suit, but that won't matter since I can inhale it out," Marco Antonio said as he swiftly pressed the edges of his fingers together and sealed his new gloves to his sleeves. The process was surprisingly quick and painless, but Ann worried that the seals might spring apart or form a leak.

Ann overlapped the edges of the pants and worked down from the crotch to his ankle, and then started at the top again and worked her way down the other leg. She took a rectangular piece of the stuff, set it on the floor, and helped him place his foot in the middle. When she tried to mold it over his shoe, it was too awkward, so he slipped his shoe off and she molded it to his foot. Remarkably, tucks and wrinkles smoothed themselves out, and where it was a trifle too short to reach his pants at the ankle, she just pulled it, and it stretched to fit. She watched as the doubled-over, wrinkled part eased into the thinner material over his instep, molding itself into boots of approximately even thickness.

"This is really remarkable stuff," Ann said. "This is *way* out of my price-range! Is it plastic?"

It looked like thick plastic wrap was molding to his body over his clothes. Marco Antonio reached out to touch her, and his message came through only barely muffled. "No, it's a life form. It's conscious, and has been bred specifically for this purpose. This will work, Ann. Do not worry about equipment failures. My suit *wants* me to survive, and it will give me plenty of warning if any part of it is weakening. Please don't fret about my safety."

"OK, I won't. I'll just bottle up my terror for later. I'll schedule that in right before my complete nervous breakdown. In the meantime, what should I be doing? Besides sleeping?" She continued to rub the seals, checking for possible holes or weakness, but there was none. It was completely smooth.

"Stay in touch with Questor. I'll try to talk to you directly, but if I get inside, I may be cut off. Questor is much more sensitive to my messages, so he'll show you what's happening. Don't freak out, baby. We need to get this information if we're going to stop this thing from wiping out the dominant life forms of this planet," he said, stroking her face with his Saran-covered fingertips. The plastic was wrapped up to his chin and over his head. The only part of his body that was not encased was his face. His hair was slicked down to his head as if were wet.

"Is this thing pumping air into that bag?" Ann asked, noticing that a bag had formed on his back. It was slightly moving rhythmically on his back.

"Yes. Questor is replacing the cabin oxygen and nitrogen from his tissues, so you will have enough. When it is full, I'll close my faceplate and leave. You can lie down in one of Questor's vacuoles and take a little snooze. Before you know it, I'll be back!" He smiled and winked at her.

"Kiss me while you still can," Ann said, reaching for his face. "Have I told you today?" she whispered.

"What? You have told me several things, querida."

"Have I told you how much I love you?"

"In many ways. And I love you even more."

The clear covering started to close down around his face, obviously trying to seal. Ann backed up and let it enclose Marco Antonio's perfect visage. It didn't cling to his skin, so the air from the bubble on his back could reach his nose. She was glad he didn't look like a burglar with a nylon stocking over his face, squishing his nose and changing his features. No, Marco Antonio looked as perfect as he always did, but now he was behind a window fitted to his face and body.

"May I stay awake so that I can hear you? I'll remain calm and I won't move unless you tell me to. If we start running long on time, I'll let Questor put me under. Is that OK?"

"Yes, but I want you lying in this vacuole. We'll leave the emergency procedures in Questor's hands. I trust his decisions. I know he likes you and will do anything to keep you safe. Don't argue with him, or fight him in any way, and you can stay awake. Deal?"

"I'll be a good girl," she said, feeling like a child climbing into the coffin-like hole about to be tucked in. As soon as she was in, Questor closed the top and she had a sudden feeling of claustrophobia. She lifted her head, and when she felt the top tap her forehead, she reached up to touch the lid, discovering that it was within a half-inch of her nose. A sudden overwhelming terror grabbed her, and she wanted to claw her way out.

Instead, she took three breaths, closed her eyes, and thought about being safe in an airlock. Questor would have to open the compartment for Marco Antonio to leave, and whatever air was still in it would escape. "I am safe. I am safe. I can breathe, and I am safe. Thank you, Questor. I am safe." She repeated this like a mantra and forced herself to relax.

"You *are* a good girl, Ann! You are showing amazing self-control, and I'm proud of you! Stay focused, baby. OK, I'm off!" Marco Antonio just pushed off from the rover and headed directly toward the massive hunk of metal in front of him. He could not miss, but Ann still would have preferred a rope around his waist, in case he had to be jerked back to the transport.

Why didn't I insist on a rope? That was so stupid! What happens if he loses consciousness, or if he gets zapped by the ship?

Ann's anxiety levels skyrocketed as she thought about all the horrible things that could happen to him with no way to retrieve him. Suddenly, a thought broke through to her, clear as a bell.

I am tied to Questor, Ann. We thought of everything you are worrying about, and I tied myself to my transport. I won't float away, and if I lose consciousness, Questor will recover me. Do not distress yourself, my love.

"Thank you. I'm glad one of us is on the ball. Sorry for the oversight. If I had been in charge of this mission, you'd be floating around like a dead fish. I'm embarrassed," Ann said aloud. She kept her eyes closed and tried to make herself calm.

Don't be. That's why we work in teams.

"Are you there yet?"

Yes.

"Is there a way in?"

Not so far. Let me concentrate, querida. Perhaps it will come to me. Marco Antonio whispered into her mind.

Ann didn't really understand what he meant, but she gathered that he wanted her to shut up and get out of his head. She tried to concentrate on her breathing and her mantra, "I am safe. It's OK."

Yes, but you are too harsh. Quiet yourself, little dove. Think quiet thoughts. Calm yourself; mantenga la calma.

Although Ann tried not to think about it, she knew he was really concentrating on something else if he spoke to her in Spanish. She tried to remember how she had felt once when she had had an MRI; this was no different, except she did not have the benefit of piped music to distract her. She tried to think of something she played on the piano. A Chopin Prelude came to mind, so she played it mentally. Twice. It was pretty cool because she didn't make any mistakes, as she would have had she had a keyboard in front of her. Then she played a little Bach, and then the second movement of the Beethoven's Pathetique. She knew the first and third movement would have been too hard to remember without the printed music in front of her, and the thought brought a smile from Marco Antonio.

Now who's not concentrating? Am I distracting you?

Only slightly. I think you're adorable, thinking that you would need the printed music. It's all there in your brain, and has been since you were 15. Your fingers might not remember it perfectly, but your brain will.

Concentrate! Get out of my head! We'll run out of time!

Ann thought she felt movement, but she immediately assured herself that it was a hallucination. Questor would never fly off leaving Marco Antonio outside. Never.

Suddenly, Marco Antonio was out of her head. She hoped that he had entered the ship. If they were not separated by distance or thick metal, he was gone. Injured or dead.

Instantly, Ann was overcome with panic and fear. Almost immediately, she directed a picture to Questor of Marco Antonio entering the huge chunk of metal next to them. Questor sent her "good feels," which assured her that he was all right and inside the ship. She exhaled.

She tried to resume her mantra, but it was impossible. The terror kept creeping back, and she could not stop it. *Time. This will take time, and I must only wait, and he will be back, bugging me. His presence will feel like background music in a movie. Enjoy the silence while you can, girl.*

She couldn't. Worry turned to fear, and fear turned to terror. She wanted out of this box so she could feel Marco Antonio in her head again. *Where is he? Is he alive? Oh, God, what if he is injured? Get him out, Questor! Get me out! Bring him back! He'll run out of air and be trapped, as I am trapped!*

Unconsciously, she began to wiggle. She wanted to free herself from the vacuole she was encased in, but as soon as she tried, her arms dropped to her side and she felt herself sliding down, down, down into oblivion.

CHAPTER 4

When she woke, Marco Antonio was holding her. He was sitting in a chair, and she was on his lap, her head on his shoulder. Conveniently, Questor had widened the pilot's chair and had raised the armrest so that her legs draped comfortably over it as Marco Antonio held her tightly.

"We've left the ship, querida. You're safe again," he whispered. She could feel his breath on her forehead. The lights were very low, and everything was very quiet.

"Sorry I got scared. When you disappeared from my mind, I thought you might be dead. Questor tried to tell me that you were OK and just in the ship, but my imagination ran away with me," Ann said. She was mortified that she had lost it. She had never been a screamer, nor was she given to hysterics in any form. It simply wasn't her style, and she was ashamed of herself.

"I know. I'm sorry. I didn't mean to frighten you. I've never felt you so upset. Even Questor was surprised that you were so frightened. He put you to sleep, ostensibly to save oxygen, but I know that it was really to soothe you. He was quite concerned, as I was. Are you all right now?" He didn't try to look at her. He just held her and whispered.

"Just embarrassed. I usually have better control," she said, her face lifted up so she could look into his eyes. "Never mind me—what did you discover within the ship? Were there any people there?" Her humiliation aside, she needed to know what he'd discovered.

"No. We were right; it's a drone. I think it's here to 'cleanse' the planet before their dominant species gets here. They're not going to completely drive you into extinction; in fact, they're looking forward to meeting you. They just want there to be far fewer of you, so that you can share the natural resources of the planet with them. Probably as their servants, or possibly as their snacks."

"How did you find that out if there was no one there?" The whispering seemed nice, and it did calm her, but she studied him as he spoke. She loved looking at him. He was gorgeous.

"I listened. Within a few minutes, I was able to break into their major computer system and get the general gist of their attitude and intentions. It's not good," Marco Antonio whispered back.

"Can you show me what you felt from them?"

"Yes, but it will exhaust you. You were pretty overwhelmed, and you are fragile now. You need to sleep so that your brain can rest and realign your neurotransmitter levels. Being upset saps them, which makes fear exhausting. Rest, querida. Go back to sleep." He gave her a gentle body-squeeze, which felt wonderful to her. Cattle-squeeze tranquilizing chutes flitted through her mind, but she immediately dismissed the wayward thought.

"So just tell me in words. I know it will be slow, but I need to know as much about them as quickly as possible. I'm sorry I freaked out on you! I did OK until I thought you might be injured. That made me crazy, as it would if you were actually hurt. Then the claustrophobia overcame me. I lost it. Sorry." Ann said. "Talk already."

"I can't give you anything more than general impressions, querida. I know they want specific organic compounds that can only be found on a planet which has had life present for several hundred million years. They can get inorganic metals from asteroids, Mars, or any number of planets in different solar systems," he said, kissing her hair and stroking her leg and butt as he held her. She felt safe and loved being snuggled in his arms.

That's how you're always supposed to feel, querida. When you are upset, I have failed.

No, that's my job. I am supposed to make you feel secure. But let's stay on the subject.

"Like gas and oil?" she said out loud.

"Yes, like gas and oil, among other things. There are many different compounds that can only be found on a planet with volcanism and liquid water. The list is long, and Earth is rich in those things."

"Can we stop them?" she asked. "That's the $64,000 question. Will we be overrun with invaders when we are so weakened that we cannot defend our planet? Or has that already happened, and we're just too stupid to know we've been conquered?"

"Perhaps. I may have to speak to the President before I can ascertain that," he said calmly. He mentioned it as if he was going to speak to her brother.

"Are you really going to do the 'Take Me to Your Leader' thing? Are we on our way to Washington, D.C.?" she said, pulling away from him enough so that she could look into his eyes. She was very surprised that he would even consider it.

"I don't even know if he's still alive. I would imagine that he was put into a secure place when the West Coast was first bombed. I doubt if there's much left of Washington, D.C., so locating him might be the biggest challenge." He looked directly at her and spoke in a normal, calm voice.

Invigorated by the thought of meeting the President, Ann stayed upright on his lap. "Will you be able to convince his guards that *he* wants to talk to *you*? And then will you be able to make everybody forget all about it? That could be hundreds of people, lots of recorded video tape, endless phone pictures—nothing happens around the President that isn't well documented. The days of secret meetings are over, I think. Especially with history-making events like these," she said, once again putting her head on his shoulder and nestling into him. They were both silent for a moment, lost in their own thoughts. "Whatever you decide, I'll be right behind you. Or not, if you prefer. I'll stay out of sight if you want me to."

"I'm not sure. However I can keep you safe. Once I 'come out' and present myself as an alien, everyone, including and especially the military, will assume that we are responsible for the bombings. They do not believe in coincidences, and they will not want to accept the fact that they have been hosts to alien scientists for centuries," Marco

Antonio said, kissing her on the temple. Without even being aware of it himself, he started to release sexual pheromones. Ann was in his lap, and his nose was in the curls on her head. He inhaled deeply, reveling in her smell, and he stroked her butt and leg which were draped across his lap.

"How many alien species have observed us over the years, Marco? Were the Monitors the only ones?" She pulled out the arm resting against his chest and wrapped it around his back. She wanted to hug him, and to hold him closer. She was beginning to want to climb into his body, or have him climb into hers. "It is becoming impossible to concentrate, Marco Antonio. You are releasing pheromones, I think."

"Not I. It must be you," he whispered into her ear as he nibbled on it. Then his lips worked their way across her throat and to her lips as his arms caressed her whole body

"Slow down, cowboy," Ann said breathlessly. "My body doesn't release pheromones. You know I am innocent," she said. . "Maybe the oxygen level is up."

With every word, her lips brushed against his. She could feel him react to every touch of her lips against his until she decided to send her tongue out to taste his mouth. His mouth covered hers, sucking her tongue into him between his teeth as he groaned.

Ann pulled away from him and stood up. He released her, but his eyebrows shot up in the middle, wrinkling his forehead and making him look like she'd hurt his feelings. Quickly, she sat back down, straddling his legs. "You look like an abandoned puppy, my love," she said.

"I thought you were going away, just as I was feeling, um, secure," he said, giving her that shy smile he saved for their most intimate moments.

"I don't want you to feel so 'secure' that I don't get my question answered," she said, putting her arms behind his head and pushing him back. Questor immediately adjusted the shape of the chair and they reclined. "Were there other species visiting us, and if so, how many?"

"Always curious, querida. Can I not divert your attention, as you do mine? I can answer a million questions telepathically, but I need my whole body to show you how much I love you. I need my fingers to touch you, my hands to stroke you, my arms to hold you and squeeze you and to bring you to my mouth so I can kiss you, like this," he said, holding her face and bringing her head to his mouth.

Willingly, she kissed him back, running her fingers through his hair. It was as if each wanted to possess the other's skull, but Ann dropped her arms beneath his arms and ran her hands down his sides. When her hands reached his ribs, he twitched.

"You're ticklish!" Ann said, smiling.

"You just startled me," he whispered.

"I'm going to file that away for future reference. You're still stalling. Answer the question, please!" She sounded like a teacher.

"I have talked to other species several times, but we Monitors were the only ones, to my knowledge, to hang around and observe you for a long time."

"Why? And how do you know? Did you meet any of them and ask?" Ann said, pulling away from him so she could see his face. She decided to change her tone. She was sounding too teacher-ish. "Have you discussed us with a third species?"

"Most other creatures who have come here did not find your kind interesting. You are a young genus. Your planet is rich with available minerals and biologically-based deposits, but most visitors who have mastered interstellar travel only interact with others who have achieved faster-than-light transportation. Recently, you have become too dangerous, and most xenosociologists believe you will destroy yourselves," he said, looking at her hair. "I can't blame them. You have always been a very pugnacious group. They don't want to be here when World War III breaks out."

"So somebody sent a drone to eliminate most of us so we won't destroy ourselves?" she said thoughtfully. Marco Antonio shrugged slightly and didn't respond. "Well, radioactivity is a bitch, I guess. Ruins the whole neighborhood, eh? That would be a major boo-hoo for them, wasting a perfectly good planet," Ann said sarcastically. "Better not to take the chance. Just get rid of the rubbish before it makes a big mess."

"That's about it in a nutshell, querida," he said, reaching up to touch her soft curls.

"They have no right, and it really pisses me off! Let's go home, talk to the President, ask him for a couple of nukes and Questor can bring them up here. You can get a real spacesuit and float them over there, set a charge for later, and let them blow that thing straight to hell. How's *that* for a plan?"

"Sounds direct and simple, but there might be complications," he said, twirling her hair with his fingers.

"Like what?"

"Well, if they sent a scout, they may expect it to return. If it doesn't come back, they might send another, or several."

"Can you get it to just go home?"

"Yes, I think so. We need to send a note home, as well. We need to tell them they found nothing worth revisiting. This planet is not a place they would like. Unfortunately, my computer skills are not sophisticated enough to send such a note, and my linguistic skills are inadequate for the task. I am not conversant in their language," he said, running his finger along the outer edge of her ear.

"Well, that's not surprising, since you've never actually met them nor talked to them. Was there anything you could read? In fact, how did you figure out anything at all about them?" Ann ran her finger over his ear lobe, mirroring his action. Her eyebrows were drawn down into a deep frown, until her right eyebrow cocked in curiosity.

He sighed. "This will sound very metaphysical to you. I hesitate to try to explain it to you in words because it will make me sound like I was over there having a séance."

"I can suspend disbelief long enough for you to let me feel what you felt. When you think I am ready, you can show me, but for now, just tell me. I promise not to laugh," Ann said, as she reached up to run her fingers through his hair.

"And no eye rolling or smirking," he said, abandoning her ear lobe and returning to her curls. He had that half-smile that he wore when he was teasing her.

"I can't promise no eye rolling, but I'll try very hard not to smirk," she said.

"OK. Here goes. When I am in a location, especially where there is electronic equipment, I can sometimes pick up traces of the people or creatures that made it. I get a feel or an image of what they were like. Sometimes I can almost hear phrases or echoes of language, and I can understand some of what they were trying to communicate to one another."

"Like ghosts?"

"I suppose so," he said, abandoning her hair and putting his hands around her waist.

Ann half expected him to start bouncing her on his knees, but he didn't. She was relieved because that would have been very distracting, and they were finally having a real conversation. She was glad her neurotransmitters were low; sometimes having a weak brain could be a blessing. "If you'd had more time, could you have picked up more vibes from the ship?"

"Perhaps. I did what I could in the allotted time," he said, sliding his hands down each leg. Ann had never sat on his lap in exactly this way, and he liked it. "It was time for me to return to Questor. Please do not think that I cut short my mission because of you," he added, almost too quickly.

"It never entered my head," Ann said, stroking his neck. "Questor put me to sleep a little sooner than he had planned. That's all."

"OK. I just know how you think, and if there's any way you can take responsibility or feel guilty, you do. I did want to be here when you woke up, but that was only because I didn't want you to be anxious."

"I thank you for that. It was quite nice waking up in your arms. I was so afraid something had happened to you! When I could no longer feel your presence, I was terrified," Ann said. She had moved her hands up to his jaws, and she held his head in her hands as she looked into his eyes. *God, you're gorgeous! I could sit and look at you all day.*

You are the beauty, my love. "I knew. I could feel your fear and anxiety. Up until the door closed behind me, you had done very well controlling your claustrophobia. I commend you for that; once again, I could feel your strength. You are a very brave woman. You feel the same emotions as everyone, but you don't let them overcome you. I must learn how you do that so that I will be able to control myself when jealousy threatens to make me act inappropriately," he said, cupping her butt, his very muscular forearms resting on her thighs. *May I kiss you again?*

No, because I'm going to kiss you first. She pulled his head towards her as she leaned in to kiss him. She knew she should be getting him to answer about a million questions while he was feeling loquacious, but kissing him was infinitely more interesting than any subject she could think of at the moment. *I am so weak, I can't even carry on a conversation when you touch me. Oh Marco Antonio! You play me like a violin!*

Only because you are a Stradivarius! I have never gotten the responses from anyone that I get from you. You are impossible to ignore. I so seldom get you alone, all to myself, and when we are alone, I want to play you exactly like a violin. Every note, every nuance, every response is different every time, but you are always beautiful.

You promised not to compare me to your million other lovers.

I've only had one real lover, and that's you. The rest I just fucked. There is no comparison possible. I love you as I've loved no other woman in eight centuries.

The world is at war, and all we want to do is screw. What a pair we are!

Yes. But there is nothing we can do until we get home.

Oh. In that case, I think we have too many clothes on.

Yes, Mrs. Jacob. I think we do.

We'll think more clearly naked.

No doubt.

Take your clothes off and pretend you're a violinist, baby.

Let's play.

CHAPTER 5

Ann was standing between Marco Antonio's legs, pulling his jeans off when Questor's communication device vibrated. As she tugged at the cuffs of his jeans, Marco Antonio lifted his butt off the chair. He reached over, picked up the box and held it in his hand. He was silent for a few seconds, then he said, "Miguel, find out where the President is. Yes, I'm sure he's in hiding, but they would have put him somewhere safe after the first explosion. Get Paul to help you—he knows his way around a computer. Yes. I need to talk to him. Any news from NORAD? Have all available people tuned into what's happening with the national defense. Has the U.S. sent any missiles their way? WHAT?" Marco Antonio froze, his receiver in his hand, listening in absolute silence. Ann could tell he didn't like what he heard. He patted the seat next to him, and she sat down, dropping his jeans onto the floor.

Damn!

At last, he put the receiver on "speaker" so she could hear what Miguel was saying. "...completely jammed. Some local television stations are broadcasting, but all VHF channels are blocked. That includes the internet and telephones. Only local computers are functioning; they are not communicating with one another. It's really weird predicting which services will work and which will fail. So far, the electric grid is still up in California, but there are a lot of holes where cities used to be."

"That would mean a lot of cell towers are down, too, right?" Marco Antonio asked. "I note that this system is only broadcasting in sound. Was it damaged as well?"

"Yes. We can call across town, but not to LA or San Francisco, where most of their towers are down. Our system is working underwater and up to the coast, but it was damaged in San Francisco. We only have the power to reach the rovers in sound, so you might have to translate for them."

"How about Sacramento?" Ann asked. Although not as populous as many of California's coastal cities, it was the seat of government for the sixth largest economy in the world. She wanted to know if they were going after governmental centers or merely cities of a certain size.

"We'll check and get back to you, Ann."

Suddenly, there was a blast, followed a few seconds later by a loud BOOM! Marco Antonio reached down to touch Questor immediately, and reported to Ann, "That was an atomic bomb sent by Earth which exploded well out of range of the City Killer's ship. No damage. It did not reach its target. Questor is reporting that there are at least six more ICBM's aimed at that ship, and he recommends that we get far away from the kill-zone. I concur."

Both Ann and Marco Antonio became seated, which was a good thing because Questor took off heading southeast at an incredible speed. Their chairs automatically swiveled to face the direction they were travelling, so that the g-forces pushed them against their padded chair. Only rarely had Ann felt acceleration or deceleration inside Questor, but she felt it now. She had no idea how Questor controlled inertia, but this was the second time she had felt like she was about to be plastered against her seat or thrown to the floor. That could only mean that he was moving very, very fast.

Exhale!

Ann did as she was told, instantly. The pressure was so great that she could not inhale. At least her lungs were not exploding in her chest, but she wasn't too sure her brains wouldn't be splattered across her headrest. She was about to lose consciousness just as the pressure let up. She inhaled.

Push! Like having a baby!

Well, that's about the dumbest thing I've ever heard!

She did it anyway, and the dizziness passed. She could feel Marco Antonio examining every part of her brain and body without touching her.

His anxiety was palpable.

I'm OK, sweetheart. I just got a little dizzy there. Ann tried to soothe him before he jumped out of his chair and started doing his doctor thing.

Thank God you do as you're told!

"Yes, I do. I've heard that this is rare in most women," Ann said aloud, hoping to relieve some of his fear.

"Almost unheard of! You frightened me when you thought my directions were 'the dumbest thing you'd ever heard!' I was afraid you would lose consciousness, which could mean that you might not resume inhalation when the g-forces went down."

"Yes, and that might mean you'd have to resuscitate me. That would be a bother, wouldn't it?" She was purposefully being a smartass so he'd lighten up.

"Indeed! Mouth-to-mouth breathing can be quite unsanitary, too, I've been told," he said, smiling at her. He knew exactly what she was doing, and he responded by toning down his anxiety levels and backing off from his invasive mental checks on her physical and mental condition. He'd also turned off the pheromones during the message from Miguel.

There was another blast, followed by a mighty roar of sound. "Is that another atom bomb?" Ann asked nervously.

"Not exactly, but yes. There are five more to go, but Questor says the City Slayer has diverted them off into space, towards the sun, he thinks."

"It's a good thing they're not exploding onto the arctic ice sheet or into the forests or tundra of Siberia. What were they thinking, sending SIX, for goodness' sake? That's really overkill! If they had all gone off, we'd all be glowing well into the next century," fussed Ann, still sitting in her chair.

"It's interesting that they did not merely divert the nuclear bombs; they flung them away from the planet. Clearly, they don't want the planet to be 'glowing' at all," Marco Antonio mused.

"They want it nice and clean when they move in," Ann noted. "We need a better weapon. ICBM's are not getting the job done. Any new arrows in your quiver?" She looked at him hopefully, but fearing to hear more about how Monitors don't pick sides.

"I think we just need a better delivery system. I need to talk to some head of state and offer my services as a delivery man."

"Do you really think that ship would let you enter it with a nuclear bomb under your arm?" Ann asked incredulously. "The more I think about it, the less I like the idea."

"It may be worth a try," he said.

Ann turned around in her chair so that she was looking directly at him, a look of shocked disbelief on her face. "Perhaps we had better reconsider. I think it's too dangerous. There is no way I'd let you re-enter that ship carrying a massive bomb. The second it sensed metal and electronics, it would ignite the bomb and watch you go 'Poof!'" Ann was still turned in her chair, looking at him. "I'm not letting you go on some suicide mission like some nutcase on a jihad!"

"You are so cute when you're incredulous, my love," he said, grinning at her. "It didn't shoot at me the last time I entered. Why would it shoot at me this time?"

"The last time you entered, you weren't wearing even a belt-buckle. Nothing metallic at all! Even your space suit was living tissue! Do you think they won't notice that it's a bomb in your suitcase? I think they will! Even if you wrap it up in the belly of a hippo, their sensors will be able to tell that what's inside is radioactive and metallic." She shook her head slightly, saying, "No way, Jose. Let someone else do the Trojan Horse thing with an atom bomb. Not you!" She crossed her arms and shook her head.

"You do have a point. We should probably experiment with other metallic objects before we try an explosive of any kind. Besides, it might take us awhile to find a Trojan Horse big enough to swallow a bomb-carrying hippo," he said, smiling at her.

She was once again bathed in a wave of his warm goodfeels. "Well, OK, I guess I did mix my metaphors. But we don't even know if it would let Questor near it if he were carrying explosives, cannons, or guns, let alone a nuclear device." She uncrossed her arms slightly.

"We could shield it," Marco Antonio said quietly.

"You could try. We have no way of knowing how sensitive its sensors are towards metals or radioactivity. Do we?" Ann suddenly realized that she had no idea what the Monitors' shields were capable of. *Oops! How good are your shields and sensors, anyway? I have no idea about that, either. Oopsy-boopsy! My bad!*

Marco Antonio laughed out loud. "Oopsy-boopsy? Really?" He shook his head and smiled at her. "You never cease to amuse me, Mrs. Jacob."

"Well, I suddenly realized that I didn't know what the hell I was talking about. It's embarrassing to catch myself being so sophomoric, especially around someone like you." Ann averted her eyes, feeling like a child who had just said something silly and naïve.

"Someone like me?" he asked, his eyebrows raised.

"Well, you're correct there, too. There isn't anyone quite like you on this whole planet, is there? Oopsy-boopsy again!" Ann felt like she was really putting her foot in her mouth and hopping around on one leg. *Stupid old lady!*

"You make me sound pretty weird. I'm just your regular 800-year-old man., sitting here in my underwear," he said gently, trying to defuse her embarrassment.

"You said you were 700 years old!" Ann said, finally looking at him. At last, a small grin crept onto her face as he spoke.

"I lied about my age. I was afraid you'd think I was too old for you. Maybe you only like young guys." Marco Antonio sounded like a kid making up reasons why some chick would never give him the time of day.

"I suspected. You have a little wrinkle right there," she said, pointing at his eyelid, which was as flawless as a 20-year-old's, "that gave you away. Definitely over 700. And you're unique in other ways besides your age, obviously. You're drop-dead gorgeous. And you're a helluva good dancer. So tell me about your shields, baby. I need to hear it." She felt back on level ground again.

"I need to run some tests to ascertain the sensitivity of their sensors—you're right about that, but I can tell you about my shields right now. Hold my hand, and I'll show you."

Ann took his hand and smiled at him. She wanted to convince him that she was fine, but he was in her mind so far beyond her consciousness that she could never fool him.

You are fatigued, my love. I will make this quick and easy. He showed her how Questor and all the other transports bent the light around them, making them visually imperceptible. All of their metallic objects were coated with a spray that absorbed sonar and radar wave lengths or misdirected them, so they did not bounce back to the sender. Ann got the general idea, but she clearly saw that it was much more intricate than she understood.

Do you understand, querida?

Well enough, I guess. I understand quantum mechanics, too, and at about the same level. Light waves and optics can get very convoluted very quickly. I get the general idea. Are you confident that it will work?

It has before, under similar circumstances. You grasped the concepts quickly. When did a history and English teacher become exposed to light waves, optics and quantum mechanics?

I read. I watch science channels on TV, and my dad did research on infrared detection in the 1960s. Why are you always so surprised when you discover that I'm not as stupid as I look?

Most people who are well educated know a lot about one or two specific areas of interest. You have one of the broadest backgrounds I have ever encountered. It is rare among your species. And you do not look stupid.

"You do. Your pants are off. Is there someone at home who can help you set up a shield? Or build or borrow a nuclear device, or get any of this other stuff done? Aren't most of the Monitors into the biological sciences?" Ann asked, too tired to send him the message telepathically. She was beginning to babble. *So many questions! Will we be able to help at all?*

"I think so. Try to rest for a while. We will be home soon, and this is a good time for a little nap. Besides, I must speak to Questor for a few minutes," he said, touching her chair, which immediately reclined and lifted her legs into a reclining position.

"Put your pants back on, then use your magic, Mr. Sandman," she said, and he touched her eyes and put her to sleep.

CHAPTER 6

When she woke, it was as dark as the bottom of a cave at midnight. She was flat, so she was probably in a bed. That meant that Marco Antonio was also sleeping, she surmised, so she tried not to stir. He needed to sleep as much as she did. He had neurotransmitters that also needed to be rebalanced, reproduced, or recalibrated. Whatever.

He had a lot more brains, so he probably needed a lot more sleep, although they had never discussed it at length. He just slept about as much as she did when they were home together. Which wasn't that often, come to think of it. Unless he was working in the lab, which he usually was.

Actually, she had to nag him a little to get him to rest or eat, or take care of himself at all. He had not had anyone who wanted to take care of him, and he was unaccustomed to it. Getting a regular supply of blood for him to eat had been a real challenge; all Monitors were very private eaters, but sanguinary eaters especially so.

As a vampire, he had hidden in dark places, eating from live donors (whether willing or unwilling) in isolation. He had used sex as a tool to get female donors alone in dark places and they had willingly allowed him to use his little sharp straw which he kept hidden in his cheek above his gums. With it, he would pierce their carotid artery, suck out enough to satisfy him but not enough to weaken them, and heal the wound almost instantly.

He could erase the memory, and they would not remember what exactly had transpired. They would, however, remember the joy and satisfaction they had experienced when they were with him. He could make their body orgasm on command, and the emotional glow persisted long after the memory of the activity was forgotten.

He could feed from men, too, of course. His mental control could freeze anyone with a simple touch. He would whip out his little straw, withdraw whatever blood he needed, heal the hole, and then convince them that they had been talking about the weather, sports, or religion. They would remember whatever he told them, and they would remember being happy in his company. All he needed was privacy and a little time.

The first time he fed off me, it was wonderful! Face it, Jacob! I was a fat old lady, and he was an Adonis. Because I didn't even try to resist, I felt so guilty! I had betrayed Tim in his very own home, as he slept in our bedroom just a few feet away.

Ann had asked Marco Antonio not to erase the memory, so she would remember to stay away from him. The shame was the price she needed to pay for the ecstasy he had provided. It wasn't until much later that Ruth told her that she had had no choice; her body obeyed his command. She could not have refused, even if she had wanted to.

I did not try very hard to refuse him, and boy, I felt really guilty! Tim was a wonderful husband for 43 years! I never even wanted to cheat. He didn't deserve a faithless spouse. We had both been completely loyal for a lifetime.

Ann had vowed never to be alone with Marco Antonio again. He would never have the opportunity, and she would never have the temptation. Because he was a Monitor, he dealt frequently with Ruth and Gabriel, the Jacobs' neighbors, but she avoided him. Most of the time, he was in South America or at the Monitor's main outpost at the bottom of the Mariana Trench.

Every Monitor respects him. They defer to him in all things, and I soon saw why.

After Tim's death, Marco Antonio was such a help! He seemed to appear from nowhere, and he took care of so many details. He helped me to deal with the terrible pain of grief, and he asked for nothing in return. I realized that I had misjudged him, but not myself. He was always patient and understanding, but I still took no chance of ever being alone with him.

MONITORS OF DESTRUCTION

The irony is that now I want to be alone with him every second, so that I can act upon every temptation possible. I love him so! I have become such a shameless hussy!

And I am so glad that you are!

Ann's intake of breath belied the stillness of her body. She should have known he would awaken when she did and be aware of her thoughts. She was glad that it was dark so he could not see that her cheeks were red.

"One of these days I'm going to be thinking that you're a green monkey, and you'll overhear my thoughts. It would serve you right!" Ann whispered into the darkness.

"It would still be a happy thought. Nearly all your thoughts are happy, even when they don't concern me. I love to tune into your mind to see what happy thoughts you're thinking. I know it's rude, but I too am shameless." Like Ann, Marco Antonio whispered, and made no effort to have Questor turn up the lighting. The darkness meant that the day had not begun, and they could be alone with each other. Confessions are best made in the dark.

"Yes, you are. You will soon discover that my thoughts are pretty boring and mundane, and you will tire of listening to drivel. Then you'll tire of me and find someone with more interesting thoughts. No one can be fascinating 24/7." Ann had turned toward him, but was not touching him. Her touch would end their conversation and begin a totally different type of communication.

"I can't imagine you ever becoming boring." He reached out his hand and took her hand, entwining his fingers in hers.

"I can't believe that you think I have happy thoughts! You have been with me through the worst times of my life—the Yellowstone Mega-volcano, the death of my husband, the death of my son-in-law—the list is endless and all pretty horrible! I'd hate to imagine the miserable thoughts other people must be thinking if mine are happy by comparison. Good grief!"

"Yet you keep bouncing back," he said, letting go of her hand after giving it a little squeeze.

The list of personal catastrophes which had plagued Ann and her world made her more aware of the fact that right now, they were lollygagging. They couldn't remain whispering in the dark while the planet was being bombed. Surely they should be busy!

Realizing that there were more important things going on than her thought processes, Ann made an effort to sit up and start the day, but he gently pulled her back. They were both silent for a moment, but then she said, "Speaking of bouncing back—what's happening on the world-domination scene? While I was snoozing, did they just go away, or did we become extinct?" Ann said, "Please catch me up with the latest activities of the City Killer and our efforts to thwart its dastardly plans."

Marco Antonio pulled her next to him and put her head back on his shoulder. Clearly, he felt they could talk in the dark, cuddled up to each other. "We have sent another ship with two men to run tests on the metal-shielding capabilities of the City Killers' drone. They will be accompanied by an unmanned rover carrying metallic objects approximately the size and weight of a large nuclear bomb. The manned ship will measure the range of detection devices utilized by the drone against both metal-bearing and non-metal-bearing rovers. Both rovers will be unshielded except for the usual visual shielding they utilize when they are within range of human beings."

"You're using Questor as your hippo to see if they'll detect metal within him?" Ann asked, content to lie in his arms if that was what he wanted.

"More or less," he said.

"So why are you sending two men in a second rover?" she asked.

"I'm not sending Questor, but yes, I'm sending two other rovers. They are living beings, as is a hippo. They can actually be your Trojan horse, at the same time. The two Monitors will be able to do their monitoring jobs as well," he added. "They will have EVA suits equipped with much larger air tanks than I had, and they will attempt to enter the drone where I did. Hopefully, they will be able to learn more about the species that built it, its purpose, and their future intentions towards Earth. With luck, they might be able to leave a message to take home or get into its computers or guidance systems. Who knows what they'll be able to do? They are very competent."

"Are they going to pose as humans or admit that they are also extraterrestrials?" Ann asked, wondering what role the monitors actually planned to play with the new invaders.

"Humans. But they'll have some of our capabilities, of course."

"The best of both worlds, I hope," she added. "Not like Jason or Doris. They'd have made a deal with the City Killers, and split the profits."

Marco Antonio did not like her to make references to Jason or Doris. As the leader of the Monitor outpost, Marco Antonio had been obliged to deal with the sociopaths in his own midst. He had grave misgivings about the things he had had to do to cover-up the horrors committed by his own people.

His hesitation to respond told Ann she had hit a sensitive nerve. "Sorry. That was tacky," she said. She hadn't meant to poke him in a sore spot, but his reference to their "capabilities" sounded a little too pretentious to her.

You're right. It was pretentious. I didn't mean to be supercilious.

No, I shouldn't be so sensitive. Clearly, your species is superior to ours. You've had about a million years to genetically alter yourselves, and we've just discovered DNA in my lifetime. We're babies compared to you guys! But it did sound a bit supercilious and arrogant.

I don't mean to be condescending, querida. As you say, 'my bad.'

That's OK. It's part of you that I love. You truly are superior, so humility certainly wouldn't suit you.

How so? Please explain.

"Well," she said aloud, so she would be able to gather her thoughts before she expressed them, "it's like loving a person who is very rich."

"So you love me for my money?" His head had pulled away from her head as if he were looking at her. She was acutely aware of his body pulling away from hers, although it had been a microscopic movement.

"No, not really," she hesitated. "You are who and what you are. You are a very rich, very smart, very good-looking alien. If any of those things were different, you wouldn't be the same man you are.

Well, the same creature or person that you are." She took a breath to see if she was being clear. "Well, the man I fell in love with."

"So if any of those traits changed, you would no longer love me?"

"Yes, I would. I will always love you, even if you suddenly become poor, ugly, or stupid. Once the commitment is made, the vows spoken, it's for life. I love those ancient vows: 'To have and to hold from this day forward, for better for worse, for richer for poorer, in sickness and in health, to love and to cherish, till death us do part.'"

"That holds true for about half of the people who choose to marry. The others get divorced, and half never bother to marry in the first place," he pointed out. "At least in America in the twenty-first century," he quickly amended.

"We're not talking about them. We were talking about me," Ann said.

"But you haven't taken that vow with me," he said. After a brief pause, he asked, "Would you like to?"

She could feel him looking at her again, if only at the top of her head.

"Is that a proposal?" Ann asked, and then quickly back-stepped. "Or is it a hypothetical question?"

"I suppose it is both. We've never discussed it, have we?"

"I committed myself to you in Argentina, when you said you would stay here until you found a cure for Marie's Disease." She paused, realizing the full implications of that promise. "I guess you've done that, so this might be a good time for you to bail out if you want to," Ann said. She held her breath, hoping that was not what he wanted.

"I changed my genetic structure so that I would be monogamous. I felt that I made a commitment when I did that. I thought that would show you that I do not want to 'bail out' ever. You seemed very insecure about my sexual history, so I hoped that my actions would speak louder than my words. I have no desire to be with anyone else. I want you to be with me for as long as I can keep us both alive. I've told you that many times." He was beginning to sound irritated. "Would you like to have a formal commitment ceremony like a wedding to make our relationship public?"

It wasn't the most romantic proposal she'd ever received. She had, in fact, received several, over a dozen. While she was at UCSB, she had worked for one of the first-ever computer dating companies. Although an office assistant, her boss had asked her to go out with several potential customers to show that it wasn't a sham or a bordello. She was always on her best behavior, and there was no sex involved. Several of the mostly-young-engineers she went out with were so lonely that they proposed on the very first date.

In order to sell the product, Ann would cast her eyes down, murmur "This is so sudden! I'd want you to meet women you have truly been matched with before you make such a hasty decision." They always signed up, and they rarely called back. That was fine with Ann; she was in love with another lonely engineer who broke her heart.

Really? I didn't know you'd worked for a dating service. I don't blame them for falling in love with you immediately. They recognized a perfect wife when they saw one.

Please get out of my head. I'd like to think about this for a moment alone.

Of course, querida.

She felt him leave her mind and she blinked. The cabin remained absolutely black and silent. She felt alone, even though she reminded herself that he was lying in the seat next to her and her head was on his shoulder. "How long have we been asleep?"

"Only a couple of hours. We have about another hour to go before we arrive at our destination. Unless things change, of course," Marco Antonio said calmly.

"What is our destination?"

"I'm not really sure. I think it's somewhere in the Atlantic Ocean, but I could be wrong. I'll have to place a couple more calls after the shield tests are completed."

"Is there anything we should be doing besides discussing wedding plans?"

"I can think of several things I'd like to be doing, but there is nothing we *should* be doing," he said, then added, "unless you're hungry or thirsty."

"No. I'm fine. Do we have any updates? Has the bombing stopped, or at least slowed down?" She felt guilty. This was a world *crisis*, and they were napping and chatting! Snuggling in the dark felt like such a guilty pleasure.

"I don't know, and I don't want to know because there's nothing we can do about it. But for you, I'll ask Questor for an update."

"No—don't! I don't want to know either," she said, and burrowed into his shoulder.

Ann put her hands on Questor to see if he was OK. She also got a blast of goodfeels from Questor, who loved to do things to please her. If he'd had a tail, it would be wagging.

"I don't want to get any more bad news while you are holding me," she said, rolling her leg over his.

"This is nice, isn't it?" he said, wrapping his other arm around her as she put her leg on his. His shoulder was bare under her cheek, as was his leg.

"Now that we are all snuggled, let's see what's been happening. I can face bad news much better like this than alone in a coal-black room." While she was in his arms, she could face anything.

Unready to face an unpleasant situation, Marco Antonio lay quite still, except for his fingers gently stroking her arm. "Would you like the lights up?"

"No. Now I like the darkness. It's so rare!"

"We are very visual creatures. Without light, our most important source of information is cut off from our brain, and we must depend on the others senses," he said. "It is more difficult for me to 'stay out of your head' when I am holding you in the dark, but it is good discipline."

"What does Questor have to report?" Ann asked, afraid of what he might say. All she had gotten was the wagging-tail report.

After a brief pause, he said "Good news! The bombing stopped shortly after our nuclear bombs were deflected towards the sun. Everything has been silent since then, but it has not moved away.

Our rovers are nearing the City Killer's ship, and it has not responded to their approach. So far, so good!"

"God, what a relief! Maybe they'll just go away!" She raised her head from his chest to look at him, but she couldn't see anything, so she put her head back onto his chest. She could feel the hairs on his chest, and she rubbed her cheek against it.

"That might not be such a good thing. I really want to get in and crack their systems before they leave. I don't want them to come back with bigger guns or more ships. Although the first effort was not successful, we have shown them that we're willing to fight back. That is sometimes a mixed message."

"Yeah, they might bring their bigger brothers to finish the fight. What do you think we should do next?" Ann asked, hoping it would involve sending for the Monitor cavalry.

"Wait and see what the two rovers discover."

Necessary, but not what she'd wanted to hear.

"And then go find the President. Or maybe go find a nuclear submarine?"

"Perhaps both. Or perhaps neither."

"Very obtuse," Ann said. After a second, when he did not explain his vague response, she said, "I miss you. It's so quiet without your running patter in my head. I miss your goodfeels, and your nosiness."

"What are my 'goodfeels'?"

"It's when you send your approval, your pride in me, your 'ahhh, so cute!' feelings like a proud papa or pet owner. It's hard to explain in words, but it arrives in my head like little squirts of goodfeels," she said, rubbing his chest gently. "Questor does it too, especially when I do something that pleases him. Like a pat on my head and a 'Good girl!'"

After a few minutes, she thought, *I'm glad you don't have a shirt on.*

"I felt stupid sitting without my jeans on, just wearing my shirt and shorts," he said, with a tiny shrug, which she felt. "And I am not your papa, and you are not my pet. But I think I understand the feeling you describe. I do think you're very cute. You amuse me."

"Get out of my head!" She pulled a few hairs on his chest, and he flinched.

"I'll try harder," he promised.

She ran her fingers through the hair on his chest, saying nothing. He remained silent, too, but his hand stroked her arm gently.

"How would your peers react if you married a human?" she asked quietly.

"I really don't care," he replied.

"I do. I don't want to make trouble for you. Could you just convince them that you're experiencing some quaint mortal ceremony to please your pet humans? Some ritual to placate my family by following our social norms?"

"Probably. What would it mean to YOU if we were to marry, Ann?"

"I'll tell you what it would mean to me if you tell me what it would mean to you first. Members of your species don't mate for life, do they? Do they love one person over another? How would it be different for you to marry me than, say, Ruth?

"Yes, we bond with one another, but not only for reproduction or sex. We join to share experiences in rituals which vary widely in the number of participants, the length of the union, and its purpose. We celebrate some accomplishment, or to join up to set out on an adventure. Most of our celebrations mark the end of a project or some achievement more often than declaring to set out on an enterprise, so we don't really have anything like a wedding ceremony. I think they'd find it interesting." Marco Antonio gave her arm a little squeeze. "Your turn."

"Not good enough. You told me about your culture, not about your personal feelings. What do *you* want?" She still idly stroked the hair on his chest.

"I would do anything to please you. If being formally married would ease your anxiety, I would insist upon it. Rationally, you would make a good mate if only because you are the first human woman who will not age and die. The worst part about having a long life is that I have outlived many people I cared about. It made me want to become a recluse. Of course, I've never loved anyone as

I love you, but I have had to bury many friends, and it was difficult. Since there is no reason for you to age, the chances are good that we can be together for many human life spans. You are a suitable choice. Better?"

"Much." She gave him a little hug. She appreciated the fact that he could list practical reasons for marrying her. She already knew the romantic feelings they had for each other.

"Your turn. What do you think about marrying me?" He kissed her hair.

"I think my children would be rather surprised if I married you; they see us more like co-leaders of the Monitor-Human Axis of Goodness." She could feel his smile because her forehead was touching his cheek, and he squeezed her arm gently. "I think they would disapprove of my marrying anyone besides Tim. No one is good enough for Mommy except Daddy. They're adults, so I think they could get used to the idea eventually. Maybe we should ask our families how they'd feel about it? There's no rush. We've already committed ourselves to this union. I feel like your wife, and you feel like my husband, so why should we have to publicize it?"

"We don't have to do anything. The question was, do YOU want to marry ME? Would you feel more secure emotionally or financially if you shared my estate and all my worldly goods? It is a legal union which you took very seriously with your last husband. Whatever you want to do is acceptable to me. If you feel there are reasons that compel us to take this step to be fully joined as man and wife, we will do it. However, if you don't want to marry, I will make no demands upon you." He remained motionless throughout that little monologue, but she got the feeling that he was leaning pro-marriage.

"Let's think about it, let me talk to my children while you talk to your cohorts, and we'll decide later. Fair enough?"

"OK. I just want to make you happy and to show the world that you are mine. I have noticed that wedding rings serve a real purpose of warding off suitors, and I'd like you to wear mine," he said, still trying hard to remain immobile, if not passive.

"That sounds very possessive."

"It is. I don't want anyone else, especially any other man, to try to take you away from me. You are mine and only mine. Don't you feel the same way? It's part of monogamy, I think."

"Yes, it is. But you must remember that jealousy can be an ugly side-effect of possessiveness. Trust me, and have confidence that I will not betray you. I feel possessive about you, too, but I am not jealous because I trust you." She knew he was very powerful, and when he was jealous, he was very dangerous. "I feel pity for the females who look at you and instantly want you. Too bad for them. You are MINE!"

He gave her arm another squeeze.

"Sometimes I want to stick my tongue out at the really beautiful women and say 'Neener-neener! You can't have this one! He's taken, and you cannot tempt him with your sexy beauty like you do other weak men. He won't pant after you, needing a dribble bib. I won this lottery, not you! For some completely unknown reason, he loves *me!* You lose, sister! Go swing your hips, flip your hair and flaunt your cleavage at some other bag of testosterone!"

What about the ugly women?

"I just feel sorry for them. But they're used to it. Now, get out of my head! You promised!"

"OK. I was laughing too much to talk! I'll try harder!"

Her hand started moving down from his chest to his abdomen. She could feel the scars where she had operated on him, removing the bullets that had lodged in his brain. She remembered being so shocked when she had opened up his abdominal cavity and found the twisted mass of cerebral cortex instead of intestines. That was when she realized that part of the "customizing" of his body was in replacing digestive organs with neurological tissue. Brains for guts.

Of course! A vampire doesn't need intestines—duh!

"Has everything grown back?" she asked, knowing that he would know she was referring to the neurons that had been damaged by the bullets and by her clumsy efforts to remove the metal pieces surgically.

"Yes. All better now," he said.

"I'm sorry I did such a sloppy job of stitching you up. I can feel the scar," she said, running her finger along it. Her fingers gently touched his flat belly, and he flinched. Smiling in the darkness, she repeated the movement, and he flinched again. Ann was surprised that she could not feel her hand; *she* did not have to flinch. Normally she felt everything he felt, but he was not in her mind, so she could only feel what her own hand and fingers were experiencing.

She could feel the pheromones acting upon her, and she knew that he was aroused. His hand had tightened on her arm, but he had made no real attempt to embrace her.

Oh, this could be fun! If I can just control myself, I could make him crazy. That will teach him to nap in the nude!

Gently, she continued to let her hand work its way down until she reached his pubic hair, which she curled between her fingers. He moaned and reached to embrace her, but she said, "No touching! You just lie there, and let me do all the work. And stay out of my mind!"

"You will make me crazy!"

"I intend to. If you manage to stay out of my mind, you won't know what I have planned for you. Just feel it." She started kissing his neck, and brought her hand back up to his belly, gently playing with the hair.

"Oh, Christ! You are torturing me, Ann," he said, and he touched her face and hair. It was still totally black in the cabin.

"No touching! Lie still and hold onto your seat, baby. Questor might also have a message for you," she said, taking his hand and placing it at his side. Leaning up onto her elbow so that her head could reach his chest, she started kissing his neck and moved down to his chest. When she reached his nipple, she bit it gently and then sucked on it.

With every inhalation, she could feel the pheromone levels rise. She brought her hand up to his other nipple, gently tugged at it, and traced around its aureole as she sucked on his nipple. She let her hand travel back down his belly, up to his chest, and back to the hair at the base of his belly. Back and forth, up and down, she traced her fingers at the bottom of his abdomen from his navel down.

Relentlessly moving, stroking, gently pulling his chest hair, running her hand up his side. Her hand would wander up to his neck, around his ear, through his hair. Then back down his chest, across his belly, through his pubic hair. Still, she had not gotten *there*, although she had been close, so close. This time, she went around it, to his thigh, and down as far as she could reach.

Her arm brushed against his erection and he jumped, growling deep in his throat. With her mouth pulling on his nipple, she gave it a tiny nip and let it go, as her hand gently touched the skin and hair on his thigh and then over to his other leg. And back, and then to the other leg, but never to where he really wanted. Just touching, stroking, feeling his skin and hair, kissing his chest and belly. Tirelessly, endlessly, never in the same place very long, but never quite *there*.

"I feel you, Marco Antonio. With my fingertips and my mouth, I feel you. With my nose, I smell you. With my mouth, I taste you. With my body, I worship you, for better or worse, in sickness or in health," she said slowly, between kisses, as she worked her way lower. At last, she touched him *there*.

His breathing was heavy, and the growl turned into a moan as he said, "Oh Ann. I want to touch you. Everywhere. Please let me hold you!"

"Not yet, my love. Tell me what you want me to do to you," she said, sitting up and taking off her shirt and bra.

"Uh! Come back!" he said when she sat up. He quickly realized that she was removing her shirt and bra, and waited. When he felt her hand again, he continued. "What you have been doing is just fine. Very fine. You are so gentle! You could do this to me forever. Never stop. What an angel you are!"

He paused, moaned as she resumed kissing his chest, her breasts rubbing up against his side. "And what a devil! I want to touch you, I want to feel your skin upon mine. I want to be in you, and on you, and around you. I want to know your thoughts, feel what you feel, smell what you smell, taste what you taste. Everything! Denying me that is torture, you know. Soon I will explode."

She continued kissing him and running her single finger around his thighs, between his legs, and *there*. One finger, slowly and gently.

"I will give you half of me—the top half. Chest to chest, skin to skin. But your hands must remain off of me. Can you do it?"

"No, I don't think so. You're killing me, Ann!"

She chuckled and resumed kissing his chest and belly, where she paused. At last, she let her hand completely encircle him as her nose rooted in his pubic hair. He gasped and then groaned.

Ann pulled away from him and froze, not touching him anywhere.

He was completely motionless, holding his breath. She had never done this to him before. "You are mine!" she said, and she took him into her mouth as she took the base in her hand and squeezed.

His head and shoulders came up from the bed and his hands grabbed her head in a reflex motion. As if remembering, he flung his hands to the sides and threw his head back down onto the bed. His body became rigid in an effort at control, and when he had regained it, he relaxed, and she resumed motion. Gently but firmly, she set up a rhythm which his hips responded to.

Fast and hard, then slow and soft. The rhythm varied as she would bring him to the edge and then back down, letting him cool off a little.

"Oh, Ann—you ask too much! I cannot control myself much longer! Please let me bury myself in you, or be ready to let me go."

"Trust me, and let me bring you all the way home. I can do this for you, to you. Let this just happen to you, like a dream in the dark. A living dream over which you have no control. Lie back, and let it happen."

At last, he let it go. The growl in his chest increased to a roar as his back arched completely off the bed several times, finally freezing in mid-air for several seconds, and then collapsing in a quivering mass.

Before Marco Antonio said a word, Ann slid up his body and kissed him on the lips. His arms and legs encircled her and her brain was flooded with many messages. Chief among them was "I love you," and she was overwhelmed at how many ways he expressed that emotion. She also received feelings of surprise, a little shock, and a great deal of respect, which she had not expected. The strength of his mind was blasting her until she had to warn him to tone it down.

You feel pleased, but don't tell me so hard. You're so strong. Back off a little. Please, Marco Antonio. She could hardly think a coherent thought. It was a little scary, but she loved pleasing him. It felt like taking her third curtain call to a standing ovation at Carnegie Hall. She was thrilled that he was so ecstatic.

Sweetheart, you're crushing me! Not so tight!

Instantly, he let up and stopped squeezing her so hard. He broke off his endless kiss, too, and whispered "I'm sorry. It was so hard not to touch you! That was truly incredible. What an amazing woman you are. Even Questor is euphoric," he said.

"Questor? Can he feel us making love? Really?"

"Let's just say he is aware. He shared my emotions as you were making me crazy with lust. I don't think he truly understands what is going on, but he certainly likes it."

"Imagine! A horny bed! Or a sexy space ship, whichever." Ann said and giggled.

"I think he is in love with you, too. If he could take human shape, I would be so jealous! One more man in love with my woman! I might have to hurt him to protect you!"

"'Raped by a Rover!' It would make a great title or newspaper headline, to say nothing of the medical and police reports."Ann said as Marco Antonio stroked and nuzzled her. She remained lying on top of him. "I'll certainly never feel comfortable using the toilet vacuole. That's creepier than looking up my skirts." She giggled again, which relieved some of her tension. She didn't want to rush him, but she was more than ready. "I have noticed that it doesn't take him long to make up the bed. This rover can do the fastest reconfigurations I've ever seen!"

"Put your hand here, and you'll feel another fast reconfiguration." He led her hand down and she wrapped her hand around his man-part. It expanded like a balloon on a helium tank.

"My goodness, mercy me!" she murmured. The pheromone levels rose again, but Ann certainly didn't need it.

"Your turn!" he said salaciously.

"No, you have suffered enough. Together. Let's feel each other and share everything. I told you that I miss you—come back into my head and body." Immediately, he flipped her over onto her back and slid into her, and they both moaned.

Questor sent them both goodfeels and then continued his flight to the east coast, or what was left of it.

CHAPTER 7

The bed vibrated. Without a pause, Marco Antonio put his hand flat onto the bed. "We must finish, Ann. We're almost there!" he said.

"I certainly am. Go for it, lover!" Ann said, feeling the sudden build-up deep in her belly. She put her head back and concentrated on the feelings she was sharing with Marco Antonio, who had picked up the speed of his hips and raised his body up so that his hand could reach her happy button. Every bell and every whistle was activated in both their bodies and minds, and the orgasms were titanic.

Even before she quit panting and quivering, she managed to say, "What did he say?"

"They got in, but they could not crack their computers. There were not enough clues to absorb the language, either," Marco Antonio said aloud while his brain sent massive messages of love, appreciation, and goodfeels that made it difficult for her to concentrate on what he had said verbally.

Ann avoided saying "Huh?" by a millisecond and only by concentrating on what he was saying aloud. Then she just lay back and glowed for almost one whole minute, which is a long time during a verbal conversation. Finally, her mind managed to drag itself away from her crotch and back to the previous conversation. "What about the metal-carrying rover? Did it get busted?" She wiped the sweat from her brow with her hand.

"Yes. The City Killer detected the metal contained within the rover and was about to fire upon it, but the rover identified the energy build-up aimed at it and escaped, much like Questor did when I fell on you. It will not be possible to plant a bomb within the City Killer, at least not a metal one."

"Are there any other kinds?" Ann knew very little about bombs and ordinance.

"Yes, but not big enough to blow up a ship that size." He was still breathing heavily, as was she.

"OK. Do we have an alternate Plan B?" Ann asked, snuggling up to Marco Antonio. She still needed some skin-time.

I agree. Skin-time is very nice, especially after great sex!

I'll bet you didn't usually get much post-coital cuddling, did you?

No. Not much pre-coital skin-time, either. Nothing like what you did to me today. This was very special.

So pretty much just fucking and feeding, eh?

Pretty much.

"Back to plan B," Ann said. *Should we turn up the lights and get dressed?*

Not yet, querida.

OK. Better to think in the dark?

Better to tell you about Plan B in the dark. You're not going to like it.

"What part of it am I not going to like?" Ann asked suspiciously.

"I think I may have to follow them home."

She was silent, thinking. Then, to straighten out her thoughts, she spoke them aloud. "That would involve interstellar space, which will involve a lot of time. Will I go with you?"

"Our interstellar craft is not set up for human bodies. I would go in my Monitor body," he said calmly.

"I have got to go to the bathroom, Marco Antonio. I'll be right back," she said, trying to stay calm about all the ramifications of what he had just said.

At the end of the cabin, a soft light began to glow over a newly built seat in a cubby of the bulkhead. She got up and walked to the light and sat down on the chair beneath it. Conveniently, a hole had appeared beneath the seat in the bulkhead, creating a potty chair into which she released her urine. The potty chair closed up, sealing her liquids and reabsorbing the entire chair into the wall. The glow went out as soon as she was done, and she was enclosed in blackness again.

In the complete darkness, she felt her way back to the bed and sat on the edge. "So will I ever see you again?" she asked, a quiet terror beginning to seize her as she returned to lie by his side.

"Oh yes! I would never leave you forever. I promised you that!" he said, holding her entire body.

"Do you have warp drive or something? You've never told me how you get between stars. Why haven't I asked that?" Her body stiffened. "How can I NOT have asked you about your star-drive before now?" Ann pulled away from him and sat up. "Of all the things I have wondered about throughout my entire life, faster-than-light speed has been *way* up near the top of my want-to-know list! What did you do to me, Marco?"

"Of course we have faster-than-light travel, but clearly, we cannot discuss it with humans until they discover it on their own. Just like the 'prime directive,' I'm not allowed to tell you how it works," he said calmly.

"Not good enough. You haven't answered my question. WHAT DID YOU DO TO ME?" She remained sitting, and she was angry. This time, she would not be put off.

"That's the first time I've ever heard you raise your voice, Ann. OK, I'll tell you. I just dampened your curiosity a little and redirected your questions. Rationally, you accepted the fact that we couldn't discuss it, and you agreed not to 'push it' by asking too many questions we couldn't answer. That was one of them."

"So every time I told myself, 'don't push it, Ann' that was your thought, not mine?" She had lowered her voice, but she was still outraged at being manipulated.

"Possibly. Well, OK--probably. However, your own natural urge to cooperate and be helpful made it very easy to convince you that you wouldn't understand it even if I told you."

"Try me. I'm not as dumb as I look, remember? Surely you could give me the children's version or something. There has to be a 'warp drives for dummies' book somewhere, isn't there?" Her voice gradually lost its tone of anger and began to sound disgusted and sarcastic. She hated begging him for knowledge, which was something she had never done. *Part of the "don't push it" belief was that you would tell me in time. Please tell me that now is the time!*

"All right, querida. Calm down. The concept is fairly easy, but the math is daunting, even for me. Let me hold you, and I'll show you the basic principles, which you will never discuss with anyone, right?"

OK, but I'm really mad at you for messing with my mind and making me beg.

In the total darkness, she once again slid into his arms and put her head on his shoulders. He kissed her forehead, and she began to get images of the galaxy, with stars shining brightly. Between the balls of light there were trails of black, inky stuff swirling in streams and joining into rivers, There were whirlpools and eddies and fantails of darkness churning between the stars. They seemed to become more solid between the stars, but mere fluffs and plumes around the planets.

"What is that dark stuff swirling around?" she asked.

"Your people have just discovered it. It is dark matter and dark energy," he said. "Actually, you have never seen it because it is invisible. It doesn't look like this, but I am showing you this picture so that your mind can grasp the concept. Your physicists know it must be there to account for the differences in mass your math clearly shows. Your scientists are trying valiantly to discern it because they know that it must be very important."

"I've read about it. Dark matter takes up almost three quarters of the mass in space, and dark energy even more. Why is it significant, Marco Antonio?"

"Einstein explained the universal rules very succinctly when he said E=MC squared. What he explained was the universe of *light*. However, there is another universe where light does not exist, so the laws of light and time do not apply. There are areas of greater density, which I showed you as dark swirls, but it is everywhere, even within planets and stars. Like light, it is spread unequally, but it is omnipresent regardless of the presence or absence of light."

"Some of our science fiction writers refer to it as 'hyperspace,' right?" Ann asked aloud, trying to tie the new knowledge to something she already knew.

"Yes, but they don't really know what they're talking about, either. Darkness is not just the absence of light. In dark matter, time and distance do not exist, nor does light. Once you enter dark matter, you can come out wherever you choose, if you can do the math. Once you exit the routes of dark energy, you will reappear in time and space, again governed by Einstein's rules. Then the speed of light will dictate your speed, and the force of gravity your weight." While he was telling her in words, he was showing her mentally, but she was still limited in her ability to learn that way. He had discovered that if he presented information rather like a TV show, with pictures and a background narration, she could grasp it readily. She was a child of her world, and he had to deal with her within the realm of her experiences and abilities.

"So you will get into a ship that will hop into dark matter and use dark energy to propel you to your own sun, or to the City Killers' sun, and then just pop out into their light?"

"Basically, that's the idea. But remember that the names your scientists gave them, 'dark matter' and 'dark energy,' are an unfortunate misnomer. It all really has very little to do with light or its absence, because both dark energy and matter are everywhere. Yet we must use the location of stars and suns as a reference point, so we can get from sun to sun, galaxy to galaxy. We do not want to re-enter this reality in the middle of a sun or planet, so we try to re-emerge close to the sun or planet we want to go to. By far the greatest travel time is spent within a solar system, not between the stars, so it's best to find a stream of dark matter as close to the solar system you are heading for, and calculate from there." Absentmindedly, he kissed her forehead, then went on. "The science behind it is pretty complicated, but your people are on the road to understanding it. They have come a long way in the last one hundred years. Let's hope the City Killer didn't eliminate your best scientists."

Ann was silent for a moment, trying to assimilate it. "If your math is off, you could be in serious trouble, I'd imagine. What would happen?"

"To try to prevent that, we keep careful notes so that we could get back to where we started, hopefully," he said, trying not to say how totally lost they could be. He didn't want to mention the changes in time they might experience. He knew she would worry about him, and she didn't need any more information right now.

"So how long will you be gone, do you suppose?"

Yes, there was Ann, his pragmatist, getting right to the point. "If I go, it will probably take two to four weeks, depending on how close to their home planet we emerge and how far away from our sun is their entry point. We could be weeks in normal space, traveling at sub-light speeds within solar systems." He didn't mention that it could be months if they entered this solar system out by Saturn or Neptune.

"You have a huge project to oversee here, too. We have to organize, develop, and distribute the bacteria and worms all over the planet, and the political fallout from that could be daunting. Could you send someone else? If not, who will be in charge of this project?"

Ann had a good point. This was not a good time for him to leave. "All that is yet to be seen, querida. We are on a fact-finding mission. Information we gather on this trip will decide what we do in the next few weeks."

"I'm just happy to be along for the ride. I feel much better knowing that you are not going to leave me forever. That really scared me. As long as we're together, I can handle it," she said, hugging him.

"I think it's time for me to do my 'take me to your leader' thing, as you call it. The events of the last twenty four hours involve interstellar war, and I think I should confer with this planet's leaders. Even though he is not the leader of the most people, I think the U.S. President will be able to speak on behalf of your planet. What do you think, querida?"

"I may be biased, but I'd agree. Have you ever done this before?"

"No. Of course, there has never been a challenge to the entire species, nor has there been a world-wide leader, although many petty kings of Europe and Asia certainly considered themselves the world's leader."

Ann thought about that for a moment. It would be pointless to interact with some petty European king or an Eastern potentate. Their world-view was very limited, at least until around the 19th Century. England was just a part of one small island until the 18th Century, and even China had been isolated until the end of the 20th Century. What was the point of talking to

Suddenly, Marco Antonio sat up and said, "I think it's time to get dressed. We can't face the president naked, can we?"

"No. It would shock his secretary. Lights, please, Questor?"

Immediately, the whole cabin took on a gentle glow, and Ann and Marco Antonio both started to find their clothes and put them on. "If I'd known I was going to meet the President, I would have brought a dressier change of clothes, and I'd have worn my make-up. We both look like we've just screwed our way across the continent." Ann said, trying desperately to comb her curly hair down with her fingers. "Terminal bed-head, and whisker burn to boot!" She jumped up and headed for the section of the ship where Questor had covered her over-night bag.

"You look fine, my love. He will understand that we are coming in under non-ideal conditions. This is not a formal meeting. Who knows? He might have bed-head too!" He had packed dark gray slacks and a long sleeve dress shirt.

Once his clothes, shoes and socks were back on, Marco Antonio looked like a New York lawyer without a tie.

He placed his hand on the bed, and it immediately started to fold itself back into chairs and thin its walls into glass-like substance through which they could see.

Everything looked green and lovely, but there was a lot of smoke in the distance and the air was even grayer than usual. Ann could not tell from the countryside where they were, so she put her hand on Questor and asked. She got a message she could not understand, so she asked Marco Antonio, and he said "South of Boston, heading south."

MONITORS OF DESTRUCTION

"Has Boston been bombed?" Ann asked, tucking her shirt into her navy blue slacks. They needed pressing. *Oh, well. Better than jeans.*

"Yes, but just the downtown. Many of the people have survived." They were both looking out the window Questor once again provided.

"The countryside here looks unscathed," Ann said hopefully.

"The pattern seems to be to hit just the economic and military centers, at least on the West Coast. If they hit Lemoore Naval Air Station, you can bet that Norfolk is toast. Let's see what they did to New York City," he said, touching the ship again.

Questor took them to the Big Apple, which was down to its core. Most of Manhattan Island was completely flattened, but the housing in the Brooklyn and Yonkers areas looked untouched. Clearly, this was 9/11 on steroids. Instead of a collection of skyscrapers surrounding a bombed-out scar where the twin towers had stood, this was a bombed-out island surrounded by fairly low-density housing.

"There are a lot of dead lawyers and bankers down there," Ann said. "I'm sure a few of them were good people." She was trying hard not to think of all the death and heartbreak below her.

"Not a fan of lawyers and bankers, I see," Marco Antonio answered.

"Not since 2008. Before that, I suspected many of them were sociopaths, but after the big financial crash, I was sure of it. The fact that none of them were punished for knowingly bilking innocent people was a tragedy and a total failure of the justice system." She paused, gazing out the window. "This seems like justice on a biblical scale, however. I'm certainly not happy to see New York in ruins. Most of the people were innocent, as usual." Ann looked down at the ruins and added, "It looks like pictures of Hiroshima after the atom bomb fell."

"Yes, it does. It's horrible," Marco Antonio said quietly.

"It's not just the buildings, it's the people in them. My God! Millions of people have become carbonized ash in just a couple of seconds. So many things and people are gone and can never be replaced," She paused. "I didn't mean to be flippant, Marco. This is a disaster." Ann's voice grew softer with every word as the horror of the scene overtook her. Out of respect for the dead, silence seemed the only honorable tone. Words were inadequate, so they both just looked down mutely.

There are no emergency vehicles, no sirens, no noise. Everything is so still.

"There are no roads left. See—there are ambulances over there, but they can't drive into the city because the roads are covered with what's left of the buildings." Ann whispered. A few seconds later, she pointed out the window and said, "Is that Central Park?"

"Yes."

"Sweet Jesus!"

"Let's go see what's left of Washington," Marco Antonio murmured, and Questor picked up speed.

Within minutes, they were at another pile of rubble. There were no craters, but there were some flat, white areas with little debris on the gray, powdery surfaces. At one end, there was a taller heap of metal and stone.

The Washington Monument.

Oh, God. May they rot in hell forever!

Ann was not thinking of the people of Washington, or the monuments. She was cursing those who had flattened the greatest symbols of her great country.

Gradually, they could make out where the White House had stood, and the Lincoln Memorial. Because the buildings were not so densely packed, it was a little easier to figure out which pile of rocks and twisted steel had been which memorial building.

On the outskirts of the ruins there were still many red brick buildings, most with their windows blown out, but there were people alive and well. Emergency vehicles could be seen, but most were not going anywhere very fast in the confusion. People were in the streets, and cars were inching along. The gridlock was almost total, but both Ann and Marco Antonio agreed that it was a relief to see so many people.

I wonder if the President survived?

Yes, he's alive.

"I can't say that I care about the Congressmen. I liked them about as much as the bankers and lawyers, but it's a damn shame about the buildings." Ann muttered aloud. She knew that Marco Antonio was in her head, so she didn't need to explain her droll comment. He knew how deeply she was grieving the loss of her government and its capital.

Let's go find him. Marco Antonio sent that message to both Ann and Questor, and they headed out to sea.

CHAPTER 8

Marco Antonio finished tying his shoes and took the few steps to the current "front" of the vessel. Since Questor travelled in every direction as easily as any other, the internal configuration of the large vacuole in which they rode changed as needed. What was recently a bed had turned back into chairs which were oriented so that they faced the direction they were currently travelling.

Marco Antonio put his hand on the bulkhead in front of his seat, but he moved it along the wall until he was to the right of Ann's chair. Questor opened his side to produce a small box which had been enclosed within yet another vacuole. Ann wondered how many other things were enclosed within Questor besides their luggage, their lunch, this box, the toilet—*Oh, my! How does he keep it all separate and remember where everything is?*

He's not just a flying sponge, querida. He is a carefully designed and bred creature we have been developing for thousands of years. We've had a lot of time to make improvements.

Marco Antonio held the dark box in his hands. His face took on a quiet look, but she could tell by the slight wrinkle between his eyes that he was concentrating on his communications with that box or whomever he was conversing with through it.

Ann stood quietly, trying not to interrupt. She knew Marco Antonio could carry on several conversations simultaneously using words alone, but the Monitors used many more means to send messages than mere words. In fact, he might be communicating with several information sources, including the human's World Wide Web, the military and intelligence systems like NORAD, the FBI, CIA, and the Secret Service as well as the Monitors' outpost located at the bottom of the Mariana Trench in the Pacific. If there was a way to locate the President, he'd find it.

Marco Antonio had been observing human communications for centuries, and he was current with every source of information ever invented on the planet. If there was information available, he could access it. Unfortunately, the City Killer had completely wiped out several entire communications systems within the last few hours, so Marco Antonio could only hope that all the redundancies he had built into his observation systems would provide him with the up-to-the-minute information he required to locate the President of the United States.

Ann could hardly stand it. She had never seen Marco Antonio so still for so long. Clearly, he was having trouble making connections. She didn't want to seem like some kid going "Are we there yet?" but she wanted to know what he was experiencing every second. Because she knew she could never keep up, she concluded that she could be the most helpful by just letting him do his job.

She decided to clean herself up a little. She could put on her face, comb her hair, or perhaps change her clothes. Granted, she had been out of them for most of the trip, but if she were going to meet the President, she could be better groomed, at least. She put her hand on Questor and asked where her suitcase was. Part of the wall opened and dropped down to form a shelf in front of her suitcase. It reminded her of a drop-down desk she had had as a girl, but she also remembered how she would close it up quickly, jamming all the papers inside so her room looked tidy before she asked her Mom if she could go somewhere.

There were no homework papers in Questor, just her tidy weekender suitcase and a place to open it. She took out her make-up bag, set up the small mirror she had brought, and started wiping off her smeared eye shadow with a damp towellette originally designed to clean baby's butts.

Best to start from scratch. She would have loved a shower, but even Questor had his limits. She scrubbed her face clean and decided she'd clean her other parts when she got to a proper toilet. She didn't want Marco Antonio—*or Questor either, for that matter*—to see her cleaning herself. *He'd probably feel like I do when I see a dog licking himself. Yuk!*

No, I wouldn't. And Questor wouldn't even notice.

Get out of my head. I'm trying to stay out of your way so you can work. Besides, someone has to lighten up the mood in here before we both become catatonically depressed.

I just don't like it when you compare yourself to a pet. It's becoming a pattern. You are not my dog or cat.

Just your bee-atch! Your main squeeze. Yo' mama-ho. She did a brief two-step and wiggled her butt, her hands in the air, fingers snapping.

You are so funny! I've never heard someone call themselves so many names! Don't call yourself my whore, either. That's no better.

Get back to work and find the President. This hobag is nearly ready for him.

I'd get back to work, but I know where the President is, and he is expecting us, so finish your right eye and put your lipstick on. We're almost there.

Ann froze, looked at him, and peered out the window.

Oh, my God! Where is he? We're over the Atlantic ocean!

He's on a submarine beneath us.

She finished her eyeliner, and then asked "How did you do that? Why haven't they blasted us out of the sky, or sent a million escort planes? They're not going to just invite us on board the submarine carrying the President of the United States during a time of war!"

Questor made the floor clear like a window just as Ann finished putting shadow on her right eyelid. She grabbed the neutral shade of lipstick she usually wore and put it on quickly. Turning to look down through the window, she strained to make out what she was looking at.

"The only logical place left was a submarine. There are certain pre-planned and organized protocols regarding governmental continuity in case of war or invasion. I checked each one, eliminating the various responses to different scenarios. I thought that the best choice would be to get the President onto a submarine, along with other key governmental personnel, where the leaders would be safely isolated."

Slowly, a huge shadow emerged, darkening as the submarine rose from the sea. "Why haven't they shot us out of the air? How can they be expecting us?" Ann asked.

"Well, they're not, exactly. I took over their controls and all electronic instruments. The only thing they can still do is surface, so we might talk face-to-face. Their radios, telephones, sonar—nothing works. The only way they can shoot us is with good old fashioned bullets shot manually, and the only way they can communicate with anyone is by speaking to us."

"Are you jamming their equipment?"

"I'm jamming everything. I'm hoping that seeing Questor will provide enough shock and awe that they will talk before they shoot."

"That would be nice," Ann quipped nervously. "Someday, you'll have to tell me how you found the particular sub in which the President of the United States is hiding. That has got to be the most highly protected bit of intel in the world right now."

"It's my job to know, querida. I must admit that knocking out so many information centers made it more of a challenge. Luckily, I have associates who were able to swim to their side and disable their equipment. Don't forget, not all of Questor's friends were bred to fly in the atmosphere; some are specifically designed to work in water. The submarine has been rendered inoperative. Now, let's see if they'll talk to us. Be prepared to get a little damp, querida," Marco Antonio said as he watched as Questor lined himself up with the hatchway. They stood there watching the huge black ship, looking like a sleeping leviathan basking in the sun.

It took several minutes before the hatch opened and four sailors in dark blue coveralls with some sort of inflatable life jackets as an outer garment emerged. Under the life jackets they wore a harness, in addition to enormous M14 rifles in their hands, which they kept pointed down. Next, an armed guard in a gray suit stepped out. Clearly not in the Navy, he tried to keep his sidearm inconspicuous, but it was impossible not to notice that he too had a gun. Behind him came someone who clearly *was* in the Navy. His gold anchor collar pins on his coveralls made him look experienced and authoritative. If he had a gun in his uniform, Ann couldn't see it.

Mr. Gold Anchor Pin looked up at Questor, clearly measuring the danger of the large blob floating in front of him. Ann leaned forward, smiled and waved, in an effort to placate the man's suspicion. With a look and a nod from him, all of the men with him detached one end of a line from their harness and slipped it over a track flush with the deck which ended near the hatch.

I didn't want you to have to get his attention.

Why?

Because a smile and wave from a woman can defuse a volatile situation.

True. Few pirates bring their girlfriends, I suppose. Besides, you're cuter than I am.

No. I just have the sex organs missing from most of the people on that ship.

Questor opened his maw and formed steps, which Ann always thought looked like a weirdly folded tongue. She tried to stifle the thought, thankful that Questor probably couldn't read her mind through her feet. Could he?

Can Questor read our minds through our feet, or any other part of our body?

Sometimes.

Oh my God! Ann felt truly shocked and embarrassed. What did the rover know about her? What had her thoughts blabbed about her while she was standing--or sitting—inside the rover?

Smiling, Marco Antonio took her hand, but stepped in front of her to descend the steps first.

Thank you. I'll expect you to catch me if I fall.

I will, querida.

Are they going to shoot us?

I certainly hope not. I'm counting on their curiosity.

Ann smiled softly at the image of her rolling into Marco Antonio and both of them landing on the submarine. Maybe on top of the President.

You worry about the strangest things, querida.

"Permission to come aboard Chief?" Marco Antonio said to the armed uniformed man who approached them first.

"We would like to see your credentials, sir," the Chief said.

Ann made a mental note that the guy to whom Marco Antonio was speaking was a Chief.

Why didn't they blown us out of the sky? This doesn't seem like a good day to come calling on the Prez.

Marco Antonio reached into his jacket pocket and withdrew a folded piece of paper. Ann had no idea what was on it, but she thought it was blank. She just stood behind him and said nothing while Marco Antonio reached out to hand the chief the paper. When the man touched the paper, Marco Antonio smoothly took his hand, saying "My name is Marco Antonio Polo, currently living in California. May I present Ann Jacob, also from California."

"Welcome aboard, sir!" the Chief responded, but he didn't take his eyes off Marco Antonio. The gentleman in the suit turned to take Ann's outstretched right hand as she stepped onto the small deck. "Welcome aboard, Ma'am," the officer said.

"We are here to see President Blake. We are unarmed, which you are welcomed to confirm," Marco Antonio said, slowly holding his elbows slightly away from his body so that they could see that he had no gun. "He is not expecting us, but under the circumstances, we're hoping that he will work us into his busy schedule."

"We come in peace," Ann said. She had always imagined that would be the appropriate thing to say, and she was thrilled to be the one to say it. As soon as it was out of her mouth, however, she felt silly and melodramatic.

The man in the uniform reached Marco Antonio and patted him down thoroughly but inconspicuously as he put a safety harness on him. When it was on, his harness D-ring was clipped to a flat bar on the deck.

Ann held her arms over her head and turned around slowly as the man quickly and smoothly ran his hands over her body. There was no hint of sexuality; she could have been a six-year-old as far as he was concerned. She stepped into the leg straps of the harness and slipped straps over her chest and shoulders and she, too, was attached to the bar on the deck.

"This way, sir," said the officer, leading the way toward the fin. Marco Antonio took Ann's hand, and she followed behind them. The ship was sturdy, with no hint of it being a huge hollow metal cylinder. The surface was black, non-skid and solid, but there was a gusty breeze that made Ann very thankful for the safety harness. At least the ocean was calm and the submarine rode very smoothly in the water, which seemed far too close to suit Ann.

They walked about fifty feet until they came to the largest hatch. *This is the torpedo hatch, querida. It's also called the midship hatch. OK. Good to know.*

They had seen other hatches, but they were closed and their handles were flush to the deck. The entire ship was very sleek, with nothing to cause turbulence. At the torpedo hatch, the officer unclipped his safety harness from the track, grasped the grab rail firmly, and stepped down the ladder. Marco Antonio then slipped off the end of the D-ring at the end of his safety line from the track. He grabbed the grab rail exactly as the officer had done then turned and unclipped Ann's safety harness, and she followed him down onto the fairly short ladder and through another hatch into the ship. They stepped through another hatch. One by one, they turned and went down some very steep metal stairs. Ann held on tightly to the stainless steel handrail and tried her best to mimic everything the men in front of her did. She was excited about meeting the President, but her mind was a little diverted by thoughts of Questor knowing her every thought. She could feel Marco Antonio mentally smiling at her, amused by her unexpected trains of thought.

They descended a full story and turned down a passageway which was narrow and low. Ann noticed that Marco Antonio shook the hand of three officers who showed them the way to a room with a table down the center and red fake-leather benches down one side and chairs down the other. Another body guard stood at the far end of the table. In a chair at the end of the table sat the President of the United States, Mike Blake.

The President rose and extended his hand. He remained silent, waiting for Marco Antonio or Ann to say something. Marco Antonio shook his hand silently, holding on a few seconds longer than normal. Ann knew he was communicating his greetings telepathically, establishing his *bona fides* instantly. Aloud, he said, "Marco Antonio Polo. I am honored to make your acquaintance. May I introduce my associate, Ann Jacob?"

Ann shook hands with the President, whose eyebrows raised slightly. "How do you do, Mr. President." When she saw the question on his face, she added "Yes, I am human. Since there is no equivalent human word for Dr. Polo's species, we call them Monitors."

"Thank you, Ms. Jacob. You answered my first two questions," the President said smoothly. "I have many, many more."

"For reasons of absolute transparency, I would prefer to deliver my message aloud, in words," said Marco Antonio. "Feel free to record any of our conversations."

"Thank you Dr. Polo," said the President. "Let me introduce the captain of this vessel, Commander John McDaniel," he said as he motioned towards the officer to his left.

The captain extended his hand, and Marco Antonio shook it, also holding it a few seconds longer than the proscribed customary time. McDaniel's expression changed dramatically into one of shock. Trained to be a warrior, he quickly formed a frown and glanced at President Blake. Ann wasn't sure if he was checking for guidance or to certify that the President was unharmed.

"Please have a seat," said the President smoothly.

Marco Antonio motioned for Ann to slide in first. It was a gracious, inclusive gesture, but sliding across benches was something Ann hated to do. She always felt very awkward galumphing down a bench.

I feel like a seal, and not a Navy one.

You don't look like a seal, querida. No one looks good scooting down a bench. You did fine.

Scooting is very difficult when your feet don't reach the floor. It's very unladylike, especially in a dress. Thank God I'm in pants—it could be worse! I could look like a walrus on an ice flow. Oh, never mind me. I'm still thinking like a fat old lady. I'm not a pinniped!

Seating us on the bench side was designed to make us uncomfortable and unable to bolt. It was very clever of them to turn us into pinnipeds.

"All our electronic devices are out of commission, Mr. Polo. I don't suppose you know anything about that, do you?" asked Captain McDaniel.

"They'll all work now. Turn them off and then on again, and that should do it," said Marco Antonio. "I wanted to talk directly to you and the President without going through a lot of red tape. I'm sorry for the inconvenience."

"You have attacked a United States Naval vessel, sir. That is an act of war, not an inconvenience," said the captain.

"What do you know of these attacks upon our cities, Mr. Polo?" asked the President, taking charge of the meeting.

"Not much more than you do, sir. Let me reassure you and Captain McDaniel that we Monitors had absolutely nothing to do with these horrendous events. We are not a violent people," Marco Antonio said quietly and confidently, "and we did not attack your planet nor your ship. We simply made it impossible for you to attack *our* ship."

"I am very relieved to hear that. If not you, then who has been bombing us?" demanded the President.

"Mrs. Jacob has dubbed them 'City Killers,' which I will also call them until we learn their actual names. Directly after the first attack of which we were aware, we took our Rover, Questor, up and approached the attacking ship. Immediately, we noticed that they ignored our existence until we hailed them. Then, their response was to fire forcefully, aiming at precisely the location from which we hailed them. Fortunately, we were no longer in that location. They did not pursue nor fire again."

Captain McDaniel's lips grew thinner, and he interrupted to ask the obvious questions. "What type of weapon did *they* use? What is their caliber and range?"

"My sensors indicated that it was an energy beam, and not a projectile. It was clearly of lethal strength, even though our hail had been a greeting. We had intended to make contact, not to make a serious attack. They did not pursue us; however, I could not immediately ascertain whether or not they were able to track us down. After further investigation, I tend to think they cannot perceive non-metallic targets."

The President nodded curtly. "What else can you tell us about them, Mr. Polo?" asked the President once he gathered that Marco Antonio was finished. By the look on the Captain's face, he gathered immediately that their transport was "non-metallic," and was almost visibly considering the ramifications of that fact. He wanted to ask, but the President's questions took precedence. Ann half expected him to raise his hand and start jumping in his seat, but he controlled his desire to interrupt.

"Their ship is unmanned. It is basically a drone. When I entered the drone, I did not see any mechanical devices designed to land on the planet, so I surmise that it is for aerial attacks only," Marco Antonio said calmly.

"You entered it?" said the Captain, clearly excited by the prospect.

"Could you get any inkling of its intentions? Why has it attacked us?" asked the President, without the "Wow!" factor the Captain was unable to conceal.

May I tell them what we discussed?

Of course! That's why you're here, my love.

"We have discussed this at some length," said Ann, leaning in. "We think that it wants to remove the highest concentrations of human life and enslave the rest. It may even suggest a partnership deal to mine our natural resources. By lowering our population numbers, they are lessening the probability of our fighting them or each other, polluting our planet even more than we have. They want a non-radioactive, pristine planet with a well-educated but poorly organized population clearly able to extract organic materials and valuable metals to give or trade. At least, that is the scenario we feel most likely," Ann said.

"And who, exactly, is 'we'?" asked the President.

He reminds me of the caterpillar in Alice in Wonderland *who said, 'Whoooo are youuu?' Can't blame him, I guess.*

"Mrs. Jacob and I went unaccompanied in our rover to meet and observe the beings which were attacking the Earth," Marco Antonio said smoothly.

"Dr. Polo and I had several hours during our journey to investigate the City Killer drone to discuss the ramifications of this attack. You, of course, may come to a different conclusion. When the City Killer deflected the ICBMs aimed at it towards the sun, rather than back towards the planet, we decided they did not want radiation to fall on the Earth. We think they want it as pristine as possible when they get here." Ann replied.

"So why are they bombing us?" The President said, hurt and confusion on his face.

"They want us disorganized and isolated, so they eliminated our communications and destroyed our economic and government centers. To them, they took out the trash," Ann said, "by cleaning out the infestations."

There was silence for a brief moment. The President looked shocked, and the Captain looked angry. They both spoke at once, but the Captain backed off immediately. "How can we stop them?" asked the President.

"For the moment, I think they have stopped," said Marco Antonio. "Perhaps they have done enough damage, or maybe they simply ran out of ammunition. Now we must decide what to do when they take the next step," said Marco Antonio. "It is about this that I wish to confer."

"What do you propose we do?" asked the President once again asserting control, by asking advice from an underling. He leaned forward, placing his forearms on the table and gazing intently at Marco Antonio.

"I would like to have your permission to speak on behalf of the citizens of Earth." Marco Antonio simply looked at him. Ann looked at both the President and the Captain, but both men remained unreadable, at least to her.

"What would you say?" asked the President, not eliminating the suggesting or taking offense that a Monitor would presume to speak for the whole planet.

"I will follow this drone back to its home planet, supposing that it will return directly. I would seek out the project's leaders, and explain why it is not in their interest to return to Earth except perhaps to apologize and to help rebuild your cities. This planet is not open to invasion, colonization, or any type of exploitation. I will make it infinitely clear that we Monitors will not permit any further violence against this planet."

"Do you have forces strong enough to enforce that?" asked the Captain, who positively *ached* to know what those forces included. Even Ann could see that clearly.

"We are not a militant race, Captain McDaniel. We do not fight wars or conquer other civilizations. But yes, we can certainly stop them from doing so."

"Why didn't you stop them before they killed millions of our people?" the President asked pointedly.

"We have only a scientific outpost here, sir. We are only prepared to observe your species, not to interfere in any way. This is why I wished to speak to you before I take any action on your behalf," Marco Antonio said in his most diplomatic tone.

"And I appreciate that," said President Blake. "Although I am not empowered to speak for the whole planet, I feel it's safe to say that the other world leaders would concur with my request for whatever help you can give us. In turn, if there's anything we can do to improve the relations between humans and Monitors, please let us know."

"So far, the relations between humans and monitors are excellent," Marco Antonio said. "Ms. Jacob and her family have been very helpful, demonstrating a spirit of cooperation you can be very proud of, sir."

You just like the way I give you blowjobs, lover!
Indeed!

Marco Antonio had a big smile that had nothing to do with national pride. Ann couldn't help but smirk, but she wiped her expression clean when the President turned his attention towards her.

"You are a credit to our species, Ms. Jacob. Have you been working with Dr. Polo long?"

"About five years. Several Monitors came here just before the Yellowstone Eruption to observe our country's response to that natural catastrophe. We helped them get settled and set up their home, just as most neighbors would do anywhere. Since then, we have had many opportunities to help each other, and we have grown very close in the process."

"It's to know there are other Monitors, and I hope we have the time to debrief you about them and to get to know Dr. Polo as well. Let's hope this is the beginning of a long and warm relationship!" said the President, sounding like an over-eager vote-getter.

"Dr. Polo can show you in seconds what I'd take hours to tell you."

"So I noticed when I shook his hand." The captain turned to Marco Antonio and said, "Are you telepathic, Doctor? Can you read my mind?" To his credit, the President's question sounded curious, but not fearful.

"Not usually. I can converse with you through touch, but rarely through the air. We usually use spoken speech because these bodies are not equipped for non-verbal communications. Your brains become exhausted quickly."

"Some of the brain's neurotransmitters run low, and you must sleep for a while. It's quite tiring, but very interesting and much faster," Ann explained.

"Besides, we have no time now to get acquainted. That drone might leave at any moment, and I must be ready to follow it. We must take our leave, sirs," Marco Antonio said as he rose to depart.

Everyone stood but Ann, who was busy trying to scoot to the end of the bench. Marco Antonio extended his hand, and she took it, trying at least to stand gracefully when she reached the end of the table.

"Will Ms. Jacob be going with you when you follow the City Killer?" asked the Captain.

Guess where he wants to go?

"No. My ship is not designed for human bodies, unfortunately." When Marco Antonio said that, both men seemed to slump a little.

"Perhaps we could visit with her, and she can tell us about you Monitors while you are off saving our world?" President Blake said.

Careful! Tricky question! They might lock you up while they "debrief" you. I won't let them waterboard you for information, querida. Aloud, he looked at the President and said "I do not know what her plans are. She may do whatever she wishes while I am gone." *Well, almost. No other men but me.* Marco Antonio glanced at her from the corner of his eye.

Oh, darn! Here I planned to have men—especially politicians—line up at my bedroom door! Ann looked right at him and gave him a gleaming smile.

Vixen!

Could I introduce the President to Ruth and Gabriel, or some of the other Monitors while you're gone? It would help a lot to get his cooperation spreading the bio-material to treat Marie's Disease. Your call, lover.

You've already told them we live nearby. In for a penny, in for a pound, but be careful, my love. They will seek control.

"There is one more project I wish to discuss with you, sir," Marco Antonio said. "As I'm sure you are aware, there has been a vast increase in lung diseases among the people of Earth. Both humans and animals are increasingly coming down with a condition called hypertrophic pulmonary osteoarthropathy, also known as HPO or Marie's Disease, due to the volcanic ash in the atmosphere. Because this condition is affecting all vertebrates, including us, we have broken our own policy of non-intervention to find a cure for this disease. We have succeeded. In fact, we were having a small celebration when the City Killers began their attacks."

"I am aware of the vast increase in lung diseases. I know the CDC in Atlanta has been working on it, as well as most of the drug companies. I'm sure they would welcome your help," said the President.

"We are entering the production phase. Since it is not a medicine or drug, we won't have to go through the FDA process. It is strictly a biologically-based cure which will be produced and delivered worldwide," Ann pointed out. "On a non-profit basis, of course," she added. *This could be the biggest mistake we've ever made. We could be buried in red tape.*

If so, we'll do the manufacturing in other countries.

"I will be en route to the home of the City Killers, but Ms. Jacob will be able to familiarize your scientists with the species we have developed to remove the lung shards which are plaguing the world. She has been of great help to me during the development stages," Marco Antonio said. "Please do not hinder her progress in this project. If you do, we will simply remove the labs from your shores and reestablish production centers in other parts of the world. They, of course, would be served first."

"We look forward to working with you, Ms. Jacob," the President said smoothly. He caught the veiled threat and responded like any good politician would.

So you're not going to tell him about Miguel and the others?

Not yet. If you're buried in paperwork, the others can melt back into the woodwork. I don't want him to think we have invaded.

Right.

"Clearly, we must deal with those you call the City Killers first," said Captain McDaniel. "How will you convince them to leave and not return? Will there be retaliatory strikes? What should we do immediately to shoot that ship down?"

"The drone has good defenses. I don't think we *can* shoot it down. It responds to all non-biological attacks," Marco Antonio began to explain.

"So you think we should use biological weapons? I thought it was a drone," the captain said. He couldn't help but show the frustration any military man would feel when his entire planet was under attack. Clearly unwilling to let Marco Antonio go until he had learned more, Ann thought for a moment that they might try to detain them on board the sub, but she said nothing.

"It is, so it is not susceptible to viruses or bacteria," Marco Antonio answered smoothly. "Since it does respond to anything metallic, it cannot be shot with conventional projectiles such as bullets or bombs. It is well shielded. However, it does not react to living material, like my rover. It allowed me to enter while I was in a biological EVA suit. If it does not leave soon, which I strongly suspect it will, we might be able to attack it with a strong acid sprayed on its surface or deposited into its cargo bay. My rovers could deliver such chemical compounds, carried in plastic, glass or ceramic. It might be possible to get some into the interior."

"We have such compounds, I believe. I'd have to check with my military advisors, of course. We are in constant contact," said the President.

"Your ship is alive?" asked the captain.

"Yes."

"Are all UFO's alive?" asked the President, sounding shocked.

"Well, all our rovers are alive. Thus, they can approach the City Killer drone without arousing its defensive reactions. It is metallic, and our ship is not."

"Unless they carry a metal bomb. We tried a reverse Trojan Horse approach, with a living being smuggling in a metal weapon, and it didn't work," Ann interjected. "It's very sensitive to metals. It wouldn't let them even get close, even though the bomb was inside a living ship. We tried that first."

"You have tried to deliver a bomb in your UFO? On your own?" the President said. "Was anybody hurt?"

"Thankfully, no. It simply didn't allow us to approach with a large metallic object aboard. It did fire upon us, but we dodged its fire. Which is why I want to follow it home to negotiate with whomever sent it. I think it is out of bombs and will leave soon, and I want to be on its tail," Marco Antonio said.

"So you have interstellar warp drive capabilities? Can we send an emissary with you to represent Earth, or at least America?" asked the President.

The President sounds like he would like to go himself. Can't blame him. I want to go, too.

"No, I'm sorry. Our ship is not capable of sustaining human life. I will have to go alone, which is why I am seeking your approval and asking for your permission to negotiate in your stead. It is a decision you must make immediately, before it leaves and I can't track it," said Marco Antonio, standing there looking like he was about to bolt. With all four people standing in the doorway, they were quite close, and Ann had to look up at all of them. There was a definite feeling of haste.

"I approve, of course. Anything you can do to help us against this heinous attack would be most welcome. I will inquire about chemical weapons right now, in case it sticks around for another attack. How do we contact you?" asked the President.

Aww—he wants your phone number! I think he wants to be your friend!

I'm not that easy.

You're not cheap, but you ARE easy, sweetheart. Ann looked up at him and smiled, but Marco Antonio maintained a poker face.

"I'll be in touch. If you stay within telephone range of the coast, you could reach Ms. Jacob's cell phone, and she can contact me. Thank you for meeting with us, sir, and thank you for allowing us aboard your ship, captain. We must be going," Marco Antonio said, holding out his hand to shake.

"We have many questions about you and your, um, fellow Monitors. I hope you will be willing to meet with us again soon under better circumstances," the President said, shaking Marco Antonio's hand.

"Oh, you'll hear from me again," Marco Antonio said, shaking the Captain's hand, but looking directly into the President's eyes.

Ann reached into her pocket and withdrew a card with her name and cell phone number. She placed it on the table, shook both the Captain's and President's hand, and followed Marco Antonio back down the narrow hallway.

CHAPTER 9

He is a pig, and he's lucky I didn't kill him.

Ann felt his ire clearly as she approached the ladder to go out of the submarine.

WHO is a pig? What are you talking about, Marco?

The President. He was very attracted to you, and he has improper intensions about you. I don't want you anywhere near him. I almost took your phone number away. I don't like the fact that he can contact you.

I rarely hang out with him, so don't worry about it. Besides, we don't live in the same neighborhood.

Wordlessly, they mounted the steep stairs, then the ladder. Once again, they were hooked up to the safety lines, and they walked back to Questor's steps near the bow of the ship.

Ann couldn't stand it. She wanted to turn and wave good-by to the men at the torpedo hatch after she unhooked her safety line before she started up Questor's steps. "This is so cool! They are so jealous!" Ann gushed. "They want to see inside Questor and take a ride in a real UFO. I am a very lucky lady!"

"I'm glad you enjoyed it, querida. I didn't. The President wants to get into your pants, and three of the sailors think you have great hooters. It was difficult for me not to be jealous. I wanted to sink the entire ship after I drained your President of every drop of blood in his body." Marco Antonio was absolutely surly.

"You did very well, then," Ann replied, trying to mollify him. "I'm glad you realized that they are sailors who haven't seen a woman for several weeks at least, and that the President is under a huge strain, since his country is under attack. Sex is one of the perks of power, and he's feeling pretty helpless right now. He's just trying to reassure himself," Ann answered. "I'll never be allowed to be alone with him, even if I wanted to be, which I don't. Don't worry about it."

"I do worry about it, every minute of every day. The idea of leaving you here alone to work with a man who wants you makes me crazy." Marco Antonio looked out the window, trying to find something to take his mind off the men on the submarine.

"Get over it, Marco. Trust me. I am NOT going to have an affair with President Blake! Most probably, I'll never see him again. I'll have to deal with the people in his bloated entourage, answering endless questions," she said, sitting down in her usual co-pilot's chair. "Now, I have a few questions of my own, like where's your interstellar ship? How can I help you prepare for your journey?"

"The only thing I'll need I can get from the Mariana Outpost. I won't be travelling in this body, so it will be in stasis." He was still grumpy, and she hesitated to talk to him.

Hoping that she could get him talking about Monitor methods, she asked, "How in the world did you find and actually get through to the President of the United States?"

"I said, 'Take me to your leader,' of course," he said, smiling one of his half-grins. He wasn't angry at her; he was trying to overcome his own emotions.

"Really? No, c'mon! How did you find him and get permission to board a submarine during a time of attack? If I hadn't been there, I wouldn't have believed it!" She used the same tactic every smart woman has used for centuries: she appealed to his ego. It worked.

"Ann, I am a Monitor. My chief job is to monitor your species, which includes socially, politically, and environmentally. I always maintain knowledge of the whereabouts of every world leader and ways to communicate with them. It's my job, querida." He tried to sound nonchalant, but just a tad of pride leaked through. He was pleased to have surprised her, especially since it showed his superiority to the President. It bolstered him to see that she was impressed with something he had done to outwit this politician, whom he considered an opponent for Ann's affections.

"Oh wow, have I ever underestimated you! All this time, I thought you were merely the galaxy's greatest bio-geneticist and xeno-sociologist! Hah! Have you ever contacted him—or any other President—before?" She really *was* impressed, and she took the opportunity to show it. He needed the reassurance to beat back those green-eyed monsters that plagued him.

"No. I have tried to stay out of all political systems. I let your leaders take care of their own political structures and organizations, and then I watch what they do." He calmed himself by remembering that Mike Blake was just another politician. He had seen hundreds of petty officials come and go during his stay on this planet. Most of them were not nearly as smart as they thought they were, and many were very dangerous. He didn't trust any politician, especially one that found Ann attractive.

"So how did you know he was on a submarine? I thought he was supposed to be on Air Force One or buried in a mountain fort somewhere." Ann wasn't going to let him off that easily.

"Don't forget that we live in the ocean. Our main outpost is in the Mariana Trench, which is still in the Pacific, but we also keep tabs on what's going on in the Atlantic. We monitor the human activity by tapping into the radio waves, microwaves, and by the water displacement of moving objects in water. We know where every whale is, every submarine, and every ship on the water, in addition to the sounds they generate on purpose to communicate with each other. Your computerized methods of conveying information via satellites, radio waves, and other electronic methods are pretty basic and easily intercepted."

Ann felt like a child showing off chalk drawings on the sidewalk to Michelangelo. Sometimes it was hard for her to remember that a species one and a half million years old might consider all human communication systems to be about on that level. "How do you filter out all the noise and background information?"

"Our filtering systems have no problems with one-or-two-component sources," he answered. She had no idea what he meant, which he saw immediately by the look on her face. "Sounds and pictures," he explained.

"OK. But what kept them from blowing us out of the sky as soon as they figured out that Questor is a UFO? This was not a good day to come calling. I would have assumed they would be more protective and suspicious on any day the planet was attacked, taking for granted that the new aliens in town were the same ones who blew up the Earth's cities," Ann said. "Did you really just *hope* they wouldn't shoot us because they were *curious? SERIOUSLY?*"

"I also completely disarmed everything electronic, with some help from my friends who gave them a little electro-magnetic shock. The President's protectors could beat us up with clubs or shoot us with guns, but they had to rise to the surface to do that. I made sure they were still able to ascend so they wouldn't panic."

"Sweetie, you have a lot more faith in the power of curiosity than I have. Besides, most submarine captains carrying the President of the United States would shoot first and ask questions later," Ann noted. After a second, she chanced an observation she thought Marco Antonio might not have realized. "You showed a lot of faith in President Blake's control of the situation and his rational response to a pretty scary state of affairs."

"Actually, he's one of the better leaders. I've had to deal with others who were completely irrational and unpredictable," he admitted. "I respect his political ability. I just don't like him around you. There have been some real sociopathic kings and generals that were totally erratic and impulsive, but fortunately, he's better than most."

"That had to be hard at times," Ann said, leaning over to touch his arm. *Watching mass murderers like Hitler committing genocide, or Stalin letting 20 million of his own people die.*

It was. I've watched your political and religious leaders do some heinous things. Sometimes it was difficult not to want to step in and stop them.

You watched and could do nothing. That had to be horrible!

I could and did help the people in my immediate vicinity who were important to me, but not to history. Your people had to make their own mistakes and survive them. Hopefully, even learn from them. It was doubtful that your species would survive long enough to overcome the consequences of your own stupidity and superstition.

"So why are you stepping in now?" Ann asked aloud. She looked at his face, trying to see if there was an answer there.

"There's a third party. That changes the rules," he answered, taking the hand that was running through the hair on his arm and kissing her wrist.

"Back to questions! Make me stay on task, or I'll jump you again!" She thought about it, but quickly brought herself back in line, saying "There's too much to do! How much do you want the government to know about the Monitors?"

"As little as possible. I don't want them knowing anything about the Mariana Outpost. I think they should know nothing about how we find bodies; they will never believe that we choose the sick and dying. Too many stories like *Invasion of the Body Snatchers* I guess."

She smiled at his reference to a movie. No, two movies; it had been made twice, and both were excellent. She was surprised that he would make a movie reference. "You can bet I won't mention that you and Miguel are sanguinary eaters, either. *WAY* too many vampire novels and movies for that!"

"I would agree, querida. I wish they wouldn't come to your house, but they probably will. Now that they have your cell phone number, they'll track you down and keep you under surveillance."

Before you can say "Jack Robinson!"

Why would I say "Jack Robinson"?

"Never mind, dear. It's just an old saying showing haste. I agree they'll be there. In fact, they may be there already, if there's communication with California. I think I'll just let them come, and work out of my house. I'll invite them in, but I'm certainly not going to show them the basement or the Smith's house next door."

They both sat silently for a moment, looking out the window Questor had made for them.

"There's a problem, though. They'll want to see our research. We'll have to show them a lab *somewhere*, and it might be easier just to show them your house. There's no reason to show them your neighbor's house, however. Let's just keep it at you and me," he said aloud.

That's not fair to the other Monitors. Why should we get all the credit?

I'll see that they get all the credit on our home planet. They'll all be going home soon anyway. It's best that they stay out of the limelight.

"Not Miguel. He intends to stay for a long while. Besides, if he's here openly, they'll have a Monitor to interview and to answer their questions. Let's give him the glory. It will make it a lot easier for you and me to slip off quietly."

"I was going to give you all the glory, querida. You deserve it!" He turned his chair to face her. He looked at her, reached out, and took her other hand.

"Me? No I don't! I'm not a scientist, and I don't want the credit. Besides, all the papers you've published have your name and Miguel's on them. Not mine." She shook her head in denial. This was something she had not earned and would not accept.

"We could not have done it without you," he said. "You know that."

"OK, I'll take credit for doing your laundry. I can't even take credit for feeding you. You're both vampires. I haven't done much to help you."

"Except when we most needed it. You have saved both our lives, more than once." He looked at her earnestly. He knew that she didn't think her own actions had ever been very significant, but they certainly had been. She had turned her entire life over to him and to the Monitors, and she had never asked for anything for herself. She had no idea how rare that was.

"Well, you gave me back my youth. I'd be dead from a heart attack by now if not for you. Seems like a fair deal to me," she said, nodding and winking at him, as if they had just made the deal. "I think Miguel must be included both in the credit department and the dealing-with-the-government department."

"All right, querida. You're probably right," He felt slightly defeated. Once again, he had failed to convince her of her own worth. She always assumed that her own contributions of effort and moral support were to be expected, and therefore nothing special. When she dealt with her own species, she was confident and assured, but when she interacted with him, her sense of inferiority kept reappearing. She thought devotion was a natural attitude, and not a rarity. Ann had no clue how most humans had treated him in the past.

"So where are we going next? I think we should head home, unless there's something else we should be doing on the East Coast," Ann said, feeling suddenly at a loss. She felt like she should be busy doing something to defeat the alien attack, but there really wasn't much she could do.

"Questor has been heading west. I have some arrangements I'll need to make on the communicator. This would be a good time to do that," he said, his voice somewhere between hopeful and apologetic.

You're afraid I'll be bored? Really?
I don't want you to feel ignored while I work.

"I'm going to fix myself something to eat, and then I'm going to settle down with my Kindle. I'll be fine, lover—you don't have to entertain me."

"But I love to entertain you!" he said quietly. That tone of voice made her want to purr.

"It's a long trip," she said, smiling smugly and winking. She got up from her seat to take out a sandwich for her and a bag of blood for him from the vacuole where their food was packed. As she passed him, she kissed his forehead and squeezed his shoulder, and he patted her arm.

I'm OK, Marco. You do what you need to do.

Before Ann could get her lunch (or dinner or breakfast; she had lost track hours ago), her telephone rang. Her cell phone did not disclose the sender, but Ann had a pretty good idea what it was about.

"Is this Ms. Ann Jacob?"

"Yes it is," Ann said in a pleasant, but not-too-cheery voice.

"Please hold for the Secretary of Defense," the voice said.

The voice changed after a two-second wait. "Ms. Jacob? This is Stanley Pickering, the Secretary of Defense. The President asked me to obtain information about certain chemical compounds, which I have done. I am calling to ensure you that we could have sufficient quantities properly bottled within two hours." Mr. Pickering paused, and then went on, "Would you like me to prepare them?"

"Yes, thank you. We are going to use the first approach suggested by Dr. Polo. However, if he cannot leave immediately because the quarry remains in a stable position, we will prepare for both pick-up and delivery in, say, twelve hours. I think it would be safer to prepare for that eventuality as soon as possible."

"We will have the product ready and waiting at a destination of your choosing, either on the East or West coast. However, I would rather not discuss specific arrangements over an open phone line," Pickering said.

Ann had a strong suspicion that he wanted a direct line to Marco Antonio more than he wanted a "secure" line. Oh, well. "There's no time to establish secure lines. The West coast would be far easier, but only if the products needed and the packaging necessary are available there. You are the warrior, sir. You decide how much we will need and we will provide the transportation and delivery," Ann said. She was surprised at herself that she could talk to the Secretary of Defense about delivering acid to a UFO in such a calm voice.

You're doing great, querida.

"Everything needed is available there. May I speak to Dr. Polo please?" Pickering's tone made him sound like he wanted to talk to her Daddy.

"I'm sorry, he's on another line. Leave me a number, and I'll have him return your call," she said, knowing that he wasn't often put off by someone he probably considered a secretary. Ann just decided to establish the pecking order right at the beginning, but she had no pencil or paper. She was afraid she might not remember ten numerals; seven was usually all she could manage. *I'll say them aloud, and Marco Antonio will remember them.*

No worries, querida.

"My line is a secure one. We'll call you back in a few minutes. I'd like to discuss Dr. Polo's means of delivery and his ship's, hmm, class before he leaves the, uh, neighborhood."

Love it! He stammered first! Ann grinned.

"That would be fine. Thank you, Secretary Pickering," Ann said as she discontinued the call.

Good job! You are very good at handling politicians. Don't be too eager.

"I hung up first! Do you think that was too much?" Ann asked anxiously.

"No, querida. You established your position, at least with him. Now, the President is another matter. He will try to dominate you. Don't trust him, and never be alone with him." Marco Antonio had seen what men of power and prestige were capable of. In fact, he had experienced it personally, and he wanted to avoid those very unpleasant incidents for Ann.

"Think about this, oh Jealous One. The President of the United States is not going to rape me or any other woman. He might make a pass at me, but I will refuse. Right? Do you have any doubts about that, Marco Antonio? Do you?" She was literally right in his face. She wanted him to realize the absurdity of his jealousy.

"No, you're right, querida. But he has no right to make a pass at you. You're mine, and I will defend you and keep you safe from men who think their position gives them the right to prey upon women. Of course, I trust you to refuse him," he said and reached for her. She stood up and stood between his knees. He put his head against her chest and held her to him as she hugged his head.

"No worries," Ann said. She gave his head another little squeeze, let go, and headed back across the narrow walkway to get her sandwich and his blood.

He let her go, and tried to assure himself that this political leader was not like the kings and princes of just a few years ago. Ann was naïve, as were most Americans. They had no idea how recently all leaders had based their power on institutionalized violence. The "divine right of kings" was alive and well less than a century ago, and there were still many places on this planet where women were not safe from men.

How thin was the veil of civilization? How soon would males revert to the notion that "might makes right?" Her innocence and the confidence it engendered made him very nervous. She had no idea how dangerous men were—all men, including and especially rulers. Mike Blake might have been elected, but he liked power, and that made him dangerous to everyone, particularly women.

"Choose a place to pick up the acid. Edwards Air Force Base? Lemoore Naval Air Station? Let's make the call. I vote for Lemoore, or what's left of it. Of course, there might not be any runway left; we'll have to check," Ann said as she poked a straw into his blood bag just as she had poked into a thousand juice boxes. She handed it to him and turned away. "Maybe Fresno Air Terminal. The runways will take jets, and I don't think it's been bombed," she mused.

She started taking her sandwich out of its baggy. Without looking back at Marco Antonio, Ann poured herself some iced tea out of the plastic bottle into a paper cup, taking her time about it. He hated it when she saw him drink blood, so she returned the bottle and fumbled around for the nectarine she had put in there. Taking out a knife, she slowly and carefully sliced the nectarine onto the plastic bag the sandwich had been in.

"Is your space ship at the Mariana Trench?" Ann asked as she finished up slicing the nectarine. She doubted it was anywhere on land, but it might be stored at the outpost at the bottom of the ocean or on the dark side of the moon. She had wondered about it many times, but had never asked. She had put it in the "don't push" categories, but now she wanted to know.

"Yes. I'll have to get it checked out, which is one of the many calls I have to make," he said.

"Got it. I'm quietly eating over here. Not talking. Not interrupting. Reading," she said, putting the plastic with the juicy fruit slices on the control console in front of her seat, and returning for her sandwich and iced tea. Questor enlarged the table in front of her seat. She grabbed her Kindle and got comfy in her chair.

It bothered her that she hadn't asked him to enlarge the dashboard into a table, but she had wondered where she would put her glass.

Oh, god! Questor does read my thoughts through my feet! Too creepy! Read your book, my love. He'll ignore you.
You, too, Mr. Telepath. Get to work and get out of my head!

MONITORS OF DESTRUCTION

OK.

As soon as her mouth was full with a big bite of sourdough sandwich, her phone rang. She picked it up, knowing they would soon be out of range.

"This is the Secretary of Defense calling for Dr. Polo. Is he available?" asked a male voice.

"No, sorry. He's eating his lunch. Give him five more minutes," Ann said with her mouth full, and then she hung up.

Gotta establish a few things, right from the get-go. One is that you eat, like everyone else.

I suppose so. Besides, I can get a lot done in five minutes.

Well then, go, go, go

CHAPTER 10

"Just as I feared, it is leaving. Damn!" Marco Antonio said. "Let's hope it is not in too much hurry to leave this solar system." He was holding his black communication box in one hand and his blood-bag in the other.

"Will you be able to follow it?" Ann asked anxiously, her sandwich still in her hand.

"I think so. We'll meet our ship and I'll exchange bodies over land. That way, I can leave sooner, and you'll get your chance to see my true form. Prepare yourself. I'm not pretty." He was very nervous about appearing in his natural state in front of Ann.

"How much time before you leave?" Ann asked as calmly as she could.

"Just a few minutes. I'm sorry, Ann."

That means that your interstellar ship has been coming towards us for quite some time, doesn't it?

Yes. Since before we met the President.

You're a clever bastard!

"I wanted to keep our good-byes short. And you said you wanted to see my native body. This is the only way, since you can't go to the bottom of the ocean." He glanced in her direction, trying to judge just how angry she was.

Not very. She was more frightened than angry. "I'll try not to cry and carry on, but you know I will. This scares the shit out of me," she said, taking the empty blood bag out of his hand and putting it in the trash vacuole.

A colorful image, querida.

In your dreams, sugar.

Marco Antonio smiled. Few humans beside Ann understood that Monitors shared defecation rituals the way people here share feasting. He liked that about her; it was one of many, many things that made him love her.

"Will you guard my body while I'm gone, Ann? It'll stay here in Questor. I'll be in stasis, which is like being in a coma. He'll take care of all my physical needs, so there will be nothing for you to do." He was trying hard to be calm, so she would be calm.

"Will you need any blood to eat? Miguel will be able to help me get some, and I'm not above changing diapers. You know I'd do anything for you, Marco Antonio." She was trying to be reassuring by offering her services. It was so like her to assume that he would allow her to care for his body while it was in stasis.

"I know you would. No, Questor is quite accustomed to guarding my human body while I'm deep underwater at the Mariana Trench, so he'll take care of me for the few days I'll be in space. If you would like to check on me, just ask Questor, and he'll make my stasis chamber clear so you can see me sleeping. I won't be visibly breathing, of course; he provides what oxygen and other gases I'll need, as well as my food and water. We've been doing this for millennia, so don't worry, my love."

"Hold me, please," Ann said, standing and reaching for him. "I'm so glad we took advantage of the time we had together."

He stood and embraced her. Silently, he sent her detailed instructions on how to build the laboratories for production of the tiny worms and the bacteria they would feed upon. In a few minutes, he instilled in her biological and genetic data that would have taken her months of hard study to learn. He knew he had flooded her brain with more than she could possibly process without sleep.

"I'm here," he said, and kissed her gently.

A little rummy, Ann melted into his kiss, not understanding what he meant. When he started taking off his clothes, she was a little taken aback, confused by his completely non-sexual disrobing. She stood there silently, watching him, until she groggily started unbuttoning her pants. His hand reached out and stopped her.

"Not you. Just me. It's easier for me to take off my clothes while I am still conscious. We'll walk to the other ship, where we'll exchange bodies."

"OK," she said, exhausted by the brain activity she had just experienced as he had downloaded information. She stood there, weaving slightly, and watched him take off everything except his shoes and socks.

"Come," he said, and took her hand. Questor formed a ramp, and they walked out of the rover into the night. It was dark and windy. There were no stars visible as they walked into the blustery breeze, and there were no houselights, streetlights, or car lights anywhere.

I see why you wore your shoes. For a while, I thought you were just making a fashion statement. Brrr! It's cold!

I'll take off my shoes and socks before I'm put into stasis. I just figured it would be rocky out here, and it is. Besides, I wanted to leave a hot memory in your mind.

Oh, yeah! Naked men in dress shoes and black socks do it for me every time.

He smiled down at her, a little surprised that she could still joke. A ramp opened a few feet in front of them, and a light shone down upon them. Marco Antonio led the way into the ship, and Ann followed, holding his hand. She was still groggy, but she really tried to focus on what she was seeing.

I think I'm the first person alive to see the inside of an interstellar space ship.

Yes, you are, querida.

There wasn't much to see, actually. Much like a big rover, there was a chair which looked like it could change shape since it was constructed of the same material (or creature) as the bulkhead and most of the walls. There was a big bench along one wall which was clearly made of different material than the Questor-like chair and walls of what she had been able to see of the ship's exterior. She was surprised at how small it appeared to be; it seemed strange that an interstellar ship would be scarcely bigger than Questor.

"Is this another creature like Questor?" Ann asked.

"Part of it is. The chair, the floor, and much of the walls are like Questor. The exterior is more solid, and far less likely to change shape. In fact, it was designed *not* to change shape. It can withstand greater heat and cold, and it can travel much longer in a vacuum. There's a great big computing brain living in here which will help me make the computations so we can travel through the dark matter using dark energy. We'll calculate where we should enter, and where we should leave."

Marco Antonio walked toward the bench and sat down upon it. Ann sat down next to him and took his hand.

Small, cramped, depressing. For weeks? Oh my god!
Probably much less. I'll be OK. Will you, querida?
I'll manage. I'll have plenty of company. Lots to do. You?
I won't have to put up with government bureaucrats.
Oh, yeah. Them. Ugh!

"Are you ready to see the good-looking me?"

"Sure. Bring him on!" She smiled at him, thinking he was kidding. She felt like she had pulled two all-nighters in a row. Positively rummy.

"I'm afraid you'll think he's a monster. Once you see him, will you ever be able to see me again? Can you ever love a monster?" He sat there, unabashedly nude, with black shoes and black socks on, looking at her face with terror in his eyes.

For the first time, Ann realized what a risk he thought he was taking. If she was truly frightened or grossed out, their relationship could be over. Did he know her better than she knew herself? He was the smartest man on the planet, after all.

She thought about it for about two seconds.

Bullshit! I will love you no matter what you look like, or what form you take! I am not afraid of looking upon you. Touch me, even if you're icky and slimy. I'll feel love through your tentacles and your big googley eyes. I'll know it's you.

"OK, Ann. Don't be afraid—I'm just sleeping in stasis. Try to remain calm and give me a chance, baby," Marco Antonio stood, took Ann's hands until she stood next to him, and then he lifted the lid of the bench. She looked in and saw a large squishy-looking invertebrate that looked like it had no shape at all. He was cradling a pointy-headed-baby-shaped thing, which was clearly made of something else, in his arms, although the rest looked dead. Marco Antonio never took his eyes off her face.

Ann stood next to him, peering into the box. "What's he holding?" she asked timidly. She was afraid she might guess something insulting, so she tried to keep her mind blank.

"That black 'squishy' thing is me, holding my vial," he said, holding her hands, watching her expression.

"The vial is what makes it possible for you to change from one form to another, right? Could you make the transfer without it?" she said, glancing up to his face.

"No. It is what helps us sort the form of our thoughts within our brains. It keeps my left parietal lobe transplant in the left parietal lobe, down to the tiniest neural connection. Every thought, every memory is either stored in my vial or in one of my brains." He was monitoring her every thought and expression. So far, he could not detect a single sign of fear or disgust.

"So you'll have some memories left in this body?" she asked, sounding hopeful and pleading.

"Yes, I will. Some memories do not need to be transferred. Glow patterns, sound patterns, swimming moves are not needed on dry land; how to ride a bike is an unnecessary skill underwater. I sort them out and leave the memories and skills that I don't need in the abandoned body." He kept the explanations simple because he could tell that her brain was already over-stimulated by the information he had infused it with earlier.

Will you remember loving me?

Of course! I have memories of you in both bodies. You are everywhere inside me. Both me's.

"I'm sorry—that was me being really needy," Ann said, embarrassed that she had even thought the question. Even as she apologized, she felt him smother her in goodfeels, reassuring her. While he was flooding her brain with endorphins, and oxytocin, she felt a brief moment of fear from him. Inhaling, she looked up at him as he looked down at the object in the bench they had been sitting on.

"Remember that both forms of me love you completely," Marco Antonio said as he perched on the edge of the stasis chamber and picked up the vial. Both the ends of the vial were conical, and much larger than a baby. He leaned down and put one edge of the cone against the dark mass of goo, and the other on his forehead between his eyes.

Almost immediately, a long black tentacle emerged and wrapped itself around his naked body, holding him upright. Still sitting on the edge of the box, his shoulders and head were turned towards the casket-shaped stasis chamber from which the dark object rose, and he was still leaning into the vial.

Ann was holding her breath, afraid to even think any coherent thoughts for fear of interrupting the process. She was not afraid of the creature; she was merely afraid of doing something to ruin it. His vial didn't look anything like a baby now. It looked like a giant, fat straw, or maybe a great big pencil pressed between his eyes and the dark gooey-looking package of gelatin in the box.

Nothing happened. There were no glowing lights, no visible but ephemeral clouds floating between them. Marco Antonio simply sat with his eyes closed, and his hands holding the vial point resting between his eyes. After what seemed like hours, but was no more than five or so minutes, the huge dark shape began to shimmer and take on colors. The colors were mostly shades of dark and royal blue, but occasionally there were others flashes of reds and yellows. The blob turned slightly, and suddenly two huge eyes opened and looked directly at her.

Hi, Ann. Please don't be afraid. It's me, Marco Antonio.

Of course it is, silly. Who else would it be? She smiled.

I am going to move now. I'm going to carry my body back to Questor and put him into stasis with our vial. Please come with me. Do not be afraid; I'm certainly not going to hurt you.

You're far more beautiful than I had imagined. And bigger. I expected you to be the size of an octopus, but you're much bigger.

The creature started to shimmer in many shades of iridescent blues, silvers, and gold. *Yes. I am large for my species, and very old. It pleases me that you are not afraid and that you find me beautiful.*

Silently, it slid over the edge of the coffin-stasis chamber and moved toward the center of the room. Two of its arms carried Marco Antonio in a relaxed sitting position. He looked like he was asleep. Ann just stood there and watched them, a huge grin on her face.

I have about a million questions about you and this ship, but I can't think of any of them right now. After you leave, I'll be so mad at myself because I've just gone completely blank, enjoying looking at you.

You are very generous. Actually, your brain is overwhelmed. I downloaded a great deal of information, and you are in shock, but positively so. I don't want to overload you any more, querida. Just enjoy the experience. As you noted before, it is a unique one for humans.

She had thought that Marco Antonio had flooded her with messages before, but now she felt them very strongly. The creature next to her was barraging her with goodfeels. If he felt like a source of mental background music before, now he felt like a crescendo of the biggest battle scene played with the soaring music at the end of the biggest action movie she'd ever seen. It was almost painful.

The room was silent, but he was so *loud!* Everything about the creature next to her was alive with power unlike any she had ever seen or felt before. Ann felt like she was on the verge of hysteria, yet she was not excited with her own emotions. The power was emanating from the huge glowing creature next to her. She felt like she was standing in front of giant speakers which were on and humming and about to blast her away with sound she would feel in her bones and throughout her body. He was a freight train of energy held back by a spider web, a molten pool of lava whose heat was contained behind the merest layer of ice.

I am sorry. You are very sensitive and quite fragile. Come, my love, and I will take you back to Questor before I hurt you.

I'm fine. What big eyes you have!

The better to see you, my dear.

You sound like the Big Bad Wolf. Sorry, that was a dumb thing to say. Of course you have big eyes—you live in dark water!

A bad joke. Sorry. I feel a little awkward.

I don't. I'm fascinated by you. Awed. Entranced. I just want to stand here and watch you move so I can realize that you really are from a different place. I guess I'm staring. Sorry. I'm a little overwhelmed.

That's all right. I'm just glad you're not hysterically screaming in terror.

Do you know what I'd really like?

No.

I'd like you to hold me. Well, at least touch me, unless that's something that your species finds distasteful. Do you touch each other?

Rarely, but I'd like to touch you. If you want me to.

Ann held out her hand, and he put the end of one tentacle into it. There were four smaller boneless fingerlike appendages at the end which wrapped around her hand, enclosing it. She took his hand in both of hers and examined it carefully, noting that the four fingers were at almost right angles from one another. Clearly, they were prehensile and could each cross the palm or meet in the middle. They could stretch out and become longer, or contract and become smaller.

Without thinking about it, she lifted his hand and kissed it. Immediately, he shimmered even more brightly than before in slightly different colors.

Oh, sorry! Was that disgusting? I know you don't put your mouth parts on anything else.

No, I liked it. It was so like you—such an 'Ann' thing to do! I must be careful, or I'll flood you with 'goodfeels.' You are so fragile!

I'm trying not to gross you out.

Nothing you could do would gross me out, Ann. But we must go. The City Killers' ship gets farther away every second.

OK. Will you just walk over to Questor?

In my own fashion. I'll carry my other body and my vial so I can put them both into stasis on Questor. Come, querida.

He appeared to roll smoothly towards the door, which opened as he approached. He wasn't rolling, of course. He slid as if he were a skater on ice. The ramp was still there, and he glided down it, supporting Marco Antonio's body in a leaning/sitting-up position.

His head was leaning against the creature as if he were asleep in an airplane seat. Ann watched them descend down the ramp, thinking how cute they were together. At the bottom of the ramp, the huge creature turned and extended one of his tentacles to her in a graceful, gracious movement.

"Cute?" You never cease to amaze me, Ann. I expected almost anything but that. "Cute" is something no one has ever called me. You are truly unique. Come, my love.

Ann smiled and accepted his outstretched arm. The breeze blew into her face and she turned her head away. The tentacle dropped her hand and wrapped around her body. It lifted her from the ship's entryway down to the ground and enveloped her within its other tentacles and held her next to its body. Together they moved toward Questor. Ann didn't even have to stoop, but she did, just so she could stay out of the wind and be in closer touch with him as he glided smoothly along.

You feel good. Warm and soft. Thank you, Marco Antonio.

As always, it was my pleasure, querida.

When they approached Questor's ramp, the huge creature spread himself out like a caped vampire in an old movie to shield Ann from the wind. She ran into Questor and hopped into her chair, turning around so she could see them. All she could see was a huge dark mass pushing itself through the entryway. It seemed to ooze apart as the body unfurled like a giant blue flower. She watched as Marco Antonio's naked form appeared, complete with his black shoes and socks.

Cool trick! You can compact and expand yourself as needed. Nicely done!

Once again shimmering blue, the creature set Marco Antonio's body into one of Questor's handy vacuoles, which the creature had opened with his other arms. While he was gently placing Marco's head and shoulders into the box, his others tentacles were removing his shoes and socks. They rolled each sock, put one into each shoe and placed them neatly into another vacuole which had formed near the door.

You are so graceful! I see now why Marco Antonio is such a good dancer.

Red and yellow shades appeared among the midnight blue shimmers.

Are you smiling, Marco?

Yes. You are cute, too.

So red and yellow means you're amused?

Very good, querida! You have a new first! You're the first person on Earth who can read a native Monitor!

All part of being the only person to have seen one. Is blue your natural color?

Only when I am under tight control. I have to be quite still so that I don't over-power you. We are very close in here, and I have to remain very calm, or I will overwhelm you with my feelings. You are very fragile, and I love you so much!

One tentacle reached up and touched Ann's face gently, as two other tentacles carefully placed the vial next to Marco Antonio's completely naked body. Even though his gigantic eyes never left Ann's face, two of his arms closed the lid on Marco Antonio's stasis chamber and several supported his gigantic head. They bent like elbows, and where he would have cheeks, he rested his head against his hands.

May I hold you once more before I go?

I'd hoped you would. I think we both need a little skin time.

Indeed. Take care of Questor on the way home and while I'm gone, and he'll take care of me. Please don't open the stasis cover. You can look at me through the clear top, but opening the box changes the humidity and chemical contents of the air.

I'm glad you warned me.

His many arms encircled her and brought her next to his huge head. His two huge eyes closed and she could feel his tentacles each striving to touch her, like little kids reaching for some beloved object they all wanted to hold.

Let me know if you feel claustrophobic, and tell me if I 'gross you out.'

No. You feel great. In fact, I could get used to this. Eight arms are better than two arms and two legs.

Good, because that's all that will be available to you until my return, and I don't want any other man's arms and legs surrounding you. Guard yourself, and stay away from the President. Beware of being alone with any man, even Miguel. They all want you, so don't give them a chance by being alone with them.

Trust me. I'll make certain not to let opportunities arise for all the sex fiends to jump me. No dark alleys, no orgies, no private meetings. And who knows? Where you're going, all the females may find you as irresistible as I do, and you'll never want to come home.

She could feel his smile, even though her eyes were closed.

A highly unlikely scenario, my little vixen. I must go. I do hate to leave you with so many responsibilities, in such a horrendous state of affairs. I do trust you. I shall return as quickly as I can. I'll call, and you and Questor can meet me here, where we will once again exchange bodies. Oh, and bring blood, for I am always very hungry when I first re-enter my body, and it is dangerous for me to feed off you. By then, I will want to devour you in every way possible!

Promises, promises. Go! You're burning daylight! Go find some dark matter and dark energy or hyperspace. Whatever. Shoo! Go kick some City Killer ass, and tell them that this planet is already taken!

His elegant navy, royal, and midnight blue skin shimmered with many red and yellow highlights. His tentacles unwrapped, and he glided out the door without sending another message. Clearly, he was maintaining tight control over his nine brains, for nary a thought was leaking out.

Ann was grateful for that. She knew she was about at the end of her strength. It had been a long, long day, one filled with horror (the City Killers' attack), thrills (the President AND a space ship AND Marco Antonio's native body), and she was exhausted. She had no idea what time it was, but it was dark outside. She had gotten in a couple hours of sleep, but it felt as if that must have been yesterday.

"Take me home, Questor. Back to Hanford, please. I'm going to take my baked brain, put it on a pillow, and hope it has enough time to manufacture a whole bunch of neurotransmitters. Right now, it's a couple of quarts low."

Questor flattened out the two chairs and exuded her favorite afghan and pillow from the vacuole between the chairs. Ann grabbed the pillow and afghan and crawled onto the bed.

Sleep well, my angel.
Night-night.

CHAPTER 11

When Ann awoke, it was still pitch black within Questor. She felt like she'd slept a long time; her mouth was dry and she felt logy.

"Lights please, Questor," she said. She fumbled around for her phone and checked the time: 10:45 a.m.

"Are we in Hanford, Questor?" she asked, and when she put her hand down on the bed, she got a tail-wagging affirmative. "Door please," she said aloud, and a ramp appeared. They were in the Secret Garden at the Smith's house, next door to hers.

She jumped up, put her hand on the bed and thought of chairs, and folded the afghan. "Thank you, Questor. Take care of Marco Antonio and yourself. I'm going in to take a shower, and I'll see what I can do to get you a bath, too." The bed began separating into two chairs, and there was a storage vacuole between them in which she put the pillow and afghan.

She virtually ran down the ramp and across the yard. She just hoped that her bedroom door was unlocked so she wouldn't have to go around to the utility room door. It felt great to be able to use her own bathroom without fear that it was aware of what she was doing.

Who wants a toilet to be aware of what you're doing? I like porcelain toilets that flush. Lots of hot water in my own shower, private thoughts. It's good to be home.

While she was washing her hair, she realized that she hadn't even announced her presence. Nobody knew she was home, and she probably still had a houseful of Monitors. She decided to forgive herself for stealing the fifteen minutes or so she was granting herself to bathe and go to the bathroom. Then she realized that she should probably take the time to dry her hair and put her face on; she might have to talk to the President again today, and who-knew how many soldiers and generals and industrialists.

She had turned off her phone before she went to sleep last night, and she was afraid to even look at the messages and missed calls she probably had. Her phone might be the only way Marco Antonio had to reach her, so she was going to have to leave it on in case he wanted to talk to her. On second thought, he would probably use the Monitor communication device, at least as long as he was in the solar system. The telephone system he had used to circumvent the Monitor's system was probably still at the Mariana Outpost, five or six miles beneath the sea. She had no idea about how he would communicate from dark matter/hyperspace, if that were even possible.

Besides, why would he want to hide his calls from the Monitors? The bad ones are either dead or in stasis. (Good!)

It really was nice to be able to think about anything or anybody, using whatever foul thoughts and words she wanted to. She could even use her imagination and fantasize about whatever struck her fancy.

I could even think sexy thoughts about the President. He's not bad looking, and Marco Antonio said he wants to have sex with me. Imagine—screwing the most powerful man in the world. Hell, I already do that. Still, the President of the United States of America....

She tried to visualize what it would be like. He was a big man, and she imagined he'd be dominating, probably demanding. She doubted that he would be very considerate, and he would probably sweat, and huff and puff. Besides, he was middle aged and a few pounds overweight, so he could certainly not do anything physically demanding. In fact, she'd probably have to do most of the heavy lifting, and even then, he might not make it over the hill.

Not even tempting, even if I were single. But it was nice to be able to fully consider it without Marco Antonio getting so possessive that he would explode the brains of the whole neighborhood in his wrath.

She finished her hair and face and went into the kitchen for a cup of coffee. The pot was empty, of course, so she made some, and then popped in some toast. She hadn't expected anyone to be in the kitchen, since Monitors avoided cooking and hated to be caught hanging out near food.

Well, we don't hang out in bathrooms, either. I guess it's for the same "yuk" factor.

She walked into the living room and noticed that one of the broken windows had been replaced, but not the other. She was pleased that they had put in double-paned glass; if they weren't too busy, she'd have the side panels replaced as well. The large window was a bay window, which made rehanging the drapes almost impossible for her. Luckily, the workmen had carefully placed the drapes across some chairs, to get them out of the way, and the blast had not hurt them.

When she checked on the other window, it was still boarded up. It made that end of the living room dark, but at least it kept out the cold. Actually, it was a pleasant surprise to see that so much work had been accomplished in such a short time. It could have been a lot worse.

Impatient for the coffee to be done, Ann headed down to the basement. She wanted to get Miguel caught up with everything before strange uniformed men in limousines started knocking on the front door.

The basement smelled stale, like a lot of people had been spending a lot of time there. Sure enough, there were four men working at a table, doing something with jars and packing boxes. Miguel was perched on a stool behind a large microscope, peering at a slide. As she watched, his eyes seemed to lose their focus, and then they seemed drawn up to the stairs. They didn't focus again until they were looking into her eyes, where they locked on as if they were magnetized and she was made of solid iron. He smiled broadly.

Hi, Ann!

"Hi, Miguel!" she said quickly, hoping to mask her other thoughts. "Thought I'd check in and see how things are going. I've also got to tell you about meeting the President on a submarine. Come up and get a cup of coffee. We need to talk."

She turned back up the stairs, closing the door behind her. She knew that Miguel, the only other sanguinary eater among the

Monitors, could speak to her telepathically if they were close. He had been across the room, and he had sent her a very clear message. He might be able to pick up on her thoughts, too. *So much for privacy. Shit!*

She returned to the kitchen and poured two cups of coffee. Her toast was up, so she "dressed it up," as Tim used to say, with peanut butter and jelly.

Miguel joined her at the breakfast table. "So tell me about meeting the President," he said, stirring two big spoons of sugar into his coffee.

"I was very surprised that he would see us, since he's supposed to be in hiding while we're under attack. But Marco Antonio talked him into it somehow, and Questor put us right down on top of the submarine. It was a brief conversation, really. We told him what we knew about the City Killer ship, and then Marco Antonio asked his permission to represent the Earth in negotiations with the City Killers' home planet. The President said OK, and we left."

"Did Marco Antonio touch him?"

"Briefly, but I don't think he told him much. Marco didn't like the President, so I think much of the interaction between our government and the Monitors will have to involve you," Ann said, and took a bite of her toast.

"Why? It's not like Marco Antonio to turn over diplomatic matters to me."

"Well, I think the President made the huge mistake of admiring something about me, and Marco Antonio wanted to kill him. Actually, I think I need to stay out of all formal discussions that Marco Antonio is involved in." Ann was careful not to talk with her mouth full. Monitors thought that was really disgusting.

"I know he is extremely possessive about you, but I didn't think it would influence his negotiations," Miguel said, looking a little worried. He took a small sip of his coffee.

"He is more than possessive; he is jealous. It's a side effect of the genetic changes he's made in his human body so that he will remain monogamous. I'm giving you fair warning not to think of me when he's around. He would go medieval on your ass."

"What does that mean?"

"Sorry, it's a movie quote. He would become violent. He gets really worked up about it, Miguel. He just sees red if anyone is attracted to me in any way, so don't even think nice thoughts. It's really scary, Miguel." Ann was really hungry, and she wanted to take another bite of her toast, but she waited.

"We have discussed this, and he warned me to keep away from you. Does he know that we will be working together?" He raised his eyebrows and looked at her, studying her face.

"Yes, which is why I want to warn you to watch what you say or think. I certainly don't want to cause hard feelings between you two, and I think he will be calling in." She just couldn't wait. She took another small bite of her toast.

"Oh, he has, several times. I didn't know you were home yet. Your phone has been ringing, too. Look," he said, standing up so he could see the house phone's main connection, "You have 47 messages!" He sat down again and looked at her as she chewed her toast.

"Oh, God! I'm going to be on the phone all day! I'll call him first, if I can. I don't want him to be worried. Questor let me sleep until 10:30 this morning. I didn't even know we were home. Oh—that reminds me! If there's anyone around here with nothing to do tonight, Questor could really use a bath. That poor creature has flown for days through grit and smoke, and he needs to be washed down," Ann said. Hoping he would say something, she took another bite.

"How were the East Coast cities?" Miguel asked.

"Oddly horrendous," she said, and swallowed. "They'd be completely leveled in some spots, and virtually untouched a block or so away. New York City's Manhattan is gone, but most of Brooklyn appears to be all right. A lot of people are dead, Miguel." As she said it, her eyes and throat started to swell, and she knew she was going to cry, or at least get "misty" as Tim used to say during sad movies.

"Show me," he said, taking her hand.

Ann closed her eyes and thought of Boston, and how the flattened part of the city was right up to the edge of the housing sections. Then, she showed him Manhattan, where there were only piles of powdered rubble. Then Washington, D.C., where the Washington monument sat pulverized on dead grass. She snuck in a view of the submarine, the walk along the deck, and meeting and talking to the President and the captain of the ship.

"You had quite a day! We were down here breeding bacteria and worms; then we got to listen to your phone ring all night," he said, only half joking.

"I'm sorry about that, Miguel. I gave them my cell phone number, and they must have just looked up my house number. It's been in the phone book for about 50 years," she said, giving his hand a little squeeze. "Well, maybe not that long, but for quite a while." She had to amend her guesstimate, remembering how literal Miguel was.

"I'll go get you Marco Antonio's messages and a comm. device so you can call him. They're probably still within lightspace," he said as he downed the rest of his coffee and started to rise.

"Explain that term, please," Ann said. She heard herself, and realized she sounded like a teacher.

Miguel froze and sat down again. "I'm surprised Marco Antonio didn't explain it to you. We're using that English term because your scientists have dubbed the other, greater part of space 'dark matter' and 'dark energy.' Space has many parts or forms. There's solid, liquid, and gas, with which you are familiar, and light and dark. Physics explains most solids, liquids, and gasses, but starts to fall apart dealing with light. They have discovered that light can be either photons or waves, and one of the properties of these parts of the universe is that nothing travels faster than light. Up until recently, that has been the totality of your understanding of the universe," Miguel explained quickly as if he were merely reviewing obvious knowledge.

Ann felt like she should reassure him that she understood, so she said, "OK," and nodded.

"What you call 'dark matter' doesn't follow the rules of light. It is more like foam than either particles or waves, and it expands and contracts like foam. The speed of light has nothing to do with foam, so the rules of your physics do not apply. Time and space are measured and moved-through using very different rules. He must locate the strand of foam used by the City Killers to leave this solar system, which is dominated by the rules of light. He'll enter and leave by the same path as the City Killers, and he'll reach the same destination." Miguel said it all as if it were a quick review of something she understood previously.

"Will they be in the same time as we are?" She hoped that was an intelligent question. It was better than the "Huh?" she had been tempted to utter several times.

"If he does it right, he'll come out in their space and time and re-enter this solar system in our space and time. Of course, their time might be quite different when measured by ours, but that won't matter. They might live a billion years ago or in the future, but who cares? Unless you want to get there in a slower-than-light vehicle, of course. Then, time and space only go in one direction—forward. You can't set out today for a sun and hope to reach it a billion years ago if you're travelling through space-time."

"What if he re-enters our light-time at a different place? Would he be in a different time, as well?" That idea was both fascinating and terrifying to Ann.

"Yes, but he won't do that. He's a much better mathematician than that, and so is the ship." Miguel assured her.

"I like your confidence, Miguel. I won't think about his appearing during the Middle Ages or living without him for five hundred years until he pops back out of the dark foam."

"I would take care of you if that happened, Ann. You have my word," Miguel said, the last sentence almost drowned out by the ringing telephone.

Ann got up and answered it, troubled by Miguel's last sentence. A male voice said, "This is the White House. We have a call for a Dr. Marco Antonio Polo or a Mrs. Ann Jacob."

"This is Ann Jacob. How may I help you?"

"Please hold for the President of the United States."

Ann put her hand over the mouthpiece and said, "It's my buddy, Mike Blake. God, I wish my kids were here!"

"Do you want me to get them?" Miguel asked innocently.

"No. I just wanted to impress them."

"I'm impressed!" he smiled broadly at her.

"Good! Somebody needs to be!" Ann said, smiling back. She waited, tempted to hang up. *I suppose it's his turn to show who's the boss. I've yet to return one of his calls.*

"Mrs. Jacob! This is Mike Blake. I trust you had a pleasant journey home?"

"I actually got a chance to sleep on the way! I just walked in my back door a few minutes ago. I haven't had a chance to call anyone yet, but I was about to listen to the 47 messages that are on my answering machine," Ann said pleasantly.

The President ignored her excuses. "I hope our friend got off on his journey in time to catch up and meet his acquaintances," he said in a clearly-rehearsed statement.

"Yes, I believe he did. At least I saw him off at the airport, and he's on his way." *So we're talking in code. I get it.*

"Good, good! We have the gifts we were going to ask you to deliver, but he left before that happened, so I just wanted to check with you."

"Well, I imagine that at least one of my 47 messages is from him with a more recent update on his whereabouts, so I'll have to get back to you with more recent news as soon as I have a chance to listen to my messages." Ann said all in one breath. "I don't believe we'll be able to deliver the gifts. Hopefully, they won't be returning to receive them."

"Let's hope our friend is successful. Mrs. Jacob, please let me know where we can meet in person. I'd very much like to talk to you about our mutual friend. I have associates who would like to meet you, as well, of course. Unfortunately, I am among the countless homeless people in our great nation, but you can be sure that as soon as I am established in a new home, a new White House, you will be one of my first guests."

Not if Marco Antonio has anything to say about it! And he does.

"I just hope he's home soon. Successful, of course. We'll be very busy here working on the manufacturing and distribution of the lung-cleaning agents developed by Marco Antonio and Miguel. Perhaps I should call them Dr. Polo and Dr. Olivas."

"Oh, does Dr. Polo have a, um, compatriot here? I would very much like to meet him and any other friends they might have. We have much to discuss," said the President. His tone went from excitedly enthused to cautiously thoughtful in three sentences.

"I know how difficult flight has become, so it would be much easier if we came to the east coast. Once you get you and your family re-established, we can meet again. You have your plate full, sir, and both Dr. Olivas and Dr. Polo plan to stay here for quite some time. Rebuild your home, and then rebuild our cities, sir."

"You're right, of course. But I also have a duty to welcome our first guests."

"I understand. I'll make certain they visit you as soon as possible, sir. As an American, I think they need to get to know you. They wish to maintain a very low profile, however. They live quietly and secretly, and that will not change. They will not involve themselves in international politics. They only came out to you because Marco Antonio felt that the rules had changed when a third entity arrived. Once that danger is ameliorated, he will go back to simply watching and recording how we deal with crises," Ann said. She didn't want the President to think they were going to be bridge buddies or political supporters.

"We'll be forever grateful for their intervention, especially if Dr. Polo is successful in chasing off the City Killers forever. How do you think he proposes to do that?"

"I have no idea, sir," Ann said, *and I wouldn't tell you if I knew.* "I do know that the Monitors are a very ancient and powerful people who do not fight wars. How they have avoided that for over a million years, I don't know. They are very honorable, as you've witnessed, but my best advice to you is not to cross them in any way," Ann pointed out.

"Oh, I don't intend to. Mutual cooperation would be much better!" the President gushed like the politician he was.

"Not really. We have nothing they want. They don't want money, objects, trade, status, women, booze, power. Absolutely nothing. They just want to learn about us, and watch us grow." Ann hated to disabuse the President of visions of forging the first interstellar treaties.

"They are paternalistic about us? Do they think they are superior to us?" asked the President rather defensively.

"They ARE superior to us, sir. They have controlled their own genetics for over a million years. They have removed all the warts and wrinkles, and have become exactly what they want to be. We didn't even plant wheat until ten thousand years ago, almost a million years after they had discovered interstellar travel." Ann decided to shut up before she said too much. She did tend to get carried away.

"All the more reason to get to know them, and for them to get to know us. We can certainly learn from them, Mrs. Jacob. Our scientists would welcome the help, as would our astronauts. Our doctors are thrilled that Dr. Polo says there is a cure for what they're calling "HPO," which is reaching epidemic proportions."

"It's also known as 'Marie's Disease,'" Ann interjected. "All I'm saying is that the Monitors are not going to rebuild our cities, or clean up our air. That's up to us. They found a cure for Marie's Disease—HPO—because it also affects them and all animals with lungs on this planet. They are observers, scientists, and we are the subjects, sir. Accept that, and don't ask for more, or they'll slip away and you'll never hear or see them again."

"That would be unfortunate, particularly for you, I would think," he mused.

Ann thought she caught an implied threat. She didn't like it. "Indeed, sir. I am their favorite, and they would protect me with their last breath, and with yours, too. Please don't think that they don't fight wars because they are not powerful. They don't fight wars because they are so powerful that no sane creature would dare cross them. Be very careful, sir." Ann wanted to warn him that his dreams of manipulating Monitors was a dangerous one. It was like an ant hoping to handle an elephant.

"Oh, I merely meant that Dr. Polo obviously thinks highly of you, and you of him. I'm sure you would miss them greatly if they 'slipped away,'" he said hastily. "I'm sure we can all be friends. You have shown us the way, and we will follow your lead, Mrs. Jacob."

God, he sounds like a car salesman. Or a politician.

"You have the greatest responsibility any President has faced since Lincoln. You have a war-ravaged nation reeling from a natural catastrophe that cut our continent in half. Now, most of our cities are gone—not just in ruins. Gone. Our infrastructure is in tatters, our communication system is spotty, our economic and political centers destroyed. Good luck, President Blake. Be excellent, and demand excellence from everyone. Be grateful that the American people are behind you, and they want to follow your lead. Just remember that you are being watched."

"That sounds a little creepy, but thank you, Mrs. Jacob. I needed to hear that. I'll call again in a few weeks, unless we hear from Dr. Polo again, of course. Please notify me immediately if you hear from him. I am most interested in the results of his journey. You and Dr. Polo and Dr. Olivas will still be the first dinner guests at the new White House. Until then, good-bye, Mrs. Jacob."

"Thanks for calling, sir. I will be in touch. Good-bye."

Ann put the phone back on the charger and walked back into the breakfast room. Miguel sat and looked at her, his mouth slightly open, as she walked back and took her seat. She picked up her toast and took a bite thoughtfully.

"Wow!" Miguel said. "What a conversation THAT was!"

"Yeah, it really was, wasn't it? I wish I had recorded it. That whole part about his responsibility was pretty good, wasn't it? I sure hope the part about you guys being super powerful was true! It's true, isn't it, Miguel?" she said hopefully.

"I guess so. I never really thought about it. We haven't fought a war in thousands and thousands of your years, but I haven't thought about our being powerful," he said thoughtfully. "Wars are so *primitive* that we haven't run into another warlike race in millennia. This would be a good topic of discussion at our next defecation ritual." He sounded like she'd be included, so she'd care what was on the agenda.

"What's so shocking about everything is how *fast* everything has happened! My life, my country, my planet, possibly my galaxy all changed in the last 24 hours. Well, maybe a little longer than that, but not much." Ann took another bite of her cold toast and threw the rest away. "I'd better not think about it, or I'll cry."

"I'll go downstairs and see if I can contact Marco Antonio. Unless you really are going to cry, and you would like me to stay here and comfort you," Miguel said, looking at her attentively, watching for clues to her emotional state.

"No, but thank you, Miguel. I'll listen to some of these messages and take notes. I'm fine, really. Too much to do to cry now. I'll do it later." She went to the desk to retrieve a pencil and paper. Since her desk had legal papers all over it, she returned to the dining room and grabbed the kitchen phone.

"If you're sure, OK." He walked toward the hall and the door to the basement. When he got there, he turned to her and said, "By the way, I did record the conversation. I can recite it for you with the voice tones, in writing, or in parts. I thought Marco Antonio would want to hear it."

"Thank you so much, Miguel! You are a prince among men!" Ann said, beaming at him. In so many ways, he was almost autistic, but he had a wonderful, warm heart.

"You are welcome, Ann. You sound pleased," he said, turning to descend the stairs in some confusion.

"I am VERY pleased! Thanks!" Ann said. Smiling, she began the long process of listening to her 47 messages. Many, she found, were repeats from the White House (which she found sadly ironic, since there was no White House,) so she didn't have to write down that number more than once. The Secretary of Defense had called several times, apparently ticked off because she had turned off her cell phone to get some sleep. There were several other official-sounding voices who had called from various medical centers with acronyms like the CDC, and UCLA.

Before she was finished, Miguel came upstairs with the small version of the Monitor communication device. It was designed to be held in their four-fingered hands, but not held up to ears or mouth. Monitors heard just fine from any of their tentacles, and could send messages through them, as well. This particular unit had been adapted to send and receive verbal communication. Wordlessly, Miguel handed Ann the small black box.

"Hi, lover! Where are you?" Ann asked.

"Chasing the City Killer drone through this solar system. He hasn't gotten away from me yet! In fact, my ship seems a trifle faster than his, and I have managed to close the gap considerably, so I am confident that I should be able to enter dark space, dark matter, black foam, hyperspace—whatever English speakers are going to call it—right behind him. You really need to get together with your astrophysicists and agree on a term for non-solar space, Ann."

"I'll get right on it, sweetlips. Most science fiction writers have called it hyperspace for about a century, so I personally vote for that term."

"Fine. Hyperspace it is! Who have you talked to this morning, querida?"

"Questor let me sleep in until 10:30, so I've only talked to your favorite President, Mike Blake. He's invited us for dinner, as soon as he finds another white house. The poor guy is homeless, you know." She kept a big smile on her face because Marco Antonio could hear a smile easily. He was not smiling, but he sounded as if he had a slight grin.

A neat trick for a celphalopod.

"Yes, I know. What else did he say, besides hitting on you for a dinner date?"

Still a slight grin.

"It's not me he wants to get to know. It's you and Miguel, of course! He'd step on my face to get to you, and I wouldn't blame him. I told him to back off and not to mess with you," she said, maintaining her grin so he would hear that she was teasing, being a tough guy.

"Good advice, but he'd better not step on any part of you."

No more grin. Oh oh! He needs reassurance. Change the topic.

"I also told him that you were not in the business of helping us, nor of fighting wars for us, so he cannot expect you to do either. But I did say that just because you don't wage war doesn't mean you can't.

Miguel said he recorded the conversation, so he can play it back for you."

"Good! It will give me another opportunity to hear your voice. I'm lonely without you."

"Of course you are, as I am. Do you have things to do, Marco Antonio? That is such a tiny space for your big old self. I worry about you going completely batshit from the isolation," Ann said, seriously concerned about his mental and emotional health. She was always concerned about those things, and he never seemed to be.

"I have a great store of information I should study. I also have innumerable math equations to do, but much of that can only be done once I see where they enter hyperspace. There are many sources of intellectual stimulation available to me here in the ship. I have never had a problem concentrating before, but I find that I keep thinking of you. It is really quite distracting, and I will have to discipline myself. Now that I know you have returned home, I feel much better, querida."

"Surely you trusted Questor to get us here safely, Marco Antonio. Your other you is still onboard him as we speak!"

"Of course."

"Oh, and by the way, I asked him to stick around until I could get him a good bath tonight, which seemed to please him. I hope that's all right," she said, mostly to take the sting out of reprimanding him for implying that Questor might be untrustworthy.

"He'll like that. I think he should stay in the Secret Garden so he's available to you on a moment's notice. He's never had anyone who worries about him the way you do. Nor have I, for that matter."

The smile has returned. Good.

"I find that hard to believe, Marco. You are a very lovable man, and I can't believe that no woman has ever loved you before now. People who love each other worry about each other. It's part of the package."

Pillow- talk voices. Better.

"So you love Questor now? I suppose I *do* have a reason to be jealous of him! I should banish him to the North Pole before he whisks you away and hides you from me."

"Honey, hot cars have always turned me on, but horny rovers? Not so much. 'Sexy' and 'UFO' just are not synonymous terms to me. Now, maybe if you could find me another hot cephalopod, I might be interested."

Ann was making a joke, but the silence she received almost prepared her for his response, but not quite.

"Your house is full of them."

Oh, shit. He's mad at me. "You're the only one I want."

"Yes, but I'm not the only one who wants you, *querida*."

Too serious! He's so damn suspicious!

"They can all just line up behind Questor. I've got no time or energy for more than one man, octopus, squid, Monitor, rover or whatever. Not even a movie star or a president could tempt me." Ann paused, and then said, "I'm sorry I made a bad joke. I was teasing you, but I never meant for you to take it seriously! If you made a primate joke, I wouldn't worry about all the gorillas or chimps in Africa."

"Good. They don't attract me too much. Now the bonobos, I hear, are sexy little beasts…."

"Now I'll spend the day in a jealous tizzy, picturing you with a furry black female primate who might swing down and capture your attentions at any moment." Ann was much relieved when he lightened up and teased her back.

"I can't imagine you in a tizzy."

Oh, good. We're teasing again.

"Oh, baby, I can throw a tizzy-worm fit about 30 yards, and it's not pretty. You do NOT want to make me jealous over some hot little bonobo chick!"

"They're primates, not birds, but I'll bear that in mind the next time I go to a zoo or to the Congo," he said with a smile in his voice.

"You won't be going to either place without me, sweetie. I'm taking no chances. And stay away from any female City Killers, too. I'll know if you go messin' around," Ann said, hoping to have cheered him up a little by her silliness.

Usually, it worked, and it appeared to have worked again until he said, "I'd know too. You cannot lie to me. Ann."

God, he's SO MERCURIAL!

"Of course you would! But it's not fear of your wrath that keeps me faithful, you know. It's honor and trust." She was quiet a second, and then continued in a softer, more intimate tone, "Nothing you could do to me would be half the punishment I would give to myself if I betrayed you in any way. Loyalty is a huge part of my character, as I've told you before. I have no reason to lie to you, so you can trust me, as I trust you."

"As you said to me, 'that was me being needy and insecure.' Sorry, Ann."

"It must have been the thought of all those bonobos and cephalopods. I shouldn't be silly in such harrowing situations. My bad."

"It is a part of you that I love. Your cheerfulness is catching, and I needed a lift. Is that your phone ringing? I should let you go answer the President's call, and all the other clingy government bureaucrats who will be pounding on your door. You will be too busy to do anything inappropriate. At least you'll understand why I have evaded working with governmental leaders. They will try to control you, and possibly even imprison you and the Monitors so that they will have absolute control over you and your actions. Be very careful, my love. If you feel pressured in any way, hop on board Questor and flee."

He sounds like my father, warning me about boys in cars and how dangerous they could be. Hmm. Daddy was right, at least at drive-in movies....

Marco Antonio continued, not having caught her thought. "Have the other Monitors leave today and return to their outposts. They must set up their production facilities and start making enough worms and bacteria to cover the planet. When the military, police, or government scientists arrive, they should find only you and Miguel working in your basement. The fewer Monitors they know about, the faster this work can begin and end. Their so-called aid will only interfere with the process and slow us down." He slowed down, but she knew he had much more advice to give her, most of which she already knew. He was not used to governing from afar.

"Answering 47 phone messages will slow me down. At least, it will keep me out of the kitchen! I'll call Carmen, and have her cook for your clan. I will pack clean clothes, food, and blood into Questor, and have him ready to bolt at a moment's notice. That's good advice, my love, and I'll see to it," she said, hoping to reassure him.

"They will want to study us, which is a luxury we do not have time for. Beware of men who are used to being obeyed. They do not tolerate independent little ladies flinging tizzy-worm fits thirty yards. They might lock you up, thinking that they can achieve their desires faster. You are in a position of weakness, querida, and once they know it, you are in danger."

What a worrywart! "We've built in several escape routes which they won't expect, Marco. We can take the tunnels to the Secret Garden behind the Smith's house and get into Questor and take off before they can ring the doorbell. Besides, I've warned them about my badass boyfriend, whom they've met, and I don't think they'll cross you if only because they don't know enough about you. The fact that you can hop on your horse and take off after the bad guys makes you someone they want to please. Right now, humans have neither a horse nor a saddle, and we've just been seriously spanked by people not from our neighborhood."

"I just hate the fact that I have left you virtually unprotected. It terrifies me."

He's admitting to being scared? Wow! But he's only afraid for me. Reassurance time, Annie!

"Don't worry—Blake is afraid of you. If he needs a little demonstration of your badass powers, I'll have Miguel bring someone to their knees across the room with a thought. I don't think it will be necessary. We'll be all right as long as they need us. Everyone's curiosity will not overwhelm their good manners until they feel safe and protected." Ann knew that Blake was afraid of Marco Antonio, not of her.

Who could blame the President for being afraid of the only extraterrestrials he had ever met after his planet had been bombed out by a different set of ETs? Had they been caught in the middle of a No-man's land in a war between two sets of aliens? Everyone was terrified; bombs were dropping out of the sky and annihilating them!

The house phone rang. "Damn, there's the phone again! I'm going to start taking a few of these calls and returning others, lover. You go do some math problems or crossword puzzles or something until the City Killer enters hyperspace. I'll keep this comm. unit with me, and your calls will take precedent over all the rest, of course. Remember that I love you above all others, always."

"You remember that you are mine. I love you, too. Be safe."

CHAPTER 12

Marco Antonio flexed his eight arms and did a few head lifts, just for the sake of keeping his body supple. He allowed himself a few seconds to wallow in the tactile memory he now possessed of having Ann enclosed within his arms. Every finger, every tentacle, every inch of skin that had touched her now had that memory fully encoded within its individual brain, and he could play with her smell, her warmth, and every memory of her. He could imagine what she would feel like if she were here, enclosed in his body so that his senses could feast upon her. He had never touched a living, conscious human in that manner. He had only prepared the sick and dying to be inhabited by a Monitor.

It was tempting to dwell upon the sensations, but he had many tasks to complete while he was still within the solar system. The first thing he did was to prepare a report of the events that had transpired on Earth, which he had sent to his home planet. They had to be apprised of his course of action so that they would be prepared to enforce his threats if necessary. He could only serve as the emissary; it was not his task to eliminate the enemies.

The message had been recorded within a physical object, much like a CD or DVD. Radio waves, like light waves, did not travel predictably through dark matter. Although it was theoretically possible, it was far easier to transmit a message-bearing solid object than a set of waves that travelled at their own speed and with their own constraints. Quantum physics was just too unpredictable, and the speed of light and radio waves was just too slow.

It had taken him only a few seconds to imprint the entire situation onto a communications box and to deposit it into the "mail slot" designed for that purpose. The ship had computed the route through the dark matter, the "hyperspace," and had delivered it directly to his home planet on the other side of the galaxy.

Almost immediately, a similar box had appeared in his "inbox" with his instructions. It contained warm greetings from his compatriots, many of whom he had not actually seen for centuries. They urged him to deliver in person whatever further facts he might discover about the City Killers. They wanted to catch up on the many experiences they had not yet shared about his other work on the planet that had so captivated his interest, Earth.

He made another comm-box outlining the work they had completed in genetically engineering the tiny worms and the bacteria which would enclose the obsidian pieces that were currently killing every species with lungs. He pointed out that he had left that project in the hands of Miguel Olivas and a human female, Ann Jacob, while he attended to this interplanetary attack. He would make the visit home as soon as most of the crises at hand were under control. He made sure to add feelings of regret in addition to a big dollop of urgency to the message, and popped it back into the mail slot.

He actually was relieved that he had a good excuse not to return to his home planet. He had been avoiding a return trip for decades. The last one had been an endless cycle of symposiums, speeches, data drops, and defecation rituals. His fame and knowledge of bio-engineering and xeno-sociology was unparalleled, and there was a long list of eager students willing to cram their knowledge into the humans' tiny craniums. They wanted to go to Earth and study this infantile species under the great Marco Antonio. Rarely did a new species evolve rapidly enough to be observed. They were emerging like a chrysalis, and the speed of their emergence was breathtaking. They had gone from being a horse-riding species to being on the verge of interstellar travel in less than three generations! Although they had been a warrior race, constantly fighting amongst themselves, they had avoided Armageddon and had emerged as cooperative seekers of peace and prosperity in one generation.

Marco Antonio had predicted this change, and it had happened despite the massive setback of the Yellowstone Eruption. He had said that they would not revert to deistic explanations for volcanic eruptions, and they had accepted the truth that they were an unlucky generation to have been alive while the tectonic forces of their planet erupted once again. Bad luck, but they would overcome it with class and panache. No powerful governmental or major religious leader had claimed that Yellowstone's eruption was a result of god's wrath.

Although Marco Antonio was what Ann would call "quite a star" on his home planet, he eschewed fame and all its trappings and demands. He would far rather be on earth with Ann and her family. They were the best example of humanity's strengths he had ever come across, and he reveled in being unashamedly loved by Ann, which made him part of their milieu. He was loved by the best woman in the best family in the finest town in the richest state of the best country the world had ever known. Why would he want to leave?

Yet here I am.

The ship suddenly alerted him that the City Killer's drone had blinked out of light space. It had automatically marked the exact exit location, and his ship's sensors were trying to ascertain its path. He was less than one Earth day away from the spot it had escaped, and he was limited by the light-space laws of physics regarding his speed. He programmed his ship to release a comm-box home with the matrix figures he would devise as soon as he could ascertain the direction the City Killer drone had taken.

Tracking through hyperspace was tricky, since it didn't involve space at all. Thinking about it in human terms was extremely taxing, since most of the vocabulary had not yet been invented. The basic concepts had been grasped by the most advanced human physicists within the last few years, and they were trying to come up with the most basic terminology and math symbols. He slipped easily into his own language which actually used very few words or written cryptograms. His people thought in concepts and processes, so translating math terms (especially into marks on a blackboard) was very difficult, in addition to being stultifying.

While he cruised through space towards the spot just short of Mars where the City Killer had disappeared, he mused on trying to invent symbols to show the concepts and processes used to explain hyperspace/dark matter/dark space. He had not considered inventing such a system of written symbols because he had never intended to teach humans about interstellar travel. He doodled with a few ideas until he received a message from Hanford.

It was Miguel, not Ann. Marco Antonio instantly felt disappointment and fear for her safety, both of which he struggled to conceal from Miguel. Within seconds, Marco Antonio learned that the other Monitors were leaving with plenty of samples of the two strains they had to nurture and produce by the ton at various locations on the planet. They had the plans and equipment lists necessary to accomplish that task, but some were returning to complete wastelands. Where there were cities, there were now barren, burned out ruins. They would have to relocate and set up vast growth tanks or sheds from locally available materials.

There were surprisingly few human refugees. Those who lived and worked in cities were eliminated; those who commuted left vacant homes in the suburbs, but there were no milling hordes of displaced people. They were either dead in the city or alive in their homes. The attacks had been almost surgical in their precision, and most rebuilding would require the replacement of the skyscrapers and the infrastructures which served them. No patching or temporary structures were needed or wanted; how could one replace the Empire State Building with a tent?

Marco Antonio and Miguel mused for a few minutes, speculating about which cities would take advantage of the opportunity to put in subways and adequate sewer systems before attempting to replace the edifices which would house the people. For that matter, were there still working subways anywhere? Water systems? Sewers? Electrical systems? Who would return to the same locations where the cities had been, and which sites would never rise from the ashes? They could only speculate, but clearly there would be much human activity to observe. How each human culture reacted to the loss of their cities and military sites would interest future Monitor students for centuries.

At last, Marco Antonio asked casually how Ann was faring with her many telephone calls, and Miguel sent him exact recordings of them, so he could review them at his leisure. The overall message was that most of the governmental people wanted her and as many Monitors as possible to meet with them on the East Coast, but she was sticking to her guns that they could exchange whatever information they needed by phone.

She did agree to get the biological samples to the major universities still functioning on the West Coast, and she would prepare samples as the other centers for medical research called in. Since most were located in the largest cities, most were gone. Basically, she was waiting for the pecking order to be established before she ran around delivering samples. Besides, she wanted the Monitors to have a chance to get established in their home countries again. She wanted to de-centralize the whole treatment effort and establish a worldwide system of production and distribution that would eliminate the possibility of monopolies being established. No one was to get rich off the distribution of these creatures, and all species with lungs would have equal access.

Oh, she is smart! She knows her species well, and is preventing those who would seek to profit from doing so. My clever, clever Ann!

Most of the country's surviving leaders were struggling to determine the extent of the damage. Not only were the cities obliterated, the institutions within those cities were also eliminated. The damage had been so exact that it was difficult to know which universities, for example, had survived virtually untouched. Boston was destroyed, but surely M.I.T. or Harvard had survived. Los Angeles was down, but was UCLA still there? If so, which biological, chemical, or medical researchers had survived? So many scientists were reeling from personal losses that they had not yet shown up for work and so were presumed to be missing.

Marco Antonio seethed with frustration at being stuck in a ship approaching the orbit of Mars when the planet that he had come to love was in such turmoil. For centuries, he had watched the stalwart people struggle against the forces of nature and the chaos they brought against themselves. Just as they were succeeding and maturing beyond their puerile natures, a natural catastrophe greater than any their species had ever seen struck the continent which had their most technologically advanced culture, creating planet-wide hunger and the political upheavals caused by the inevitable famines. The Yellowstone Mega-volcano had changed the planet in ways no one could have predicted.

Once a thriving planet, Earth's major problem had been overpopulation. At over seven billion, humanity had threatened many other species on the planet and had already created the biggest animal die-off in millions of years. When Yellowstone had pushed over one hundred cubic kilometers of ejecta into the air, the sudden cooling and the endless winter conditions had made farming impossible on much of the planet, in addition to completely burying the entire central section of the North American continent in three to ten feet of volcanic ash and rock. Over half of the planet—*3.8 billion* people—had died of starvation or the plagues brought on by famine, including war.

Yet the millions who had survived in America had not regressed as most had expected. Oddly enough, this famine was far worse on the continents not hit directly by the mega-volcano. Even though America's bread-basket and major corn-producing areas were buried in volcanic ash, the coasts on either side were relatively untouched. The countries which normally received the tons of grains produced in the plains states of America, however, could not support their bloated populations, and hunger soon haunted their distended metropolitan areas. The cold air made their own farmers' crops stunted, and emaciated farmers tried in vain to hoard their meager crops from the starving cities. Civil wars and border clashes soon followed, causing further destruction and agony. Northern Europe had been especially hard hit with well-educated people struggling to obtain enough food for their densely populated countries. The Danes, the Dutch, the Swedes, and even the English were desperately short of food.

Nonetheless, out of the ashes had arisen strong, noble people who cared for each other and who demonstrated the maturity of their cultures. They had established trade routes and made deals with the Southern Hemisphere countries whose farmers grew suddenly rich. The seas were now filled with ships laden with wheat, corn, and rice rather than manufactured goods. Salmon and shrimp fisheries clogged the mouths of nearly every river, trying to provide protein for a starving world which could no longer afford to feed beef and pork. The crowded, hungry northern hemisphere had adjusted their diet and lifestyles, and they had survived.

Now, they were struck down by drones sent by a species that clearly was still in the adolescent stages of imperialism. Marco Antonio chafed at being stuck tracking down the juvenile bullies who still preyed upon other species whom they assumed to be inferior to them just because they were weaker. He should be back on Earth helping Ann sort out the chaos left by these unworthy socially pubescent tormentors.

He had studied many intelligent species, and never had there been one to come so far or so fast as humans. They had matured from warring barbarian zealots in mud huts to the brink of interstellar travel in under 10,000 years. Just as they were about to make the leap, a series of catastrophes impaled them back onto the dirt. He could not stop a mega volcano like the Yellowstone eruption, but he could see that Earth would not be bombed again by punks with big toys.

In spite of the Yellowstone Eruption, science and technology had changed at a dizzying pace, even for him. Clearly, humanity had reached a turning point, and knowledge growth had taken on a life of its own. Learning had once again become a challenge which they met joyously, jumping from topic to skills to knowledge, eating it all up at dizzying speeds. Materialism had been replaced by information, which was much cheaper. Granted, much information was useless pap, but many folks would pursue knowledge just to satisfy their curiosity. Marco Antonio read constantly, and could look up information on his telephone in seconds. Now that he had access to e-books, he was never without his Kindle, and their Amazon bill was huge. Everything was fascinating to him, especially since they had successfully bred the new lung cleaners. Before that, he was absolutely dedicated to finding a way to curb Marie's Disease. Finally, he could lift his head and redirect his passions towards learning, and watching his favorite species blossom before his eyes.

MONITORS OF DESTRUCTION

The burgeoning rate of discovery in almost every field was now in jeopardy, so the Golden Age of human discovery was threatened, if not completely ended. Most of the museums, libraries and great universities were gone, along with many of the greatest minds—evaporated in great mushroom clouds. Would the information stored in the "world wide web," the "cloud" or on various surviving hard drives be enough to maintain the pace of discovery once achieved by the people of Earth? Would this loss of the urban centers cripple the cultures and bog them down in the mire of rebuilding, or would it act as a cleansing agent, a sloughing off of moribund ideas and institutions?

Miguel had never seen Marco Antonio so upset. Clearly, the more Marco Antonio thought about it, the angrier he became. In the eight centuries he had spent on this planet, he had become very fond of these people.

Miguel was aware of other feelings as well, most surprisingly, fear. Marco Antonio was afraid that Ann would be endangered by her own species now that she stood between the scientists, politicians, and businessmen and the Monitors. She had jokingly pointed out that they would step over her to get to the Monitors, and that was precisely what he feared they would do.

Miguel could also sense that Marco Antonio was even afraid to leave her with the Monitors, too, although Miguel certainly couldn't understand why.

They communicated for a long time, at least in Monitor terms. Miguel was pleased to have so much of the master's time to exchange ideas. Marco Antonio had been very concerned with the biogenetics involved in finding a cure for the HPO crises, and when he did have a spare moment, he spent it with Ann. Miguel couldn't blame him for that. Marco Antonio had spent many days with long hours in the lab trying to find or breed a species which would clean the tiny obsidian shards from lungs. He drove himself and those around him with a monomania which rivaled Ahab's search for Moby Dick, sure that he could find or design some organism to clean the lungs of all of the long-living vertebrates who were threatened with painful extinction from Marie's Disease. His work was his passion, his determination was his addiction, and success was the only acceptable result.

Marco Antonio's ship was approaching the exact spot where the City Killer's drone had left light space. His ship located both the exit location and directional path its heat had left, as well as its speed, weight, and the exact materials which made up the hull and contents. Everything had to be factored in before his ship could follow; a single mistake could send him millions of miles off course or several centuries off the exact date. Any error could create many problems for everyone involved.

He popped into hyperspace and popped right back out far away from Earth. The drone had hardly moved, and both ships nearly occupied the same space and time, which would have resulted in a violent integration of their materials and speed. The rapid energy release would have created a gigantic explosion which would have blasted him and both ships across the galaxy. Luckily, the math variables eliminated that event.

The drone seemed to have come to a full stop near a yellow sun much like Earth's. There was an Earth-sized planet hanging nearby which clearly had large oceans and an oxygen-rich atmosphere. The planet even had a single moon encircling it closely—too closely for Marco Antonio's taste. They were too near the sun, and the planet was bearing directly down on them. Either this species was very confident of their mathematics and hardware, or they were naïve about the dangers. He suspected the latter. Those variables were too close for comfort.

After adjusting his location, and sending a comm-device with the coordinates to his home planet, he started an analysis of the radio waves being emitted by the people of the planet. As he would have expected, there were also plenty of types of frequencies, making it easy for him to collect data on their communication systems. Like humans, these people spoke with vocal languages—many of them. He narrowed the recordings down to the three main languages. His ship could break down the sounds to their individual words and phrases, as well as the tonalities, pauses, inflections—all the thousands of things that make up a spoken language.

MONITORS OF DESTRUCTION

There were many different types of projections of the creatures who inhabited the planet. Unlike Earth, there were several species vying for domination, and he had to watch their TV equivalents for quite a while (at least in Monitor terms) to pick out the dominant native class. Not surprisingly, there appeared to be a strong warrior class, but these creatures were not the same species as the majority. This appeared to be a conquered world.

As usual, most of the inhabitants of the planet, whether native species, conquerors, or visitors, were bipedal vertebrates. Some wore armor, and a few seemed to have natural chitinous shells like insects and turtles. All of the species seemed to wear some type of clothing, if only a scarf which seemed to denote a status or role. The largest species wore gaudy uniforms, complete with capes, gold trim and bright colors. These seemed to hop much like kangaroos, but their upper bodies were far more muscular. Their arms were longer than a kangaroo's, too, and they had a long and powerful tail which they could equip with a whip, blade or club. Their heads were larger than a kangaroo and were equipped with muzzles outfitted with incisors which would make a wolf jealous. These were the conquering carnivores.

Marco Antonio was studying three of the lingual systems when a message directed to his ship arrived from the surface. As expected, it was in the warrior-class language.

"State your planet of origin and your purpose for being here!" demanded an apparently male voice.

"My name is Marco Antonio Polo, and I am here representing the planet Earth, which you have just bombed. Although I am not an Earthling, my species has directed me to inform you that Earth is a protected planet, and all efforts to conquer or colonize it must cease immediately. To whom should I address this message? Please put me in contact with the military or political leader in charge." Marco Antonio mentally smiled, thinking of Ann's phrase, "Take me to your leader." That one was apt, but her "We come in peace" was not exactly accurate.

"Our leaders are very busy and do not respond to every off-planet visitor. Your ship is apparently unarmed, so you may put it into a high orbit about the moon of this planet, and a member of the administration will contact you within the hinz."

"I am unfamiliar with this term. Is a *hinz* a location or a period of time?"

"It is period of time."

"Describe the length of this *hinz* with a different reference, please."

"There are 23 *hinz* of the moon within 1 solar rotation of Venden."

"How many planetary rotations will occur during one *hinz* of the moon?"

"Seven."

"Is your species native to this planet?" Marco Antonio needed a different reference. It still sounded as if they were in no hurry to talk to him, and that receiving visitors was not a significant event in this person's life.

"Absolutely not! I am from Venden!"

"What is the name of this planet?"

"This chunk of ugly rock is Kudtz."

"Tell your Venden leader that a Monitor has arrived. I will speak directly to the governor of this planet before you take nourishment again, or I will leave. If I leave, every member of his family will die within one solar rotation of this planet, as will every Venden in a leadership or decision-making role."

"You are threatening the life of the Venden governor?! That is punishable by death, sir. Good-bye." His threat was not merely boastful; he meant it. Still, he did not disconnect the call, so Marco Antonio continued his message.

"Know that any attack on this vessel will be ineffectual. Just put me through to your leader, son. You will shoot and shoot, and miss every time. You do not want to look foolish." Marco Antonio was fairly confident that his ship would be immune to any type of physical attack. Either an object, like a bomb or a bullet, or a force, like a laser beam or sonic pulse, would pass right through his ship as it automatically floated into dark matter. It would phase out at light speed and reappear once whatever matter or energy source had passed beyond its position.

Of course, this particular ship had never been tested in battle. A Monitor interstellar ship had not been hit by anything in over 800,000 years. He could only hope that this ship would not be the first.

"We shall see!" said the soldier, as he disconnected the communication.

The fact that nothing happened immediately told Marco Antonio that this person was of low rank, unable to make an attack decision on his own. While he waited, he studied the local time-measurement systems. As he had expected, a *hinz* was roughly equivalent to about a week.

Most planets that had developed intelligent life had one or two moons, but their rotations varied. Because all moons affected tides, their cycles were important. Two large moons with conflicting orbits could cause tidal sloshing that could make life difficult, if not impossible. Both of the planets in this solar system had single moons, and both had water and enough oxygen to support fire. *Unusual.*

He felt the ship phase out as an explosion burst around it. They had not used a concussive projectile, but instead they had exploded one just in front of them. It didn't matter, since the ship just disappeared and let the explosion pass right through it and everything within it. His body had just been bombed, too, but he wasn't there at the time.

"I told you, son. Now, get the governor before I lose my patience! You don't even want me to start shooting back at you!"

There was no response for several minutes, during which he returned to studying the language of this species. As more conversations were recorded and analyzed, his sentence constructions would improve. This was a fairly wide-spoken, ancient language, so its grammar would have been simplified over the centuries. The really difficult grammars and syntax systems were those of isolated languages spoken by non-literate people.

"Who is this? Where are you from, and who do you think you are, threatening the rightful Vendenese governing body of Kudtz?!"

This voice contained a threatening growl that the other had not, typical of self-important, officious dominators across the galaxy. Apparently, his message had been bounced up to the next level in the hierarchy.

"I am called Marco Antonio Polo by the humans of Earth. Your drone has just returned to Kudtz after striking many of the large cities of Earth. This unprovoked attack will not be repeated or followed up on in any way. The humans of Earth are a sentient species capable of interplanetary flight and on the verge of interstellar flight. I am a Monitor of this planet, and as such I am telling you not to return—ever—to Earth. It will not be colonized or contribute in any way to your empire. You may not conquer them, and your warlike violent attack upon this planet has terminated any chances of peaceful interactions." It was tempting to add a mental growl that would fry their brains, but Marco Antonio controlled himself. Threatening them, or better still, killing a few would only impel them to more violence. Still, they deserved it, and it would make him feel better. *I've been surrounded by hierarchical thinkers too long. I'm beginning to feel anger, too.*

"I have never heard of you. The Venden Empire claims Earth as a vassal state. We will spare them further invasion if they submit immediately to our authority and peaceably cooperate with us. If they resist, we will eliminate their entire species. Is *that* understood, Mr. Marco Antonio Polo?" The growl was far more apparent now.

Oooh! You've struck terror into my heart! You big bully! Part of Marco Antonio's several brains could almost hear Ann's voice, but he knew she would have come up with a much more imaginative name than "bully." *God, how I miss that woman!*

Remaining placid, he said, "They are not going to wage war with you or anyone. If you attack them again in any way, you do so at your own peril, sir." *But I WILL fry your brains, you non-intimidating tyrant wannabe.* Better, but still not up to Ann's level.

"If the Monitors of Earth protect them, they declare war on the Venden Empire," growled the officer as threateningly as he could.

"Monitors do not fight wars. We eliminate those who declare war on others. Not their soldiers. Not their sailors. Them. So, if you are the leader of the Venden army, you will be the first to die. Next will come your immediate superior, and his superior on up to the political or religious head of your society. Is this clear to you sir?" *Shit does NOT roll downhill in our world, nutbreath!*

"There are millions of loyal soldiers who have sworn to die in the name of the Venden Empire! We will not be cowed by a few vile terrorists who fight in dark corners, killing innocent leaders and their families. You have no honor, sir!"

Marco Antonio could hear the outrage in his voice. "That is absolutely true," he responded placidly. "We will not support rule by violence. We do not condone governments who institutionalize violence and who give a state or a religion the right to kill its citizens or another group of citizens. We do not kill soldiers; we kill generals, emperors, popes and kings. Anyone who asks others to fight to defend their rule or their god forfeits that rule." He knew that he must remain calm, even in the face of their efforts to terrorize another whole species, one that he loved very much.

"So you are an anarchist, and you think we should fear you? I think not, sir!"

I think so, sir! "We are not against government if it serves the people. We are against governments where the people must serve the state." *If I wasn't positive this is being recorded, we would not be discussing political philosophy, labia-lips.*

"We are not afraid of you! You are cowards who threaten the leaders of a great league of nations. Our valiant soldiers enforce our laws and protect our leaders! Tell Earth that they are coming!"

Bullshit! "No, they're not. There will be no more soldiers. How long will your government last when the soldiers simply go home? What if you call for a war, and no young people will die for you? What if you have to go fight it yourself? How long will you last without the lives of the poor, the young, and the uneducated? That is the price you must pay for the lives of the millions of human beings you have killed this week on Earth! You have just lost your army." *Try not to cackle. Remain calm.* Marco Antonio knew he was enjoying this far too much. He was imagining what Ann would be telling herself.

"What are you talking about? We have a magnificent army! We have brilliant engineers who have designed war drones so that our soldiers no longer have to die to protect our way of life. You cannot simply push a button and our army disappears. WHY AM I EVEN HAVING THIS CONVERSATION WITH A MADMAN? BLOW HIM OUT OF THE SKY!"

Marco Antonio felt his ship phase into the reality of hyperspace as the sudden release of energy pushed solar-based atoms through the dark matter envelope which surrounded and encompassed his ship. He smiled. Marco Antonio had spoken to this pompous windbag long enough to be able to return a message directly into his brainstem, shutting down the creature's heartbeat and breathing. Surrounded by over a dozen highly trained soldiers, the man dropped to the floor, dead.

"How did you do that?" yelled a soldier after several minutes of harried activity in the background. Clearly, he had picked up the microphone after ascertaining that the officer was dead.

"Easily. Bring me his superior, and I'll do it again," Marco Antonio responded calmly. "He ordered you to shoot me and my ship, right? Is there any other officer there who will issue a similar order to kill?" Now, he was beginning to achieve some level of satisfaction. *Shame on me!*

"Not me! Don't kill me! I was just following orders!" The soldier virtually shrieked.

"I know you were. You had better go tell the base commander about the death of this officer. He will want to know immediately, I'm sure."

"Of course. Do you intend to kill him, too?"

"Should I? Will he order you to kill me?" Now, he felt like he was talking to an hysterical child.

"Absolutely! I'm sure you are in the crosshairs of every gun on the planet. There are airships coming your way as we speak. You will soon be killed, and every battleship in our armada will be sent to Earth. We will kill everyone there in retaliation for killing Officer Shtung. His death marks the first of this campaign, and you have made him a hero!" Instead of growling, this guy's voice continued to rise. Clearly, he had not mastered the art of intimidation, but he was trying to be a toughbutt. His screaming was not very impressive, however.

"Don't start. He's not a hero, nor am I. He tried to kill me, and I killed him instead. That's what war is, only he would have preferred that I had killed you instead of him. How do you feel about that? Should I have killed the soldiers of lower rank before I killed him?" It was a stupid question, but Marco Antonio thought he'd give the old Socratic method a try.

"Yes, of course! Officers are far more important than soldiers, so their lives must be protected!"

"Are you an officer or a soldier?"

"I am a soldier, but I would die protecting my betters. I am loyal!"

"You are stupid! Now, go tell your officers that they are doomed, and watch how quickly they leave this planet, giving you the opportunity to be heroically dead for the empire." So much for Socrates. These guys were completely brainwashed. At least he'd tried.

"I will not put them in danger, sir. You must kill me first!"

"Just put the phone down and walk away. You will soon change your mind." *This is getting boring.*

By now, there were many Monitor ships blinking into existence near Kudtz. *At last! Come on, guys! Do your thing!*

These Monitors had been trained to destroy empires from within. Some were accessing every major water system on the planet. Other ships were cruising above the deserts and land masses, releasing tiny carrier-viruses into the air. Everyone would soon be drinking or breathing in the virus which would attach its DNA to the DNA of every cell on the planet.

With several million years of study, the Monitors had become experts at handling every nucleotide in the double helix of life. They had discovered that the structures of the four basic building blocks of DNA are the cornerstone for every living thing in the universe. As basic and common as the atoms in the periodic table of elements from which they were made, the pattern of all oxygen-breathing life forms was found in the double-helix pattern. While many configurations were possible, they were all combinations of genes common to every creature. What humans first thought to be "junk" genes in the codes of some Earth creatures were frequently in use on other planets. The Monitors had decoded nearly every possible covalently bonded combination of nucleotides, and they could alter them at will. Thus, they could alter DNA patterns of every creature they had encountered so far.

This new link being spread by the Monitors simply awakened certain existing DNA patterns so the Venden would imprint on the next bit of information presented. Like a newborn duckling imprints on the first creature it sees, these brain cells would permanently encode the next bit of knowledge presented to them. For 24 hours or so, the planet would be covered with eager learners who would never forget the next lessons accessible to them.

There were many Monitor ships patching into every communications system on the planet. Every radio, every television, every telephone came the message that violent behavior cannot be expected, and anyone who would try should be the recipient of their own orders. From their interstellar ships they could convince every soldier that they would no longer fight for this empire. In fact, they would kill the next officer who gave them an order to do anything violent. It was unthinkable to do otherwise.

Mechanics who worked with armaments would defuse every bomb, unload every gun, and disconnect every system of destruction. Soldiers would turn in their knives, bayonets and swords. Engineers would devise ways to shut down the electronic firing devices and reprogram the computers, most of which they had designed themselves. No orders of attack would be followed except in the reverse.

Every television set, every radio, and over every computer network, the message was the same: War is wrong. Violence is wrong. The only ones who could be attacked are the ones who attack us; defense is acceptable, especially if someone in power is forcing us to do violent acts against anyone else. "Friendly fire" was to be avoided at all costs, since the innocent should not suffer at the hands of their own leaders. Thus, the recipient of an order demanding violence should calmly and quietly end the life of the person who gave the command.

There were Monitors especially trained to ferret out political leaders, and Marco Antonio was one of them. He knew that a culturally universal rule was: the higher the ranking, the more isolated the leader. It required experts and knowledge of the social system and the communication hierarchy.

Marco Antonio had been able to locate the President of the United States hiding on a submarine because he was in touch with every method of verbal and electronic interaction on the planet. He had watched it grow, and had monitored the political, military and industrial systems as they grew. He was able to study the communication system and zero in on the elite, and his knowledge of Earth systems helped him interpret those of Venden. Compared to Earth's carefully encrypted programs, these were child's play. Before a single ship was able to leave Kudtz, the Venden leaders had been located.

Marco Antonio started in at the top. As he had expected, the Vendens were racists who firmly believed their species was superior to everyone, but especially to the two Kudtzan races that had lived together in relative harmony for hundreds of thousands of years. Descended from predators, the Vendens had a military culture that was strictly hierarchical. Most of their science had involved military engineering and weapons construction. Their communication systems were predictable and easily tapped.

Marco Antonio sent his analysis of the language and the communication system to the other Monitors. Within seconds, they had tapped into the location and whatever unique call sign they could use to talk to each one.

Using the Monitor's language, Marco Antonio sent his cohorts the information he had gathered in just a few hours of observation. He sent them images of the pictures he had intercepted from their equivalent to Earth's televisions, edited and described wordlessly with his impressions.

The two Kudtz species were smaller and physically weaker than the Vendens, but their scholars were much more intelligent.

One species living on Kudtz consisted mainly of farmers and insect breeders. They called themselves the Viodtzen. Placid by nature, they produced a variety of crops and insects to feed their scientists and professors, the Trin. (Although the Trin had an ancient name that was much longer and more descriptive, the Viodtzen only called them the Trin.)

The Viodtzen lived simply. Their lives centered around a polytheistic religion within which every activity and relationship rotated. There were many holidays, and they spent most of their time discussing the many adventures of their many gods. Every time they ate, drank, began or finished a task, the activity was dedicated to one or many deities. Without temples or churches, the Viodtzen were satisfied with small altars, sacred trees, groves, or rocks, and so were their gods. With no written language, the Viodtzen did not need a divinity school to produce clerics, and there were no priests. They lived without fear of death or dying, since they had no concept of heaven or hell.

The Trin shared the planet peacefully with the Viodtzen. Religion was a non-subject for the Trin even more so than the Viodtzen. The only competition to be found anywhere was around getting funding, usually for research grants. Most Trin worked in groups, and it was considered impolite to compete with one's peers. Pride of accomplishments was allowed, but gloating was boorish and rude. Group cooperation was highly valued as was friendship. Marriage had not been invented because monogamy was rare. Sexual relations were simple; when a female became fertile, she chose three or four males and copulated with them as often as she liked. It was unimportant which male was the actual sire, since she might have a litter of four or five infants, and they might *all* be fathers. They would all supply the female and her brood regularly with an assortment of insects and other foodstuffs until they were grown enough to enter nursery school. Few females had more than one litter, so many famous scientists were females.

Marco Antonio had too little time to really analyze the social lives of the Trin and the Viodtzen, but he recognized the similarities of his own culture and that of the Trin.

The Vendens, however, were diametrically opposed to the Trin. The Vendens valued competition and conquest, and they valued money and artifacts without any sense of fair play or ethics to hinder their collection of money or power. The only deity Marco Antonio could make out in the brief time he had to listen to their radios and television shows was a war god who didn't seem very demanding. There were no temples or art works devoted to this war god, and Marco Antonio could not even find a reference to his name.

No one on either planet seemed particularly pious.

About two Earth centuries earlier, the Trin had begun to investigate their solar system. Like humans, they quickly developed satellites spinning around their planet and had finally sent a manned spacecraft to their neighboring planet Vender. When the local Venden king saw it, he immediately opened secret negotiations with the Trin leaders, requesting them to send emissaries to open trade and exchange scientific information with *his* kingdom. Eagerly, the Kudtzans, both the Trin and the Viodtzen, had voted to comply.

Vaguely justified by their religion, the Vendens had only journeyed from their planet to Kudtz, in ships supplied by the Kudtz. The Venden king had immediately imported Trin engineers and had begun to build transport ships to import new objects. Their major export from the Vendens had been soldiers and weapons.

Easily conquering the Kudtzans, the Vendens had encouraged the Trin scientists to work on creating interstellar travel based on dark matter physics. The Vendens had only the barest understanding about the physics involved, but they agreed that that was what Trins were for. Willing to supply the Trin scientists, there appeared to be a total lack of ethical considerations regarding the astronauts who died during the many experiments. Within two decades, the Trins had worked out the mathematics and had sent an unmanned ship out of the solar system and had returned it unscathed. They were richly rewarded with medals, titles, awards, and positions on many boards and committees. They were heroes of two worlds.

Both the Viodtzen and the Trin were omnivores who ate mainly plants and insects, but the Vendens were carnivores who now ate mainly Viodtzen. The Vendens had imported large herbivores from their home planet, but they found it easier to dine off their farming neighbors, keeping their delicious home bred herbivores as delicacies for the elite.

The Vendens had set out to conquer an empire. Equipped by the Trins, they sent out drones to weaken their enemy, and swooped in later with Venden troops to mop up whatever defenses were left. They set up a colonial government and basked in their power and glory. If it had not been based on the deaths of millions and the enslavement of billions, it made two species of two neighboring planets within the same star system very happy.

Except for the Viodtzen, of course. They objected to their children being consumed, but there was nothing they could do about it without the help of the Trins, who really didn't care as long as they kept getting their grant money. If they were free to do research in well-equipped labs and were rewarded with honors and titles, they were happy to munch their crunchy bugs and live very simple lives. They wore no clothes except for the scarves the Vendens insisted they put around their necks to identify which organization they worked for. One Trin female was as attractive as the next, and they weren't interested in literature, music, or the theater. Besides, the Viodtzen had far too many children anyway.

Marco Antonio analyzed the social structure of the empire quickly and sent his report to every Monitor on site as well as to his home planet. His report lacked taste, smell, and had very limited color tones, but it was compact and clear. He apologized for the brevity, and added that he was sure his cohorts would do a much more thorough job and correct what he imagined to be his many errors. After all, he had only had a few Earth hours for observation, and he had never actually visited either planet. He hoped that his ship's analysis of the chemical compositions and optical information he was including were accurate.

One of his compatriots contacted him directly, anxious for the chance to exchange ideas directly with such an expert.

How did the Vendens become so powerful so rapidly sir?

MONITORS OF DESTRUCTION

Why don't you call me Marco Antonio? That is what my human friends call me, and frankly I've found it quite handy to have a verbal name. Do you have a name?

Not a verbal one, no sir. No one has ever honored me in such a manner.

Try it—it makes a quick reference easier, although not as rich as our complete identification. You'll have no color or shimmer, and your smell will not be clear, but you'll be recognizable in an instant.

Would you choose one for me?

Sure. I'll call you Kristen. Is that all right?

Oh yes, sir! I am honored to have that name, sir!

What did you want to discuss, Kristen?

The Vendens' rise to power. It was so sudden—within a few generations! How did they become so addicted to power so rapidly?

They are predators who met up with a culture that did not value power. It was inevitable, really. The Vendens are very violent, vicious hunters who were in a constant state of war.

Why?

Hierarchical predators love to fight. They fight over territory, money, jewels, sex, status, or any combination of things. Fighting and killing were even their main sports. When they met up with species they could easily conquer, they stopped fighting amongst themselves. When the Trins arrived on their doorstep, the Vendens jumped at the chance to subjugate their peaceful neighbors.

Neither the Vendens nor the Viodtzen were a match for the Trins' intelligence, but neither had the will to fight. The Viodtzen had no weapons, and the Vendens were happy with an unlimited food supply, as well as a new source of status. You can see it in the development of their body adornments. Suddenly, they had very fancy uniforms, capes, hats, make-up—it all became very elaborate to delineate the nuances of power. I'm sure you've noticed that neither the Viodtzen nor the Trin normally wear clothes. Only their size and the sleekness of their fur denote their health and vigor.

I hadn't realized the significance of their costumes. Thank you, Marco Antonio. I will be able to apply this to other cultures, won't I? Is it a cultural universal?

Yes. It is also an indication of the cultural immaturity. The Vendens are an immature bunch of strutting bullies who are looking for other planets to conquer. Without the Trin, they would not have developed the equipment for interstellar travel until they were more ready for it. They needed to have a few centuries to develop other interests and a great deal more wisdom before they were handed so much power.

So their maturity comes in stages, like physical growth?

In many ways, yes. They adopted the Trins' scientific wisdom before they understood the Trins' emotional and cultural values. They are still in the "might makes right" stage of development. They have a long way to go.

What else do they need to indicate social maturity?

Well, they have no art, music, or literature. Those things allow individuals a chance to fantasize about other realities, to try to imagine how others think and feel. Right now, they don't really care how others feel. Kristen, I must return to my tasks, as you must. I have enjoyed talking and reflecting on these issues with you.

Thank you, Marco Antonio. I have much to think about, and many new ideas to help me analyze this and other societies. Good bye! And thank you for honoring me with a name. I shall treasure it.

Marco Antonio turned to the comm-box that had just popped into his ship from his home planet. The message, sent in pictures and complete thoughts, boiled down to the fact that they had agreed that the Venden soldiers should all be returned to their home planet which would be off limits for any Trin scientist for at least an eon. If the Venden scientists could design and build their own ships, trade could resume, but no military ships would be allowed to leave Venden for a thousand years, if ever.

Furthermore, if the Vendens had conquered any other planet, they were to leave immediately. Venden war chiefs would be eliminated until compliance was achieved. Venden soldiers would be imprinted with non-hierarchical, non-violent lessons. For seven generations, they would be monitored to see if they reverted to militarism and to follow their progress in science, mathematics and engineering.

Marco Antonio agreed that this was a fitting punishment for the invasion of Earth. He would return directly to Earth and inform the government there of this decision and leave the other highly trained Monitors to implement and enforce it.

They responded that they had hoped that he would leave Earth and direct this project, since it would take an expert sociologist and an organizer of his experience to oversee this dual-planet mission.

If Earth had not just been the planet attacked, he might have seriously considered the move. He was right in the middle of creating and dispersing two bio-engineered species to cleanse the lungs of all the vertebrate species, which was doubly important now that they had even more dust in the air. As soon as that task was completed, the effects would have to be observed and evaluated. Besides, there were dozens of cities that had to be reconstructed worldwide, and this was a crucial time in humanity's development. He was anxious to see which goals they would set and how they would achieve them. It was a turning point in human development and a defining moment in their future cultural and social development.

He explained this in great detail, and his cohorts agreed that it was a difficult time for Earth. Perhaps if he could come and show them personally, they would have a clearer idea of the situation.

As he was about to reluctantly agree to visit his home planet, he became aware of a change around him. It felt as if something had once again attacked his ship, but there was a difference. A living being was attached to his ship. He could feel it.

It was alive, but barely. Its life indicators were low, and its mental function was almost non-existent. It was clinging to the outside of his ship. He tried to hurl it into space, but it was incapable of receiving a mental message. Thus, it would not push itself away from the ship.

The ship itself tried to blow it away, but it was already attached to the side of the ship and was now in dark hyperspace itself. Like the ship and himself, it could not be affected by light-space atoms or waves.

Another creature grabbed onto his ship and clung. Marco Antonio did not understand how these creatures could have entered hyperspace, but if they were here, he would leave. He gave the ship the request to leave hyperspace by moving ten centimeters in whichever direction it chose.

There were two large explosions, and two holes appeared in the sides of his ship. A large section of the wall shattered and blew into his body, badly slicing into his right side. Instantly, the ship decompressed and he was pulled in two directions. The cabin was small, and he stretched himself, filling the holes with two of his tentacles. The pressure inside them was immense, and even though the ship's hull immediately healed the outer layer, one of his legs had been ripped beyond repair. His entire body expanded until it almost completely filled the cabin. He tried to decrease the pressure within his tissues by blowing as much air and water out, trying to equalize the forces.

The pain was severe, and he nearly lost consciousness. His legs expanded within the holes, filling them as they exploded into the vacuum. The outer skin of one of the tentacles burst, and the tissues shot out in a spray of gray and red. The brain at the joining of that leg and his body was scrunched as all the muscles of that tentacle constricted in an effort to keep itself from blowing his insides out through the hole in his skin. Like a helium balloon, the opening had to be squeezed shut before all the helium escaped from the end. His insides wanted to explode through that leg's tear and escape to the freedom of airlessness.

In less than ten seconds, the decompression had ceased and the ship had recompressed the cabin. Marco Antonio examined his tentacles and his side, and decided that one leg would have to be completely removed and regrown. He slid into his chair and sent out a bulletin to all the Monitor ships in the area and reported on exactly what had happened to him. He made no recommendations because he assumed that they were better updated than he on the capabilities of their ships.

How did they attach living creatures to the ship while it was in hyperspace? Clearly, there are some updates to be made by Monitor engineers....I wish Ann were here to take out the bullets and stitch me up. She could hold me and give me some "skin time," and put me to bed where I'd sleep in her arms. Sleep and feel, querida mia....

His many fingers started pulling out the shrapnel from his body. Some bits were too small and too deep, and he needed medical attention to stop the leaking of his body's fluids from pouring out the huge gash in his body. His ship, too, needed to be repaired with greater attention than he could give it, so he realized that as soon as it was healed enough, he would go directly to his home planet.

Strangely, the one thought that kept invading his mind was of Ann. When the explosion happened, the first thing that he felt was gratitude that Ann was not there. He knew she could not survive such a decompression; her weak human body would explode. When he decided to go to his home planet, two thoughts had zipped across his consciousness: first, he would have to tell Ann, and second that they needed to give his home planet a name. He had always thought words were limiting, but now they seemed like a valid shortcut.

It was ironic that "He of the Massive Brain," as Ann had referred to him once, found shortcuts to thinking useful. If he had been in his human body, he would have smiled.

Comm-boxes snapped into the cabin in quick succession. He could not grab even one of them. Not one of his legs would obey him, so he decided to remember what it had felt like holding Ann against his body. Some of his tentacles remembered, but several were completely numb. He remembered her smell and how the wind was blowing her hair. He had encompased her completely, and he would do it again.

By the time the other Monitors found him, he was unconscious and barely alive.

CHAPTER 13

Ann spent much of the day on the telephone, as she had expected to do. It was slow, and she had to repeat the same information with every call. She was tempted to change the answering machine's message to a status report, but she didn't have time to draft a good one and get it recorded. No time to save time.

After every call, she stood up and saw to some task in the house. She wanted to pack each Monitor at least a good lunch before they left, but the most she could do was give them a frozen burrito and a juice box. Even peanut butter and jelly sandwiches required more time than she had, and she wanted to get them on their way before governmental or military officials arrived.

The doorbell rang, and Ann walked to the front of the house, the phone at her ear. A man she didn't know stood there in a Navy uniform, and she opened the gigantic screen door and motioned for him to enter.

"Excuse me, Dr. Dutra. I have a Naval Commander at my door, so I'll have to continue this conversation at a later time. Please give me your address, and I'll have a sample of the biological entities delivered to you for you to study. Also, we're putting the research information onto a website so you'll be able to peruse it at your convenience," Ann said, walking to the game table in the living room, taking a pen and paper and writing down his address.

The Naval officer stood in her living room, awaiting instructions. Ann motioned for him to take a seat at the game table and finished her conversation with the scientist.

"Yes. Yes. We'll be in touch with that information today. Goodbye, Dr. Dutra." Ann pushed the red button on her phone and started to sit down across from the officer.

Holding out her hand, she said, "How do you do. I'm Ann Jacob, and I apologize for the terrible welcome," she said.

The officer started to stand as he took her hand and replied, "That's quite all right, Mrs. Jacob. I'm Nick Marshall, and I'm not a Commander. I'm a Lieutenant Commander, but I'm the best they could rustle up since Lemoore was bombed. I was not on base when it happened, so I'm available."

"I apologize. Actually, I was just guessing. Please have a seat. Could I get you some coffee or tea?" They both sat down from the half-standing position they had taken to shake hands. Ann adjusted the pillow behind her so she could sit comfortably.

"No, thank you, Ma'am. I have orders to make contact with Dr. Polo or you regarding the defensive plans undertaken by Dr. Polo. For the time being, I'm the liaison between the United States Navy and the Monitors. Has there been any word from Dr. Polo, Ma'am?" He sounded confident, although she could sense there was something sad about Lieutenant Commander Nick Marshall. His eyes were slightly swollen. He either had an allergy to something, or he'd been weeping not long ago.

"Yes. The last thing I heard was that he was about to enter hyperspace. The City Killers' drone had just blinked out, and he was in hot pursuit," Ann said, as if it were a daily occurrence.

"That's awesome. Do you know how he enters hyperspace, Ma'am?" He sounded enthusiastic in spite of himself.

"Not really, and it's a military secret. Sort of like the 'prime directive' from *Star Trek*. They can't tell us, but I hear we've almost figured it out for ourselves," Ann said rather proudly.

"I understand, Ma'am. How long have you known Dr. Polo? Is he really from outer space?" Mr. Marshall was trying to be as polite as he could be, but it was his job to get as much information out of her as possible. At least he was being polite about it, and she found his enthusiasm disarming.

"Oh, yes. I've known him several years. And you don't have to call me Ma'am. It makes me feel old. Just call me Ann, or Mrs. Jacob if you'd prefer. I was a teacher, so I'm used to that."

"Fine, Mrs. Jacob. How many of them are here? Can I meet one?" The excitement in the officer's voice and body was rising, although he was doing his best to remain officious. At least, he wasn't sad any more.

"They are scientists, Commander. They study us the way we study insects or lions. As I told the President, they are not warriors, and they will not wage war for us." The sooner he understood that, the better, Ann felt.

"How did you meet them? Did they just show up on your doorstep, or were you taken as study subjects?"

These are the questions I had when I first met them. I'd sort of forgotten how exciting the whole prospect was. "Study subjects" makes me want to make up a story about anal probes. Ann suddenly realized that Marco Antonio couldn't hear her thoughts or lame jokes. It made her miss him even more.

The phone rang again, and Ann glanced down at the phone she still held in her hand. It was the White House.

"Excuse me, Commander Marshall. I must take this. It's the President," Ann said with a little shrug, showing a "Whatcha gonna do?" attitude. She winked at Commander Marshall, amused at the look on his face.

"This is she. Yes, I'll hold." Neither Marshall nor Ann said a word as they waited for President Blake to speak. As they were waiting, Miguel came up from the basement and through the kitchen. Coming through the dining room, he held up the comm-box, and took the phone from Ann's hand as he traded devices.

"This is Miguel Olivas, sir. How do you do? Yes, sir, I am a friend of Dr. Polo's. Mrs. Jacob is receiving a message from him right now, but I can tell you what is happening. One moment please, sir." Miguel turned to Commander Marshall and said, "Excuse me, sir. Who are you?"

"Lieutenant Commander Nick Marshall, sir, United States Navy. I am here representing the military forces of the United States of America," he said, sounding very self-important.

Ann had stood, and started wandering towards the kitchen, the black box in her hand.

Miguel resumed his conversation with the President. "Have you sent a naval officer here? Does Lieutenant Commander Nick Marshall represent the military forces of the United States?" He waited a moment before resuming. "All right, then, he may listen to this conversation. Dr. Polo was in negotiations with the City Killers at their home planet. Other Monitors have been notified, and they are undertaking steps to insure that the City Killers will not return to Earth. Unfortunately, Dr. Polo's ship has been attacked, and he has been injured. He will not be returning directly to Earth, but will return to our home planet for the medical attention he needs. Until his return, I will be in charge, along with Mrs. Jacob, of course." Miguel was silent for a moment, and then said, "Yes, I am also a Monitor, but I cannot tell you that, sir."

Miguel glanced at Ann, and saw her sink into one of the dining room chairs. "May I continue this conversation at a later time, sir? I must help Mrs. Jacob now," and he disconnected the line. In about four long steps, Miguel was at Ann's side. She stood and he embraced her. She would not relinquish the black box, so he held her with one arm.

The officer remained in his seat, at a loss as to what to do. He had just watched two people, one a human and the other apparently a Monitor, hang up on the President of the United States. He could only guess that whatever news was coming in on the black box in Mrs. Jacob's hand was bad. He didn't want to be intrusive, but it was his duty to get as many military details out of them as possible. He decided to just wait silently until they noticed him or kicked him out. He watched as Miguel tenderly kissed Mrs. Jacob on the forehead as he put his hand on the box being held between them.

"Do you need me to translate, Ann? Did you understand what they said to you?" Miguel asked, pulling back so that he could look at her face.

"I got the main idea, Miguel, but I would appreciate it if you could clarify the medical terms for me. How bad is it, Miguel?" Ann said, her face beseeching him to tell her that it was not serious.

He couldn't do that. "His ship decompressed, and he had damage down to the cellular level from that. In addition, he was badly injured from the explosion, which cut into his body, injuring his right frontal cortex, and he nearly bled out. Two of his legs were ripped off, so they will have to regrow. He needs to spend some time in a depressurizing tank." Miguel spoke in a quiet voice, but Marshall heard every word. Miguel never took his eyes from Ann's face, which searched his for any sign of good news.

"They said something about his vial that I didn't get," Ann said.

"It would go much more quickly if they had his vial. I will send Questor to meet the ship they will send for it." Miguel took the black box from Ann and cast a quick glance at the Lt. Commander, who was sitting quietly in the living room, his hat in his hand.

"Is there anything I can do for him, Miguel?" Ann asked calmly.

"No, not really. I have just sent Questor," Miguel said quietly, trying to say as little as possible in front of the officer in the living room.

"He'll return with Marco's body, won't he?" Somehow, the thought of losing the human part of Marco Antonio would finalize things. As long as she could hold on to that, she could believe that he would return.

The phone rang again, but Ann ignored it. Miguel walked to the living room, picked up the phone, and said, "It doesn't say who it is."

"Let it go to the answering machine," Ann said, noticing the officer for the first time in several minutes. She returned to the living room and sat down. "Miguel, perhaps you can explain some of the things that happened at Kuze, or Koots, or whatever they call the City Killer's home planet."

"I suppose I can tell you about them. It is right that you know who attacked Earth and why," Miguel said.

"Yes sir, please. Who are they, and what did they want?" asked the officer.

"They are from the planet Venden, which conquered their neighbors on Kudtz. It was the scientists on Kudtz who developed interplanetary travel, but as soon as they got to the neighboring planet in their solar system, Venden, they were conquered by them. The Venden are barbaric carnivores who were quick to take advantage of their more peaceful, non-violent neighbors' scientific expertise to create an empire." Miguel explained calmly, but Ann felt his anger when he mentioned the Venden.

"So there are *two* other species attacking us?" asked Commander Marshall.

"Not really," Miguel explained. "The species that developed interstellar travel did not attack you. They were non-violent, on a scientific mission. They were easily fooled by the Vendens, apparently, into constructing large ships for trade between the two neighboring planets. Within just a few years, the Venden had constructed enough weapons and ships, and they successfully invaded and conquered the Kudtz. The Kudtz were conquered by the Vendens because the Kudtz had virtually no weapons or defense tactics. This is what happens when a species that is not mature enough gets their hands on technology they are not ready for, Commander. There are certain cultural and sociological developmental stages that every species must go through before they are ready to interact with other creatures."

"But look what happens when an innocent world is attacked by a vicious one! We should have been able to defend ourselves. We don't want to be like the Kudtz, who could not. Perhaps with your help, we can still defeat them," Commander Marshall said, sounding like the warrior he was.

Ann tried valiantly to concentrate on what Miguel was saying, but it was very confusing to her. All she could think about was that Marco Antonio had been wounded, severely. He's had two arms *ripped off?* He'd been injured to the cellular level? What the hell did that mean? If his right frontal cortex had been injured, it meant that he'd had brain damage, which was horrendous. Marco Antonio's brain was everything to him; he could live without all eight arms, but he needed every cell of his humongous brain. *Oh, god! If he's brain damaged, he might be so damaged that he can't come back to Earth, even if he survives everything else.*

Ann tried to focus her eyes on Miguel, so that she could follow what he was saying and pay attention, but no matter how hard she tried, she couldn't help be distracted by the terror she felt about Marco Antonio.

Miguel continued answering the officer's question. "The Venden will not bother you again. Their attack was very sudden, and we were unprepared for it. For that, we can only apologize. Many human beings died, and a great deal of history and human culture has been obliterated. It is very sad," Miguel said. Although his face remained passive, Ann could feel Miguel's misery. In fact, it was pulsing out with so much force that she was almost overwhelmed. His distress and guilt was heartbreaking, and she was about to lose it.

Please calm down, Miguel. You are flooding me with messages that I can't take in right now. We must both cope with this.

Oh, I'm sorry, Ann. I will control myself.

Miguel's eyes dropped from the stare he had been exchanging with the officer to the brown carpet at his feet. He became quiet and took several deep breaths. Ann also tried once again to calm herself. The news was bad on top of worse, covered by horrific.

"How can you be so sure that the Venden will not attack us or others again? Mrs. Jacob said that you do not fight wars. What did you do to them?" Marshall hoped Miguel would tell him, because he *needed* to know. It was his job to find out, but his need was more visceral than professional. Ann watched him and knew that he, too, had experienced tragedy and was in great pain. Nonetheless, in her heart of hearts, she didn't really care about the Vendens and the Commander, or anyone else. She wanted to yell, "Who gives a shit? Nothing matters except Marco Antonio!" She took a deep breath and tried to calm herself so that she could absorb the situation in all its complexity.

"Wars require soldiers and sailors, Commander. We make sure that the soldiers and sailors will not fight or die at someone else's orders. If that doesn't work, we eliminate the leaders. The combination is very effective," Miguel said mildly. To Miguel, the answer was obvious.

"I'll bet it is. I don't see how you can change the entire species' morality that quickly, however. Clearly there was some battle, or Dr. Polo wouldn't have been injured. How did that happen?" Marshall was pushing now, not to be put off by vague philosophical conversation.

A very good question, Miguel. At last! Something she truly cared about!

"We are uncertain. We will analyze the ship's records to see exactly what happened. Only Marco Antonio's ship was attacked, apparently, but his observations about the method of attack were confusing and vague due to his injuries. You are correct about the necessity for haste," Miguel said. "We must analyze his ship carefully to see how exactly it was damaged, so that we can guard against it ever happening again. Right now, all indications point to the fact that the Monitors have neutralized the Vendens' leadership capabilities, and their soldiers are being de-programmed as we speak."

"So you killed all the officers? Good!" Commander Marshall said with a small nod of satisfaction.

"We didn't have to. We programmed the soldiers to kill whoever gives them a kill order. The punishment fits the crime, and the perpetrators are the former victims," Miguel explained calmly.

"As long as you give the leaders fair warning, it seems like a good plan to me. If someone had killed Hitler, there'd have been no holocaust. Believe it or not, sir, I am absolutely against war. It's my job to maintain the peace, so I understand your plan to eliminate the warmongers. I have one more question, if I may?" asked the Commander. He sounded as if he expected his question to be offensive, but he would take the risk of asking it anyway.

"I'll answer if I can sir," Miguel replied graciously.

"How is it that you look so human? Are the Monitors all exactly like human beings, or do you just adapt your bodies to whatever planet you happen to be on?"

"That is exactly what we do. My native body does not look like this one, I assure you. In fact, you would probably think me quite ugly. Our work just goes much more smoothly when we can blend into the native population. Unfortunately, I cannot explain the process, which is very complicated, but necessary. We have learned millennia ago that to truly understand the play, we must eventually get on the stage."

The phone rang again, and it was a number Ann recognized as that of Raul, one of the Monitors.

"If you gentlemen will excuse me, I'll take this in the kitchen," Ann said, and left the room. She hoped they had more news about Marco Antonio, or would be willing to tell her more about his condition than Miguel had been able to while the naval officer listened.

"Yes, I have heard that Marco Antonio has been injured, but I don't know how he's doing. Please tell me anything you have heard, Raul," Ann said, keeping her voice low.

"He was gravely injured, but he will recover. There is much concern about brain damage, both in his central head and in at least two of his neuronal centers at the conjunction of his head and tentacles. He will lose some of his abilities, and perhaps some memories. There's hope that the decompression and liquid loss, well, it's like your blood, Mrs. Jacob, you know, we hope it hasn't killed too many cells to cripple him," Raul mumbled, becoming increasingly vague.

"Do you mean he'd be physically handicapped, or mentally damaged?" Ann asked. She could not imagine either, but she didn't really know how much coordination it took to move his huge body.

"Well, a lot of cells exploded, so we're not sure if they were neurons or muscle cells. His skin will regrow, of course, and his legs will be regrown. That's easy. It's just not clear how many neurons exploded, and where they were. They'll be able to tell more once they have his vial. Most of the cells can be replaced, but a lot of the information stored on them might be too damaged to recall. It's a wonder that he survived at all, Mrs. Jacob." Raul's tone was supposed to be comforting, but she was hearing "What do you expect?" from him, as well.

"How long does Monitor recuperation generally take?" Ann asked, trying not to sound as timid as she felt. She was afraid of the answer. She missed the background music of Marco Antonio's thoughts; everything was so gray and silent and lonely.

"Nobody's ever been this severely wounded and survived. He may end up as a big bag of water, or he may come back just like he was before the explosion. Who knows?" Raul said, finally sounding confident enough to at least tell her the truth. Monitors were unable to lie, and even selecting some truths while masking others was extremely difficult for someone as young as Raul.

"A big bag of water? Seriously?" Ann said, placing her head on her hand on the table.

"Oh, sorry, Mrs. Jacob. Probably not that bad. I was exaggerating, I think," Raul stumbled on. "He's so huge and brilliant, even half of him would be smarter than all of me. He'll be fine, I'm sure. We have really good doctors." Raul stumbled on, trying to take back his colorful but terrifying metaphor.

Ann couldn't take any more. "Thank you, Raul. Stay in touch," she said, and she ended the call.

The image of Marco Antonio's huge, blue, shimmering body deflated back to the black mass of goo she'd seen in his stasis chamber had become a real possibility. She knew that his life force was what she loved, not his body—either of them. If that were damaged, if he were brain damaged so that the *self* that she loved was gone, well, she didn't know what she would do.

Yes, she did. She'd take care of him, of course. If he were wheelchair bound, or needed diapers and a dribble-bib, she would tend to him. Would they let him return to her if he was mentally damaged? Would he want to? Almost any permanent damage would involve brain damage: the largest organs in their bodies were brains. In fact, they were brains and eyes on legs.

Her mind raced with a million questions, and she wondered if Miguel knew any of the answers and was just trying to spare her.

When Miguel came into the kitchen, he saw Ann sitting at the kitchen table staring out the window. "I asked the Lieutenant Commander to leave, Ann. I have his phone number, and I promised to let him know as soon as we receive another report. Are you all right?"

Ann looked up at Miguel and rose, saying, "That's good. I've got to get these samples boxed and ready to be delivered to a dozen universities. I think I'll go to Walmart or Target and buy some plastic refrigerator boxes with tight lids. No, I'll send Ruth. I've got several more calls to return." She looked to the floor and pursed her lips, trying not to fall apart.

He's alive. That's all that matters. The future comes one day at a time, and I'll just have to deal with him in whatever shape he's in when he gets home. He's alive.

She had decided how she would handle this. Every time the glue started to come out, she'd think, *He's alive!* She'd put herself back together, try to concentrate on what she had to do, and get on with it. It made her very fragile, however. Too fragile to deal with all the "what if" thoughts that kept washing over her, so she would just have to stop that. *Get a grip, girl!*

"Ann, I know you are upset. You are worried about Marco Antonio and afraid that he will die. So am I. He is my leader, and my friend. He has saved my life several times, and I will do whatever I can to save his. We all will." He approached her, but he did not touch her, for which she was grateful.

"I know that, Miguel. I am trying very hard not to worry. Raul mentioned that he might be handicapped in some way, either mentally or physically, and that kind of scares me. But we'll take care of him, no matter what shape he's in. Right?" Ann said, needing the reassurance that his species would care for their invalids. It had crossed her mind that they might not; she didn't know what they did with their handicapped.

"If he is very damaged, he might not be able to enter his human body. That is quite a strenuous process. Even if he could only return to the Marianna Outpost, you would be able to talk to him. He would like that." Miguel paused, and took her hand. "As I have told you before, I will stay here to care for you, Ann. You will not be alone; there will be Questor and me. We will guard you, and I will live here with you. You need never be alone." He patted the top of her hand and looked deeply into her eyes.

"I am not afraid of being alone, Miguel. I have my children and grandchildren, and many friends. You are one of my dearest friends, and I know you'll help me. Thank you, Miguel." Ann looked back outside. Looking into Miguel's intense stare was too much, and she didn't like the way this conversation was going. They'd been here before.

"I will arrange for more containers for you now. How many should I buy? Which type would you prefer?" Miguel asked, clearly wanting to change the subject.

"I have the feeling that we are going to have more visitors today, and your presence might be required. I don't want anyone to know that Ruth and Gabriel are also Monitors, so right now, it's just you and Marco Antonio. Let's let Gabriel go to the store for us. He's our friendly neighbor, right?" Ann said, as she reached once more for the ringing phone.

"This is she. No, I'm sorry, we have heard nothing more. To the best of my knowledge, they will not be returning." Ann listened for a few moments, making soft responses, and then said, "I'll certainly let you know as soon as I hear anything else. Which number should I call to get directly to you?" she said, writing it down on her note pad. Thank you. Uh-huh. Indeed. Good-bye." She made a note on the pad of notes she was keeping. It had the time and the number next to "Homeland Security."

As soon as she disconnected from Homeland Security, she looked up at Miguel and said, "How do you feel about euthanasia?"

"It is sometimes a valid choice, but not one Marco Antonio would choose for himself. Is that a concern for you?" Miguel answered as if she had asked about a favorite color.

"No, not really. I just wanted to know if that would be something your people might consider if he were severely handicapped. Would they?" Ann asked, trying to be as cool as Miguel. The welling of the tears in her eyes betrayed her, as they always did.

I am such a sponge!

"He would have to be very near death, with almost no hope of regaining the function of his mind or body. Our doctors can heal or replace almost every body part. They have his complete genetic record and will have no problem regenerating new legs for the two that were injured. He can control his own pain, but if he could not, they would not let him suffer as humans must. Your pain control methods are very primitive, and your brains cannot control the amount of pain your body is subject to. I know. Remember when you found me in the alley, living off of the blood of rats while they ate me, too?" Once again, he looked into her eyes intensely.

"Of course, I remember. You were so brave, Miguel! I'll never forget that!" She remembered vividly, and it took her mind off Marco Antonio for a moment.

"Yet it did not occur to me to kill myself because I was in pain. I knew that Marco Antonio would find me eventually. It never occurred to me that *you* would find me and save my life by feeding me the blood from your own body. I will always be grateful for that, Ann," he said shyly.

"It was no big thing, Miguel. You were in terrible shape, and you needed human blood. Anyone who knew you would have done the same," Ann said. To her, it was an obvious action that she would do for any creature, but especially visitors from another planet. She didn't want any Monitor to die on Earth, if for no other reason than it was very bad advertising.

"I tried to thank you, but Marco Antonio didn't like it," he said, avoiding her eyes and smiling shyly again.

"Few men would like another man to give his woman an orgasm, even under those chaste conditions," Ann responded, also smiling. Miguel was so naïve!

"I would do it again, any time you feel the need. Just let me know. Or, if you just need to be held and stroked, I will be happy to do that. Perhaps to music, as we did in Argentina. It seemed to comfort you. I know you are under great stress now, so tonight I will hold you and pet you in a non-sexual manner, if you would like."

"Oh, Miguel. You are a sweetheart! I know that your intentions are good, but I think we had better not soothe each other physically. Marco Antonio gets very possessive and is quite jealous, and he would certainly object. I will do nothing that he would object to, but thanks for offering. You're a really nice person."

Sometimes dealing with Miguel was like dealing with a child, or someone who was slightly autistic. He just didn't understand about jealousy or possessiveness, and had clearly never experienced those emotions himself. He was completely amoral, especially about sexual matters. He had no moral norms at all, and human rules and feelings about sex and love were like a minefield that he was cheerfully wandering through, clutching his teddy bear. Especially around Marco Antonio, Miguel might say or do something that would cause everything to blow up around her.

"If ever you change your mind, let me know. I will always be here," Miguel said quietly.

This whole conversation was making Ann very uncomfortable. "I will always be here to help you, too. But right now, we have to worry about getting these samples out to the universities and medical labs. Would you please go ask Gabriel to buy some of those Ziplock or Gladwrap boxes? The baggies might work, too. Come here and look at these—what do you think?" Ann said, fetching some plastic bags out of her kitchen drawers.

She was very relieved to have that discussion over. They had had that very conversation several times before, and every time, it was the same. It made her extremely anxious. Marco Antonio would turn green with jealousy if he ever heard Miguel make those cozy little offers. When Marco Antonio got jealous or possessive, people died.

As Miguel took the baggies and left to get Gabriel, Ann wondered about him. Did Miguel really think she would change her mind about something like that just because Marco Antonio was injured? If so, Miguel really didn't understand the whole concept of monogamy, possessiveness, or jealousy. Ann could hardly believe that any race, especially one as ancient as the Monitors, would be so naïve, yet they were.

Perhaps they didn't understand the concept of betrayal. Their race reproduced sexually, but not on a basis of a pair-bond. They were notified when there was a need for more Monitors and asked for either their male or female contributions. If they unilaterally decided that they would like to reproduce, they simply contributed their sex cells and requested a specific partner or put in for a general match. The number of babies born each year was predetermined by the reproductive branches of the government.

If a couple wished to privately reproduce, they could do so. They could raise their own children, or send their babies to specialists who would gestate the eggs and train the infants with basic skill-developmental experiences to maximize their growth. Each baby was individually nurtured by an adult for at least a year, when they were exposed to other babies in a nursery school-type setting for several more years. Surely thoughts of loyalty and constancy would be common when they were raising children together? Perhaps not.

Every Monitor was expected to reproduce at least twice sometime during their life. The reproductive history of every Monitor was public knowledge, and the genetic make-up of every individual was carefully recorded. Yet they rarely tinkered with most matches. Monitors were an ancient race, and they had achieved enough wisdom to leave well enough alone. Unless there was a known genetic abnormality, which they fixed long before the infant matured to childhood, most pairings were left up to chance.

Specific characteristics could be requested, of course. For the most part, however, it was unnecessary. If one combination didn't work very well, it could be changed after the fact. The genetic make-up of Monitors had been tweaked for hundreds of thousands of years by millions of parents and scientists, so everyone generally got exactly what they wanted.

There were conditions under which specific types of Monitors were desired, but that was rare now. They were capable of breeding Monitors who would be comfortable in a very dry environment, like a desert. Many times, they designed creatures to live undersea, frequently considering the salinity or acidity of the water when the babies were developed. Most Monitors were capable of living either under water or on land, and their genetic make-up could be altered as needed long after they were born. They could—and did—alter their own genes to maximize their efficiency under specific conditions.

All this had been explained to Ann long ago. She knew that love was not unknown to Monitors, but they thought that mixing love with sex showed the quaint, primitive emotions of a very young species. Perhaps she was the one who didn't understand. Love, marriage and children had always meant loyalty and fidelity to Ann. Maybe she was the one who was confused.

Both Miguel and Marco Antonio had used sex as a positive reinforcer to get blood. Because female humans are smaller and weaker, Monitors rarely chose female avatars. To feed off males, they typically waited until the men were asleep, but not always. In any case, both male and female donors remembered a positive experience, even if they couldn't remember the actual event. Thus, they looked forward to seeing both vampires. Unlike the movie vampires, neither Marco Antonio nor Miguel would ever drain a donor to a danger point; they wanted to be able to return and feed again.

Erotic love was new to Marco Antonio. Ann had spent a lot of time thinking about Marco Antonio's declaration that he had never loved anyone as he loved her. Clearly, love and sex were separate to Marco Antonio and to Miguel as well. Apples and oranges.

Maybe Miguel knew that Marco Antonio would only be available over the phone or the comm-box because he was too damaged to return to his human body. Maybe Miguel was offering his stud service because he knew that Marco Antonio's body would remain unavailable to her forever.

Oh, God.

CHAPTER 14

The comm-box made its noise again, indicating that the Monitors wished to speak to Ann or Miguel. Hoping it was news of Marco Antonio, Ann picked it up and instantly all thoughts of Monitor reproduction left her mind as she was swamped with messages of the City Killers, the Trin, the Vendens, and several dozen Monitors.

"Wait a minute! Back off for a second; you're talking too fast. I'll get Miguel in here, and you can tell him the updates with the war, but right now, all I'm interested in is Marco Antonio's condition."

She was met with a blank silence. Clearly, the Monitor on the other end had never talked to her before and assumed that she could sort out the multiple-layered messages that they could deal with. She tried to imagine Marco Antonio's native body, hoping to convey his persona. She remembered seeing Marco Antonio's human body lying next to his vial.

With one hand on the comm-box, she grabbed her cell phone with the other and dialed Miguel.

When he picked up, Ann said, "I've got a message on the comm-box that I can't understand. Can you come back and answer it for me please?"

"I'm at Ruth's next door. I'll be right there," he said, and a few seconds later she heard the front door open.

Silently, she handed the box to him. He stood there silently, his hair hanging over his forehead, his green eyes looking down at the carpet. His jeans were black, and his shirt was tucked in neatly, showing his flat stomach and broad shoulders. She couldn't help noting that he was an absolutely striking man, beautiful in an artistic sense. She could admire his beauty as if he were in one of her classes.

Gorgeous, but as untouchable as a Rubens or a Van Gogh painting on a museum wall.

Ann tried to read Miguel's face, but he gave away nothing. She was anxious to hear what was happening with the City Killers, of course, but her prime concern was Marco Antonio's condition.

Ann's cell rang, and it was Samantha, her daughter. "Hi, Mom. I was wondering if you could get Johnny from soccer practice. I have a department meeting today, and I completely forgot. He can hook a ride from Ashley's mom to soccer from school, but he'll need a ride home. Molly will be home with Jacob, but I might be late, and I hate the idea of his being alone down at the Soc.Com. That soccer field is not in the safest part of town." Sam said it all like it was one continuous sentence, so Ann knew she was stressed.

"Of course, Sam. What time exactly?"

"They're supposed to be through by 4:30. You can just take him to your house, and I'll swing by and pick him up as soon as the department meeting is over, so you won't have to drive him all the way home. Besides, that way Molly will only have one of the boys, not both." Samantha answered, still sounding like she was hanging by a thread. Being a soccer mom was hard enough with two parents, but being a working widow made it really hard.

Ann never took her gaze away from Miguel. "Status non sweatus, sweetie. I'll be there at 4:30. No, maybe I'll send Ruth or Gabe, but he'll be picked up on time. We've got it covered. Relax." Ann said. Normally, Samantha would be the first one Ann would turn to for help with her own anxiety about Marco Antonio, but not today. No, not today.

"Thanks, Mom. See you around five-ish. Bye."

Let's see. Return the calls to Homeland Security and the President of the United States, determine the state of an intergalactic war, worry about whether or not the love of my life is a bag of jelly, and pick up my grandson after soccer. No sweat. All in an afternoon's work.

She pressed the red button and ended the call.

He's alive. Deep cleansing breaths. He's alive.

Miguel was waiting patiently for Ann to finish her conversation with Samantha. Before he could begin, Ann said, "Please remind me to pick up Johnny from soccer at 4:30. I mustn't forget."

"Certainly."

"Now, what's the news?" Ann asked calmly. *Spread the responsibility, and hang on.*

"Most of the leaders of the Venden army have been removed from power. The soldiers directly under them are organizing the return of their troops to Venden from Kudtz. There is one other colony of pre-interstellar cultures the Venden had conquered and enslaved that have been identified, and the Venden rulers have been ordered to retreat immediately. It is doubtful that they will comply, so in approximately twenty-four hours, Monitor ships will arrive there to insure their compliance." Miguel sounded like he was giving the weather report.

"What about the Trin? And the other guys from Kudtz? What's going to happen to them?" Ann asked. She tried to remain as calm as Miguel was. She just wished she could channel her thoughts as well as he could. Her brain kept bouncing around from crisis to crisis, from Samantha to Marco Antonio, to the City Killers, to the President, to the Marie's Disease project, back to Marco Antonio, to what to serve for dinner—bouncing back and forth endlessly. Every thought had its own train of emotions, every situation engendered a hundred questions to which she rarely could get answers.

"The Viodtzen," Miguel replied. "They will no longer be eaten, I suppose, since the Trin are mainly insectivores. The Trin are a much more interesting species. They are very alert scientifically, but they are mostly theoreticians. Having developed interstellar travel marks them as a very developed species, however. The Monitors will be opening a dialogue with them on Kudtz, if only to see how they attached the explosive-packed Viodtzen to Marco Antonio's ship while it was in dark space, or hyperspace, as you prefer to call it." Miguel relayed this information as smoothly as a six o'clock newsman, and Ann thought that was exactly what he should be.

"Let's get this information to the President, Homeland Security, the Pentagon, and everyone else who should know. They will be very interested in this news. Can we put it on Skype or on a conference call? I don't want to get anybody's nose out of joint because we ignored them. Better yet, let's let *them* arrange the conference and notify whatever international bigwigs they want to include. That should raise their political brownie points score," Ann said thoughtfully.

"What are 'political brownie points'?" asked Miguel.

"It will give the illusion of control and cooperation. I think the Prez needs that about now, don't you?" Ann said, reaching for her home phone. Before she dialed, she asked, "Any news about Marco Antonio?"

Oh yeah, him.

"No. They're working on him. They said that having his vial will help. His stasis box was also gravely injured due to the rapid depressurization, so the vial and his human body will help restore many of his brain cells," Miguel said.

"I don't think the President needs to know those details, do you?" Ann said.

"No. If he asks, I'll simply say he was injured and is recuperating," Miguel said.

Ann dialed the White House number she had been given, and it was picked up after the second ring. "This is the White House. Is this Mrs. Ann Jacob?"

Surprised to be identified immediately, Ann felt important for the first time. Before she was put through to the President, Ann said, "We have an update on the City Killers situation, and we would like to have a conference call set up. We'll leave it to President Blake's discretion, but we suggest that several world leaders and Homeland Security, the Pentagon, and whatever branches of the government he deems necessary be made aware and ready to receive this update."

Surprisingly, President Blake spoke right up. "Good idea, Mrs. Jacob! It's very dicey politically right now because so many of the capitals and leaders have been blown up. Others are in chaos. The U.N. building is destroyed, and so is Parliament and Paris. I appreciate the heads-up. Give us ten minutes, and we'll connect as many leaders as we can. I would rather they hear it from you than from CNN," he said, catching Ann as she was about to suggest exactly that.

"It's more important than that. Only the American government has been contacted directly, and many world leaders are extremely suspicious of the Monitors. They want us to produce one before they'll believe them, or me, for that matter. They want to see little green men, I think," the President admitted.

"That never occurred to me! I just wanted you, our government, and the world's leaders to feel empowered, sir. They need to feel included in the latest info," Ann said, mainly to let him know that she knew what she was doing. "News this important shouldn't be received on You-Tube or Facebook."

"Exactly, exactly! How is Mr. Polo, or should I say, Doctor Polo? I understand he was injured?"

"He is recuperating, I am told. Thank you for asking," Ann said, doing her best to sound like a politician. *Actually, it's easy. Just say as little as possible in as many words as possible.*

"And Mr. Olivas? Is he there too?" asked the President, as if he was checking up on the wife and kiddies. When he admitted that he hoped Miguel would be there for the conference call, he sounded a little more desperate.

"Yes sir. He will be making the report. As a Monitor himself, he is much more adept at interpreting their messages than I. In fact, he could make the report in any of twenty-nine languages," Ann said, killing time, waiting for the call to be set up. She didn't feel like she was giving away any Monitor secrets by letting the President know that Miguel was multi-lingual. In fact, she hoped it would help to convince him that the Monitors were a superior race, although she didn't know why she needed to.

Am I just proud of him, or am I being defensive? He feels like my son. He's a geek, but I love him. No, wait. Neither of my sons are geeks. Miguel just feels like a child to me; he has so much to learn.

"I just wish he could send out one of those picture-messages like Dr. Polo did. Then, they'd believe him," President Blake said hopefully.

"I don't think he can do that, but who knows? I'll ask. Have you had any luck in the real estate market? I understand you're looking for another White House," Ann said, trying to make pleasant conversation by joking. What she really wanted to say was "Shut up and arrange the call!" She knew, of course, that his staff was doing it, but she wasn't used to having a staff.

"Ha ha," chortled the President politely. "We're not exactly on the street, as so many of our fellow citizens are. Mrs. Blake and myself are in a lovely home which has been graciously extended to us, but right now, its location is a secret."

"I understand. You and Mrs. Blake were very fortunate to be out of town when the City Killers bombed Washington. I think you'll be pleased when you find out what is going to happen to the Vendens," Ann said. She wanted him to think positively about what the Monitors were doing.

"Whatever they do will be more than we're capable of at this point. Even though I'm the leader of the greatest nation on Earth, I feel pretty helpless. They really kicked our butts. I think it was a cowardly attack against innocent people. We didn't deserve to be victimized, and I'm mighty glad the Monitors have stepped up to protect us from the bullies in our galaxy."

Ann was genuinely shocked to hear the President admit to anyone—least of all her—that he felt helpless. She didn't quite know what to say, so she decided to be supportive.

"Here here!" Ann said. "What Marco Antonio did for us was courageous beyond your wildest dreams. He stood up and faced the whole empire totally alone."

"Really? I'm anxious to hear the story!" the President said. "Weren't there other Monitors there to back him up?"

"Not at first. They're there now, mopping up. The Venden Empire has been shut down, once and for all. They've been sent home, their tails between their legs, and they won't be allowed off their planet for a thousand years." Ann couldn't help but brag. She was so proud of Marco Antonio, and she knew that Miguel would understate the scenario. By their very nature, the Monitors would downplay the events, for to do otherwise would contribute to the fame and glory of militarism. Her people needed to feel vindicated; they needed a hero after the horrible losses they had suffered.

She knew that the "missing and presumed dead" lists continued to grow. In so many ways, life and death had hinged upon location, not guilt, status, money, or religion. It all depended on where they were at the time. Every victim was innocent, since not one human being had done anything to provoke the attack.

"However they did it, we'll be forever in their debt. How did you meet Dr. Polo, if I may ask?"

Clearly, Mike Blake is used to getting answers to his questions. Let's give him something to talk about.

"Well, the first time I met him, he slept in my bed," Ann said. *If they only knew the real story....*

"Oh, really? This sounds like a tale I'd like to hear," the President said.

"He was visiting the neighbors next door, but they were remodeling, and there was sawdust everywhere, so I invited him to stay with us. He took us up on it, stayed in the guest room, and we've been friends ever since." Ann said, making a joke out of it.

"Your husband, Tim, was there too, I presume?"

"Of course. It's not really as racy as I can make it sound. Being just a good neighbor doesn't make a good story," Ann admitted, noting silently that she had never mentioned Tim. Clearly, the President had vetted her. She didn't care.

"I know what you mean. You're lucky to be in the position where you can still make such jokes. In a few days, you'll be so famous, you won't be able to."

"I'll always be able to, since I'll never run for office, and I don't care what anyone thinks of me. I am as free as a bird, Mr. President." *And no one can blackmail me, least of all you.*

"I envy you then," he said.

Ann heard voices, and then he said, "We have as many leaders tuned into this line as we can get on such short notice. Of course, it will be taped so that the world can hear it soon."

"This is a report, sir, not a speech. You'll not hear 'I have a dream' or 'Four score and seven years ago.' Just the facts. Let me introduce my good friend, Dr. Miguel Olivas. He will explain the latest situation concerning the City Killers. Go ahead, Miguel," Ann said, and handed him the phone. She ran into the living room and grabbed the other unit.

The President was introducing the other people on the line and identifying which country or arm of the government they represented.

After greeting everyone in their native language, Miguel related the situation exactly as he had to Ann, but she took over to explain the complicated relationships of the species involved. She tried to avoid politically "loaded" terms, minimizing the fact that the Viodtzan had been eaten by the Vendens. She admitted not knowing the names of the citizens of the other planets conquered by the Vendens, but she warned that they had made other conquests before attacking Earth. She could always add information, but once it was out, it couldn't be rescinded.

When the President asked about Marco Antonio, Ann let Miguel handle it. He said that his ship had received two blasts resulting in rapid decompression resulting in severe injury. He was currently in a recompression chamber and awaiting surgery to replace a limb which was blown completely off. However, it was expected that he would recover.

I notice that you never mentioned that his "limb" was one of eight, not four.

Miguel looked at her and smiled slightly. Ann winked, glad that every expression was not being visually recorded, because she knew every vocal nuance would be analyzed for years.

"So the Venden leaders will be removed if they do not return directly to their home planet, is that correct?" asked the Prime Minister of the U.K. "What if they refuse? If they wounded Dr. Polo, they clearly have the ability to resist the Monitor's ships. What will they do to make them comply?"

"They will be eliminated on an individual basis. Their crews will no longer obey an order requiring violence. In fact, they will rebel and kill whoever issues the order," explained Miguel.

Ann reached over and touched Miguel. *Oh, oh. They're not going to like the sound of that. It sounds like mind control. Be careful!*

"The Monitors are very good at infiltrating the ranks and finding those who have second thoughts about colonial conquest. These key personnel will be supported in their efforts to challenge authority. After a few token assassinations of the most public military leaders, the rebels can set the example and discourage further genocide," Ann interjected. She wanted to avoid the idea of mind control so that all the nutcases wouldn't wear tin foil on their heads so the voices would come in more clearly. Any hint of mind control had to be minimized.

"So they're going to foment a revolution? How do they know so quickly who the ringleaders are? It isn't always the most famous political head," asked President Blake, letting his helplessness show a little.

"That's why Dr. Polo went himself. He is a famous sociologist among our people. He can analyze an entire society very quickly by studying their communications systems," Miguel commented. "Also, he doesn't need to know who the leaders are; he must know the people who do know and who have access to them. The lowest private knows who the general is, and if all the privates refuse to fight, the generals lose their power."

"He doesn't need a translator?" asked someone Ann didn't know.

Trust the guy with the thick accent to ask that question, she thought.

"No. He listened to the radio messages and learned the dominant tongues."

"I noticed that you greeted us all in our native tongues, and Mrs. Jacob said you speak twenty eight languages yourself," said President Blake. "Very impressive!"

"Yes. We learn languages very quickly," Miguel admitted humbly.

There was a few seconds of shocked silence as that sunk in.

"How many Monitors are here on Earth right now?" asked someone with a French accent.

"Very few besides myself and Dr. Polo. We have been observing your adjustments to the Yellowstone eruption which created many new problems that required new coping skills. We have also been doing some research on lung diseases which are the direct results of the Yellowstone Mega-volcano. Usually, we merely observe other worlds; we do not interfere," Miguel pointed out. "We are biologists, so that observation usually includes microbial and genomic studies."

"So you have helped the Americans after Yellowstone?" asked someone Ann did not recognize.

Here it comes. "The Americans were successful because they had outside help. Boo-hoo! You like them better than us!"

"No. Neither politically nor economically. We do not interfere in human affairs, even during disasters. We watch and study. In fact, we have had nothing to do with any political leaders, and, except for the Jacob family, we have not provided food or any type of aid to Americans." Miguel remained calm, although he had caught Ann's thought and looked aside to smile at her. "The reality of the situation is that the Jacobs helped us, not the other way around," Miguel said.

"I can vouch for that. The first time I became aware of any Monitors was a few days ago, during the bombing, when Dr. Polo and Mrs. Jacob asked my permission to intercede on our behalf. I assured him that our people would be most grateful if he would negotiate with the City Killers. We had been unsuccessful in our efforts to talk to them, or to retaliate. The Monitors have been straightforward with us. Completely. Dr. Polo came to me to ask permission to negotiate on our behalf." President Blake sounded utterly convinced that the Monitors were the good guys. Perhaps too much so. He sounded as if he might have been "brainwashed," he was so adamant.

"How would we know if we had been brainwashed? If they can change the minds of a whole conquering army, what might they have done to us?" asked another person Ann did not recognize. He sounded a trifle panicky, Ann thought.

Ann felt it was time she defended Miguel before they blamed him for everything bad that had ever happened to them down to and including the zit they wore to their senior prom. They were eager to find a scapegoat.

"Gentlemen, I will tell you exactly what I have told President Blake. You are correct in your assumption that we would be at the Monitors' mercy—completely. They are more advanced than we are in every way, which is precisely why we need not fear them. We have nothing they want. They can't be bought, seduced, blackmailed, or conquered. They just want to study us the way we study other species. We're interesting, but only in a primitive way. The only reason they have stepped forward and made themselves known is because a third party has attacked us, which they won't tolerate," Ann responded. "The Monitors consider the Vendens bullies, and they will put them in their place, and then back off again and leave us to live our own lives and make our own mistakes."

There was silence, so Ann continued. "You have nothing to fear from the Monitors. If you make demands on them, they would simply leave. They will let us fight each other like squabbling children until we grow up and learn to cooperate."

"You, too, could have been brainwashed, Mrs. Jacob," another voice said.

Miguel said something Ann did not understand because it was in another language which sounded like Russian.

"If they had brainwashed us, they'd have done a better job," Ann continued. "We are certainly not perfect people! But we have far too much to do to fight amongst ourselves now. We have cities to rebuild, diseases to cure, people to feed. Let's show them that we are worth saving."

"So how did you get to know the Monitors, Mrs. Jacob?" asked the Director of the FBI.

"They moved to Hanford before the Yellowstone Eruption, and we helped them get established in our town. We were just being good neighbors, and eventually they trusted us enough to ask our opinions of certain events. We are friends, and we help each other. And look—nobody's tried to take over the planet! Well, not until now, and it wasn't our friends, the Monitors."

"Is there anything more you could tell us about these Monitors, Mrs. Jacob?" asked a man whose name Ann had forgotten. He sounded Chinese, or from somewhere in the far East; she couldn't tell.

"Yes, I do. The Monitors are an ancient race. They were around over a million years, and we started to settle down in cities and towns less than 20,000 years ago. We weren't very interesting until just recently. The main reason they have been watching us closely is because we have made such rapid progress for being such a young species. The breakthroughs in the last century, I've been told by my Monitor friends, has been phenomenal. I am very proud of that. We will overcome the huge setbacks, both the Yellowstone mega-volcano and the attack of the City Killers. I'm sure because Marco Antonio would not have risked his life to save us if he had not been convinced that he has been observing the emergence of a great species who will soon take their place among the citizens of the cosmos," Ann said, and she turned to Miguel, this time for his support.

"Mrs. Jacob is correct, as she usually is," Miguel said, smiling at her.

"We will all say a prayer for Dr. Polo's swift recovery, and we thank him for his intervention. Thank you, too, Mrs. Jacob for arranging this call," President Blake said, clearly about to terminate the conversation.

"You're welcome. I must go pick up my grandson at soccer practice. I'll be in touch if there is any further news. Good bye, gentlemen," Ann said, and she hung up.

Ann had to take a few breaths. She had gotten a little carried away at the end. "I should have let you close the meeting, but I didn't want Blake to do it. That would give him way too much power. I just hope the headlines read, 'Soccer Granny Calls Meeting of Political Bigwigs' rather than 'President Blake Directs Interplanetary Conference Call.'" Ann sat back and tried to relax.

"You don't have to pick up Johnny for another hour, Ann," Miguel pointed out softly.

"I know. I was being petty, I guess. Mainly, I was getting emotional, and I didn't want to lose it in front of that 'good ol' boys' club. And I didn't want to listen to anything suspicious or threatening. They should be licking your boots, Miguel, not running around saying 'they're controlling our minds! They made me do it!'"

"Made you do what?" he asked.

"That's the whole point! They'd blame the Monitors for every mistake they've ever made since kindergarten! I just wanted them to come back down to earth a little. We still have to pick up kids from soccer practice, do the laundry, fix dinner. All that stuff. Life is made up of daily chores, not by interplanetary conference meetings."

Ann slumped in her chair and said, "Maybe I'm just reminding myself."

CHAPTER 15

Ann got busy packaging biological samples. She had compiled a list of universities with biological labs that were still functional and she wanted to get samples off to them to study as soon as possible. She knew that, at least during normal times, all the research that Marco Antonio, Miguel and their teams of Monitors had done would have to be replicated.

Of course, they were not going to wait for anybody's rubber stamp. Unlike most medicines, the microscopic worms and the bacteria which would accompany them would not have to be field tested; they had already been tested by the finest genetic engineers in the solar system, or the galaxy, for that matter. Nonetheless, Ann and Marco Antonio felt it was essential that the Earth's experts be apprised of the newest creatures in the realm.

The Monitors who had so recently been dancing in celebration were now being put to work building facilities in which the creatures could flourish. Designed to live in lungs, the sheer numbers required meant that more than just a few Petri dishes would be needed. Thousands of factory buildings all over the world would be constructed where shallow pans of blood would be kept warm and dark. By the time the blood coagulated, the tiny worms would have reproduced several times and then encapsulated due to dehydration. These would have mixed with bacteria within the blood which coincidently reproduced and encapsulated at approximately the same rate. The "coincidental" part had required several years and the expertise of the best genetic engineers doing thousands of trials to synchronize.

The blood could be from almost any animal, so the factories would be located near slaughter houses or butcher shops where pigs or cattle met their end.

The little beasties grew quickly when they were warm and had plenty to eat. Hoping to be blown away and inhaled by any passing animal with lungs after the encapsulation process, these friendly worms and bacteria were vacuumed up, packaged, and spread as far and wide as possible. This powdered cleansing agent was far too valuable and essential to be left to drift in the wind.

The original plan was to disperse them over cities, where human beings would be the first species to benefit from their lung-cleansing services, but the City Killers had altered that plan somewhat. Towns and villages would be flown over with small planes and balloons to spread the powdered cleansing agents to people who were unaware of what they were receiving from on high.

Ann wanted to develop much more sophisticated means of delivery, along with an information barrage on all the television stations, explaining what was happening. She wanted to have small aerosol spray bottles available to every school, office, or shop where people gathered. In addition, bottled nose-sprays needed to be sold at very low cost in every pharmacy or shop, hopefully with returnable bottles. The sick, the old, and the young should be served first, but total coverage was the goal.

Wildlife was at risk, too, as were long-lived creatures. Since lungs never stop collecting dust and obsidian, the longer the creature survived, the more likely would be its death from lung damage. Deer, wolves, bears, and coyotes would all suffer painful bone deformities caused by lung damage. Young children faced a lifetime of inhalation and a youthful, painful end from hypertrophic pulmonary osteoarthropathy just because they took so long to reproduce. To become fully educated usually took the first 25 years, and unless the custom of child marriages was reinstituted, most moms would have very thick, painful ankles and thick, ugly brows and jaws. There would be no grandmothers, since they would have died before grandchildren could be born. Eventually, mankind might very well become extinct.

Let's see...the population has gone from 7.2 billion to about 3 billion before our cities were bombed. That knocked out at least half the rest, so we're back down to about the population of the planet when Christ walked the Earth. That's in about five years.

Pondering mankind's problems, Ann heard a knock on her door. When she opened it, a well-dressed woman was standing there, briefcase in hand. Her hair was long, but neatly tied back in a low ponytail. She wore enough make-up to look like a professional: not so much she looked like a salesman, but more than a missionary.

"How do you do? I'm Casey Ranefield. Are you Ann Jacob?" Taken back a trifle by the sudden introduction and the fact that the woman knew Ann's name, Ann nodded, and the woman continued. "I've been sent here by the President to help you set up an office and to act as your legal counsel."

"President Blake did not inform me that you were coming, but please come in." Ann showed Ms. Ranefield in and sat down with her at the round game table in the living room. "What did Mr. Blake have in mind for you to do, exactly?"

"I understand that you are currently manufacturing a biologic cleansing agent for the treatment of lung conditions. I'm here to help you get set up. I'll handle the legal and business end of production, if that's all right with you. My services have been paid for by the government," she added.

"Well, good! I've been working to set up the production of the, uh, product, but I haven't gotten around to the bottling or distribution yet. Since this will be a world-wide project, it's a little daunting. I could use the help, but I'll tell you right now that I'm very hesitant to get involved with the government," Ann said.

"Why is that, Mrs. Jacob?"

"Government is synonymous for red-tape, and people and projects can get buried in that almost instantly. I would far rather work with the private sector to create a product we could make and sell at cost as quickly and cheaply as possible."

"That's exactly what I'm supposed to do. I'll keep you legal, but help you grow the business so that it gets up and running as quickly as possible. I understand that you are the president of a public benefit non-profit corporation in the state of California?"

"I am," replied Ann. "But I didn't intend for the two projects to overlap."

"OK. Good to know. Why don't you tell me what you had in mind as a marketing strategy for this project, so I can help you get it off the ground?"

Ann explained what she, Miguel and Marco Antonio had spent hours, days, and weeks discussing. Things that had been dreams had to become realities if people were to be saved. As Ann spoke, she became aware of what a huge task this was going to be. Somehow, she had assumed that Marco Antonio would be in charge of pulling his magic tricks and making it all just *happen*.

Ann and Casey spoke for over an hour, and Casey said she would return the next day with business plans, outlines for corporate structure, and lists of possible board members. She also said she would investigate office buildings and staff.

When Casey left, Ann walked downstairs with a pot of fresh tea for Miguel. He was right where she had left him, still processing the biological samples, getting them ready for shipment.

"Hi, Ann. Oh, tea—good!" he said, going to the downstairs refrigerator for the milk. He and Ann both preferred their tea "white," with milk. "I'm going to have Raul take his rover Euripides` and deliver these back east. Hopefully, he won't have to explain how they got from California to Massachusetts overnight if he's in a UPS uniform. Who was that?" he asked, handing her a cup with a little milk in the bottom and grabbing another for himself. He put four teaspoons of sugar into his cup before the tea was even poured into it.

"Euripides? The guys have really gotten into naming their rovers, haven't they? I love it!" Ann smiled, pouring tea into her cup as she watched Miguel spooning the sugar into his milk. *I'm going to have to get him a bigger sugar bowl.* "That was Casey Ranefield. The President sent her to help us set up the legal structure for the lung bugs."

"Speaking of names, we're going to need one for the 'lung bugs.' That term is inaccurate, Ann," Miguel corrected, smiling at her.

"Not a big seller, eh? I agree. Maybe we should put Raul on it. He came up with Euripides, which is Greek to me," Ann said.

"Euripides was a Greek name. Do you want a Greek name for the 'lung bugs'?"

So much for Shakespearean references. Oh, well. "Not particularly. Anyway, Casey sounds like a very smart young lady, and it was nice of the Prez to send us a paid-for consultant. We need one—I don't have a clue what I'm doing."

"What makes you think she's paid-for?" Miguel asked, a trifle incredulous.

"She told me so. She is at our disposal. Just a little Presidential perk for saving the world, I guess. Of course, she might be more trouble than she's worth if she starts generating tons of legal documents. Lawyers do that, you know," Ann said pensively. The more she thought about it, the more overwhelmed she felt. *I miss Marco Antonio! Thank God he's alive!* She thought her mental self-calming mantra again for the thousandth time that day. She stirred her tea, thinking.

"It is nice to have friends in high places, isn't it, Ann?" Miguel said. "Especially ones who can send you corporate lawyers."

"Amen!"

"That was not a prayer, Ann." Miguel sipped his tea, testing the temperature.

"No, I was just seconding your thought. It's sort of like saying 'I agree!'" she said absently, still stirring her tea. Explaining the obvious had become second nature to her years ago.

"Thank you for explaining things to me, Ann. By the way, I heard some news about Marco Antonio. He is doing very well. His legs are growing very nicely, and he is concurrently 're-booting' his brain with the help of his vial, which they received from Questor. His progress is exceptional, and they foresee a complete recovery." He took a big drink of his tea.

"That was fast! I expected it would take longer than a day for him to recover! I am so relieved, Miguel!" Emerging from her lethargy, Ann took a sip of her tea and then took a deep breath.

"So am I. Talking to all those people was difficult," he said.

"Well, you did very well! Dropping comments in several languages was a nice touch which, I think, added credibility," Ann said, just before she heard the back door slam and heard Johnny talking to someone. She looked at Miguel with guilt and surprise as she realized that she had completely forgotten to pick up her grandson after soccer practice. Wordlessly, she turned and ran up the stairs.

"Hi, Nana! Gabriel showed me some neat stuff at his house. Look at these spider eggs! Inside this ball there are *jillions* of them!" Johnny said.

"Oh, thank you, Gabe! I was talking to that lawyer, and I lost track of time!"

"No problem, Ann. Miguel remembered, and I figured Johnny would recognize me because we're old friends. Right, buddy?" he said, looking at Johnny.

"Show me the egg case, Johnny! How was your game?" Ann said, bending over to see a small fuzzy white ball. *That looks like a Black Widow egg case. Ugh!*

"Gabe got there early and got to watch me kick a goal! They called me Big Foot and I got to do a dance like this!" Johnny said, doing a victory dance that he'd probably spent more time rehearsing than he had the kick.

"Lookin' good, Johnny!" said Gabe. "Big Foot, eh? I'll have to remember that!"

"Did you learn to dance from your Mom?" asked Miguel, joining everyone in the kitchen. "She showed me a few moves, too," he said, moving his feet and hips in a recognizable dance move.

"Not bad, Miguel," Ann said. "Would anyone like some popcorn and lemonade?"

"Yeah!" said Johnny, doing another victory dance, just for good measure.

"You'll have to show me where you found that egg case, Johnny. I'd like to look at the mama spider," Ann said. "It might have been a Black Widow."

"Oh, it was!" Johnny gushed. "That's why Gabe showed it to me. Those spiders can *bite* , so I have to watch out for the mamas.

Sometimes they eat the daddies, too! That's why they're called 'widows' instead of 'witches.'"

Johnny wandered over to the microwave and watched the popcorn bag expand as it popped.

"I've got a movie about spiders taped, if you'd like to see other spiders. Some of them are *really* mean, but just to other bugs. They don't hurt us, like Black Widows do," Ann said, stirring the lemonade powder into the pitcher of water.

"I'll watch it, too!" Miguel said. "I'd like to learn more about spiders. I think they're cool, the way they make silk and webs." He took Johnny's hand and they started to walk into the den. "Maybe we should wash our hands before we eat popcorn. Mine are pretty dirty," he said as he examined his hands.

"I recorded it, if you want to go find it, Miguel. I'll bring in the popcorn and drinks in a minute," Ann said.

"I've got to go. Ruth has a bunch of chores for me, I'm sure. See you later, Big Foot!" Gabe said, and he left out the back door.

Just as he was leaving, Samantha came in. "Hi, Mom! Do you have a small beast here that you'd like to get rid of?"

"No. Actually, Big Foot was just about to watch a spider video with Miguel. Want some lemonade and popcorn?"

"Sure! I called Molly, and she and Jake are home with their eyes glued to computer screens. I said they could play games for one hour, since she said they both had their homework done. The English department meeting went quickly. I just had to hand out some info on the next 'Common Core' in-service, and listen to each one give their concerns. For once, nobody complained about anything! Woohoo!" Samantha raised one hand in a victory sign.

"If the first one doesn't start with a complaint, the others are far more likely to pass when it's their turn to gripe. Come on in and I'll tell you about the lawyer the President sent." Ann got ice from the refrigerator, poured one of the lemonade drinks into a sippy cup, and replaced the lid.

After they delivered the popcorn and lemonade to Miguel and Johnny in the den, Ann and Samantha got their own lemonade and sat down to chat in the living room. Within minutes, they were swapping outrageous stories and laughing.

It's good to hear her laugh again! Her load has been heavy since Aaron died. She has such a great sense of humor!

Soon Miguel appeared in the doorway, bringing his lemonade with him. "I thought I heard a party in here. May I join you? Johnny fell asleep."

I'll bet he had a little help in the snooze department. Miguel would far rather spend time with Sam than with Johnny. Good for him!

"Tell Miguel about the McClintock girl, Sam."

"It's the mom! I just wanted to tell her that if her precious daughter, whose almost my age now, was beaten up by her girlfriend, it was probably because her daughter was a bitch like her Mama! Even back in the day, girls didn't beat each other up unless they'd done something heinous. But Mama's innocent little angel was ferociously attacked by a vicious witch, the way Mrs. McClintock told it. I nearly lost it when she went on to tell everyone at the meeting that she actually went to the other girl's house and demanded that they pay for the visit to the doctor for a Band-Aid. If McClintock had done that today, she'd be wearing the other mama's ring on her cheek! Things have changed, and the mighty McClintock name doesn't carry the weight it did back when the McClintocks ruled the town. If one of them had pulled some of their uppity, holier-than-thou shit, and they would take her and her mother *down!*"

Sam took a sip of her lemonade and went on. "Can't you just see Mrs. McClintock huffing up to the door, banging on it, and having the girl's mama come to the door, her tattoos all sweaty, her nose ring dripping, saying, 'You want me to pay for WHAT?' I wanted to say, 'It's a different world out there, girlfriend. It might just be that your princess was taken down a peg because she's an uppity bitch like her mama!"

Ann was laughing so hard at Samantha's exaggerated accent and facial expressions that she nearly spilled her lemonade. Miguel laughed too, but he was laughing mainly because Ann and Sam were—their glee was contagious. They shared story after story about the meeting Sam had attended the night before with the scions of the city. Sam had grown up with their children, so she had intimate knowledge of the families' relationships to one another as well as their social connections throughout the last quarter of the twentieth century and the years before Yellowstone.

"You are so funny, Samantha! You can talk in so many accents and voices, you sound like different people. Do you not like these women?" Miguel asked as Sam finally prepared to gather up little Johnny and go home.

"Oh, I love each and every one of them! I can laugh at them, but nobody else but Mom is allowed to," Sam explained. "They built this town, actually."

"It's part of growing up in a small town, Miguel," Ann explained. "We're like a family, and most of us don't take each other too seriously."

"We laugh at those who do think they are all that and a bag of chips. And I needed a good laugh," Sam admitted.

"It is good to see you laugh with your mother," Miguel said.

"Actually, you've never seen us laugh together. I guess you've only seen me crying or dancing," Samantha quipped.

"Yes, and this is much better," Miguel said, and then quickly added "although you are a wonderful dancer!"

"Honey, you just saved yourself from a world of hurt! Don't even *imply* that I'm not a great dancer—I might have to hurt you!" Sam said.

The comm-box jingled, so Ann ran downstairs with a "Gotta get this!" Miguel carried Johnny as he walked Samantha out to the car. He put the sleepy child into his car seat and helped Johnny attach his seat belt.

Well, that went well! Good to see Sam happy. Widowhood sucks!

Breathlessly, Ann picked up the box in both hands, hoping it was Marco Antonio. Instead, she instantly got a clear picture of what a Venden warrior looked like, and it took her breath away.

Dinosaurs! They look like dinosaurs in Victorian costumes!

They are similar to some of your extinct species, yes.

Ann studied the picture that had appeared in her mind as clearly as if she were looking at a screen. She was "looking" at a T-rex with a floppy wig on. With closer inspection, what appeared at first to be long hair were ears hanging like a basset hound's. The snout and teeth looked like the T-rex, but above the hooded eyes was a square-ish dome much larger than any dinosaur head she had ever seen. The two eyes were large and set beneath heavy brows, which made it look like it was scowling. She could not tell if it had feathers or fur, but it was colorfully striped, much like a tiger or a zebra. At least its head was striped, because she could not see most of its body, which was covered in a breastplate of metal above a red shirt. Beneath the shirt was a skirt covering its legs and muscular tail.

Soon, another T-rex appeared in a different outfit. This one also had the breastplate armor, but it had an additional bright crimson cloak hanging from its shoulders. The cloak was trimmed in some kind of black fur, and the skirt appeared to be made from the same black fabric or fur. This one had its ears pulled back and connected with a scarlet ribbon, displaying holes beneath the ears. Two holes, in fact, one beneath the other. As the image rotated in her mind, Ann wondered what the holes were for.

The lower holes are nostrils for air intake, and the upper holes are ears. We have not had the opportunity to study them carefully, but that is what they told us. Note the lack of nostrils at the end of the snout. We have yet to ascertain its olfactory capabilities or its hearing acuity. Its vision is binocular and capable of perceiving well into the infrared range, so we presume its night vision is good.

Is there any way to get a drawing or photo of a Venden warrior? I would love a two-dimensional picture we could show on TV. Several different ones, in fact. It would mean a great deal to my people if we could put a face on our attackers. We would feel less helpless, and I don't think it's good for my people to feel like victims.

Would you like two dimensional pictures of the Trin and the Viodtzen as well? They are the native species of Kudtz, the first planets conquered by the Vendens. The Trin are the engineers whose technology was stolen by the Vendens and used by them to victimize the people of several planets.

Absolutely! Can you download pictures to my computer? May I send these pictures to the President and to the people of Earth?

They are on your computer now, along with written descriptions in English, French, Spanish, Mandarin and Russian in Cyrillic. You may distribute them worldwide if you choose.

I'd take videos, too, if you've got them.

Of course. You will be able to see how they move and communicate.

How is the situation progressing? Any encouraging updates I might add in my report to the President?

There have been many local changes in leadership. It will take many weeks to transport all Venden soldiers back to their home planet, but that process has begun.

Please add that to your written reports. That will encourage my people. Is Marco Antonio's recuperation progressing as hoped?

Yes.

May I talk to him? Is he conscious?

No. He is in stasis, which is the best place for his reconstruction to occur.

Please have him contact me as soon as he is able. His disability is very upsetting to me.

All right. He will be notified as soon as he regains consciousness; however, he may choose not to respond to you first. His knowledge must be shared as soon as possible. We, too, are anxious for his reports.

I understand. His companions here on Earth are all very concerned about his health. I would like to comfort them and ease their concerns as well. Hearing his voice would accomplish that instantly. I thank you for this update. I also thank you and all your people on behalf of every human on this planet.

Do you have that authority?

Yes, I do. I met today via communication devices with as many of the world's leaders as could be reached. The Venden attack did great damage to our communication systems, but we reached many of my planet's leaders directly, and the others have all been contacted by now, I'm sure. Would you like to speak directly to the President of the United States?

No. We wish to limit our contact.

That is what I was told by Marco Antonio. The only Monitors to directly speak to the humans have been Marco Antonio and Miguel. I am trying to maintain that situation, but I'm sure it will become increasingly difficult if the press corps becomes aware of where the information is coming from. That is why I have not contacted the news teams directly. I am allowing the political leaders to release the information to their people. Does that meet with your approval?

We wish to remain invisible, if possible. Would it be more convenient if we appointed one Monitor to speak directly to your leaders? When this situation has been dealt with, that Monitor will leave and terminate the relationship.

That would be far easier for me, but I do not want to lie to my people. They deserve to know that Monitors have saved them. Otherwise, they will live in constant fear that the Venden will return and rain bombs upon our cities again.

Since you have already reported to other political leaders, it is no longer possible to convince them that the Americans or the Russians or some international group of humans has eliminated the Venden threat. Is that correct?

Yes. Too many scientists know our level of development. It would be impossible to convince them that Americans chased them off. Besides, I do not wish to tell them untruths. Of course, if you gave us the technology for interstellar travel, we might convince most people that it was a human discovery under development at some secret facility that scared them off.

We do not disclose that level of technology. Each civilization must discover it on its own. If they are not ready, they become empire-builders, as the Venden have shown.

That's what I thought. You are very wise. We humans are at an awkward phase. We are too smart to lie to, but not smart enough to figure out hyperspace or how to protect ourselves. Establishing that humans chased them off would necessitate an extremely intricate scenario, and we could not convince people that we could discourage their return. Many will doubt that even the Monitors can prevent their future military activities.

"Awkward" could describe your situation and the relationship between the Monitor and human civilizations. However, the speed at which your knowledge is increasing is amazing. Your intelligence is still limited, but it is increasing. Your species is very young, and you have *made remarkable progress. This current generation has experienced a scientific emergence unmatched by any species we have thus far observed. Dr. Polo was correct in his assertions about the potential of your people.*

He's usually right, isn't he? By the way, your ability to converse with me has certainly improved! Thank you! My abilities are limited by my biological make up. I think mainly in words, but I'm trying to learn to understand more fully.

Your species will have to change biologically, which they will do eventually. Your brains are adapting rapidly to the many sources and the quantity of information now available to each individual. Young children know more than the wisest professors in universities a thousand years ago, and their brains learn differently and more rapidly than their ancestors' did. You have begun to genetically alter and improve many other species. Soon, you will improve your own.

I look forward to that. Not everyone on my planet thinks that is a good idea, so there will be some resistance, but it will be overcome eventually. Ah, here is Miguel! I will let you communicate with him, and I will get busy looking at the pictures. Thank you so much for releasing them to us! Good-bye!

Ann handed the comm-box to Miguel and turned to the computer screen next to her. She opened her e-mail and started looking at the pictures of the creatures of Venden and Kudtz. She was exhausted, mentally. She had received more telepathic messages in the last few minutes than she ever had before, and it made her rummy and sleepy.

For the next few minutes, I am the only human being who has ever seen extraterrestrial creatures. In four and a half billion years, I'm the only one. Now, I've seen four species from three different planets. Savor the moment, Annie.

She clicked through dozens of pictures on her laptop, studying each one, fascinated.

Wow! They look like cartoon characters! Check out those teeth! What an outfit! Freakin' dinosaurs in drag. Whoda thunk it!?

CHAPTER 16

Ann was glued to the computer screen for the rest of the evening. Miguel joined her, and together they studied the hundreds of pictures sent by the Monitors. They saw the houses, the streets, the "transports," which looked like flatbed, sideless vans and the tuk-tuks Ann had seen in India, but without seats. To accommodate the long, thick Venden tails, there was only a flat platform.

From the waist down, the Venden looked like kangaroos, but from the waist up, they looked like meat-eating dinosaurs with long, muscular arms and clawed hands. Their teeth looked sharp, and their raptor-like jaws made it obvious they were meat-eaters and gave them a distinctly dinosaur, T-rex appearance. Dressed in colorful clothing and sweeping coats and cloaks, their skin looked hairless and was either striped or black. Their large eyes sat beneath heavy brows near the front of their heads, but their ears were long and to the back, usually hanging down like hair beneath their domed heads. Not obvious at first glance, they had no nostrils, but they had flaps along the sides of their necks which hung beneath their ears. Miguel proposed that the nostril and ear covers suggested they might have evolved to protect them in windy conditions.

Although the Vendens looked like buffed, wigged raptors in drag, the Trins looked like teddy bears with long snouts and hands. They walked upright, but they had short legs with backward knees, big heads, and short fur. Their coats were mousy gray-brown, and most wore no clothes except for a colored tie some wore around their necks. They had small, sharp teeth, but their mouths didn't look dangerous. Their eyes were very large, as were their teddy-bear ears, and their skulls were too big for their bodies. There didn't seem to be any difference between males and females, unless the pictures were all of the same sex. Whatever sex organs they possessed were invisible, so it was impossible to tell.

The third species seemed to avoid urban settings since all the pictures of them were in rural areas. They were probably a related species of the Trin, but their heads were smaller and their fur seemed matted into a shell across their shoulders, hips, chests, and thighs. They were darker than the Trin, but they shared the same big eyes and short legs with backward knees. They were frequently seen on all four legs, but they appeared to walk upright most of the time.

There was so much to see and analyze, and they spent an enjoyable evening discussing the sights. Just the clothing and body adornments, coupled with the bodies themselves told so much about the cultures of each creature. Ann and Miguel swapped guesses about how these creatures lived, what they ate, how they communicated. They were both anxious to see how close their conjectures were to the actual conditions of these creatures.

The time flew by, and soon it was past dinner and rapidly approaching bedtime. Ann and Miguel said good-night, and both wandered to their own refrigerators for a snack before bed.

The pictures gave Ann something to think about besides Marco Antonio before she went to sleep. She was tempted to send all the photographs to CNN, but then she thought that SETI deserved to see them first. They'd been the most dedicated towards the belief that we are not alone. If she sent them to the President, they might end up in the CIA's Top Secret files. Sending them to YouTube would guarantee that they were seen by millions, but people might be convinced that she was making this all up, and it was just a hoax. Others would be terrified and react to the Zombie Apocalypse they expected any day.

A dinosaur in a red velvet coat, trimmed with gold braid. Really? Yeah, even I wouldn't believe that, unless I was already dating an octopus. Oh, Anniegirl, you are truly weirded-out now!

Ann decided that she did not want reporters swarming all over her house and yard, which is what would happen once the word was out that Monitors lived here with her. Totally exhausted, she went to sleep and hardly moved for the next eight hours.

Early the next morning, Ann called the White House number and within minutes was connected to President Blake.

"Hello, President Blake!" Ann said exuberantly. She was excited, and she wanted to sound excited.

"Hello yourself, Mrs. Jacob! It's always good to hear from you, but right now, your call is especially welcomed. You sound like you have good news, and believe me, I could use some at the moment." He sounded friendly, and he was very good at making someone feel special just for calling him.

"I have some pictures of our enemies I'd like to share with you, as well as some pictures of the other people, well, creatures they have victimized and enslaved," Ann said. She could have sent them last night, but this morning was soon enough. Besides, she wanted to savor the moments of being the first.

Petty, perhaps, but I needed to feel a little special.

"I'd love to see them!" the President responded, letting his excitement show. "How did you get them?"

"Well, I need to talk to you about that, sir. They're from my friends, the Monitors." This was the difficult part, explaining where these pictures came from and how they got here.

"Do they not want to share them publicly?" The President sounded cautious.

"Oh, yes. The pictures have been sent to the people of this planet. That is not the problem. The problem is mine, Marco Antonio's, and Miguel's." Ann answered, hoping Mr. Blake could figure out what she wanted.

"You don't want to be named as the source, right?"

"Exactly. I don't want to wake up tomorrow and see journalists all over my front lawn. We have other fish to fry here, President Blake, and we can't get it done if we're in the public eye." She didn't want to threaten him, but she wanted a guarantee of anonymity before she released them.

"I see. I'll just say they were e-mailed directly to me by the Monitors. I can keep your name out of it, if you would prefer."

"Perfect. No one else has seen these pictures, and I think it would be best if you just say they are directly from the Monitors, who contacted you shortly after the bombings and offered to help." Ann thought that was almost too easy. She doubted that the President could keep a hacker from tracing the e-mails back to her, but it was nice of him to try. Besides, it gave him the illusion of power, which she thought was a good idea.

"I could say that." admitted the President. "No one else has to know who Dr. Polo's friend is, and they don't have to know about Miguel at all."

"I don't think they have to know that the Monitors have been observing Earth for several years. They could have been observing the Vendens, who are the ones who attacked us and the people of Kudtz," Ann continued, knowing she was name-dropping. "They could have reached out to us and offered us their help."

"A lot of people on that submarine saw you and Dr. Polo, but it was not discussed amongst the crew. Besides being an unusual landing ship, everyone else looked human. I think we could simply stonewall any discussion of you and Dr. Polo, and they'll just assume you're both human first contacts. Now, what about the people of Kurtz?"

"It's Kudtz. There are two species there that the Vendens have enslaved, and another planet that has remained as yet unnamed. OK, here's the deal as I hear it: I'll e-mail the pictures and descriptions to whatever computer you want me to, and you make the general announcement. Let the photos and info go to CNN, NBC, or wherever you choose, but they're coming from you."

"Right."

"Now, how do I go about sending them without having them easily tracked back to my home computer? I could put everything onto a flash drive and deliver that to you, if that would be more secure. I'm not too good at this spy thing, Mr. President."

"Neither am I, but I certainly do know people who are. Let's let them do their jobs. I will try to minimize the fact that there are Monitors living among us, although I would very much like to know more about that, just for national security's sake," he amended his offer to "minimize" the Monitors' presence.

Ann knew that there would be a tidal wave of interest as soon as the news of an off-world presence was made known. There had been tales of UFO sightings for decades, and the people would be rabid about seeing Marco Antonio and Questor. Secrecy would be extremely difficult, and tales of sightings would become flagrantly imaginative. Ann feared a carnival atmosphere; the Monitors would think it was childish and undignified for so many people to lie so blatantly.

What would I have done to meet someone from another world? Just about anything. I would have looked like a teenager at a Beetles concert.

"I understand, and I expected that you would want to meet again. We're not sneaking around. We were in a scientific experiment, and as the subjects of the experiment, we have to remain unaware of being observed. Besides, I have other tasks to do, and having to answer a bunch of questions would slow me down enormously," Ann pointed out. *We have a planet to cure here. No time for adulation.*

"What I'd like to do is just sit down to a leisurely lunch with you so you could tell me the whole story. Bring Dr. Olivas or Dr. Polo or any Monitor you choose, and we can just get acquainted. You have knowledge I really want to know, and you know people I'd very much like to talk to."

"OK, but not now. I'm going to put these pictures onto a flash drive and have it physically delivered to you by Fed Ex. Where do you want me to send it?" Ann asked, becoming a little irritated. She just wanted things to be simple, but they rarely were.

Secrecy's a bitch!

"That will take several hours, if not days, even by diplomatic courier. Is there an internet café in Fresno or Bakersfield you could get to? That would mask your address, and you could send it from a different account. Send it to prez.mikeblake@gmail.com."

"OK. Check in ten minutes, and you'll be looking at creatures from a different solar system. I'm going to ask you for your first impression when I talk to you next, so please remember it. I think we'll share a couple chuckles. Call me back!"

That last sentence made it sound like they were teenagers, but it was easier for him to get through to her than vice versa.

Oh well. He's the Prez. I'm sure he's used to it.

Ann decided to talk to Miguel, and let him figure out the cloak and dagger stuff. When she went back downstairs, Miguel was again holding the black comm.box. She sat down quietly until he was through.

"Anything else I need to know, Miguel?" Ann asked.

"Not really. What did the President have to say?"

"He gave me his personal e-mail, and we can send the pictures to him, but I don't want them coming from our computers. Any computer hacker worth his salt could trace them back to us and be at our door in ten minutes. Can you hide where the pictures came from?" Ann asked.

"Of course. What's his address?" Miguel glanced at it, picked up the comm.box again, and said, "There. He has the full report. It came from an office in southern Oklahoma."

"Oh, Miguel, I should have known you could do it with the flip of your wrist! I've decided to just let the President handle it. He's agreed to keep us out of it. I told him I didn't want anyone to know that the Monitors have been living here and watching us for a long time. Every conspiracy buff would be telling stories about how they met you in dark alleys and you took them off in your space ship and did weird and unlikely things to their body."

"Some of them might be true," he said, smiling like Simon Legree.

"Only the vampire stories," Ann said, returning his leer. "And only involving you, Mr. McWeirdo!"

"My days in dark alleys are over. Now I spend my time in dark basements."

Instantly, she became aware of how long he'd been down here working. "Are you going stir-crazy in here, Miguel? Do you need to go check on your stable of old ladies? Or just get out of here for a while?" Ann was making reference to Miguel's many friends whom he visited regularly for blood donations. Most of them had become his friends who looked forward to his visits as some of their only social contact.

"I should go check up on them. I haven't visited them since the attack, and they might be anxious. If you're OK for now, I think I will take a walk and stop in on Mrs. Wilson and Mrs. Sanchez, at least." He started to tidy up the table, and he put the comm-box back in the drawer. It was programmed to ring like an old fashioned telephone, but he still liked to keep it out of sight.

"Casey's due here any minute, and she and I have a lot of work to do. Plus, the President is due to call any minute. Go—you need to blow the stink off!" she said, and then quickly amended her quip "I meant that fresh air would be good for your spirits. It's something my mother used to say, and it has nothing to do with your body odor. Sorry!"

"I knew I bathed this morning, so you were just being a wise-ass," Miguel said, feeling very smug about using that term.

"Oh, just listen to your smart mouth! Calling me, a sweet old lady, a wise-ass! I'll have to clean your mouth out with soap if you keep up the smarty comments!"

"You can take it. Toughen up, Grandma!" he said as he grabbed his coat, a big smile on his face.

"Out! Out, you young whippersnapper!" she said, smiling. She could hear the doorbell ring, so she followed him upstairs. Casey was there, and she came in as Miguel left.

Ann and Casey sat down at the game table as they had the day before, and instantly, Casey was showing Ann the business plan she had worked out. Ann was impressed, and soon they were deep into planning. They worked all afternoon, ignoring the telephone's constant ringing after Ann answered the President's call. When she saw who it was, she had taken the call in her bedroom.

"I've looked over the pictures you sent me, and they were fascinating!" said the President.

"The Vendens look like dinosaurs in drag, don't they?" said Ann, smiling.

"You'll never hear me say that, but that was my first impression, too. They look like mean dinosaur dolls that little girls have dressed up in Barbie doll formal wear! They look silly."

"Good one! I thought you'd get a kick out of them. We're about the only ones who can afford to laugh at them, so I thought we should. From now on, we'll have to take them very seriously, I suppose," Ann said. It felt good to have a secret with such an important person. He was beginning to feel like a friend.

I'd better not let Marco Antonio hear that little thought. I'd be soothing his ruffled feathers for weeks.

"I don't know. Nothing makes something less scary than laughter," the President replied. "Now, the Trin look like they could be evil little bastards."

"I agree. Those sharp little teeth look like they'd nip you if you pet them. Those are the ones we'll probably have to deal with, you know. They're very intelligent, with no sense of humor or imagination. Very dangerous, indeed. What's more, I don't think the Monitors have grounded them like they have the Venden. We'll see," Ann said, and after a momentary pause, she added, "Maybe we'll get to meet them one day. Well, I'll let you go. I just wanted to hear your take on the big, bad T. Rexes in their velvet capes. Thanks for calling, Mr. President. Good bye."

"Thanks, Ann," he said absentmindedly. He was studying the pictures, she could tell.

That evening, Ann called Ruth to see how many Monitors were still working in her basement.

"Ten? You and Gabe make twelve?" Ann felt shocked and a little ashamed that she had ignored them all day. "What did they eat for lunch?"

"I don't know," Ruth answered. "They found things to eat in the kitchen, I guess." Typically, no one had taken the responsibility to fix a meal. Food was a very low priority item for the Monitors. They lived off the dollar menu and big boxes of cereal.

"How about if I order Chinese delivered?" Ann suggested. "We can help ourselves and watch the news on TV, or I can download all the pictures to anyone who hasn't seen them yet. Whatever," Ann said, feeling a little overwhelmed by the prospect of feeding another dozen people when she hadn't taken time to fix anything but peanut butter sandwiches for herself.

"Good idea! Order Chinese, and see if Miguel will play bridge. Gabe and I are willing and able to spend an evening watching you go down," Ruth said.

Ann smiled at the double entendre, but the smile died with a sudden intake of breath. "Oh my God! I've got to play bridge tomorrow! I've got to get on the horn and find a substitute! I don't want to get away from the phone until I hear from Marco Antonio again. Besides, I've got meetings with the Prez tomorrow morning, and a contractor, and a trucking company."

"Where's bridge?" Ruth asked.

"Let's see. It's at Judy Hansen's house, unless it's been cancelled," Ann noted, checking the calendar.

"I'll go. I need to get out of the house and away from all these damn Monitors. Some of them have absolutely no social skills! They act like they have Asperger's Syndrome! Were we ever like that, Ann?" Ruth asked innocently.

Ann had to smile. "Gabe was worse than you, but you were both a little, shall we say, awkward. You've come a long way, Baby!"

"Do think I could cut it? I don't want to say or do anything 'awkward' and not even know it. If we were this bad, I don't know how you put up with us!" Ruth sounded like she really needed to get away from everyone for a while. Being hostess for a dozen child-like people would wear anyone down.

"I think you'll do fine at Judy's. Thank you! That's another dozen phone calls I don't have to make. I'll check my e-mail to see if bridge has been cancelled, and I'll call the Chinese Kitchen. Any d'ruthers?" Ann asked, relieved.

"No, just order plenty of it, so there are leftovers. They can eat rice for the next week! Call me when it comes, and I'll march everybody over with their own plates."

Ann called their favorite Chinese restaurant, and ordered huge piles of food. The next night, she ordered Mexican food, and the next night they had hamburgers, which proved to be a bad choice because there were no leftovers for lunch the next day. Every morning, Ann made a big pot of oatmeal, and there was plenty of bread for toast. Lunch was warmed-over whatever. Miguel fended for himself.

Before long, the week was over, and there was still no word from Marco Antonio. Ann felt like the phone had become part of her body. President Blake wanted daily updates, as did the Defense Department and Homeland Security. Ann tried to put Miguel in charge of relaying the progress of the war, but he needed help. Ann also had a complete production and delivery system to build. She felt like she was being nibbled to death by ducks.

The only thing that saved her sanity was the money available to her. She had stopped trying to save or conserve Marco Antonio's funds. He had told her that money was no object, and she was beginning to act like it.

Ann called Lieutenant Commander Marshall. "Hello. This is Ann Jacob. Is this Lieutenant Commander Nick Marshall?"

"It's Commander Marshall now, thanks to you, and please call me Nick. How can I be of service, Mrs. Jacob?"

"We need some help, Nick. Miguel is receiving the updates from the front, but he has some difficulty explaining things online to the brass. Could you come to my house and give him a hand? I'll supply the coffee and wine," Ann said, in case her phones were monitored. "*War Craft* is a tough game."

"*World at War* is too. It's the game most of us are playing these days," he replied. "I can come now if you're up and playing."

"Wonderful! I'll put on the coffee," Ann said.

He was there in ten minutes, once again in his uniform.

Ann met him at the door. "Come in, Commander. And congratulations on the promotion! You look wonderful, but the next time you come, please come in civvies. The neighbors will start to wonder why I have a Commander hanging out here. If you're in regular clothes, they're less likely to be noticed." She turned and walked into the living room, and Marshall was right behind her.

"Duly noted. I will notify the President that I was requested to look like a civilian," he said.

"If you have an extra uniform shirt and tie, you could leave one here and get all duded up if you have to Skype him. He won't see what pants you have on, and you can just walk out in your tee-shirt and jeans. That way you'll always look very official, which I understand is important, since everything will be taped for posterity." She sat down in the big armchair in the living room, and the Commander sat on the couch across from her. He looked very formal and a trifle uptight.

"Sounds like a good plan to me, Ann. Now, how can I help?" He looked eager, and she realized that she had ignored him for almost a week.

Ann explained the difficulties of perceiving things in four dimensions and five senses and relating them in words. With Skype, Miguel had the additional aide of facial expressions and hand gestures, but it would still take skill. Marshall had a face that was easy to read, but Miguel still lacked the emotional nuances human faces use to accomplish the majority of their communication.

The Commander asked, "What sort of communication system do you use? It sounds really new."

"Come downstairs, and I'll show you," Ann explained.

Miguel was just closing the refrigerator door when Ann came down with Nick Marshall. "Hello, Ann. Oh, the Lieutenant Commander! Hello!"

"Miguel, Nick here has just had a promotion! He's a full Commander now!"

"Congratulations!" Miguel smiled, but didn't move.

"Miguel, I think it's time you shake hands with the Commander and explain a few things to him about how the war is going. He'll be helping you make clear to President Blake and the Joint Chiefs of Staff and Homeland Security and whoever else needs to know just how the Venden Retreat is coming along," Ann said, and then backed up so that Miguel could reach across Ann's body to shake the officer's hand. Nick Marshall's eyebrows shot up and he smiled a crooked smile. He didn't drop his hand until Miguel did, but then Nick gave a brief nod.

"Got it!" he said. "Please tell me more about yourself, sir. I find you fascinating!"

Ann smiled and remembered the thrill she had felt when she had first been introduced to Gabriel and had learned that he and Ruth were extraterrestrials. It was still the greatest single turning point of her life; everything had changed at that moment. All of her silly concerns about daily tasks had become trivialized in that second, and she knew that she was put on this earth to help these people and her own people succeed. She had instantly devoted her life to that cause.

Although she had often wondered whether they had placed that devotion and determination into her mind, she didn't think so. It was *her* devotion, not *theirs*. In fact, the Monitors had always been surprised at her determination. To Ann, it was simple: history had made it hers to do.

Well, history had stepped up and tapped Nick Marshall on the shoulder. She saw it in his face: the gratitude, the acceptance, and the determination not to fail. He would take his uniform off and work in his skivvies if that was required. He would fight and die unknown, if that was required. He would wave in tickertape parades, if that was required. Fame and fortune, love and hate, prominence or ignominy no longer mattered. He would do what was required of him to see that the Monitors would lead his planet and people into legend.

Ann knew exactly how he felt, because that's how she felt. Blessed beyond belief, she had been given the opportunity to make a difference on a biblical scale. Marco Antonio didn't really understand why she felt so blessed, but Nick Marshall would. He felt it, too. Her kids didn't. Oh, they were vaguely aware that they were in a unique position, and it was really cool to personally know the Monitors, but it wasn't to the same depth as Ann and Nick felt it.

After a few moments of holding Miguel's hand, receiving information directly, Nick got on line and reported to the Joint Chiefs of Staff, who would then notify the President, the DOD, and HLS. He spoke eloquently, but explained the situation clearly. He explained how the Vendens had overpowered the people of Kudtz, and then had utilized the Trin to develop other military and ship designs. The Trin had no interest in conquest, but design, math, and mechanical engineering fascinated them, so they were not difficult to coerce. Without a cultural heritage of moral, honorable, or ethical training, their major principles and values circled mainly around research and educational honesty. To the Trins, people come and go, but a good discovery lasts forever.

Commander Marshall returned several times to Miguel with specific requests. He wanted maps of all the Venden command posts on all the worlds they had conquered, and he wanted detailed reports of how the retreat was coming along.

Miguel tried to obtain this information from the Monitors overseeing the Venden Retreat, as it was being called, and they tried very hard to comply. Explaining things to Commander Marshall was much easier than explaining things on a conference call with the Joint Chiefs and the President because Miguel could touch Marshall's mind directly, and Marshall could then explain it in the common military jargon.

Ann liked Commander Marshall, and she knew his career was getting a big boost by being the liaison to the military experts on the east coast. So many had been pulverized at the Pentagon or on the bases like Norfolk and Lemoore Naval Air Station that the entire military defense system was on its knees. One of the major jobs of the staff left was to locate whatever military personnel were still alive. There weren't many, and Marshall's star was shining brightly across the continent and around the world.

Ann could see the fatigue in Marshall's face as his brain's neurotransmitters ran low. "Nick, you need to rest now. Go home and get some sleep, so your brain can rest."

"No, I'm fine. There's so much to learn, and it takes time to explain everything Miguel shows me. I can't quit now. Besides, I'd just go back to my hotel room, where it's really depressing. I'd much rather stay and work with Miguel."

"Did you live on base?" Ann asked.

"Yes ma'am."

"Did you have family there?" Ann asked, afraid of the answer.

"Yes. A wife and two kids," he said, instantly tearing up. He blinked his eyes, looked to the floor, and said, "Sorry," as if he'd done something wrong.

Ann could tell instantly that everyone in his family was dead. "I'm so sorry! Please let Miguel help you. I know the horrendous pain you're in right now, and he can help you to deal with it. Why don't you take a little rest in that little room right over there," she said, pointing to one of the tiny bedrooms she had built in the basement for visiting Monitors. "You can take a nap, refresh your neurotransmitters, and have dinner with us tonight. We're having spaghetti. Simple, but you're welcome to it."

"I am tired. That sounds a lot better than just sitting in that room thinking about my family. It's been tough, but I'm not the only one who's lost people." He was trying valiantly to get control of his emotions, but his eyes kept welling up. It was further evidence to her that his brain was exhausted and his neurotransmitters were low and completely out of balance.

"No, you're not alone, but that's small comfort. I know this is going to sound weird, but please let Miguel kiss you on the forehead. He has chemicals in his saliva that will numb your pain for a few hours so you can sleep," Ann said.

"If it were anyone else, I'd say 'no,' and 'hell, no!' But I've seen what he is, and I'd trust both of you with my life. If you think that's what I should do, then I'll do it."

Miguel had been sitting across the lab table listening to the whole conversation, and he said nothing. He just spit into his hand and reached across the table to shake Nick's hand. "That silly woman doesn't know that men don't kiss each other."

Nick took his hand and shook it, smiling shyly.

Ann smiled too and said, "And all this time I thought you were kissing me for a reason!"

"I was. Just not the reason you thought!" Miguel said, winking at Nick, who smiled. Ann smiled, rolled her eyes, and shook her head.

"Come on. Let's put you to bed before your face hits the table," Ann said, leading the Commander to the tiny bedroom. "If you want to take your uniform off, you can put it on that chair and keep it pressed. I promise not to peek," she said. "I'll call you for dinner."

"Thanks, Ann. I appreciate this."

"No problem. Sleep tight!"

CHAPTER 17

Ann had decided to cook, so she sent Raul to the grocery store with a short list: bread, salad in a bag, Italian dressing. She had meat balls in the freezer, jars of marinara sauce, and pounds of spaghetti. She was filling the big soup pot with water when she heard the back door open. She looked up, expecting to see Raul with an armload of groceries, but Marco Antonio was wiping his shoes on the rug.

"Honey, I'm home!" he said quietly, but in the lilt men have used since Ricky Ricardo greeted Lucy in the 1950s.

Ann just stood there in shock as the water kept filling the pot. Calmly, she shut off the water, turned to him and started to cry. "Oh, thank God!" she said, and walked into his arms. They just stood near the washing machine holding each other and rocking gently.

I've missed you so, Marco! I am so glad you are home, my love!

I've been a bit stretched out. I was unconscious most of the time, or I would have called every day. As soon as I was out of stasis, I came back home. I've missed you, too, querida.

Ann could feel love emanating from him, but it was different, less intense. She could tell that he had changed in some way she could only guess at, but it was there. Overwhelmed with relief, she was happy to have him holding her again.

"Are you hungry? I think Miguel has something in his refrigerator that I could warm up, or you could feed off me."

"I do need to feed, but not from you. I might take too much. Please go ask Miguel if he has something for me. I think I'll go lie down," he said, looking down at her. He kissed her forehead.

"Lean on me, and we'll get you tucked in. Then, I'll go see what I can rustle up for you," she said. "I would have met you in Questor, as we agreed. I would have brought plenty of blood. I know how hungry you are when you first transfer bodies," she said, and then decided to shut up before she started scolding him.

He was weak, she could tell. He did lean on her until they entered the hall, where it was too narrow. He made it to his side of the bed and lay down fully dressed on top of the comforter. She took his shoes off and put his feet on the bed.

"I'll be right back. Rest." Ann turned and walked as quickly as she could downstairs, where she hustled directly to Miguel's refrigerator. There was only one pint of blood, and she took it. Miguel would awaken hungry, too, and he would have to go visit some of his friends to feed. She felt guilty taking his last packet of blood, but she knew he would have insisted if he'd been awake to ask.

She came upstairs and popped the blood into the microwave. She gave it only 40 seconds, which would make it about lukewarm. Close enough—he didn't like it hot, anyway. It was very hard to hit 98.6 degrees exactly.

Ann walked in and handed Marco Antonio the plastic bag. He scooted over so she could sit beside him, which she did. He put his finger into his mouth and withdrew his syringe needle from his cheek and poked it into the bag. The needle expanded in both width and length, and he drank deeply. She knew he didn't like to be watched feeding, but she just couldn't keep her eyes off him. He was actually home! Her mantra changed from "He's alive!" to "He's actually home! He's here! Oh, thank God, he's home!"

"You sound very relieved, Ann. I am, too," he said when he finished the blood in the bag. "Is there more?"

"No, but I'm here." She took the bag from his hand, but didn't move.

"No. I'll wait, and go out later if Miguel's not here." He put his head back down on the two pillows. She grabbed the pillow from her side of the bed, and put it under his head so he could sit up a trifle higher. She wanted to look at his face, every inch of it.

"There's a Commander downstairs sleeping, and Ruth has ten healthy Monitors next door who would all be willing and honored. I would rather it be me. I nursed all three of my children, and I miss feeding someone I love," she said, running her fingers down his cheeks, feeling the stubble. She put her knee on the bed, straddled him, and rolled over him to lie beside him on the inside of the huge bed.

"Perhaps in a moment. Let this circulate a little, so I do not drain you."

"I'm here, which is just where I want to be," she said, snuggling into his side.

"So tell me about the sleeping Commander," he said, completely without rancor, as if he had merely inquired about her day.

A trifle relieved that he wasn't jealous, Ann was about to explain Commander Marshall's role as the phone rang. Ann reached over to her nightstand, picked up the phone, and said, "It's the President. Let me take this, Sweetheart." Without waiting for his response, she pressed the green button and replied, "This is Ann Jacob."

There was a few moments of silence as she was connected, and then she said, "Hello yourself, Mr. President! How nice of you to call!" She listened silently, and then explained, "The Commander and Miguel are both resting. They have been working very hard, and I insisted they sleep for a few hours. The good news is that Marco Antonio is home and well....Yes, he's resting, too. We're about to have dinner.... That's great! I'm so relieved for you....I know. It's difficult.... I'll have the Commander call you as soon as he's awake. What would be a good time for you? Uh huh." The conversation continued for several minutes, with Ann just making general grunts of acknowledgement. At last, she said, "Hang in there. I'll give Marco Antonio your greetings, and I'll have the Commander call you back in a couple hours. Yes. Yes. All right, you too. Good-bye."

"Well, he was quite chatty. Does he call often?" Marco Antonio asked.

"Daily, but it's for war news," she said, trying to avert his jealousy.

"No, it's not. It's because he's smitten with you. Too bad for him," he said, rolling over towards her. "Can I have my snack now?" he asked. He looked at her hungrily.

"Should I lock the doors? I'm having thirteen for dinner in less than an hour, but they can wait." Ann well remembered how he rewarded women for feeding him, and just the memory made her want to purr.

"No. Let me feed a little bit, and I will ravish you slowly when we have time and I have the strength to do a proper job." He rolled onto his side and began to nuzzle her neck.

"I hate sloppy ravishing," she whispered. "Just hold me, feed, and I will go do scullery duty while you rest. Everyone will want to see you, and I'd hate to tell them that you were over-ravished and exhausted." She put her chin to the side, giving access to her neck. She felt a gentle pressure, but there was no feeling of an incision or pinprick. "I love you, Marco Antonio," she whispered as he fed.

I love you, too, querida. You still are the most delicious person I have ever tasted.

Sinful.

Yes, sinful. It's hard to stop. You're too scrumptious.

He lifted his head, pulled out his straw, and lowered his head to her neck to kiss her. When he did, he sent her an intense orgasm that rocked her world.

"Ohhhh. Thank you, sir!" she said, suddenly breathing through her mouth.

"Miguel is not the only one who can do that, you know," he whispered into her ear. She didn't respond, and he knew she was enjoying the moment.

"I think I'll rest, and you go cook," Ann said with a deep sigh.

"I'll help," he said. "Just give me another minute or so," he said, putting his head down onto the pillow next to her.

"No, you rest. I'll call you when everyone's here, or at least when they start to come in. I just have to boil water and open a jar or two," she said, still breathing through her mouth with her eyes half closed.

"Most women I've known would have been cooking for hours and be completely at their wits' end by now. You're calmly lying in bed, enjoying a languid orgasm. You never cease to amaze." She could hear the smile in his voice, but she could also hear the fatigue. Clearly, he had returned to Earth before he had completely recuperated, which both worried and thrilled her.

"Yeah, I'm the world's best water-boiler and jar opener. You just keep believing that's cooking, my dear. I've got you completely snowed."

"Completely."

Good!

She didn't want to get up or go cook. Even if he fell directly to sleep, she wanted to lie next to him, put her head on his chest and her leg over his, and revel in his touch. It had nothing to do with sex; it had to do with missing him, and finally having him home.

She heard the back door open, and hoped it was Raul. He could lift the heavy pot of water out of the sink for her. She got up, and patted his leg as she rose.

Sleep tight, lover. I want you strong.

CHAPTER 18

Ann bustled around in the kitchen, fixing the spaghetti. She threw in a bag of frozen meatballs into three quart jars of marinara sauce and let it simmer so the meatballs would heat completely. She washed six eggs and put them into the spaghetti as it boiled in the big pot. No point in under-using boiling water. She would peel the eggs once they were hard, slice them, and add them to the salad.

Peering into the refrigerator, she saw that there were few vegetables left, but there were two apples, so she sliced them up, cubed them, and put them into the salad, too. Taking a mug down, she put a cube of butter into it, melted the butter in the microwave, added some garlic powder and a little dried parsley, and then spread it on two large loaves of French bread which had been sliced lengthwise. She put some grated cheese on two of the bread halves, but left the other two with just the seasoned butter. She popped the bread into the broiler, set the timer, and decided the eggs were hard boiled, so she ran them under cold water after twirling them on the counter to see if they were done, knowing that hard boiled eggs will spin, but uncooked eggs will fall over quickly onto their sides. These spun. She tested the spaghetti, but it was still a little "boney," as her grandfather had called it. She poured a little olive oil into the boiling water and stirred the spaghetti so it wouldn't get sticky.

She wanted to make sure that Miguel brought home extra blood, so she called him on his cell phone. Normally, he enjoyed chatting with his friends and doing small favors for them, but today, she didn't want him to lollygag.

Marco Antonio's home! He's alive, and well, and home! Yippee!

Ann hadn't enjoyed cooking—hadn't enjoyed *anything* this much—since Marco Antonio had left. She felt as if a cloud of responsibility had been lifted from her shoulders, and the relief made her steps light. When everything was done, she put the food on the dining room table and called Ruth. A few had drifted in, their plates and silverware in hand, and the rest soon followed. They helped themselves to the spaghetti and salad, choosing whichever salad dressing they preferred.

Marco Antonio walked from the bedroom through the kitchen as if he'd never left. Ruth put her plate down and hugged him, and Gabe let out a cheer, which the others followed. The mood in the whole house had changed; it was as if the City Killers had never appeared, and the party had picked up where it had left off when the glass had blown into the living room and millions of people had died. Not since death had rained down upon them had anyone truly smiled.

Into this happy throng walked Commander Marshall. He looked at the dozen or so people standing in the dining room and kitchen holding plates of spaghetti and salad, trying to all talk to Marco Antonio and Ann at once.

"Nick! Come here and meet Marco Antonio," Ann said, pulling him past several others. "In fact, you should meet everyone, I suppose, and then grab some spaghetti before there's none left. Marco Antonio, this is Commander Nick Marshall, who is helping Miguel explain the messages from the Monitor reports on the Venden Retreat to the President and the Joint Chiefs."

"It's an honor to meet you, sir," said Nick, shaking Marco Antonio's hand.

"The honor is mine, sir," said Marco Antonio, holding Nick's hand several seconds longer than necessary. Once again, the Commander's eyebrows shot up and he smiled broadly.

"I'll let everyone introduce themselves later, but I want you all to meet Commander Nick Marshall. He is the voice of the Monitors with the U.S. military and government," Ann said aloud. To Marshall, she said, "Here's a plate. Fill it up, and I'll get you a glass of wine. Marco, would you like a glass of wine? I would. Why don't you sit down here, my love, and I'll get it for you," she said, and turned back into the kitchen, leaving the two men alone.

Marshall helped himself to a generous pile of spaghetti, sauce, and salad, and sat next to Marco Antonio at the big dining room table. Most of the Monitors had come up, shaken Marco Antonio's hand, holding it for a few seconds while they expressed their relief at his return, and then left to eat alone. Monitors would never eat together unless there was no alternative; even then, they would assiduously avoid looking at each other while they ate.

Ann returned with three wine glasses and a bottle of Merlot. She handed the unopened bottle and the opener which she had tucked under her arm to Marco Antonio. Without thinking, he took the bottle and opened it smoothly, a task that would have been difficult for Ann. She silently thought, *Another reason I'm glad you're home! I don't have to open wine bottles!*

Marshall or Miguel could have opened it for you. You are not helpless without me.

Ann was surprised at the tone of his thought. Before she could stop herself, she thought, *I can masturbate, too, but I'd rather have your help.*

Any time.

She felt tacky about her thought, and his response had lacked the warmth he used to send. What's more, there were no messages of exclusivity or possessiveness. She had sent him an opportunity to claim her, and he had merely offered. Usually, he was like a warrior drawing his sword and taking a fighting stance as soon as there was a hint of sex or the presence of another male. There were both tonight, and he hadn't even noticed.

You are tired and hungry, aren't you?

I'm not too tired to make love to you, but I'll feel better when I've fed again.

Miguel should be home soon, and he will have something for you. I can wait until tomorrow, or next week. I would wait for you forever, my love.

At that, he finally stopped talking to Commander Marshall and glanced at her. She took a good look at his face, and she knew that there were differences. His eyebrows were almost level, and there was no sparkle in his eyes. There was a light droop to his mouth, and when he smiled, it did not extend to his eyes. He looked flat. Deflated. Tired of life, defeated. He returned to his conversation with Marshall about the Venden Retreat, and Ann decided that she was going to put him to bed as soon as Miguel brought home some more blood.

Ann drank her glass of wine, and decided she should have some spaghetti. The wine was making her fairly woozy, since her stomach was empty, her blood sugar was low, and she had donated blood. Too bad she couldn't afford to go on a cheap drunk. She felt like having a party. "One drink, and I'll be under the table; two drinks, and I'll be under the host," was an old saying from some movie, and it was apt now, but there were too many people and Marco Antonio was definitely not up to par. She grabbed the last piece of garlic bread and started noshing on it, and then she helped herself to some spaghetti and a couple meatballs.

At last, Miguel came into the kitchen through the back door. He was dressed in his bulky windbreaker, which had plenty of room for several pints of blood inside the jacket. "Welcome, Marco Antonio! It's good to see you home!" he said aloud, and mentally, he said *Check under your pillow.* Ann heard it distinctly, as did Marco Antonio, who nodded, and stuck out his hand to shake Miguel's.

Ann could feel the messages passing between Marco Antonio and Miguel through their touch, but it went far too fast for her to catch. It just felt like a current passed between them, and she knew they had carried on an entire conversation.

"Would you like a glass of wine, Miguel?" Ann asked.

"Sure! Let me go hang up my jacket, and I'll have a glass with you. I ate at Mrs. Wilson's house. She's a great cook, and lonely," he said, and headed into the hall to go down to the basement. Ann knew he would put whatever packets of blood he had collected into his own refrigerator. She might have to move all the blood to Ruth and Gabe's house next door if Commander Marshall was going to spend much time in the basement with Miguel. It could be tough to explain why he had pints of blood in the refrigerator.

Ann started to relax. Miguel had brought food for her Marco Antonio, and her beloved was home, safe if not sound. The changes in Marco Antonio were subtle, yet profound, and she could only hope that they were temporary. With rest, he would probably return to his normal, passionate self. This man's ennui was not typical of Marco Antonio. He was her dancer, her dedicated scientist who worked around the clock to save humanity, and then set off alone across the galaxy to meet up with their enemy. He had met the army of an empire, alone and unaided, armed with nothing more than outrage.

She was secretly glad that Commander Marshall was there. Marco Antonio was asking him about the condition of the country's armed services, and he seemed engrossed in the answers. Giving her a chance to eat, she listened attentively to Marco Antonio's description of the Monitors' methods of fighting with the opponent's own troops. It was fascinating, and it gave her a chance to observe both men like a fly on the wall. There were no little asides from Marco Antonio, no passing thoughts, no slick innuendos.

She felt alone with her thoughts, as if he wasn't here. She didn't try to send him any thoughts of her own.

When Miguel rejoined them, he walked around and sat with his back to the window. "There was a message waiting for me downstairs. All of the highest ranking officers stationed on the Venden colony of what sounds like Aynara, or Einada—I couldn't make out the pronunciation—are dead. The troops are awaiting transport back home. They're afraid of being massacred by the Aynarans once they are discovered to be leaving. It is a genuine concern, since the Vendens are very guilty of many war crimes, and the Aynarans will seek vengeance."

"Will the Monitors protect their retreat?" asked Marshall.

"Probably not," said Marco Antonio. "We may try to buy them time by engaging the Einadrans in negotiations. I believe that's the closest human pronunciation, 'Einadrans.' The Vendens' troop transport ships had best move quickly, or the last of the officers will be trapped there."

"So the troops move first, and the officers last?" Marshall asked.

"Of course. There is no finer motivation for a speedy withdrawal than to make the highest ranking soldiers the last to leave," Marco Antonio said, smiling. "They see to the efficiency of the process, believe me. Especially when the barbarians are at the gates."

"I'll bet," said Commander Marshall, ducking his head down for another bite of spaghetti.

Ann watched as both Miguel and Marco Antonio averted their eyes. Both her Monitors were unconsciously far too polite to watch a stranger put a big bite of coiled spaghetti into his opened mouth, any more than she would stare at someone using Preparation H. The floor or a wall would be much more interesting and deserving of rapt attention.

Completely oblivious to the reactions of the Monitors, Marshall chewed and swallowed as quickly as he could so that he could ask, "How many other planets have they conquered?" He stabbed several lettuce leaves and shoved them into his mouth. Although Nick had eaten with them before, Ann hadn't seen him show any *gusto* about her food or anything else until tonight. She enjoyed watching him, and she knew she was the only one who did. That fact gave her pleasure, although she didn't know why.

"Only two others, besides Kudtz. Earth would have been their third, as far as we know. However, they were building two other City Killers like the one that rained death upon us. We stopped them just in time to save billions," Marco Antonio said.

"Did they invade planets without sentient beings? Surely there are oxygen-rich planets with liquid water and life that have not yet developed intelligent life. Did they go to any of them?" Nick asked.

Ann thought that was a particularly good question, because it went to the core of their reasons for conquest. Did they want or need natural resources, or were they just on a power trip?

"They sent small colonies of Trin to study those planets that they encountered without sentient life. There were only two that I'm aware of," Marco Antonio answered, but quickly added dryly, "Of course, I wasn't there long enough to validate that fact," and he gave a crooked little nod.

"Do you have to have special training to stop wars? Or can anyone of your species do it?" Ann asked. She didn't want to point out that Marco Antonio was a biological engineer and sociologist, not a whatever-he-called it. *Anti-war general? Mass telepath? Troop conscience? Studmuffin?* Her mind wandered to his many other, additional talents.

I prefer Studmuffin, querida.

Me, too! She smiled at him, vastly relieved that he had read her mind.

"We do have people who specialize in the skills necessary to control the actions of armed forces. I had sent for them, and they had arrived when I was attacked. They quickly stopped any further armed resistance," Marco Antonio said. "I was the only casualty, and our scientists are studying their methodology very carefully." He took a sip of wine. He was answering her question, but he was addressing Nick Marshall.

"Speaking of casualties and armed resistance, I want to put you to bed now, Marco Antonio. You need to rest, so no arguments, please," Ann said, sounding like a concerned mother. "Please excuse us, Commander. We can continue this conversation in the morning."

"I'd like to take a shower," said Marco Antonio. "I'll see you in the morning, Commander. Good night, Miguel," he said, standing. Then he added, "I can quell an entire species, but I dare not disobey Ann."

"Certainly not," agreed Miguel. "She can be brutal."

"Believe it! Mean, cruel, and *ugly*," Ann said, picking up her dishes to take into the kitchen.

"Not ugly," the Commander smiled and said.

There's another one in love with you.

He lost his wife and children in the attack. So no, I don't think so. He's suffering, Mr. Suspicious.

"I'll help you clean up later," Marco Antonio said, putting his wine glass down near the dishwasher.

Go eat. I'll be there in a minute, Ann responded, opening the dishwasher to empty it. It felt like she was always filling or emptying the dishwasher. After her children had grown and left the nest, she had forgotten how often she had had to clean up the kitchen, even if she didn't cook. It was endless. If she let others do it, she couldn't find a thing. They put dishes and tools away in the strangest places.

Clean-up went quickly because the other Monitors had brought Ruth's dishes, filled their plates, and returned to her home to eat. Ann got the dishwasher emptied, and when the Commander brought his plate into the kitchen, he announced that his job had always been to wash the pots and pans.

"It would make me happy to do it, Ann. It's the least I can do. You go take care of Marco Antonio. Miguel will show me where everything is. We'll manage. Go!" he insisted, while she continued bringing the cups around to the kitchen and putting them onto the shelf.

"OK. Thanks, Nick. I do want to keep a close eye on him. He was nearly killed, and he's far more wounded than we can see." She knew that to be true, but she doubted that he had a clue as to how *flat* Marco Antonio really felt.

When she walked into the bedroom, he was sitting on the chair near the bed drinking the last of the blood in the container Miguel had left beneath his pillow. "Phew! This is certainly not as good as yours, my love. This person is on several kinds of medicine, and it changes the flavor. I am not usually particular, but you spoiled me," he said.

"The meds don't affect you?" Ann asked, sitting on the bed.

"No, not in this concentration. They just taste nasty," he said, making a disgusted face which would be humanly universal as "Yuk!" He truly did speak many languages.

"Here, give me that, and go take your shower," she said, reaching for the empty baggy. "Is there anything I can do for you?" She hadn't meant to push. Really. Not exactly. Well, sort of.

"You could wash my back," he said. He looked at her out of the side of his eyes. That looked said volumes, in any human language.

"Are you sure you're up to that?" she asked, hesitantly, trying to say it wasn't *really* necessary. She'd forgive him.

"Not yet, but I soon will be, if you're in the shower with me." His crooked head said, "I could do it if you help. Will you?"

"Oh, you! I didn't mean that! I meant, well, are you strong enough? Should you be recuperating?" She really didn't want to push him to do something he wasn't strong enough to do comfortably. Not if it was work. She was a big girl, and she could wait. Sort of. If she had to. Really.

"This body is fine. My other body is in stasis, growing new arms. One of the reasons I came home was to get back into this body so that the other one can heal more slowly. It has been returned home with my vial. The doctors there are tweaking the nutrients, monitoring the reconstruction of the cells, neurons, and all that stuff while the parts that this body needs are here with you."

I know what you need, and I'm here to provide it. Honest. It's OK.

"Is this another case of having half of your memories in each body? That didn't work out so well last time, as I recall. Of course, you didn't tell me last time, so please tell me this time. I can take it if I know." *Yes. It's OK either way.*

"My mental capacity is not complete, but unless you give me some Boolean algebra problems, you won't notice. Come to think of it, I'd probably have some trouble with dark matter equations, too," he said, standing and reaching for her as if he were asking her to dance.

Ann stepped into his arms and said, "I'll try to limit my mathematical demands." Her actions told him that he sounded OK to her.

"Good," he said just before he kissed her. "But don't spare the shampoo. I can take it if I know," he whispered, mimicking her.

Ann smiled and started pulling his shirt up so he could take it off. "It's good to know that even though you are no longer perfect, parts of you are still excellent," she whispered as he nuzzled her neck.

"Actually, I'm not sure. I think an exam and experiment are required, and my doctor has recommended you to perform the tests," he said slowly in between kisses on her neck.

"And who, exactly, is this doctor?" Ann whispered, getting goose bumps on her skin and heat in her belly. She ran her hands up his back, under his shirt.

"Dr. Polo of course. There had better not be another doctor around who knows of your expertise," he said.

Ah, there you are! I was wondering where my possessive, jealous boyfriend had gone!

I am right here, waiting for you to clean me up so that I can ravish you and possess you completely. I've been in a stasis tube for days, and I want to come to you clean. As I recall, I owe you a good ravishing.

Indeed you do! I have been distinctly under-ravished for weeks.

Ann stepped back and undid his shirt buttons. Marco Antonio pulled her tee-shirt over her head. They both reached for the other's jean buttons and zippers and undid them, and together they pulled them off, their thumbs including their underwear. Their eyes never left each other's as their knees bent. Ann smiled when she could no longer reach him, and she stood up as he took her jeans down to the ground. She side-stepped out of them as he started kissing her inner thigh above her knee and continued upwards.

I, too, want to be fresh and clean. I've worked hard all day. Let's go shower, my love.

Without comment, he stood and stepped out of his jeans. He took her hand and they walked into the bathroom together, leaving their clothes in a pile in front of the chair. While he turned on the hot water and waited for it to turn warm, Ann ducked back out of the door and went into the hallway closet, where she had stored the shower seat she had bought so many years ago. It had been a godsend when her hips were arthritic and her heart was so weak she couldn't hold her hands above her head long enough to wash her hair.

What's this?

I want to wash your hair, and you're too tall. Sit here for a minute, please.

He sat on the seat while she washed his hair. She rubbed his shoulders and temples, forehead and chin as he leaned his head back onto her chest. While he was sudsy, she carefully shaved his face and neck.

You spoil me, querida. You can turn a simple shower into a tactile celebration.

Life should be a tactile celebration, my love.

They washed each other carefully, languidly, sensually until every inch of their bodies glowed. Then silky bath oil was rubbed into every pore except for their hair, which had received its own special conditioner. With big, fluffy towels, they dried each other, and then they used the blow dryer on their hair—all of it.

After they were both completely clean, they entered the bedroom, where they proceeded to get human bodily fluids spread evenly in as many areas as possible. When skills learned by decades of practice met those of an anatomical expert with super-human techniques, the orgasms were titanic.

Yet there was something missing that Ann couldn't put her finger on, even though she'd put her fingers on as much as possible. It was fun, they were both very competent lovers, and they were completely comfortable with one another.

The music of his mind was not there. She was not encircled by the waves of emotion that were at times overwhelming. She couldn't feel the fervor, just the lust. There was plenty of heat, but no fever, and she missed it.

He had been injured, and "injury" meant "brain damage" to a Monitor, since they were, for the most part, merely brains and arms. Clearly, he was not at 100%, but she vowed not to worry about it. Marco Antonio had been completely upfront about it, and she could and would accept whatever he was. He had come back to her as quickly as he could, and she was grateful beyond words. Thankful that anything survived, she would take care of him and nurture him back to health.

She knew that he would have to journey back to his home world at least to pick up his vial, where much of his knowledge and thinking ability were stored. Surely, the data stored in his vial would rejuvenate his native body and mind, and the next time he was transferred back into this body, he would be more complete.

They lay together, legs and arms entwined. He fell asleep almost immediately, but she wanted to go back into the bathroom to clean up some of the body fluids trickling down her thigh. Once up, she glanced at the clock and realized that it was too early for her to sleep; if she went to sleep now, she would arise at three or four in the morning, bright-eyed and bushy-tailed.

She put on her house coat hanging on the bathroom door and decided to clean up the kitchen and perhaps read some of the papers Casey had left for her. She secretly hoped that Marco Antonio could/would take over the business of business; she had never liked it, which was why she had become a teacher in the first place.

Get a grip, girl! I'm perfectly capable of managing the tediousness of legal and economic details. Why should he have to do it? He probably hates it twenty times more than I do.

She grumbled to herself, berating herself for being lazy about corporate and tax minutiae until she got into the kitchen and found it was immaculate. Someone had even mopped the floor, or had at least cleaned up the spot of sauce she had dripped and swept up the onion skin that had drifted off the cutting board. There was not a dirty dish or pot, and the dishwasher was in the last stages of drying.

Bless their little cotton socks! Now I have no excuses. If I could grade term papers, I can read corporate bylaws. The yuk factor is about the same....

Taking herself well in hand, she grabbed the stack of legal documents left by Casey and sat down to read them.

CHAPTER 19

Marco Antonio, Ann, and Casey worked together for many hours the next day, so Ann was particularly grateful when Samantha offered to bring over a big pot of gumbo if Ann fixed the rice. Unlike her mother, Sam loved to cook, but cooking for children was no fun. While half the world starved, the Bright kids were still picky eaters and difficult to please. Besides, it was a nightly reminder that Aaron was no longer around to cook for.

When he heard her car parking under the tree on Malone Street, Miguel popped up and rushed out the back door to help Samantha bring in the children and the dinner. There were many hugs and vociferous notifications of wondrous achievements delivered as loudly as children could yell them so as not to be ignored. The adults tried to react to each proclamation with adequate astonishment from the announcements of the boys, while they tried to address questions to include Molly, whose attention was glued to her Mom's phone as her thumbs raced over the letters. Molly's answers were perfunctory at best, and she quickly edged into the living room, obviously hoping to make a getaway.

Ann put the water on to boil for the rice while Sam set the table. Miguel and the boys had gone into the bathroom where some of the big toys were stored. They had chosen a set of Lincoln Logs and they were all playing with them in the living room. Marco Antonio was helping Sam, filling the glasses with milk or ice water. All of the adults already had a glass of wine.

"I'm afraid that neither Miguel nor I will be able to do justice to your cooking. We just had tea with a friend of Miguel's, and we ate far too many goodies before dinner. We can surely keep you company and I, for one, am very anxious to taste your famous gumbo," Marco Antonio said, bringing over an extra chair.

Ann put the bread into the oven to keep it warm. It was all wrapped in tin foil and had already been buttered. She looked at Marco Antonio and sent him a thought. *It feels enormously normal, doesn't it?*

It would if Aaron were here. Samantha misses him. Do you still miss Tim?

Of course. Every day. But I am so lucky to have had you both in my life. You didn't take his place, but having you is like getting another flower in my bouquet of people I have loved.

I think Miguel would like to join Sam's bouquet. Does she know that he is a sanguinary eater?

I don't know. I have never mentioned it. Should I tell her?

I think so. She will need time to accept that before she commits her life and love to a monster.

Ann looked up at Marco Antonio, shocked that he would say such a thing.

Why would you call him a monster?

We are sitting down to a table to eat a meal neither man here can partake in. Not only are we not the same species, we cannot even share a meal with you. We are monsters. Blood-sucking monsters who feed off the unwary.

Yes, and I am your pet. Your favorite little mammal. Not too bright, but the only one you can ride inside the house.

He looked up at her, fury in his face. He hated it when she referred to herself as an animal. She was looking at him, one eyebrow raised, waiting with an "I beg your pardon?" look on her face. The anger in his eyes melted, and he smiled.

"Gotcha!" she said out loud.

"Checkmate!" he said.

We are what we are, and we love each other for all those reasons. No insecurity allowed, right?

Fair enough. But you knew what I am before you loved me. You avoided me for over a year because I'm a vampire.

No, I avoided you because I loved you.

Really? I didn't know that.
Neither did I.

Samantha brought in the salad and asked the children to go wash their hands. Miguel stopped building his log cabin, and rose to take the boys into the bathroom to wash up.

They'd be a good match, and he could help raise the children.
I don't think she'll let a monster raise her children.
There you go with that "monster" crap again. You are an extraterrestrial creature with different culinary requirements. So is he. Get over it.

They sat down to eat, and both Marco Antonio and Miguel apologized again for having spoiled their dinner by eating at Mrs. Wilson's house. Both men tried the gumbo, and pronounced it delicious. They talked about the City Killers, the lung cleaners, the high school, and soccer. It was just a normal family conversation, complete with one four-year-old's almost-tantrum, neatly avoided by a whispered message from his mama.

The evening ended early because little Jake and Johnny were decidedly tired. Miguel went home with them, offering to help carry in the pot or the boys. He needed no ride home, since he would simply send for a rover to pick him up after the children were in bed.

It didn't take long to clean up after dinner. Ann only had to rinse the bowls and put them into the dishwasher along with the silverware and glasses. Not having to wash pots and serving dishes certainly cut down on the clean-up.

Marco Antonio turned to the computer and tried to catch up on what had been happening in his absence. Ann tried to concentrate on the book she was reading on her Kindle, but her mind kept flitting to the differences in Marco Antonio. Something about him was missing. He was quiet; if she'd had to pick out an adjective to describe him, it would have been "flat." He just wasn't himself.

She got up and put on a CD with Chopin's Etudes. If Marco Antonio listened to them a few times, it would be far easier for him to learn to play them. Her hands were too small; she had tried and tried, but many of the Rachmaninoff, Chopin, Liszt and other 19th century romantic composers were just too difficult for small hands.

That's my excuse, and I'm sticking to it.

She didn't want to face the possibility that perhaps she just wasn't good enough, or perhaps she hadn't worked as hard as she should have.

While he was scanning the Washington Post, the phone rang. Ann picked it up in the living room, and waited for the President to come on the line. Finally, she said, "Hello, Mr. President. Good to hear from you!" Ann was sitting in the deep chairs in the living room, and she had to struggle to get out of them.

"I wanted to call and ask if you had heard from Dr. Polo?"

"Yes. Marco Antonio is here. We have just finished dinner, and he's trying to catch up on the news. Would you like to speak to him?" She arose without grunting and walked across the dark brown carpet into the den. There were three doors into the den, and she went in the one behind the computer.

"Yes, please. I'd like to see if he could come to the East Coast anytime soon. I believe I owe you two a dinner at the White House, such as it is. I would really like to learn more about him and the people who saved us."

"Hold on for a sec." Ann handed her phone to Marco Antonio who was seated at the desk at the computer, and then reached across the desk to the phone there, so they could both listen in. Before turning hers on, she walked to her rocking chair in front of the television and sat down.

"Hello, Mr. President," Marco said. "As a matter of fact, I have some business with the lung cleaner production company which will take me to the East Coast early next week, and I'd be pleased to meet with you and Mrs. Blake. Yes, Mrs. Jacob will be with me. Tuesday night at seven would be fine. We'll be there. Excellent. Just a minute, and I'll ask."

He put his hand over the phone and looked at Ann. "Would you like to stay at the temporary White House? They are actually staying at some mansion in North Carolina, but he says it might be more convenient than a hotel, and the mansion has many extra bedrooms."

Ann hit the "on" button on the desk phone and answered directly. "Sure! We could sleep in Questor, but it would be nice to be able to shower. I'll pack my jammies," Ann said, knowing full well Marco Antonio would say no such thing.

"Mrs. Jacob says she would be thrilled."

"We'll have a sleep-over then," said the President, picking up on her lack of formality. "Bring your pictures! Charlotte will love to see them, and you can describe them to us in your own special way, Dr. Polo. Sounds fun! Cocktails at six, dinner at eight, if that's all right with your schedule."

"I think we can do that, can't we, Marco?" Ann asked.

"Until Tuesday, then. It sounds like a good idea. Ann will like a little time to freshen up before dinner, unpack, and rest. We'll arrive shortly after five, if that is convenient. It's a long flight," Marco Antonio said. Questor could make the flight in about half the time of commercial flights, but Marco Antonio didn't want the President to know that.

"Fine. We'll see you then. I'm looking forward to it. Good-bye, Dr. Polo, Mrs. Jacob," he said, and hung up.

"I wonder if they'll put us in the same bedroom," Ann said aloud. "I would imagine not. If we weren't already lovers, it could be quite a scandal." She walked behind the desk and stood behind Marco Antonio, looking at the computer, trying to figure out what he had been doing there. It didn't look like any site she'd ever seen. It looked vaguely like a newspaper, but not like one she'd ever seen. Of course, online newspapers never looked like their paper counterparts. "I miss the old newspapers, don't you?" Ann said, musing aloud.

"Imagine the headlines, 'Vampire in White House!' or 'I was forced to sleep with an extraterrestrial vampire in the White House!' It would definitely make the papers. Maybe that would take everyone's mind off the City Killers," Marco Antonio mused.

"How about this: "Vampire caught sneaking into the room of White House guest!' Since Blake wouldn't forbid the first extraterrestrial houseguest whatever he wanted, I could write—and sell—a tell-all article about how the President just assigned me the adjoining room to make me available to his vampire ET." Ann said. "Poor little me!" Rubbing his shoulders, she leaned down and whispered, "Oh baby, we could get rich and famous with our tell-all book!"

"So either separate bedrooms or the same one could cause quite a stir if it leaks out that I am both an alien and a vampire! Look at the power we could wield, just keeping everything secret—for a price!" Marco Antonio swiveled the chair and sat Ann on his lap. "Blackmail could be profitable, too!"

"I've long suspected you just wanted your fifteen minutes of fame on this planet. You've been waiting centuries for this chance, haven't you?" Ann teased.

"Oh, yes! Let's hope he has banners across the entry, saying 'Welcome Mr. Extraterrestrial Vampire!' That would give the news photographers something to shoot. We could have Questor de-cloak near the front door, too. The pictures alone could make us rich."

Ann said quietly, leaning her head onto his shoulder. "This could be a complete disaster, couldn't it, love?"

"Oh, yes! This could be the beginning of the end of our quiet little life together. We may have to move to Wyoming or somewhere to avoid the press."

"Wyoming is no longer there, unless you want to settle into a nice ash hill."

"My point exactly."

"Maybe we should get married. Then, at least, we'd be Dr. and Mrs. Polo. It would simplify the sleeping arrangements," Ann mused quietly. "Better than 'Vampire and Wench' on the invitations." She snuggled into his shoulder, wishing this chair would adjust like Questor did.

"More like 'Mrs. Jacob and guest.'"

"Right. Like anybody gives a damn about some old English or history teacher."

"Well, I've heard she makes a dandy pet. Nice to stroke, very good on long trips, sits and fetches well. She even is a great ride indoors," he said softly, holding her tightly against his chest in the desk chair.

"Beware. I hear she has a nasty bite, but Vampires don't mind. They think she tastes yummy." She shifted slightly to fit even more tightly under his chin, with her lips whispering against his neck. "She's loyal, anyway. Even if she's not too bright and has trouble communicating." She tried not to think about the surprise she felt about her status as a pet. Normally, it infuriated him when she referred to herself as an inferior being. He had actually joked with her about it!

They sat silently for several minutes. Suddenly, Ann said, "I have to buy new clothes, but I don't want to think about that. I don't want to think about President Mike Blake or the Washington White House that's probably brown and in North Carolina. Let's make a decision about where we're going to put the lung-cleaner factory so we can get Casey to purchase the land or find a building we can use. She'll have to hire people while we're gone, so we'd better find a place for them to work."

"For a stupid pet, you're certainly ambitious. So much for cuddling. OK, I'll find some likely listings here on the computer. Would you like to call your favorite realtor, Shannon Johnson, or should we stick to the internet?"

"My butt's asleep. I'll get the laptop and help you look. I hate to call her in the evening. I'll call her in the morning. Would it be OK with you if we let her broker the local purchases? She's very good," Ann said, stretching.

"Of course. I like to use local brokers, vendors and dealers whenever possible." Marco Antonio turned back to the computer and started typing rapidly.

"OK, Vampire -boy. Let's see who can find the best locations the fastest," she said, setting up the laptop behind him on the dining room table.

"You're on, my pet."

Both Ann and Marco Antonio worked well into the night. Since they sat within a few feet of each other, they shared pictures and descriptions of likely sites, printing up the addresses and descriptions of locations they would like to investigate further.

MONITORS OF DESTRUCTION

I wish you would play the piano for me, Ann. I have not heard you play in weeks, and I missed it.
What would you like me to play?
Something by Beethoven, I think.

Without saying a word, Ann closed the laptop and walked across the room to the piano. She took out the music to the Pathetique and started to play the first movement. For her, it was difficult, but she had been practicing while he was away, and she hoped it would be good enough. She had played it for a recital when she was 14, but that was a long time ago, and she certainly had not kept it up.

Ann got through the first movement, although she stumbled along in several places. Once she hit the second movement, she was on her home turf; this she had played regularly. Less showy than the first movement, it was easier to listen to and far less likely to make her fingers trip.

As she was playing, she felt him walk toward her, and she kept hearing, *beautiful, beautiful* in her head. As he stood directly behind her, she was flooded with goodfeels, both towards her and for the music. Soon, pheromones were mixed with the feelings.

It's nice to know this music turns you on, Marco.
Only when you play it. This is so much more beautiful than any music my people can make that it is a sensual experience on many levels.
Seriously? Your people do not have music like this?
No. Not like this.

She didn't get through the third movement. He was flooding her with messages, and the pheromones were making concentration impossible. She yearned to touch him, to run her fingers through his hair, to have his body surrounding hers. Her belly was hot, and she was so wet she was glad the bench was maple, or it would be damp. Sliding across the bench, she turned and stepped into his waiting arms. Her cheek was against his chest. She raised her chin, and he kissed her softly.

Lovely, but I want more.
More what, querida?
More of you.
Tell me what you want, and you shall have it.

I want you naked on top of me. I want to feel your bare skin, and the hair on your chest scratching my breasts as you move up and down on top of my body. I want to feel you inside of me until I am completely full, and then I want you to slide out, and then all the way in, as far as you can fit, with all the force you can muster.

Oh, my god. You will talk me into an explosion. Just your words and your music. Ann, you are very sensual!

Come into the bedroom, and I will tell you a tale about everything I want you to do, and everything I want to do to you, and how I want to feel with you.

Let's go, baby.

The next morning was Saturday, so Samantha and the children didn't have to go to school. Ann called to see if Samantha and/or Molly could help her buy some classy clothes to wear to the White House. Molly had a birthday party, and Jacob had a soccer match.

"Too many moving parts, eh Sam? That's OK Sweetie, I can go by myself. Not to change the subject, but did you have a nice time with Miguel last night?"

"Oh my gawd, Mom—I'll have to talk to you later about this. Let's just say that I did tap that, and that boy has some skills. Nice to have around, too."

"I am so glad, Sam! We will have to run away together sometime soon—we must catch up, girlfriend! Let's see what we can work out. We have to be in North Carolina by Tuesday afternoon, so it has to be today or tomorrow. Work me in for a grocery run or something," Ann said. "Well, I gotta jet. Call ASAP. Bye."

Samantha no longer felt like her daughter; she had long ago become Ann's best friend. They had comforted each other through the worst times, and they only wished each other the best. Neither one judged the other, nor did they fear being judged. Since Ann no longer looked like she was in her 60s, even the age barrier had come down.

"Could I accompany you to pick out new clothing?" Marco Antonio asked as Ann hung up the phone. He had just come in after a shower. His hair was wet, and he still looked sexy. He poured himself a cup of coffee as Ann put the phone back on the base. She looked at him in shock.

"Surely you jest! You want to go clothes shopping in a woman's clothing store?" Ann asked, taken aback. She had never known a man to want to shop for women's clothing or shoes.

"The last time we hunted for clothing was in the crushed buildings of Kansas City. I would like to see what is in the stores both here in Hanford and perhaps in Fresno. I would love to see you fit properly in one of the finest clothiers in San Francisco, if San Francisco were still there. You deserve the finest, querida."

"Clothing has never been of interest to me. My body was never constructed to make clothes look good; the goal was always to look neat, tidy, clean and well groomed. Fashion has never been a priority in my life, Marco Antonio." Actually, she had totally given up on shopping and bought her clothes from catalogues. She had not done any recreational shopping since before the Yellowstone eruption, and not much before then, when she was a chubby little old lady.

"I know, but you still deserve the finest. In everything."

"Of course I do. The next time you're near Venden, pick me up one of those great scarlet and gold capes the dinosaurs wear. That would go well with my stilettos, don't you think?" She smiled at him, mostly with her eyebrows.

"And your diamonds and rubies," he added, smiling at her.

"Ah, yes. My main goal: to wear diamonds as big as horse turds. Then everyone would love and respect me!" She approached him, wanting to walk into his arms.

"They already do, my love." He put down his coffee cup and put his arms around her. He kissed her, knowing he tasted like coffee.

"Then a plain navy, black, or red dress will do very nicely. You are the only one I need to impress. I could care less what Mike Blake or his minions think of me, but I certainly don't want to embarrass you." She leaned back, so she could look him in the eye. "I just don't want to look frumpy, Marco. I know I'll never decorate your arm like a Jackie Kennedy or a Princess Diana, but I'd like to make you proud to be seen with me."

"I am always proud to be seen with you. You make it difficult, because all the men want you, and it makes me crazy. Besides, my darling, you need to remember that it is *they* who need to impress *us*," Marco Antonio said, putting his hands around her waist, forcing her to look up into his eyes as he stared forcefully into hers.

"Damn straight! You are the man of the hour, the savior of the race. For some completely unfathomable reason, you have chosen me to sit next to the most magnificent creature in the solar system as your mate. If I choose to wear purple polka dots, and you dress in an iridescent Speedo, so be it!" she said, giving him a squeeze around his waist. Just before he kissed her, she said, "Have I told you today?"

"In many ways, and I love you, too." He kissed her, and then whispered in her ear, "Now, let's go buy you some diamonds as big as horse turds and find me an iridescent Speedo!"

They drove together to the Hanford Mall, but they didn't really find anything presidential, so they headed to Fresno. Ann missed Gottschalk's, the bastion of middle class and professional women in the valley for many years, which had closed because of the recession before the Yellowstone Eruption. There were still a few classy stores in Fresno, and they found a surprising number of very nice outfits for both of them. When he wore the dark charcoal suit, she would wear the red suit, and his tie would match. She also bought a basic black silk sheath which she could wear either during the daytime or with a gold chain at night. His other suit was black with a wine shirt and black tie.

No Speedo, no polka dots, no large jewels of any kind.

On the way back to Hanford, they drove by a fairly large warehouse in the industrial section of Fresno which was for sale. They discussed its merits as a growing center for the nematodes and bacteria they were beginning to produce on an industrial scale all over the world. They decided to buy it if only because it would provide many jobs for the homeless near G Street.

Ann called Shannon Johnson, got the description and asking price, and gave her an offer. As Marco Antonio drove home, Ann and Shannon talked over the details of the offer, and Shannon wrote it up. Ann and Marco Antonio could sign the cash offer on the way home.

"It's so much easier to deal with cash!" Ann said.

"You know a lot about buying property, Ann. I am very impressed at how smoothly you work with Shannon." Marco Antonio had never seen Ann doing business before, and he was impressed, but not surprised. "You and Tim had rentals, didn't you?"

They had never talked about money. He had given her a Mastercard and a Visa, and told her that money was no object. Once, she had gone into Ruth and Gabriel's house and taken over $80,000 in cash out of hiding, and driven it down to Los Angeles, where Ruth was in the hospital. She had replaced what they hadn't used, and had given Ruth a written accounting of every dime she had spent. He had never checked her bank accounts, and he had no idea how much money she had. She had spent very little of his money after they had finished refurbishing the Smiths' house and putting in the basement under Ann's house. She had let him pay half of that, and she had paid half, he had learned after the project was finished.

He would cheerfully have paid for the new basement, Ann's new carpet, new drapes, and anything else she had wanted, either before or after Tim died. Both of the Jacobs had been very generous with their time and expertise, and they had never asked him to pay for anything. Clearly, Marco Antonio had underestimated their wealth.

"I suppose it's time to have this conversation," Ann said, glancing thoughtfully out the car window.

Which conversation? He looked at her out of the side of his eye as he drove across the flat farmland. There were few trees, oddly spaced. Some trees would be clustered around a house that had been torn down, others lined a driveway to nowhere. Originally, the valley had been settled with small farms, but the trees these pioneers had planted had long outlasted the homes they were supposed to decorate. Now they stood as sentries, guarding the site where people once lived.

"You have told me that you have unlimited money. Where did you get it? Were you in business, do you have stocks in some corporations?" she paused for a brief second. "Here, I'll start, since I've already told you about my real estate addiction. Together, we bought and sold 97 units. Some were for my mother, when she retired up here, and some we didn't keep long. A couple of triplexes we backed out of before they closed, so if I don't count those, the total was 91. I like real estate." She added.

"I know you still have tenants who come and pay you rent. How many houses do you have now?" Marco Antonio asked casually.

"Thirteen, counting the apartment behind my house. Eleven are rented," Ann replied, glancing in his direction. "I have two duplexes and seven houses, my own house, and the little apartment. Although they're not all paid off, most are, and the payments are low because the interest rate is low. They're all rented. So besides my teacher's retirement, I have real estate in Hanford, plus Tim's insurance and retirement. All these different sources provide me with enough money to live comfortably and relatively immune to inflation, but it requires my attention. I don't need or want your money, but I should know something about it, don't you agree?" Ann had no idea about the Monitors' attitudes about wealth. This could be a moral minefield, too crass to discuss, like food.

"There's no real secret to my wealth. As you know, we are a semi-aquatic species who are quite comfortable swimming around wrecks in the water. There are thousands of sunken ships which carried treasure. I just went down and got it, a long time ago."

"Really? I guess that makes you a buccaneer! Were you ever a pirate?"

"No. I just listened to the stories, and went out and found the wrecks. There are still tons of gold sitting on the sea floor in shallow water. When we need more, we go get it." Marco Antonio drove calmly down the road, explaining to Ann how he had acquired billions of dollars of gold without stealing it or mining for it.

"Very clever, Mr. Polo. You could melt the gold down, and it would be completely untraceable. You could convert it into cash, bank it, or use it directly to pay for whatever you need. No interest earned, but the value of gold has more than kept up with inflation," she commented aloud.

"Thank you, Mrs. Jacob. Actually, your wealth acquisition is much more impressive. You and Tim actually earned it!" Marco

Antonio sounded impressed, and she was receiving background feelings of pride and admiration in the goodfeels he was sending out. "I am surprised and a little embarrassed that I knew nothing of your great wealth, Ann. I'm supposed to know these things."

"You just didn't want to pry into your girlfriend's finances. It's not nearly as impressive as it sounds. I should be much richer than I am."

"Have you lost your money? Bad investments? Scoundrels?" Marco Antonio expected to hear a sad tale of woe, and he was very surprised when he heard what actually happened to much of the Jacob family money.

"No, nothing like that. We gave it away," Ann said calmly

"To your children? To whom?" He kept his eyes on the road, but he was quite interested in Ann's story. This was a vital part of her life that he knew nothing about, and he was floored that it was so, so *significant*.

"Well, we sponsor teachers in Kenya. We run Hopewell High School, where neighborhood slum kids can go to high school for free, and we have four nursery schools, to get the orphans and poor children ready for first grade. In Kenya, no child can enter first grade until he or she has completed three years of nursery school, which is very expensive. So we sponsor the teachers, rent the buildings, and provide the money for food, uniforms, and school supplies to run the nursery schools."

"You do this on your *own?*" Marco Antonio almost squeaked, he was so surprised.

"No. Helping Other People Everywhere, Inc. runs a sponsor a teacher program, and many people, teachers especially, contribute monthly to pay the salaries of the Kenyan teachers. I'm President of H.O.P.E., so I gather up the money, wire it to people I trust in Kenya, and then go check on them. The good people of Kings County are the ones supporting the education of Kenyan girls and orphans. I just manage it."

"So you've been to Kenya?"

"Nine times. Tim and I used to go every year. When people give me money, I must be able to assure them that it is being spent for the purpose they intended. We never charged anything for management, travel expenses, wiring—nothing, and most of the time we were able to match every dollar donated. It's been hard since Tim died, but we're still sponsoring the same number of teachers and staff."

"Why is it harder without Tim?" Marco Antonio wanted to pay attention to this. Why hadn't she let him in on this project? She had never asked him for money or help with the book work or anything, and it bothered him. Maybe she felt he wasn't as generous as Tim? He didn't know himself, but he did know that if it was important to Ann, it would be important to him.

"Tim was the Chief Financial Officer, and he took care of the bookwork and the taxes. There's a million trips to the bank, thank you letters to write, presentations to put on—it takes a lot of work to give money away," Ann said, gazing out the car window, her mind miles away, remembering Tim in Africa.

"Yet you have never told me about this whole section of your life, querida. I feel like there's a completely different person here that I don't even know."

"Maybe there is. Remember, I wasn't a young girl with dreams and stars in her eyes when you met me. I was 62 years old, and I had packed a lot of living into those years," she said as he came to a four-way-stop on Grangeville.

"I knew you were very special and unique from the moment I met you. Always calm, but fiercely noble. So tell me now—what other things have you done?"

"Well, we used to trade homes with other people in different parts of the world. Teachers don't make a lot of money, and the real estate frequently made us pretty broke. But we usually got nice, fat income tax returns because of the depreciation schedules and expenses we could deduct. With that money, I bought plane tickets. We traded homes with people in the Lake District of England, one in Madrid, one in Villach, Austria, another in Maidstone, Kent, another in Harpenden, north of London, and two in Australia. We took my mother along on several of these trips, so she got to spend time with her grandchildren, too. We had some great times."

"We're home, but this conversation is not over, querida. I will want to hear everything about all these trips, these schools, the nurseries, your 97 houses. You are amazing! I thought you were just a teacher, albeit one who has eleven "Teacher of the Year" or "Outstanding Woman of the Year" or "Ruby Award for Outstanding Contribution to Your Community" up on your wall." Marco Antonio rested his left arm on the steering wheel and had swiveled his body around to face her. He looked at her seriously and she returned his gaze with a small smile of her own. "We must have many more conversations, Ann. I must know more about you."

"OK," she said, and she hopped out of the car, gathered up their many packages, loaded up Marco Antonio, and they went into the house.

They packed much more carefully, hanging their fancy new clothes on a Questor-extension in the rover's cab. They left on Saturday night, intending to stop in Pennsylvania and Kentucky to check on the Monitors and the Lung Cleaner factories being built there. It would be a brief flight from either place to North Carolina, so they could arrive clean and tidy after staying with Monitors, leaving their jeans and tee-shirts in Questor. They had much to talk about. Besides, they both looked forward to night flights in Questor. Making love in total blackness with a responsive bed was just kinky enough.

CHAPTER 20

Questor let them off just out of sight of the huge house. He had remained cloaked, so if anyone had seen them disembark, they would only have seen two people appearing out of nowhere, feet first. It was highly unlikely that anyone would see them, since Questor turned off all the interior lights, and there were no exterior lights. Unless there was a flashlight pointed directly at them, they would emerge out of the darkness unseen.

Like they were visiting neighbors, Marco Antonio and Ann simply walked up to the front door and knocked. They were met by two Secret Service men, who checked their identification, and patted them down.

"How did you get here, sir? We did not see your vehicles' approach," asked one of the nervous guards.

"We were dropped off down the road, and we walked from there," answered Marco Antonio smoothly. Ann could tell by the look on the guard's faces that they didn't buy that for a moment. Marco Antonio took the hand of the man who was patting him down, hesitated a brief second, and offered to shake the hand of the other Secret Service agent. "I'm Marco Antonio Polo and we're here to see the President and First Lady," he continued smoothly.

"There were other agents you should have encountered," mentioned one of the agents.

"We have encountered several other Secret Service personnel on the road, and they have been most polite," Ann responded.

"The two guests have arrived, sir. They just walked up from the turn-off. They are unarmed and checked out," said the first agent softly into his phone. A moment later, he turned and escorted them into the foyer, where the President and First Lady were waiting.

There was much hand-shaking and introductions were made by the President to Mrs. Blake. Both Ann and Marco Antonio shook hands with them both. They were escorted down the hall by the President, but Ann noticed that there were several other men in suits standing around the rooms and in the hallways.

While they were taking a quick tour of the house, Charlotte Blake gave them some background. The Blakes had arrived from Mt. Weather, Virginia, where they had been ensconced during the bombing by the City Killers, along with whichever members of Congress were in Washington, D.C. at the time of the bombing. Mt. Weather was designed to be the government's center in the event of a nuclear attack, and it had proven to be a tough egg to crack. "Even the crash of TWA flight 514, on Dec. 1, 1974, couldn't smash it. The plane had run into the mountain, but the huge crash had only knocked out the phone lines, and they were fixed long ago," Mrs. Blake told Ann conspiratorially. 'The government Is still run from that facility, but we decided that the First Family needed better digs to entertain the most important guest the world had ever had."

That's you, sweetheart. And she's absolutely correct. You are the most significant guest any President has ever hosted.

Marco Antonio said nothing as Ann beamed at him.

The largest private residence in the world, Biltmore House, in Ashville, North Carolina had graciously been offered to the President and First Lady as an interim venue for important ambassadorial affairs by the remaining members of the Vanderbilt family.

Welcoming the first E.T. would definitely qualify as a VIP affair, I should imaging. The dinner and overnight stay for the visit of the Monitor ambassador and his guest had been well planned by the Biltmore House staff, so the Blakes had apparently been wandering around the vast ornate estate, marveling at the furniture, paintings, beautifully carved wood, and the many elaborate fireplaces (65, they were told).

After the short tour and the intimate chat with the President's wife, they were shown into a huge room. "Tell me about the Vendens," the First Lady, Charlotte Blake, requested shortly after they had been shown into the library, been served drinks, and were just sitting down to get acquainted.

"Why don't I show you instead?" Marco Antonio suggested reaching out his hand to both the President and his wife.

"I'd love that!" Charlotte Blake gushed. "Then I'll know a little about the Monitors' special means of communication and the City Killers as well!"

Ann noted that Charlotte had done her homework.

"Might I suggest that we sit together here on the sofa so that I might hold both your hand and the President's. That way, you can both receive the same images and sounds at the same time."

They repositioned themselves so that they were all on the same sofa in the huge library. The Blakes had arrived from Mt. Weather, Virginia, where they had been ensconced during the bombing by the City Killers, along with whichever members of Congress were in Washington, D.C. at the time of the bombing.

Standing in front of the huge, ornate fireplace in the library, they were all vaguely overwhelmed by the sheer size of the room. The walls were lined with book shelves two stories high, the furniture was dark red velvet, and they stood on a navy blue Turkish rug. The entire room was ornate and over-decorated, dwarfing the four mere mortals standing awkwardly in front of the black, heavily carved fireplace, above which was another ten feet or so of more ornate wood carving surrounding a painting they could hardly see, it was so far above them.

"Should we make a circle, and all join hands?" asked the First Lady.

"That will not be necessary," Marco Antonio replied, smiling.

"This isn't a séance," Ann added. "There will be no ghosts or moving tables. It just makes it easier for your brain to receive pictures from his brain if you have skin contact. Strictly a matter of communication, and he doesn't need feedback."

They all put their drinks on the glass-covered table and took their seats on the long wine velvet sofa with Marco Antonio and Charlotte Blake in the middle. Ann had purposefully seated herself so as to hold hands with Charlotte and not Mike, so Marco Antonio would feel no untoward lustful urges from Mike. Ann wanted no jealous scenes with Marco and the President of the United States.

Strangely, she felt none of the hypersensitivity Marco usually evinced around other men. The last time he had met the President, he had been sure that the President had impure motivations towards Ann, but now there was none of that. Either the President had changed, or Marco Antonio had.

Silently, Marco Antonio poured images into their minds of the large carnivores of Venden, who loved to posture in front of each other wearing outlandish costumes to demonstrate whatever power they could wield against one another. Their social structure was extremely complicated, in a hierarchical pattern so detailed and complex that it was the main academic subject taught at battle school.

They were physically strong, and a very big part of the Venden culture was devoted to establishing and maintaining a reputation for power and viciousness. They practiced fighting throughout childhood, and competed in fighting matches and contests of strength their entire lives.

The females were smaller and plainer, but extremely fecund. They were constantly pregnant, bearing litters of two to four every year. Much like birds, the young were kept in a nest-bed for the first few weeks, fed regurgitated meat, and guarded jealously by their mothers. Once the young could walk, they followed the mother around constantly until the males were sent to battle school. There, the young were fed cooked meat for the first time, and they grew prodigiously. Females stayed with their mothers, got mostly raw meat, assisted their mothers with the next brood, and helped care for the pig-like animals raised for food.

"They seem so primitive and shallow! How did they ever conquer their neighbors? These guys are either as dumb as dirt, or they're still living in the Dark Ages. Most of their houses don't even have electricity! Yet they overpowered a sentient, scientifically advanced race?" Ann asked aloud.

"Neither planet has developed a species with ethics. The Vendens have become physically very fit, and the Trin of Kudtz have become very scientific, yet neither have developed a very rich culture. They have no music, little art, little curiosity about cosmology or religion, and no literature, at least no fiction. The empathic development on both planets is almost infantile, and they all lead shallow lives. No conscience, no guilt, no passion." Marco Antonio said aloud. "I'd really like to inspect both their brain structures; I would bet they both have stunted amygdalas, among other quirks."

"Structurally, are human brains anything like Monitor brains?" Charlotte asked.

"Yes, quite similar, actually. Your amygdala is larger than ours, at least in relation to total size, and the connections to other parts of your brains are slightly different. You are a passionate bunch, unlike the Venden or the Trin. In fact," he added, "I'd bet that even dogs have larger amygdalas than the Venden or Trin."

"I'd like to know more about your race, Dr. Polo. Please show us what your home is like, and what your people look like," asked the President.

Marco Antonio showed them images of the Monitors taking part in a defecation ritual in the Marianna Trench. They had formed into a giant ball and were sharing thoughts while glowing in waves of color. The ball was spinning slightly, and pulsing as they gave off a rhythmic sound.

He omitted the actual defecations, but he showed the ball breaking up and everyone jetting away into the abyss. Shortly thereafter, he switched the image to one of individual Monitors gliding smoothly on dry land. There was a smooth path through a dense, blue-green forest that smelled of plants, not quite like pine nor flowers, but very pleasant. One Monitor came to a clearing in the woods on a grassy knoll, and entered a transport like Questor. They zoomed off together, clearly knowing their destination.

Marco Antonio quietly withdrew his hands and placed them in his lap. The President and Mrs. Blake opened their eyes and smiled as if they were awakening from a dream. "There is much I did not show you, of course, but I do not want to overwhelm your brains with too much information. Let us relax, have dinner, and talk. I will answer whatever verbal questions you might have at dinner. You will be very sleepy tonight, so we should retire early. Your brains will need to refill your neurotransmitters and process the images I have given you."

"I still need to know how you convinced the Venden to go home. That little military secret is priceless!" said the President.

"Those squids were your people?" asked Charlotte Blake. "What were they doing in that big ball? Were they underwater? Can you breathe underwater and in the air as well?"

The President gave his exuberant wife a slightly disgruntled look, since he wanted his question answered before hers. After all, *his* question involved national security, while hers were just unbridled curiosity.

Ann just smiled proudly at her beloved as he answered Mrs. Blake's questions. At last, she got the chance to observe him with others of her kind who knew how wonderful he really was. Of course, they didn't know a tenth of his abilities, but at least they had had a glimpse of his reality. She was so proud of him! She listened to him explain what he had shown them in English, and she realized that he was trying to be inoffensive, yet clear. Their brains' abilities to process the smells, sounds, sights and messages were undeveloped, as hers had been.

Only then did she realize how much she had learned from him.

Yes, querida. Your brain has developed remarkably in the last few years.

I want to grow up to be just like you! I am so proud of you and yours, and I worship the ground you walk on. Just sayin'.

Ann felt a flush of goodfeels emanate from him to her. It was the first time he had had done that since his return. Something inside of her relaxed. *He's back.*

Ann picked up the conversation. "The Monitors have no natural enemies, and they haven't had any in eons. They manufacture their food from various types of plankton, krill, fungi, and other things we would find inedible. Food, to them, is a necessary requirement, and nothing special. They eat to live, and the food they consume is micro-managed to be completely healthful. They have real difficulty with our obsession with eating gourmet foods, or things like sugar and transfats which clearly are not good for us."

"So they never enjoy a good meal? They just eat plankton?" asked Charlotte.

"They can adjust their food or adjust to their food, as the situation requires," Ann said.

"I don't understand," said the President.

"Well, let's say that the only available food sources were too high in protein, or short on some necessary oils, like vitamins E or D. They could adjust their body so that it would require less of the things unavailable and could utilize what was available to them, at least for a time. Then, they could analyze what they needed and design a source which would fill that need. So to them, food intake is a necessary weakness, and when they consume food, they are only recharging their energy sources."

"I see. I certainly hope Dr. Polo enjoys our meal tonight," Charlotte said rather defensively.

"He has had a long time to adjust to our pleasures," Ann said, hoping they would not catch the double entendre. She really didn't like talking about food, since Marco Antonio was not a normal Monitor, and soon she would have to lie to them. Discussing the needs of sanguinary eaters might be just too much for them to get used to.

"I noticed you enjoyed a finger of fine Scotch and a glass of wine. Do Monitors all enjoy alcohol in their native forms, too?" asked the President.

"We occasionally partake of mood-altering beverages, yes," Marco Antonio admitted.

"Marco Antonio partakes of all sorts of alcohol, yet I've never seen him drunk," said Ann. "Just one drink makes me tiddly."

The Blakes and their guests went on to discuss the country's plight, just as any friends might do. Marco Antonio carefully avoided giving advice or solutions, although his opinions were sought actively by the President.

Charlotte Blake was more interested in Marco Antonio, and Ann felt a strong attraction coming from the First Lady towards Marco Antonio. Ann was almost used to it, since being with Marco Antonio was like being with a famous movie star. "So how did you come to look like you do? Can your species change their appearance at will?"

"No. I moved into this body just as he was about to die. I healed his physical problems, made adjustments for my own mental requirements, and I've been here ever since."

You certainly shortened THAT story. Very smoothly, I might add.

"What happened to your natural body? Did it die?" asked Charlotte.

"No. It is in stasis. As a matter of fact, it is on my home planet, growing two new arms and healing the other injuries I sustained at Kudtz. I can be in either body if the other one is in stasis."

"Remarkable!" gushed the President. "Is that true of you, too, Mrs. Jacob?"

"No. I have no Monitor counterpart. I'm just a human female," Ann said without rancor or shame.

"And a lovely one," the President said smoothly.

"Thank you," replied Ann.

I told you he was hot for you.

He's just being a smooth politician. Not to worry, lover. It's Charlotte who has the crush, not Mike.

There was a time when I would have tested your hypothesis, but no longer.

Are you hungry, Marco?

For you, always.

Is there food in Questor?

Yes. I will not have to seduce the First Lady.

Good. I won't have to hurt either of you then.

Ann glanced at Marco Antonio and smiled sweetly.

Charlotte caught the glance and the smile, and said, "OK, my husband is the politician, so he must be politically correct, but I can ask the question about the elephant in the room. Are you two an item, or are you just co-workers? I have *got* to know—the curiosity is killing me!"

Marco Antonio looked at the First Lady for a brief moment, saying nothing. Ann didn't feel it her place to make any romantic declarations; she'd let Marco Antonio set the public boundaries of the relationship. "Mrs. Jacob is the most remarkable being I have ever met, of any race or species. I love her totally, truly, and completely."

"Wow!" the First Lady said, her hand on her chest. "Mike, I want you to say things like that about me someday!"

"I wish I had! Well said, Dr. Polo! You do know how to charm the ladies!"

"No need to. I have found the only one I need. It took me a while, but she was worth the wait."

Ann just sat there demurely. She was well pleased, and what woman would not be? *Thank you for that, my love. I will always treasure this moment.*

It's the truth.

Let's get married. Now I really want to, if you still do too.

May I announce it?

Sure, why not? Go for it, lover!

"Mrs. Jacob has agreed to be my wife. We are announcing our engagement here and now, in your company. She has at last agreed to make my life complete," Marco Antonio said with a small dip of his head in Ann's direction.

"Well, congratulations!" the President said, pumping Marco Antonio's hand. When the President stood up, everyone else followed. Charlotte leaned over and gave Ann a hug, congratulating her. Then, she turned to Marco Antonio, and hugged him, too. "I think we need some champagne for this!" said the President, and he walked to the door, opened it, and talked to a man standing just outside the door.

When he returned, he said, "We'll be having some sparkling wine grown and bottled here at the Biltmore winery." He then asked Marco Antonio, "Would it be all right if the staff photographer took some pictures? It's his job to record activities in the White House for historical reasons, and I cannot imagine any event more historical than this one! We are truly honored at your visit, and especially so since you chose this place and time to announce the first interstellar or intergalactic marriage!"

"The photographs are all right, but we would prefer that they not be released to the press. We would like to remain anonymous so that we can live in peace, without being hunted by paparazzi. Once people know who and what I am, that will be impossible. I'm sure you understand, sir."

"So you wish to remain simply Dr. Polo and Mrs. Jacob? I think history will demand a more thorough explanation for the Venden Retreat. Everyone wants to meet the Monitors, at least so they can thank them. I don't see how you can remain anonymous after all you've done for us," the President said.

"We are just diplomats representing the Monitor species, who have returned to their own planet. We may—or may not—remain in touch with them and with the United States government for future updates, but if I am exposed as an alien, that will force me to disappear, permanently. Those are my conditions, and they are absolutely non-negotiable. Share in our joy and be our friends or lose our association forever," Marco Antonio said in a level voice, without bluster or threat.

"Mr. President, history will show that it was you who were the first President to meet and talk with extraterrestrials. Eventually, the Monitors will allow their presence to be known, and you will have absolutely incontrovertible proof that it was you who saved our planet from the City Killers' return by working with the Monitors. Everything will be documented, photographed, and recorded. Just please, let us have a few months or years in private," Ann said.

"So be it!" said the President, just as a cart was rolled into the room with champagne on ice and four fluted glasses. "But let us drink to your engagement and photograph your announcement, which is plenty of cause to celebrate together!"

Smoothly announced in front of the waiter and the Secret Service dude. He's good!

Indeed. Perhaps we won't have to move to a cave in Wyoming after all.

The waiter poured the four Waterford flutes, and both the Blakes and the future Polos took one. "To many years of wedded bliss and close friendships with, uh, us!" the President toasted lamely.

Marco Antonio reached for the President's hand, shook it firmly, and sent him a message: *I hope that's spelled in capitals, sir. We wish to be friends with the Blakes and with the U.S.*

"Of course! That was precisely what I meant!" smiled President Blake. They all took a sip of the clear bubbly liquid. "I'm just a little speechless from your announcement!" Turning to the waiter and the Secret Service man still standing outside of the open door, he added, "They're getting married! We're the first they've told. Isn't it great?!"

The Secret Service man stepped inside, grasped Marco Antonio's hand, and said, "Congratulations, sir!" right after the waiter smiled, said "Congratulations!" but did not offer his hand. Marco Antonio reached out and took the waiter's hand in his and shook it as an equal, and Ann outstretched her hand to both men, who dutifully shook it. Without further ado, both men disappeared and closed the door.

Everyone took a seat again, and the talk turned to weddings. Mrs. Blake, always curious about Marco Antonio, asked, "What types of weddings do your people have?"

"We do not usually mate for life. We are not a very romantic species; we come together to procreate, and then we go about our business. The children are raised by professionals, so we do not have families like yours."

"You're MRS. Jacob, so clearly, you have been married before. Do you have a family, and how do they feel about Dr. Polo joining them?" asked Charlotte.

"I was happily married for many years, but my husband was killed in a fire. I have three grown children and three grandchildren, all of whom adore Marco Antonio," Ann replied.

"Ann's splendid family and the warmth they share is one of many of her great accomplishments. I find the entire system to be charming and to provide support unattainable by other cultures. I yearn to be part of such a sustaining collaboration of love," Marco Antonio added.

"Oh, you *are* a romantic!" Charlotte said. "Not all families are as successful as Mrs. Jacob's. Some squabble and split, and some live in misery for years."

"Which is why I am not marrying one of them," he answered smoothly.

The door opened, and the butler entered and announced, "Dinner is being served. Please walk this way." They all rose, finished whatever champagne was in their glass, and started towards the door. Marco Antonio offered his arm to the First Lady, and the President offered his arm to Ann. They prepared to walk to the dining room arm-in-arm, much as the elite of the continent had done during the Golden Age.

The dining room they had seen was an overwhelming room. The table was huge, designed to comfortably seat twelve guests on each side, plus two at each end. The size and height of the room and furnishings completely dwarfed the two couples. Designed to express opulence, it succeeded in making everyone slightly uncomfortable. Knowing this, the First Lady had requested that dinner be served in a smaller, more intimate setting.

They were escorted to the breakfast room where an oval table was set in front of yet another fireplace, this one creamy white with Wedgewood blue panels with white cameo-style bas reliefs surrounding the hearth. Two red and gold velvet chairs were placed on one side of the table facing the fireplace, and one was on each end. The white damask tablecloth became the center of attention in the dark wood paneled room. An elegant painting of a nineteenth century gentleman in a black suit hung on one wall, and windows with heavy red and gold drapes exactly matching the chairs decorated another. Two Renoir paintings were on the other side of the fireplace.

Still elegant, the room was at least of human proportions. Nonetheless, it was intimidating, demanding sumptuous food, elaborate dress, and complex manners. It was clearly built by and for people who sent their daughters to finishing schools to learn which forks to use for oysters, not for schoolteachers in simple black dresses.

The Vendens would love this house. Their red and gold capes would fit right in, and their medals would shine in the candlelight.

I agree querida, but their tails might knock over the chairs.

The meal they ate was a simple five-course dinner, elegantly served. Ann watched Marco Antonio eat sparingly, but she also noted that he had brought a large zip-lock bag into which he put the largest chunks of solid food. She knew he had to remove it from the table, or the waiter and cooks would know he had not eaten. He could "convince" the President and First Lady that he had eaten heartily and had enjoyed everything, but the staff would know he had not. The fish and steak simply had to disappear, and there were no dogs at Biltmore.

At the end of the meal, the President once again wanted to know how he had convinced the Vendens to retreat.

"I reversed the use of violence," Marco Antonio explained.

"How did you do that? Please explain that to me," the President almost begged.

"Here, touch my hands again, and I'll try to explain it to you," Marco Antonio said as he leaned forward and gently took the President's and Mrs. Blake's hand. Silently, he ordered them to pay attention only to his words, but not to his actions. Anything he did would not be noticed nor remembered.

Leaning back into his seat once more, Marco Antonio continued. "Hierarchies are based on power, and power is frequently based on violence. In an empire, it is based on the right of *institutionalized* violence. That means that a king or bishop, for example, would have the right to imprison, torture, or kill the people they govern. Once the common people, especially the soldiers, are convinced that the government, upper classes and religious leaders have no right to harm the members of its society, they can easily be convinced that they can and should remove those who advocate brutality." While he was talking nonchalantly, Marco Antonio removed the baggy from his jacket pocket and slid his steak into it. Smoothly, he closed the bag and returned it to his jacket pocket. He continued talking without missing a beat. "Their use of violence should be reversed. Those who advocate bloodshed must be removed. Ferocity must be shown only to those advocating brutality. It is a simple message, especially for minds with undeveloped ethical standards."

"How did you convince them all at the same time?" asked the President.

"It's a simple idea. If you tell me to kill someone, I should kill you. It's the right thing to do, because you are ordering murder, and you have no right to do that. You are the President, and you serve the people, not the other way around. All government should serve the people. All officers should serve their soldiers, making sure to order the best defense possible in the face of attack. But ordering an attack against non-combatants to gain riches, land, or more power is wrong."

"You must be very powerful indeed, if you can convince a whole army—hell, a whole planet—to kill their officers and go home. That's really scary," the President said, leaning back.

"Not really. I only had to convince a few before back-up arrived. My fellow Monitors quickly took over that task. Your people have independently come to the same realization, which is why you are such an interesting species. With the advent of democracy, the institutionalization of brutality gradually was eliminated. Oh, you flirted for a while with colonialism, but for the most part, America has fought defensive wars. You *could have* taken over the world shortly after World War II, yet you did not. Put simply, you do not fight wars to conquer because that would be wrong."

"Did we come to that conclusion by ourselves, or did you convince us of it?" the President asked, still visibly shaken by Marco Antonio's power.

"Oh, quite by yourselves. And you're lucky the rest of the world has reached the same level of moral development, or they might have invaded and taken over your country shortly after Yellowstone erupted. They didn't," Marco Antonio noted.

"Did you ever defend a human group against another human group?" Charlotte answered.

"No. We are just observers. We don't interfere."

"So why did you this time? Not that I'm complaining, mind you," said the President.

"For the same reason that you stopped Saddam Hussein from invading Kuwait. As long as he stayed within his own borders, you did not interfere. Once he left his own borders and invaded someone else, you stepped in."

Seeing a quizzical look on Charlotte Blake's face, Marco Antonio continued to explain. "I was particularly outraged that the Venden had sent an unmanned ship solely for the purpose of slaughtering millions. That's wrong, and an act committed by a species with no moral development. I can only apologize that I was not able to stop the City Killers' ship before it killed so many. As an outpost, I had no defense against an unmanned ship."

"Yet your people do have the means to bring down such a ship?" asked Charlotte innocently.

"Yes, but we would prefer to deal with its makers. Taking out hardware is rarely productive for long."

"So what will happen to the Trin and the Venden now?"

"They will return to their own planets, and they will be monitored. The Trin will probably be allowed to travel at will, but not to their neighboring planet. They too will be monitored."

"So your people are the Intergalactic Police?" asked Mrs. Blake.

Marco Antonio chuckled. "Not usually. Most species have developed a post-war mentality, as you have, long before they venture between the stars. Those that do not stop warring usually destroy themselves before they leave their own planet. It is very rare for space technology to fall into the hands of a species who still seek power and glory."

"Wow! I guess we came pretty close in the 60s, didn't we? There were a lot of people who thought we'd blow each other up, but we didn't," the President said.

"Mainly because America developed the bomb before the Germans and the Russians. At least that's what I think," Ann said, realizing that her opinion was of no interest whatsoever. She decided to shut up again, especially when she noticed the Blakes' two-second blinks. They were visibly tiring.

"I agree, Ann. If a more aggressive nation had achieved nuclear power unilaterally, they would have used it, at first just to end the war. Then, America would have developed it, and wars fought with nuclear bombs would have been inevitable," Marco Antonio said supportively. "Nuclear war was averted because the original developer of atom bombs refused to use them again."

"I was wondering how you located me on that submarine. The Secret Service assured me that the City Killers would not be able to pinpoint my whereabouts. I was very surprised to hear from an off-world visitor, believe me." Turning away from Marco Antonio, he looked at Ann. "How long have they been observing us?" Blake asked Ann quietly.

"Many hundreds of years. He's had many opportunities to interfere with human development, but he never has until our species was threatened."

"Why didn't he come forward before now? Well, maybe he did, and we just didn't know it," Blake said, answering his own question. "He could have helped Washington, Lincoln, Roosevelt—whoever needed him, and they just didn't talk about it," Blake said quietly to both Ann and Charlotte as if Marco Antonio couldn't hear him.

"Yes, they might have interfered before, but they didn't. Remember, they are *Monitors*. It is his job to be able to tell who's doing what and where. His access to information precedes and includes our internet and worldwide web." The corners of Ann's mouth lifted, knowing that Marco Antonio could certainly hear the entire conversation, although he chose not to respond.

"Are the Monitors going to help us clean up this mess?" the President asked, at last looking directly at the only Monitor present.

Marco Antonio did not answer immediately. Clearly, he wanted Ann to respond for him. "That would be very unscientific. He's here to collect data on a rapidly evolving species, not to help one group defeat another, nor to help that species replace its lost cultural artifacts, treasures, or economy. The Monitors let nature take its course; if he'd wanted to interfere, he could have just designed a more intelligent species and been done with it. That's why he has to back off now. He has protected us from invasion, but he won't help us skip any developmental steps that we still need to go through."

"I guess I understand. But we've been set back so far by things out of our control that a little help wouldn't be too far out of line, I think. What with Yellowstone's eruption, a plague of HPO, and then the City Killers' bombardment—the world's population is about a third of what it was, and many of our greatest minds have been turned to dust. Our cities, our economy, our universities, so many are gone," Blake said, his voice growing slower and quieter as he spoke. Clearly, he was becoming overwhelmed with the horror of the last five years. His eyes were brimming, and when he blinked, a single tear slid down his cheek.

"Marco Antonio has already done more than you know to improve the quality of life on this planet. He and Miguel have spent untold hours in laboratories developing something to clean the ash and glass out of the lungs of every vertebrate on the planet, and they're going to produce and donate this to every species on this world. He's already breaking about a million Monitor-rules to save us from painful deaths and possible extinction," Ann said somewhat defensively.

"I haven't forgotten, Mrs. Jacob. I'm sorry," the President said. He looked down at the napkin on his lap and said, "I just get a little overwhelmed."

"So do I. Believe me, I understand," said Ann.

Clearly, the Blakes were beginning to flag. Their questions and responses had slowed considerably, and they were obviously tired. At last, the President said, "Dr. Polo has been very shy about telling us what happened to him. Will you tell us, Dr. Polo? I'd like to know," said the President.

May I tell them?

Briefly.

"He followed the City Killers' drone back to its home planet. How, I can't tell you. That would be against the Prime Directive, you understand, and way above my pay grade." Ann decided to put in an ad for science research government grants. "I *can* tell you that our physicists are getting close, and that he has confidence that they will soon figure it out, if we still have physicists or astro-physicists at our universities."

"If we still have universities," quipped Charlotte.

Ann nodded briefly and continued. "Anyway, he got back to their planet, analyzed the radio broadcasts, learned their most widely used language, figured out who was what, and contacted the leader of the Venden. He told him exactly what would happen if they did not immediately stop building and using weapons of mass destruction. Of course, he had sent for reinforcements before he had threatened them, but he started to de-program the soldiers right away."

"He was alone?"

"Yes. They were about to send out another drone, and they were preparing an invasion force to be sent to Earth. He didn't think he could wait for back-up."

"Is that when you were shot down?" asked the President, turning directly to Marco Antonio.

"Yes. Fortunately, my people were there to rescue me before I completely decompressed," responded Marco Antonio to the first direct question he had received in several minutes.

"How badly were you wounded, if I might ask?" said Charlotte.

"Well, I'm still here," retorted Marco Antonio, smiling shyly. "But it is growing late, and I am fatigued. I think it is time for us to retire. This has been a lovely evening; the food was delicious, and the company most pleasant. We will be leaving in the morning, so until then, good night," Marco Antonio said, standing up and shaking the hands of both Mr. and Mrs. Blake.

Ann knew he had "convinced" them that they had not seen him put his steak and fish into a baggie, and that he had eaten heartily. He then offered Ann his arm, and together they walked back to the single bedroom they had requested.

Ann walked into the huge, over-decorated room, trying to take it all in. "This was quite a pleasant evening, wasn't it? It's such a kick for me to watch other people's reaction to you. I think they will allow us to remain discreet, insisting that you are just a human diplomat. If we can keep the staff ignorant of your true identity, we can remain unexposed," Ann said. *God, that sounds so dramatic! It feels like we're in a Star Trek movie or a James Bond flick. "Remain unexposed."Urp!*

You seem to be enjoying it. I will have to furnish you with that Venden cloak, along with a dagger, so you can stay in character.

Ann kicked off her high heels and started fumbling with the zipper of her dress. "It is fun, and it makes me so proud of you! I know how extraordinary you are, and now others are becoming aware of it, too. I meant it when I said I will treasure the memory of this evening for the rest of my life. You made it very special, Marco Antonio. God, how I love you!"

He walked across the huge room in his stocking feet and embraced her. His pheromones virtually pulsed from his body as he unzipped her dress. Sliding it down her shoulders, she stepped out of it and stood before him in her bra and panties. She loosened his tie and slipped it over his head, and he kissed her slowly and deeply.

Ann pulled back and started unbuttoning his shirt. Slowly, she undressed him, talking just above a whisper as her fingers moved steadily down his shirtfront. "Let me worship you, Marco Antonio. I want to make you crazy with lust so you'll know how you always make me feel. I want to spend the rest of the night bringing you to heaven's gate again and again, so you'll be absolutely certain that being a human is intense, dramatic, and passionate. I want to rock your world with an intensity unattainable in any other form."

Without any sense of haste, she removed his shirt and started to loosen his belt. He kept his hands on her shoulders and watched her as she attended to him physically, taking each piece of clothing off while continuing to talk of her intentions. When his pants and shorts were around his ankles, she knelt and helped him step out of them. Then, slowly, she pulled down each sock, and he put his hand on her head to steady himself. She tugged each sock off as he balanced on the other foot.

Ann took each of his hands in hers and pressed them to her head as she knelt in front of him. She looked up into his eyes, and let go of his hands. Very slowly, she pulled his hips towards her lips and kissed him, never taking her eyes off his. When she took his manhood into her mouth, he shut his eyes and moaned.

With her head in his hands, he directed her speed and rhythm to match the natural pulse of his hips. Her hands freely wandered, tenderly surrounded, grasped, pulled, and generally made themselves useful. She wanted him to feel passion, unbridled lust, and the love that spurred the intensity of his physical responses. Tonight especially, she wanted him to adore her as she revered him.

Before he had left Earth to pursue the City Killers and had been so damaged by the explosion and depressurization, he had flooded her constantly with passionate goodfeels. The depth of his love was exalted to the point of intense idolatry that verged on being pathological. His love had frightened her because it was so possessive, and Marco Antonio's power made him dangerous. She had learned to be intensely aware of his every fleeting sentiment, living in a state of anxiety and intense emotions.

Although exhausting, it was addictive. She missed it. She had felt it several times, so it wasn't completely gone, but it was intermittent. After being deluged with constant sensations, occasional wisps of sentiment were a far cry from the hurricane of passion to which she had become accustomed.

Sexual excitement was only one side of Marco Antonio's multifaceted emotions, she knew. There was more, so much more, and she wanted him to feel it again, and to swamp her with his tsunami of emotion. She could help him learn to temper his outbursts, especially those of jealousy and rage. As his trust in her grew, his feelings of security would mitigate his furor. He had been doing well, but now he was doing *too* well.

Ann had paid attention to Marco Antonio's discussion of the lack of emotional development among the Trin and the Venden. She strongly suspected that the Monitors had allowed their passions to atrophy in their million or so years of self-design. Feelings are messy, and they handicap intellectual pursuits. Glory, anger, lust, and even love need to be present, but controlled. Borderline personalities develop when strong emotions become a roller coaster ride, yet total equilibrium is boring.

Suddenly, Marco Antonio stopped moving. Carefully, he removed himself from her and lifted her to his eye level. She had communicated her thoughts to him while she was on her knees in front of him, his hands in her hair. Ann had not intended to have a conversation, and her theories were still at the stage of undirected thoughts pinging around in her head. But he had put it together instantly, and he knew that she was right.

You are absolutely correct, querida. Since I have returned, the fires have been banked. I have not felt the joy, the elation, of loving you. I thought it was because of the wounds I had suffered, but it was not. The doctors had to reformulate many of my neurons from my vial, and the filters they used to make genetic corrections would have found the gene

I changed for monogamy. They would have eliminated it, returning me to 'normal.'

You have changed, my love. The enthusiasm you felt, your zeal for life, has ebbed. I feel your love, but I miss your obsession. I just don't want you to be so depressed. I thought that if I could make you feel lust, maybe that would spread to other things.

You are a genius, querida! I have never stopped loving you—know that.

I do.

I will fix this. I will be the crazed zealot I was! I miss it, too, and I didn't know what was wrong. But my pet, my Ann, my little human with the three-pound brain, figured it out.

So this means that you love me more than your horse?

Oh, yes. And I would far rather ride you.

He reached down, pulled her into a standing position, and then put his arm under her knees and picked her up. He placed her gently on the huge, over-decorated bed, and kissed her, sending out wave after wave of pheromones and goodfeels until she was nearly unconscious with them. The pinging thoughts she had had were now impossible, since her brain was overwhelmed with emotions until she felt drunk with them. She didn't think, she just felt.

He slipped into her, and they both moaned. Once again, he sent her blasts of emotions. Love, adoration, gratitude, awe, delight—they came singly and in groups. She returned them as best she could, but she couldn't match his power or fervor. At last, she had to holler "Uncle!"

Instantly, everything stopped. "Are you all right?" he whispered, frozen above her, around her, and in her.

She didn't want to answer. She didn't want to move, or think long enough to formulate a coherent message. She just wanted to glow and assimilate everything that had just happened. Her body was still twitching, the orgasm she had been experiencing for several minutes finally slowing from waves to ripples.

"Give me a second," she whispered.

He rolled off her and pulled her onto him, holding her still against his body. They lay without moving for several moments while her breathing slowed and her heart rate returned to merely a sprinter's level.

"I'm sorry, querida," he whispered. "I was so, so *impressed* with you, that I almost lost control."

"I got exactly what I wanted. In spades. You're back, and we know what's different, and it can be fixed. I'm so happy!"

"So am I. Sleep now, querida. I have exhausted you," he said, kissing the top of her head and stroking her back.

"No. You are not finished. I'm OK. It's your turn," she murmured.

"I'm fine. Go to sleep. I love you," he whispered. Instantly, she was asleep in his arms. Without waking her, he covered their naked bodies with the beautiful bed's fine sheets and beautiful blankets, and went to sleep next to her, comforted in the knowledge that he would soon be capable of maintaining the zest for life that had been taken from him by his fuddy-duddy doctors. Ann knew more about the joys of life than any of them, and she would soon be his wife.

Just before he nodded off, he remembered the intensity of the feelings he had had when he thought of her as his. It made him smile as he thought,

She IS mine, all mine.

CHAPTER 21

Marco Antonio woke up after only a couple of hours. It was still very dark, and Ann was sleeping soundly next to him.

He was hungry. He had eaten shortly before they had landed, but that had been many hours ago.

He also had to get rid of the meat and fish that was still in the baggy inside his coat. Slipping quietly away from Ann, he slid out of the bed on the opposite side. Sleeping next to Ann when he was hungry was dangerous; his whole body yearned to taste her delicious blood, but he knew he should not do that. She had fed him just a few days ago, and it took several days for a human body to replace the pint or so of blood he had drained from her.

There was blood in Questor, but he couldn't eat it while the President and First Lady were with them, and he couldn't walk outside without having Secret Service men and women accosting him, demanding to know what he was doing.

No, it was far better to isolate one of them and feed directly from him. As quietly as possible, he put his clothes back on and went into the bathroom. He took the meat from the baggy, ripped it into small pieces, and flushed it. He rinsed the baggy and quietly returned it to his suitcase, placing his toothpaste within the bag so as to give it purpose. Nosy maids needed explanations for every object.

He put his shoes and socks on, tucked in his shirt, and left the room. With all the cameras on in the hall, he didn't think it would take long before a guard of some type came to see what he was up to. He wasn't afraid of the guards; in fact, he was counting on them.

It took less time than he had expected. There were two guards sitting outside their bedroom who stood as soon as he opened the door. He stepped out and closed the door so as not to awaken Ann.

"I'm sorry sir, but you are not supposed to leave your suite until morning. Please return and close the door," one said quietly to him.

Marco Antonio put his fingers to his lips to shush him, then he grabbed both their arms and took one step away from the door. Both Secret Service men automatically flinched away from his touch, but the shushing motion had diverted their attention. Even through their suit coats, he was still able to freeze both men in the half-second they had hesitated.

"I need to take a little walk, and you will accompany me silently and willingly," Marco Antonio said softly.

"How can we help you sir?" asked one of the guards.

"I could not sleep, so I thought a little walk might help to settle my nerves. This has been a very exciting day for me. Dinner with the President and his wife—I'm sure you understand."

"You cannot just wander around in the dark, sir, for security reasons. The President is in residence. Please return to your room."

"No, I need to walk," Marco insisted, holding on to both their arms.

"Perhaps you could go into the library or the billiard room. We could escort you to either place if you wish," said one of the guards. Since he was in a suit, Marco Antonio decided he was employed by the Secret Service, not the Biltmore House.

"That would be fine. I just need to move around a little."

The two Secret Service men turned around and started walking towards the massive library. The hallway was dark except for faint night lights every twenty feet or so. There was plenty of light for him, but the guards carried flashlights.

Marco Antonio followed behind, but they indicated that they wanted him abreast of them. He came up to the right of the nearest guard, who was holding the flashlight in his right hand. Marco Antonio put his hand on the hand holding the flashlight, and instantly knew where the cameras were located.

None of the three men missed a step but continued walking. When they turned into the billiard room, Marco Antonio walked almost directly to one of the corners, where there was a large leather chair beneath several small paintings. The guards stopped while he examined them. Turning abruptly, he grabbed both the hands holding the flashlights. One guard turned and walked around the room, admiring every picture, painting, carving and decoration in the room. The other froze, and Marco Antonio slipped his tiny sharp straw from his gum line where he kept it. Gently, he poked it into the carotid artery of the man standing in front of him.

As it was designed to do, the needle-sharp straw slipped easily into the man's carotid artery and then expanded both in width and length. Marco Antonio put the other end into his mouth, and started drinking the blood which was coursing up to the man's brain, full of nutrients, oxygen, and everything the brain needed to function. The pressure was good, the seal tight, and the man immobile.

Standing almost directly beneath the camera, the two were invisible to the observant electronics always on duty. After taking about a pint over several minutes, Marco Antonio removed the little straw, and sealed up the hole while he completely erased any memory of the event. In fact, they had been looking at the paintings behind the chair near the door, and the guard had a sudden interest in the similarly framed pictures on the other side of the fireplace, where the other guard had been studying them with great interest.

Wordlessly, the two Secret Service agents traded places, and Marco Antonio fed from the carotid of the other guard as he studied the pictures behind the chair. Normally, Marco Antonio would have saved the blood of the second man to be consumed later, but he did not want to take the chance of having any stored blood on his person. Instead, he drank all he could hold and then sealed the hole of the second man, who also would remember nothing of the incident. In a comfortably casual manner, all three started admiring the two beautiful billiard tables in the middle of the room and hence directly in view of the cameras.

"I think I will retire now. I thank you gentlemen for showing me this room, and I agree with your comments about the artwork. It is truly magnificent, as are the tables and fireplace. If you would like, you may accompany me back to my room now, although I'm sure I could find the way on my own."

"No, we'll accompany you, sir. It's no problem."

At the door to his bedroom, Marco Antonio turned and shook hands with each man, once again assuring them that they had merely enjoyed a look at the billiard room together. As quietly as possible, so as not to awaken Ann, Marco Antonio slipped into the ornate bedroom, took off his clothes, folded them neatly and put them on a chair. Naked once more, he slid between the sheets and lay down next to her.

He had known that something was missing, but he had not realized what it was. It was a marvel that Ann had realized it, too, and it hadn't taken her long to put her finger on what was missing: passion. That one gene had brought with it changes in his entire emotional rainbow, making the intensity of all emotions far greater. Before the City Killers had come, he had worked harder, longer, and with much more zeal. Music was sweeter, colors were brighter, anger was closer to rage, and desire was passionate lust, not satisfied by mutual masturbation but only by titanic release.

Monitors felt emotions, but theirs were timid and faded, as his had been. Once he had been exposed to the zeal attached to that one little genome, which he had thought attached merely to monogamy, he realized that it was a focus for all emotional intensity. Jealousy was part of it, but it was tempered by trust. Nothing could replace the joy of possession, the desire to protect and shield his beloved from all harm and from all others.

He remembered when he had walked Ann from the starship back to Questor. He had been in his native form, and he had shielded her from the blowing wind and sand. The act of sheltering her with his body had given him more satisfaction than any other thing he had ever done. Enfolding her tiny body within his arms to save her from all harm had been more satisfying than sex, and he had relived that feeling many times during the journey to Venden and Kudtz.

Wanting to hold her once more, he rolled over onto his side and pulled her towards him. She automatically spooned into him, her back and butt pressed against him. He wanted to nuzzle her neck, but he knew if he did, he would awaken her. She would rightly assume he wanted sex, and she would comply, but he knew her brain needed the time to rest and process. He could wait. In fact, waiting was part of taking care of her, so he merely allowed himself the joy of her warmth and the smell of her skin and hair.

In the early morning, he was on his back, and she was pressed against his side. Her hand was holding the part of him which had awakened before he had.

Your turn, lover.

As he rolled over towards her, she rolled onto her back and awaited him. She was ready, for apparently he had been emitting pheromones for some time. Without further ado, he slid home from third base, and she was rewarded with an instant home run. It was fast, but thorough, and they both got out of the bed with smiles on their faces.

They showered separately because they didn't know when breakfast would arrive. Since it took her longer to get dressed and put her face on, Ann showered first. Marco Antonio was shaving and Ann was finishing up her mascara just as there was a knock on the door. Ann opened the door and helped a man bring in a cart bearing a pot of what Ann sincerely hoped was strong, black coffee, and three covered plates. Under the largest was a selection of croissants, Danish rolls, muffins, and donuts. Under the two others were plates of scrambled eggs, bacon, and sausage next to hash brown potatoes.

"If I ate even half of this, I'd weigh four hundred pounds!" Ann told the waiter. "What would you most like me to leave for you?" she asked the waiter coyly.

"It's all for you and Dr. Polo, ma'am. But if that Danish were left on the cart, I doubt if it would make it back to the kitchen," he answered conspiratorially.

"Gotcha!" she said, and winked. "Anything else?"

"No, ma'am. You just enjoy it all! I've got to watch my weight, too, you know!"

"You look just perfect to me. You're wise to watch it before you have to lose it. Smart man. Thank you for bringing it!"

"My pleasure!"

Flirting with waiters again, querida?

Waking up next to you makes me want to flirt with everyone. I'm just one happy lady.

Good! I intend to keep you that way.

Ann decided to have some scrambled eggs with one of the muffins. The coffee was delicious, and Marco Antonio soon joined her, at least for the coffee.

"I'll bet you're starving," Ann said, taking another bite of scrambled eggs.

"No, I got up and met a couple of the Secret Service men last night. We went to the billiard room and admired the art," Marco Antonio answered.

"No wonder you woke up so full of spit and vinegar," she answered, sipping coffee.

"You were not exactly a shrinking violet," he responded.

She smiled and took another bite of her muffin. "Would it be so awful to give Mr. & Mrs. Prez a ride on Questor, Marco?"

"Not this time. It's snowing, and it would be difficult for Questor to carry four in the cold."

"It never occurred to me that the cold would bother Questor. He can face the frigid temperatures of space—why should a little snow bother him?"

"He would have four people. He'd have to provide air and warmth for twice the number of people, in addition to carrying twice the weight. Plus, he's been out in the cold now for several hours, and the wind has blown all night. He can't ascend into the sunlight when the planet is turned towards the dark side. It's just a bunch of little things."

"If you're worried, I am too. We don't have to do this," Ann said, then rethought it. "We could stay here until this blizzard is over. I don't want to strain Questor. I'm sure the Blakes would put up with us for another day or so."

"I'm going to pack while you finish breakfast. We'll see how it goes. Will you want to brush your teeth before we go?"

"Yes, but everything else can go into the suitcase. I'll be right there," Ann said, taking another bite of eggs but deciding not to finish her coffee. It was her second cup, and she didn't want to have to pee in Questor, at least no more than she absolutely had to.

Soon, they were dressed, made-up, teeth brushed, and packed. They started out the door, heading towards the main front door, where the President and First Lady were supposed to be waiting for them. Sure enough, there they were, along with four Secret Service men.

"Good morning, Dr. Polo, and Mrs. Jacob! I hope you had a pleasant evening?" gushed the President, all political-good-ol'-boy.

"Good morning, sir. These are today's guards? Would you introduce me to them so that I can thank them on behalf of the American people for the excellent job they have done in keeping you and Mrs. Blake alive," Marco Antonio said, giving a friendly nod to Mrs. Blake first.

"Oh, of course. This is Mr. Larson, and this is Mr. Shiller. They have been hard at work all night, keeping us safe!" said the President, turning to point to them.

"We meet again! Thank you, Mr. Larson, for watching over the President," he said, shaking his hand and then turning to Shiller. "And you, too, Mr. Shiller. We all know you labor in obscurity, yet your jobs are absolutely essential. I know for a fact that you don't let strangers just wander the halls."

Greet them, shake their hands, say nice things. I must summon Questor.

Without missing a beat, Ann stepped forward, took the hands of Mr. Larson in her own and blathered on about how she appreciated their efforts at guarding the first family. She repeated the process as she watched Marco Antonio stand perfectly still and hail Questor.

For the first time, she could hear his message in her mind. It wasn't a whistle or a moan, but it was the thought or memory of a sound between the two. She didn't understand it, nor could she have identified it as a message without a context, but she was pretty sure that Marco Antonio had used it to summon Questor.

After greeting the Secret Service men, she turned to the First Lady and said, "It looks like we'll need our coats. I didn't think to bring a heavy one, but I have a blanket in Questor, our transport." Ann thought it was a pretty lame piece of information, but she wanted to be chatty to keep everyone, especially the Secret Service men, calm.

"We'd be happy to drive you to your vehicle, sir. It's snowing pretty hard and the wind will freeze you in minutes," said Larson.

"We'll be fine, but thank you. Let's go!" said Marco Antonio, heading for the front door, pulling their suitcase behind them. As they opened the huge door, a blast of freezing air nearly knocked Ann over, but she lowered her head and followed Marco Antonio out the door. She carefully closed the huge front door so that the wind would not freeze the President and the other people who had come to say good-bye. She also didn't want them to see that Questor was right outside.

Questor's steps were waiting for them, and she quickly walked into his warm cockpit. Marco Antonio had stepped to the side, holding his hand out to steady her as she walked up the steps and disappeared from sight. Without handrails, there was a very real possibility that Ann might be blown off the steps, but she wasn't.

Questor closed the steps-tongue-door part of him through which they entered, and immediately started repositioning what had been their bed into two chairs. Ann grabbed the quilt and the afghan they had used as covers, and placed them at one end of the bed. She put her hand on the bed, sent Questor the thought, and they were immediately encapsulated by Questor in a storage vacuole.

"Because there is such a gruesome storm on the Eastern Seaboard right now, I think we should head west, as the President suggested. Perhaps we can find some decent weather, so we can see something instead of just white snow flurries." Marco Antonio put his hand on the table and sent Questor a message. Instantly, they were surrounded by windows, and they could see they were moving rapidly. It was impossible to discern which direction they were going because the snow was blowing around them in all directions.

"Won't they be able to see light through the windows?" Ann asked.

"Not in this storm, but it does make it more difficult for Questor to cloak," Marco Antonio answered. They sat and talked about Questor's abilities to change his shape by re-forming himself, about his energy consumption, and finally about his recent interest in sex. Ann felt like she should be embarrassed or something, but she really wasn't. He felt too much like an innocent pet.

As Marco Antonio was chatting about how his people had been bioengineering species like Questor for over a million years, Ann became gradually aware that there was something wrong with Questor. She put her hand under her seat, and she sent him greetings. What she got back was lackadaisical at best; she felt no tail-wagging joy that she usually got from him.

Talking with Questor was difficult, because she had to think in pictures and feelings rather than words. She tried to ask if he was angry with her or Marco Antonio, but all she got back were feelings of confusion. She tried to picture him sick, but she didn't know what sickness felt like to him. She could envision herself throwing up, or suffering from a fever, but she didn't think either of those would apply to Questor.

Marco Antonio, I think Questor is sick. I don't know how to ask him how he feels, though. There's something wrong.

Marco Antonio gave a brief nod and put his hand to the side of his chair.

Suddenly, they were blown to Ann's left, and her stomach told her they had experienced a rapid decrease in altitude. "Well, that was a wicked downdraft!" Ann commented in an effort to hide her terror.

"This storm has become dangerous. Questor is going to try to rise above it," Marco Antonio said, sounding like the pilot he was.

What's wrong with Questor?

You were right. He is sick and weak. He has not fed nor refilled his energy storage for several days, and the weather has been unseasonably cold. Now, we have asked him to fly through a blizzard.

Can he get high enough to reach the sun's rays?

Not with this wind, if he's going to provide air, pressure, and heat.

Have him land and drop us off, and then ascend until he's full enough to take us home. We'll take shelter somewhere, and he can pick us up later.

No. You're not going anywhere in this blizzard. There is no safety down there. It's a killer storm, far worse than normal.

Could he manage if he only had to provide heat and air for you? Have him put me in stasis on life-support. Wouldn't that use less energy?

I don't think it would make enough difference to bother to set up. Getting the stasis chamber prepared takes energy, too. I'll ask him and let him decide.

The silence in the cabin became disquieting. As the conversation became internalized, the storm sounds increased. They were both acutely aware that the rover was straining, and Ann and Marco Antonio were becoming conscious of the fact that his efforts were becoming more and more strained.

Suddenly, there was a jerk. Clearly, Questor had lost power. It had felt like a cough, or possibly a hiccup, and it scared Marco Antonio more than he showed, but Ann felt his fear. She tried to mask her own, but she knew she could hide nothing from Marco Antonio.

Is there any way he can use the energy from our bodies? Can we act as human batteries so that he can at least land safely?

I'll ask him.

"Apparently, Questor is sick. I have never seen him like this, Marco, but I've only seen him in California. Never in snow or a blizzard like this one," Ann said, mainly just to make a comment. "Although, come to think of it, it was Questor who carried us to the City Killers' ship, so I know he can travel in a vacuum and in the cold. If not for him, we would have dinosaurs stomping around our world again. Only this time, they'd be wearing bright clothes and probably be eating us or killing us for sport. He's my hero, and I'm really worried about him."

"Questor is going to land now. He does not have the strength to battle these winds and the cold temperature, so he is going to set down until the storm dies down a little. I think I've located a barn he can enter until the winds die down," Marco Antonio said.

How sick is he?

Very. I'm hoping he'll be able to send out messages. At least he won't have to provide air, but it might get cold. And dark.

He can use whatever energy I can provide. We can milk energy from the barn if we can. The owners will forget us if you ask them to.

I'm considering it, querida.

"Let me get that afghan and quilt out again. We can snuggle under them, and then Questor won't have to keep the temperature quite so high," Ann said as she returned to the place she had put the folded blankets, opened a flap, and withdrew them. She covered her legs and Marco Antonio's with the afghan. She was already chilly, and she knew it would soon be worse. Hopefully, they could preserve some of their body heat while they still had some.

"Have you sent out an SOS?"

"Let's land first. Then, we'll make contact with some rescue ships," he said out loud, but Ann could feel the unspoken "*I hope*" he failed to enunciate.

"I'm going to see if I can get an update on the weather," Marco Antonio said, taking out his telephone. Suddenly, he looked much younger.

Watching you poking at your telephone screen makes you look like a teenager.

Most people have phones like this now, querida. Except you, of course.

I have you, and access to your communication and information systems. You are my smart phone; all I can handle is a dumb phone.

At last, he said, "This storm is proving to be a really big one. No one that I can raise is saying how big or how long. Sorry, not much help from the smart phone. Questor thinks he can make it back to Biltmore House. I think there is a place there where he could get out of this storm," said Marco Antonio.

Marco Antonio reached into what Ann knew to be a storage vacuole and pulled out a black communication box. Closing his eyes, he held the box in his hand and just sat quietly for a moment.

Questor coughed again. At least, that was how Ann interpreted the hesitation they experienced. Like a hiccup, the perfect fluidity at which they flew was clearly blocked, and soon after, they had an abrupt change of direction. Ann thought it was a result of a wind, but it felt like a stream of water going around a rock. Whatever it was, Questor had never done it before, and this bumpy ride scared her, not for her own safety, but for Questor's.

It happened again, and then again.

Marco Antonio—are we going to make it? Is Questor all right?

Yes. Help is on the way.

Suddenly, they were lifted by several feet, and Ann could feel the ride smooth out and speed up. It was subtle, but she could feel it.

"He seems to feel better," said Ann. "The flight has gotten smoother, or did he get a lift?"

"Yes. We will be fine now," said Marco Antonio, turning his chair around to face her. "We will seek some shelter for him, and once we find a barn or garage, he can rest through this storm. When it's over, he can recharge his energy levels. I'm sure he'll be fine, querida," he said, being purposefully vague.

"There is a school bus garage near the Biltmore property. I think I saw it as we were coming in. They could move out the busses, and Questor would fit. Here, I'll show you on your phone," she said, picking up his phone so that she could show Marco Antonio the location.

"That would do nicely if there are not too many people around. I'd rather not attract a large crowd so that he could de-cloak," Marco Antonio replied, peering at the tiny map.

"I don't think there are many people there right now. Everyone at school has been sent home until this storm is over. Plus, Charlotte told me that most of the regular staff at the Biltmore house have been sent home for the whole winter, especially since the Prez and his posse are in residence here. The Secret Service does not like busloads of people too close, and these buildings are constructed to house some of the school busses having maintenance. The tours at the Biltmore are cancelled until spring, and the school busses won't be running for a few days. It should be OK," Ann said.

"Sounds perfect, if there are no busses."

The cabin remained cold, however, and Ann was shivering.

Perhaps you should go with the Blakes and spend a couple days with them at the Biltmore. We've been invited.

I would rather stay with Questor until I know he's OK.

It might get really cold, querida. That garage is probably unheated.

Then he'll need us to warm him up somehow. Do you know what's wrong with him? Is he sick, or just out of energy?

I think he's mainly out of energy, but he doesn't know himself. The Keith's rover came and gave him a lift, but it didn't have enough energy to share with him. They just weren't bred for this cold wind!

"If I stayed with the Blakes, where would you be?" Ann asked aloud.

"With Questor, until I get him settled somewhere warm. Then, I'll come back and stay with you."

"I am definitely a California chica, with no use for ice except in a glass. But I think we should stick together, all three of us."

"OK, *chica mia*. Check on this satellite map and see if you can find anything nearer that might give Questor shelter. It would be difficult to explain to the President that we need housing for our "flying saucer," which I would have to do if I took you back. We'll find something else. Here, help me look on this. The screen is bigger and it will be easier to see than on my phone." He handed her a tablet already set to their present coordinates, and she started looking for the buildings in the immediate area she had noticed before the storm. He and Questor used whatever magic they used to find a big barn or warehouse.

Ann beat them both. She spotted the school transport center where there were over a dozen school busses parked together on a large lot. Next to it was a large metal building which she guessed was the maintenance garage. On the computer screen, the image was of a bright, sunny day, but their view was of a big white snow blur.

Marco Antonio put his hand on Questor and sent him directions to the bus garage. Questor had de-cloaked, and he flew above the road at an altitude which would make him barely visible if there were any cars, which there weren't. Carefully and silently, he followed the directions he received from Marco Antonio, who was looking at the tablet.

Once in front of the large metal building, Questor became invisible again and hovered, but no one was near. Slowly and carefully, Questor opened his hatch, rolled out his stair-tongue, and Marco Antonio went into the blowing storm to open the huge garage doors. The simple locks on the staff entry door gave him no problems, but two large square-nosed yellow busses filled the vast metallic building. Without a word, he walked to one, pried the door open, and found the keys conveniently left in the ignition. He was surprised to see Ann entering the garage before he was able to open the garage doors to drive the bus out of the building. Ann tried the light switch by the entrance and quickly saw the automatic door opener on the wall near the light switch. She touched it, and the huge doors swung open.

With a merry wave, Ann pried open the door of the other bus and entered. She, too, started the bus and drove it out right ahead of Marco Antonio's bus. She could make out a bus parked in front of her just to the right of the garage, and she pulled up next it and turned off the engine. Marco Antonio drove his bus out the door and parked near the others.

Both Ann and Marco Antonio came out of their respective busses and back into the blowing gale. Questor carefully entered the huge garage, and the gigantic door closed smoothly when Ann hit the button. She stood there and tried to shake some of the snow out of her hair, and Marco Antonio walked back to inspect Questor from the exterior as he brushed the snow off his arms. Ann started walking around the huge garage, checking out her environment to see what might be useful.

"We were lucky that both busses were ready to go. Mine could have had a rear wheel off or the engine sitting on the floor. I didn't even check," Ann said guiltily. "I think my brain is frozen."

"Mine, too. I was going to just start the engine to see if the bus I was in would run, and then I was going to check the rear to make sure they were not attached to anything or disabled in any way. I was so surprised to see you hop into the other bus and drive it, I didn't do the proper check, either. We were lucky indeed. I didn't expect you to be able to drive a bus."

"I drove a 79-passenger diesel school bus for a couple years when I worked at Pioneer until I was too pregnant with Samantha to fit behind the steering wheel. I could still steer, but the double-clutch stick shift became very awkward in my ninth month."

"Of course," was all he said in response. Ann was too busy snooping around the garage to catch the irony in his voice or the satiric grin on his face. *Why should that surprise me?*

Tim was in college, and we needed the money. I got a whopping $2.50 a run, and I made three runs a day and taught the second grade. One hour before school, and two hours after, then prepping and grading and other school stuff. I was young and energetic.

Of course.

It was frigid, and there didn't appear to be any heaters or thermostats. There was nothing with which to build a fire, which was her first idea. There was an acetylene torch, but the tank was too big to get into Questor, and the heat it generated would burn him. There were a couple of tires, but they would be toxic if they burned. She hunted and lifted, peeking in cabinets and at the backs of the shelves along the sides of the building, but she could find nothing but an electric drip coffee pot and some tea bags. *No coffee. Drat!*

Ann thought everything would be better with a hot cup of tea in their hands, so she poked around and made a pot of boiling water with the coffee maker. She found a couple of very dirty mugs and cleaned them in the bathroom sink with pink hand soap, the granulated kind that she hadn't seen in years.

As Ann put the tea bags into the water, she decided that the pot itself was hot enough to help keep them warm, so she brought that back to Questor with her. Marco Antonio came into the cabin with Ann, and they settled back to drink their tea as they warmed their hands on the mugs.

"Would it help Questor at all if we heated it up in here?" Ann asked, sitting in what she thought of as the co-pilot's chair.

"Probably, but he can't drink tea, querida."

"I know. But what if we heated up something and brought it in here. This pot of tea will cool quickly in here, but the heat it gives off can be used by Questor. What if we heated something up and let it cool down in here?"

"I volunteer. You can heat me up anytime, querida."

"You might be up for that, but I don't know if Questor is. For him, it involves changing chairs into beds, and all sorts of moving around. No, I was thinking of heating up something metal or liquid with the torch and letting it cool in here."

"I don't see anything we could heat up. What did you have in mind, oh clever woman of mine?"

"Well, there's a wheel rim over there. We could heat the metal and bring it in here to cool. We could set it on the blanket or a tire so it doesn't burn Questor. In fact, we could leave the tank outside, and heat it from the doorway, so we don't have to lift it when it's heavy and hot, nor would we have to wrestle that huge tank up his steps. Hmm, maybe he could open his port from the top instead of the bottom, so we could stand at the doorway and heat the metal of the wheel," Ann said, clearly thinking out loud. "The wheel with the tire on it might explode if we heated the air within the rubber, but we could set the hot metal rim on top of the rubber, which would act as insulation between the hot metal and Questor."

"All possible. Which should we try first?"

"It might be easiest to just heat up water. No, that would involve a million trips because the water would cool too fast to be worthwhile. We should put the chairs together, so we could share our body heat under a blanket, but it might take more energy than we produce or save. I wish we had rocks; we could heat them, and they would cool more slowly and steadily. Damn!" Ann was virtually mumbling, as she considered ideas and rejected the bad ones, which was nearly all of them.

She was suddenly surrounded by goodfeels, and she looked up at Marco Antonio with surprise on her face.

I love to watch you think. You are adorable, and very, very clever. None of those things had occurred to me or to Questor. Your solutions are always so ingenious!

Thank you. I just try to be useful.

Without saying another word, Marco Antonio put his cup down and hopped out of Questor before the steps were even all the way down. Ann didn't know exactly what he was doing, but she followed him. He grabbed the heavy wheel rim, set it on edge, and rolled it towards Questor. She tried to bring the acetylene tank over, but even on a dolly, it was too heavy for her. She jogged back to Questor, hoping to be able to spread the blankets on the floor before the wheel rim was in the cabin. The blanket was not enough insulation, so they rolled a tire up the ramp, and put the heavy rim on top and heated the rim.

Questor reconfigured the cabin so that the seats were together, like a couch. There was much jostling and heaving, but before long, there was a large tire, beneath a metal object with a can of hot water on top, both being heated with a torch.

Marco Antonio put his hand on Questor's flank to see if the heat had helped. Although it hadn't made much difference in Questor's physical state, it had done wonders for his mental health. He felt appreciated, even cherished, and he was deeply moved that Ann had come up with so many ideas of ways to help him. While he appreciated Marco Antonio's efforts, he knew that Ann had been the one who had decided to take action. Monitors didn't do things like that for their transports.

We will, my friend. From now on, we will be more aware of your needs. We have learned something from these humans, haven't we?

Marco Antonio got a loud, sharp, bright image of Ann from Questor, and the message was clear: it was Ann, not the other humans or Monitors, who had tried to help transports. She had washed him, she had warmed him, and she had made love inside of him.

Marco Antonio backed off, a trifle shocked. While he sauntered over to the workbench to retrieve Ann's lunch, he mused about the message. A part of Marco Antonio was stunned by how much Questor had appreciated those changes, so he was not too surprised when Questor's door opened to see that the cabin had been reconfigured into a bedroom with a tire rim-fire pit by the door.

"I guess he thinks it's bedtime. He just reconfigured the cabin all by himself," Ann said, reclining on the bed with her mug of tea poised carefully on the tire rim.

"I think he wants me to heat you up, querida. I think he prefers body heat to acetylene torches or bus wheels. I must say I agree with him."

There are worse ways to ride out a storm.
Indeed there are.

CHAPTER 22

The storm lasted the rest of the day and night. Marco Antonio and Ann heated up the cabin several times by heating the tire rim with the acetylene torch, and several more times with the heat from their bodies.

"Tell me more about your life, mi Chula. When did you get interested in buying real estate?" Marco Antonio was ashamed and embarrassed that he knew so little about the first 60 years of Ann's life. When they talked, it was about the crises they were dealing with at the time, or the people and experiences they had shared together.

Ann told him about their first tri-plex, which she and Tim had purchased with money from selling her Volkswagen and some she had borrowed on her signature at the teachers' Credit Union. The buyer had taken back a second mortgage, and the bank let them carry over the first mortgage. It was pretty fancy financing, but Ann had learned that there were many ways to make a deal if everyone was motivated and their credit was good. The secret, of course, was to buy low and sell high, which she was particularly good at.

Ann had borrowed money from anyone who wanted a slightly higher interest rate than they could get in a bank. She knew doctors and lawyers who had more money than they knew what to do with, and she offered them 10% and a second mortgage on whatever property she wanted to purchase, and they were pleased to get it. The Jacobs would buy properties that had been neglected, fix them up, raise the rents, and sell them at a profit, paying off their 10% notes, and still making enough to buy something else.

"I have to go to the bathroom. You think of a story about your life about how you got so rich and sexy," Ann said. She got up and Questor opened a ramp and let her down.

When she returned, Marco Antonio was deep in thought. He looked up at her as if he was afraid that whatever he said wouldn't be good enough. He was afraid of disappointing her. She had seen that look on many faces when she was a teacher, but she had the additional ability to sense his emotions, if not his specific thought.

"Just tell me about the first thing that happened to you when you arrived on this planet," she suggested, realizing that the assignment had been far too broad.

"There were two of us when we arrived. We found two bodies dying of a cholera epidemic. We entered their bodies, patched them up as well as we could by rehydrating them and killing the specific bacteria causing all the trouble. We carried our bodies back to our rover, put them into stasis, and returned to set fire to their little cottage. Then, we flew to England from France, so nobody would recognize their bodies and treat us as the people we used to be," he said, tucking in the afghan around Ann as she sat down and put her head on his shoulder.

"And lived happily ever after?" Ann said, indicating that she wanted to know what came next.

"We got a cart and a horse, filled it with trade goods, and went on the road, hoping to chance upon strangers who would teach us English. On the second day, we were set upon by brigands, who gang-raped me and killed my husband. After that, I was on my own," he said with a note of finality. "Your turn."

"You were a female?" Ann asked, sitting up so she could look at him.

"Yes."

"They raped you? The brigands? What a horrible way to enter a new culture! How long were you a female?"

"I was a female long enough to know it was much better to be a male in that culture at that time. Your turn."

"Your stories are much better than mine!" She could tell that he didn't want to talk about it, so she let him off easily. "Well, we bought two duplexes from an old, retired couple, the Edwards, who owned them free and clear. They were willing to carry back the loan and take only $5,000 as a down payment. One day, while Tim was on the roof, and I was painting in the kitchen, Mrs. Edwards came up and watched me for a while. 'Would you like to buy some more? I like the way you kids are willin' to work to fix these up. I'd sell you some more that we have, cuz ol' P.M. can't work like he used to, and he gets mad at me if I get on the roof to fix a cooler.' She was 84 at the time."

"She gave me a list of the 13 other properties they owned, I drove past them, and I made an offer on a house on Myrtle Street. Mrs. Edwards said, 'Oh no. You cain't just buy the best one! If you want 'em, you gotta take 'em all!'"

"When I explained that I had only $5,000, which wasn't enough down payment on all thirteen properties, but Mrs. Edwards assured me that it was enough. They'd take back the rest at 8%. So I borrowed a contract of sale that Mrs. Edwards had had a lawyer draw up on another property, and I typed up a contract of sale for every one of the thirteen houses, splitting up the $5,000 equally, so that each house had a down payment of $384. Most were rented and all needed maintenance, but some were beyond fixing. I had the fire department burn down a house that I'd paid $7,000 for, and then sold the lot for $20,000. See? Not very exciting," said Ann, a trifle ruefully.

But each house had a story, and every deal was an adventure. I know that you are giving me the Reader's Digest condensed version, but I want to learn of a lifetime of deals, of failures and successes, that made you who you are, querida.

For the next few hours, he and Ann swapped stories, and he told her of things he hadn't thought of for centuries. Neither of them were children, who speak mostly of the present and the future. They had a past, a history that had created them one event at a time, and the more they shared these events, the better they knew each other. Marco Antonio was very glad he had taken the opportunity to feed when it had presented itself. He had needed the energy.

Questor was another underestimated character in his life. It was true that he had taken for granted Questor's wellbeing, vastly underestimating the rover's amorous and emotional needs. Once he realized how important sex was to the happiness of his rover, he felt curious about his other needs, and more responsible for making him happy. As soon as he returned from the hospital on his home planet, and as soon as the lung cleaner was produced and released planet-wide, after the wedding, he intended to definitely analyze the emotional needs of all the transports used by the Monitors.

What are you smiling about, lover?

I'm just thinking about how many things we have to do, querida.

Welcome to my life. I'm just glad we had the chance to have some time alone with nothing else to do but love each other. Life tends to get in the way when we're at home.

They both grew silent for a few moments. Ann put her hand flat on the bed and tried to ask Questor how he felt. She got back a tail-wagging response, but it wasn't as energetic as she'd felt in the past.

She tried to sequence a series of mental images of Questor high above the clouds, bathing in the sunlight. She pictured herself and Marco Antonio waving good-bye to Questor while standing on the ground in front of Biltmore House as he ascended into the sky. Then, she tried to picture his return, but she couldn't think of any way to differentiate his state of health except by his doing a couple of completely unnecessary loops in the sky before landing.

She could feel Marco Antonio smiling. He was laughing at her, but not in a derogatory way. He was just amused at her efforts at telepathy with a non-speaking creature. She didn't take offense at his quietly observing her floundering around mentally; he was trying to be supportive, as was Questor.

Ann got a message broken up into hundreds of tiny pictures of both Marco Antonio and her in the Secret Garden behind the Smiths' house in Hanford. Then, they waved as they grew tinier.

"Questor doesn't have binocular vision!" Ann said aloud. "How could I have not realized that before now? I am such a stupid old lady! He doesn't even see in the same way I do, does he? So even if I think in pictures, he doesn't have a clue what I'm trying to show him. He doesn't see the things in the same way. Such a stupid, STUPID old lady!" she practically wailed.

"Careful, old lady! You are talking about the woman we both love," Marco Antonio said as he smiled at her. "Rovers are notoriously difficult to communicate with. For a non-telepath, you do remarkably well, querida. Questor truly appreciates the fact that you have tried so hard to establish contact with him. In fact, he recently let me know in no uncertain terms that you are the only one who does not take him for granted. In his own way, he loves you dearly."

"Well, I definitely need some remedial-transport-communication lessons. I just can't seem to get the hang of it, Marco. And it's no wonder—we don't even perceive the world in the same way. How will I ever be able to communicate with him? This is so frustrating!"

"Let's practice," Marco Antonio said. He tried to send her a message, and she would try to repeat it. Then, she would send the message to Questor, and he would repeat the message he had received to them both. At times, they would burst into laughter at each other, but for the most part, Ann learned a lot about how rovers communicated.

The point of the message was that Questor felt he could make it back to California if the weather was good, if he could rise above the clouds and into sunlight, and if he had to carry only two people. Thus, they decided to leave in the morning if the storm had ebbed.

By morning, the storm was over. They took the big rim and bus tire out, and rolled them back to where they'd found them. Questor floated out to the big, snow covered parking lot entry, the two busses were returned to their snug parking places within the garage, and everything was returned to its former location. Where the busses had been parked outside, the snow was much thinner, but the wind had been sufficient to blow snow under the busses so that only the tire tracks were obvious. Marco Antonio tried to throw some snow into the blank, dark places so that only the most observant would see where the busses had parked. Of course, the tops of the busses had about a foot of snow, making them look like Marines with flat-tops.

If the snow did not melt quickly, many people would wonder how two busses had ended up with a foot of snow on top of them.

I think we should tell President Blake that we slept in his bus garage. Anyone with half a brain will be able to see what we've done, and they'll be out looking for terrorists. Let's save some Secret Service men some frostbite.

OK, querida. I agree that it is obvious that the busses were outside last night. I'm not used to explaining my activities, but now I suppose I should. It will help show that we are cooperative. I'll let you call President Blake. It will give him a thrill to hear from you.

Yeah, right.

After Ann called the President, they took off in bright sunlight, the brightest Ann had seen since Yellowstone had exploded and darkened the skies. Questor flew above actual clouds, with blue, not gray, above them. The ground was sparkling white, and the trees bare and skeletal. Eventually, they saw evergreens covered in snow. It looked like a Christmas card for a while, but Questor continued to gain altitude until individual trees could no longer be seen clearly. They lost forward momentum, and it seemed as if they just floated.

Marco Antonio sat for a moment, his hands on Questor, until he suddenly nodded. "Come here, querida. Lie down next to me. This will be fun."

Ann had no idea what he had in mind, but she lay down next to Marco Antonio on the bed, which seemed to grow narrower. In fact, everything in the cab seemed to shrink and smooth out until there was only Ann and Marco Antonio lying together on a constricted, flat surface. Gradually, the flat surface felt like it was trying to slide them to one side as the entire ship rolled over.

Marco Antonio wrapped his arms around Ann and rolled her onto him as the ship turned. There was plenty of room in the cabin, but the bed was quite narrow and kept shifting as Questor slowly rotated in the sun. Everything that had been sitting around in the cabin had been encapsulated into a storage vacuole, so there were only the two entwined people slowly turning over on their ever-shifting bed.

"This is fun!" Ann said, holding tightly onto Marco Antonio. She could feel his pheromones taking over as she clung to him. She nuzzled his neck and reveled in his smell—he reeked of sex. But it was the smell of Marco-wanting-sex, a smell that was unique to him and intensely intoxicating. She could feel him growing hard against her and it made her want to squirm. She wanted to move herself so that she could align her body next to his, and his hands on her back and butt obviously showed that he had the same idea.

"We have to remain hooked together as Questor rotates," Marco Antonio whispered, breathing heavily.

"I could wrap my legs around you. Would that help?"

"Oh, I think it would. Let's see what else we could do to join our bodies together." He fumbled with clothing, as she removed hers, all of which quickly became enclosed in new vacuoles and disappeared. His hands were on her hips until he moved one hand to the front of her body and slid it down and in. "Oh, Ann, you are always so ready for me."

Her response was breathy and slow. "How could I not be when you hold me like this? When you smell like horny Marco, and you feel as hard as a rock? I would have to be hopelessly senile not to react to you. I think you'd turn me on if I were dead as a doornail."

"You're not. You are very much alive. And you feel good."

"I certainly do. Oh, my. Yes. Yes. Yes."

Questor continued to rotate, but the bed slowly disappeared. Instead, the cabin became one circular chamber spinning slowly, growing bigger and bigger as Questor thinned out his walls and expanded to expose the maximum number of cells to the solar radiation. Because the chamber was larger, the spinning became slower, but they continued to keep rolling over on one another.

Even as busy as she was, Ann managed to note that Questor himself was shimmering. His sides were vibrating unevenly, and it frightened her.

Don't worry. He's rotating his cellular structure so that as many cells as possible can directly absorb the solar energy. I'll ask him to be less distracting. Just feel. Don't look. Don't worry. No fear at all.

It had become completely black within the cabin, and they just rolled around, completely wound around each other. After several rotations, Marco Antonio disconnected them and turned Ann around so that she was spooning with him. This enabled him to touch the front of her body with his hands after they had reconnected. His hands knew what to do, where to go, and how to hold her, but they denied her the opportunity to touch the front of his body. She became passive, and let Marco Antonio stimulate her body in any way he liked, and he liked what she liked. He was completely aware of her every thought and response, so every repetition was in accord with her reaction.

Ann thought they had plenty of time and absolute privacy. As Questor's strength increased, he went higher and higher until they were completely weightless. They rolled over several times, trying front and back.

Ann was surprised to discover that it was much more difficult to move jointly with no gravity to help hold them together. What they expected to be concurrent movement was frequently enough to push them across the cabin.

The forces they shared were not equal. What they thought was joint movement was actually usually controlled by Marco Antonio, so Ann got pushed into Questor's side. It became a challenge for her to gauge the force she needed to counter-balance his thrusts. It was fun, but distracting.

Staying in sync with you is hard work.
Are you tired?
A little. This is fun, though.
Yes it is.

Suddenly, he pinned her against the wall. When he put his hands against Questor, two handles formed and he grabbed one and held on as he repositioned her body. She was face down, and suddenly the top of her head was half buried into the wall. At last, she had something to push against. Marco Antonio lifted her hips and placed her knees against the wall so that he was behind her and between her legs. He grabbed the handle on the other side of her head.

I will try to make this fast and hard, querida. Come for me, and let me hear you. Tell me what you want, and I will give it to you.

"I want you. You know I do. Hard and fast. Yes. Like that. More. More. Oh, Marco Antonio—come with me. Let's go!"

After they had exploded in a frenzy of twitching splendor, he pulled her up and let her go. She floated alone except for his hand, which held hers as he floated next to her.

You always said you felt like you were floating after you came. Now, you really are. Float and rest. That was hard work, but worth everything to feel you come like a rocket beneath me.

I am floating, aren't I? This is really special, Marco. There haven't been many women who have really rocketed into space. I think Questor is a true Orgasmatron. You have taught him well, grasshopper.

Grasshopper?

Movie references. All part of my shallow education. Let me float in silence while I mix my metaphors.

As you wish, my lady.

CHAPTER 23

They arrived back in Hanford dressed, rested, but hungry. Ann wanted a chili verde burrito from Jalisco's, but Marco Antonio wished to confer with Ruth and Gabriel. They offered to feed him, and since he was very hungry and the refrigerator was empty, he took them up on it.

Ann said nothing, secretly happy that he was taking no chances about finding feeding donors. While Miguel had a wide circle of acquaintances he visited regularly, Marco Antonio did not, so he would have had to approach a stranger. She couldn't help but be concerned that he would be interrupted or attacked for some other reason, no matter how often she assured herself that he had been gathering blood from unwitting donors for 800 years.

Hopefully, one day they could make arrangements with a hospital or a morgue so that they could collect the blood from the recently dead, store it, and use it at will. Ann had never mentioned the idea, mainly because neither Marco Antonio nor Miguel liked to talk about their feeding habits or sources of nourishment, so she didn't bring it up. She had been working on a plan for a major hospital to provide *post mortem* blood to the Lung Cleaner factories as food for the bacterial and nematode colonies which produced the spores used to clean vertebrate lungs. Surely no one would miss four or five pints a day from a major hospital?

Unfortunately, major hospitals occur in major cities, many of which had been eliminated by the City Killers. Right now, they were using slaughter house blood—mainly beef—but why couldn't they use human blood? Maybe they could make something up about producing superior lung cleaners for human use from human blood?

It was nonsense, but it might help establish a continual supply. She'd have to think about it and talk about it with Miguel or Marco Antonio later.

After she finished half of her burrito and wrapped the other half for later, Ann called Samantha to see how things were going, especially with Miguel. What she heard in response to her question about how the Samantha-Miguel romance was coming along surprised her and confirmed Marco Antonio's worst fears.

"Mom, he's a really nice guy, but he's a blood-eater! That immediately eliminates him from becoming part of the family. I don't want my kids raised by a vampire—that's just too weird. He makes a nice uncle and friend, but he's certainly not daddy-material," Samantha said almost flippantly.

"I thought you and he were an item, at least sexually. Was I wrong?" Ann asked, trying not to sound like a nosy mother.

"When he does that pheromone-thing, he's pretty hard to resist. I must admit I haven't always succeeded in getting him out the door before that happens. I sure wouldn't let him stay over. My kids are not going to wake up to find Miguel in my bed. Or anybody else, for that matter. They're just not ready, and I don't know if they'll ever be."

"It is a good idea to be discreet, for sure. But I don't want you to become a nun or something, Sam. You deserve to have a life that includes masculine company. It doesn't have to be Miguel."

"You're right. A little sex relieves all sorts of tension and Miguel can certainly brighten my mood. I can see why you were so taken with Marco Antonio after Daddy died. Being a widow sucks!"

"It certainly does."

"You could afford to fall in love with him, but I can't. I have three kids to think of, and if I choose someone to marry or settle down with, the first requirement would be as a father to my kids," Sam said.

"And you think a vampire just wouldn't fill that bill?" Ann asked.

"No way. A regular Monitor would be weird enough, but a vampire-Monitor? Nope."

"Would you be too shocked if I married Marco Antonio?" Ann asked.

"Not at all! Go for it, Mom! As I said, you don't have kids to feed who are already picky eaters. You don't have to explain why Daddy doesn't eat his vegetables, either. Or his meat, or his bread, or anything else Mommy cooks."

"True, and I hate that part of it. Cooking is how we show love. We've talked about getting married, and he announced it to President Blake at dinner the other night. Because we have to deal with so many people, it would just be easier to be introduced as 'Dr. and Mrs.' instead of 'Dr. and Hobag.'"

"Yeah, I can't picture you being happy as someone's girlfriend. How soon?"

"He has to return to his home planet-without-a-name first. He's got to pick up his spare body and get some fine-tuning done. Then he'll come back and we'll do it."

"God, you make him sound like a used car! Why doesn't his planet have a name?"

"Well, it does, but not one we can pronounce. The name comes with colors and a certain smell, and a sound we can't hear. We'll have to come up with something better, so work on it with me. Otherwise, the press will come up with something we don't like, and we'll be stuck with it," Ann said, adding, "I think it would be best to come up with a completely new word that has no connotations for anybody. If we use something like 'Asgard,' it comes with religious or cultural baggage. I haven't really talked to Marco Antonio about it, which I should do, I suppose."

"I would think so. They might have something that is similar to what they call it that we *could* pronounce. We've got to check. Besides, if we come up with a completely new word, it might translate into something obscene in their language. We can't have them coming from *The Land of Shit* or something. It has to be neutral, at least, and it should be fairly close to one of the sounds they attribute to their planet."

"We can't hear that sound, let alone say it," Ann reminded her.

"Well, you know what I mean. We should be careful not to offend anybody."

"I absolutely agree. For that reason, be careful what you say to Miguel. He's very sensitive about being a vampire, and he is also fairly convinced that human women need to be sexually serviced, so he might be thinking that he's doing you a big favor," Ann pointed out.

"Yeah, he's mentioned that, sort of. Actually, I kind of agree with him, and I appreciate his efforts to please. Why, has he made the same offer to you, too?"

"No. He knows I'm Marco Antonio's woman, so he steers clear, but it's come up in other conversations," Ann hedged. She wanted to squash that rumor-bug as soon as it popped its head up. Samantha did not *ever* need to know that Miguel was very willing to take Marco Antonio's place. Marco Antonio didn't need to know it, either.

The conversation continued to wander around the wedding, the Monitors, Sam's classes, and the kids. They talked for over an hour.

When she heard Marco Antonio coming back upstairs from the lab, Ann figured it was time to sign off and get some work done. There were a stack of files, notes, and documents Casey had left on her desk that Ann had not even glanced at, and she knew it was time. "Bye, Sam. Catch you later." She walked to the desk, put the phone in the charger, and looked at the pile.

Ugh!

Ugh what? Was that "ugh" for me?

Oh, I didn't feel you behind me! No, silly. I was just thinking about this stack on my desk that Casey left for me. I have to stop lollygagging around and get back to work. No 'ughs' for you!

I'll try to get to that before I leave.

He reached around her and picked up a couple of lawyer-made, tidy files and flipped open the top one.

"When are you leaving?" Ann asked aloud. She had learned to use words to mask her emotional responses to certain ideas. She knew that talk about his leaving was always surrounded by feelings of fear and loss. By saying it in words, those feelings didn't come out so clearly, so he didn't have to respond to them. She hated feeling needy; it made her feel and look weak.

"I was just talking to the doctors, and I told them I wanted that genetic alteration done for monogamy. They were quite interested in your observations that it has affected other emotional responses. They are going to direct their research into that gene to see how monogamy is related to passions for work, art, music and sex. They found it very impressive that a human being would be the one to notice such a subtle but profound difference in the ability to focus attention because of the change of that particular gene." After answering her question, he returned his attention to the legal document in his hands.

Ann knew he was hiding something he didn't want to think about or discuss. "Will you have to stick around so that they can measure the changes in you when they alter that gene?" Ann asked, looking up at him. That could take days, weeks, or years, and she certainly didn't want him to be gone that long. Suddenly, she was afraid.

"Perhaps. We'll see what they intend to study first. I won't let them keep me for too long—I have a wedding to attend." He reached over and gently pinched her cheek.

"If I may make a research suggestion, see if they can figure out a way to measure your jealousy and possession levels before and after they change that gene. They should be aware of both the strengths and weaknesses it brings."

"An excellent suggestion!" he said, perching one hip on the corner of the desk. "Monitors do not usually feel much jealousy or possessiveness, since we do not collect objects or money. We wouldn't want them to change the genetic make-up of fellow Monitors until after they have mastered some methods of controlling those violent urges," Marco Antonio said. "However, since we do not have monogamous sexual relationships, the primary purpose of changing the gene would be to focus attention, not to defend a mate."

"Have other Monitors fallen in love with creatures from a different species?" Ann mused aloud while she was trying, unsuccessfully, to concentrate on the boring contract she was trying to read.

"Not that I know of. They are very anxious to study me to see what has changed in my brain structure or function which has brought about such intense emotional attachment."

"Well, it can't be the only monogamy gene because you love me with or without it," Ann pointed out. "There has to be more to it, either another gene or a combination of them. Perhaps it is something to do with the human brain you transfer into that finds a home in your Monitor brain when you transfer back. I can only guess, but it feels like you love me when you're in your Monitor body. Is there a difference?" She felt like a cheerleader asking if he liked her pom-poms this way, or that way, searching for a compliment. It really was a question, not a needy-reassurance bid.

"No. I find you enchanting while I'm in either form. When I was nearly dying, the one thing that brought me comfort were thoughts of you, especially when I was holding you during that dust storm. I had all my legs wrapped around you, protecting you from the wind, and it was those intense feelings and memories I concentrated on."

"That's interesting! It felt really good to be completely surrounded by you. It felt like a squeeze chute they use to calm cattle, totally surrounded and safe. No—better than that. I felt swaddled like I haven't been since I was a baby. Surrounded by a protective, loving entity and completely safe. I loved it, except it meant that you were about to leave, which I hated."

What are you hiding from me, Marco Antonio? There is something you do not want me to have to deal with, so you're not thinking about it. What is it?

"The psychologists are very interested in this whole phenomenon, and I wouldn't be surprised if they sent one or more Monitors to Earth to study us," Marco Antonio said almost ruefully. He was still hiding something.

I'll bake them a cake. What else?

They might want me to stay so they can study me. It might take longer than I want to be there, querida.

"It's the price of being a hero. No good deed goes unpunished," Ann responded. *How long? Can they make you stay home?*

NO!

"They just haven't met you yet, querida. Once they do, they'll be smitten, too, and then they'll understand why I must return to you quickly. When I'm not near you, I feel like something is missing, and I have a hunger for you. You have become my compulsion."

"I can just see you around a bunch of Monitors who have a crush on me! You would be so jealous, you'd blast them all back to the Mariana outpost," she said, smiling, relieved that they could not force him or imprison him.

"You'll just have to hold me back."

Is that what they think I am doing to you?

Yes.

Am I in danger?

Not as long as I draw breath. They cannot keep us apart, and I will not let them hurt you!

Then I'm not afraid. Are you?

She sat quietly and listened. Nothing. He wouldn't lie to her, even mentally, so he *was* afraid, but he didn't want to discuss it. She tried once more to concentrate on the legal mumbo-jumbo written on the paper in front of her, but it was impossible. She decided to change the subject. "I'll take you for frequent rides in Questor, just to remind you that it's just you and me, baby, alone in weightless darkness, finding endless ways to love each other." She reached up and touched his face with the back of her hand. Some things were better said in words. She'd let his memories and imagination fill in the blanks far better than any garbled bunch of thoughts she might be able to send.

"I'd like that. Questor will like that." *Don't be afraid, querida. And I like your garbled thoughts. They're like a jigsaw puzzle with pieces missing: a real challenge. I love watching you put ideas together from such disparate memory files. They stir around in your brain, and suddenly, a clear thought emerges, fully formed. It's fascinating.*

"Bring your Monitor body, and I'll rock both your worlds. I'll show you how fascinating I could be. Clearly, I have some research to do, my love. I've only loved half of you," she said aloud. *Picture this: what thrilling things could you do if you had eight hands? You could completely enclose me, or give me a full-body massage of Biblical proportions. (Whatever that means....) What could I do to your huge soft self with only my two little hands? We haven't even begun to explore your body, and I'm curious and willing to find new ways to please you.*

"My, my. What an interesting experiment! We would truly shock the scientists."

"We could reintroduce sex to your whole species. It's probably been a while since they tried anything truly new!" Ann looked up from the legal folders and looked in his eyes. "How soon must you leave?"

Marco Antonio stood there in silence, avoiding her eyes. After a moment, he looked at her and said, "Now."

"How long will you be gone?" she said, once again looking at whatever paper she held in her hands.

"I don't know," he said quietly.

She felt like bursting into tears, but she was trying very hard not to. *What will happen if they don't let you come back?*

I don't think they would do that. We are usually free to do whatever we want to, unless they want to study us. When they are done, we are free to come and go as we please.

Is there any reason they might keep you there to "study" you?

Perhaps. Some feel that this gene is very dangerous. I don't know what they might do if they decide to stop its use. It might have to be settled by an ethics committee, and that could take some time.

Ann felt the tears start to roll down her face. Her next breath was a sob. "Have I gotten you into trouble? Do they think you are some kind of sexual pervert or something?"

"Some do. We are a very unusual couple," he said, sitting down in the chair next to hers. He reached across and caught two tears running down her face. He licked the tears from his fingers.

"I think we're a *wonderful* couple!" she blurted, more than a little defensively. "We are very happy together. Granted, we'd be happier if I were smarter, but we don't hurt anyone else. We don't abuse animals or small children or do weird dances around fires in the forest."

"They don't think we do. Besides, they would know if I did, because I cannot lie to people who can read my entire mind and body with one glance," he said gently, trying to calm her fears.

"Do they think I've led you down a primrose path? Am I the weirdo pervert who has somehow debased you? Or is it because we eat together and pee alone? What is their PROBLEM?" Ann stood up and started pacing. She was afraid, which made her angry. *Stupid sons of bitches,* she fumed. *A bunch of old Kansas matrons with their lips pursed because their lemonade is sour. Assholes. They all just need to get laid.*

Even though he loved to hear her fulminate, he didn't want to leave her when she was upset. Smiling, Marco Antonio stood and put his arms around her, calming her instantly.

Still, she ranted mentally, but her thoughts were much more coherent. *They must understand that sex is only one passion among many, and humans use all types of fervor to deal with catastrophes and to make great discoveries. Musicians and artists become obsessed with their craft and create masterpieces. Nothing great was ever created by indifference. When I return, we will show them a thing or two about passion! And love. And sex is pretty cool with passion. Excitement, enthusiasm, delight, all that stuff. They're wrong to think we're perverts because we get emotional.*

Ann was winding down, as he knew she would. He didn't want to leave her when she was anxious or angry. It was his job to protect her and to make her happy.

"I'll have to learn to master my negative emotions, too, querida. I must control my rage and fury when I feel jealous or fearful of your safety. My outbursts and furor can be dangerous, and I must learn to control my strong feelings. You are a patient teacher, and I will learn to channel my furies," he said, his chin resting on her head. "I must convince them that I can learn control."

"Oh, I think I can civilize you. If you come back to me."

"I will, querida. I will."

He leaned back a little and raised her face with his hand cupping her jaw. Gently, he kissed her, and then he kissed her again, with greater zeal. She froze in his arms, arching her back as a huge orgasm swamped through her, creating crashing waves of contractions that literally took her breath away.

Oh, my god! Oh, Marco Antonio!

Before she could think of anything else, he kissed her again and she collapsed in his arms. Gently, he put one arm beneath her knees, picked her up, and placed her on the couch. He smoothed her hair back from her forehead, kissed her sleeping eyes, and left quietly out the back door.

#####

Helping Other People Everywhere Inc. (HOPE Inc.) is a non-profit public benefit corporation set up by the Johnsons after one visit to Kenya. These are some of the projects we have completed or are on-going. Much of the funding for teachers' salaries are donated by Kings County teachers in a monthly automatic deduction program, but many other projects have helped feed and educate the children in Kenya. HOPE Inc. pays no salaries to corporate officers, and the Johnsons pay all their own expenses, including the nine visits we have made to Kenya. All donations to HOPE Inc. are tax deductible. All profits earned by books written by Darleen Hayball Johnson will be contributed to Helping Other People Everywhere, Inc. (HOPE Inc.)

Accomplishments of Helping Other People Everywhere, Inc. 2002-2018
Our On-Going Projects
Hopewell High School, Nakuru, Kenya

From 2001 to 2007, HOPE sent thousands of textbooks and reading books to Hopewell High School and Lewa Children's Home. In 2007, the U.S. Post Office eliminated book and surface rates, and everything had to be sent airmail. The price of airmail coupled with the increase in duty made sending books and clothing to Kenya. HOPE built a large library to house the books and contracted with Ngala School for the Deaf to build tables, chairs and book shelves. Rotary International helped to fund the furniture with

Sewing projects provided thousands of skirts, shorts, and dresses to seven orphanages in Kenya, and used shits and jeans were purchased and mailed. Uniform skirts were made here and boys' shorts and shirts were purchased in Kenya and distributed to orphans and needy children. These projects were also cancelled in 2007, when postage made shipping impractical.

- Completed construction of 4 additional classrooms, two science labs, and an office.
- Resurfaced floors in 5 classrooms and the library.
- Sponsor a Teacher Program paid salaries and wages of all teachers, cooks, maintenance and support staff
- Coordinated several Kings-County-Hopewell school projects, such as "change for chonies" drive to purchase underwear for girls
- Coordinated community fund-raising to support "Freedom for Girls" project to purchase sanitary napkins for girls in Kenya. Over 8,000 presentations of one year's worth of pads have been made by August, 2013. Walworth-Fontana Rotary Foundation is spearheading the continuing program with support from HOPE.
- Coordinated the "Seeds of Hope" program which supplied seeds, fertilizer, pesticides and farm tools for the school garden.
- Bought new pipes and hoses for Hopewell's drip irrigation system
- Coordinated the Girl Scouts sponsorship of three orphaned girls at Hopewell
- Paid much of the hospital bill and medication for the Superintendent's surgery.

Little Saints Nursery School (around 87 students) Nakuru, Kenya

- Sponsor a Teacher Program paid salaries and wages of all teachers, cooks, maintenance, and support staff
- Paid rent for the building and grounds
- Provided two meals a day for every student and staff member
- Made and sent 60 skirts and ties for little girls' uniforms
- Made and sent 4 red skirts for teachers

- Bought and mailed 59 white polo shirts for boys' and girls' uniforms tops
- Paid for 15 boys shorts and 25 red skirts
- Paid for all teaching supplies, sports equipment, and children's school supplies

Lewa Children's Home (about 67 children), and Kabi Turkana refugee camp, Eldoret, Kenya

- Sponsor a Teacher Program paid nursery school teachers at both locations
- Made and mailed skirts for girls, and play clothes for boys and girls

Nygoon Ladies Self-Help Group (near Eldoret, Kenya)

- Buy uniforms, shoes, and school supplies for 80 orphans living in the community
- Installed pipes and foot pumps for irrigation at the Orphans' Garden
- With Seeds of HOPE program, provided seeds, fertilizer for the Orphans' Garden.
  Helped raise money for an orphaned graduate from Hopewell High School to attend Kings College in London where he studied and completed his Master's Degree. His scholarship paid for his transportation, visa, vaccines, tuition, room and board, but he needed warm clothing, shoes, school supplies, books, laptop, subway and bus fees and some spending money for unforeseen expenses. (Note: after a brief internship in Bangkok, this student returned to London with another scholarship to earn his Ph.D.)

Helping Other People Everywhere, in Hanford On-going Projects

Coat Reclaiming Project, 2006-2018

- Collect "Lost and Found" jackets, coats, and sweaters from Kings County schools
- Collect all abandoned physical education uniforms, shoes, towels, etc. from all Hanford High Schools and Lemoore High School
- Wash, sort, mend and store all clothing
- Redistribute clothes to those who need them.
  Summer give-away of shorts and tee-shirts
  Fall and Winter Coat Giveaways (over 2,000 jackets reclaimed annually)
  > Rotary, Churches, Kings Community Action Organization, Cornerstone Men's Recovery Systems, Pentecostal Church Homeless Outreach
  > Kings County Child Protective Service, Commission on Aging, Salvation Army, St. Vincent de Paul,

Pentecostal Church Homeless Bathing Facilities

- Collect used but serviceable towels and bathmats from Kings County residents and schools
- Pick up wet and soiled towels, washcloths, and bath mats
- Wash, dry, fold and return clean used towels and bathmats as needed for the shower facilities for the homeless twice each week

Christmas Projects

Santa Claus

- Bell-ringing for Salvation Army
- Gift delivery at Shelly Baird School, Episcopal Church Free Lunch Christmas Toys, Senior Citizen homes and events

Christmas Surprises supplied for

- Commission on Aging
- Child Protection Service
- Foster Care children
- Homeless

Provided a free home for a graduating senior who had aged out of the foster care program. She stayed with us for three years, commuting to Fresno State. We co-signed for a new Hyunda, but she made the payments. Although we charged no rent or utilities, she decided to move in with her boyfriend for her senior year. She graduated in four years, got married and moved to Missouri to settled in his hometown.

Provided a free home for a recovering addict. She lived in our little mother-in-law apartment, got a full time job, and moved into a larger house with her father after a year with us. She has maintained her sobriety for over two years and has been promoted at work.

Annually give $500 scholarships to one student from each of three high school in the Hanford Joint Union High School District.

www.ingramcontent.com/pod-product-compliance
Lightning Source LLC
LaVergne TN
LVHW021651060526
838200LV00050B/2306